THE
HAMMERHEAD
CHRONICLES

SCOTT GOULD

THE
HAMMERHEAD
CHRONICLES

SCOTT GOULD

UNG

UNIVERSITY *of*
NORTH GEORGIA™
UNIVERSITY PRESS

Blue Ridge | Cumming | Dahlonega | Gainesville | Oconee

Published by:
University of North Georgia Press
Dahlonega, Georgia

Printing Support by:
Lightning Source Inc.
La Vergne, Tennessee

Cover design by Sam Caldwell.
Book design by Corey Parson.

ISBN: 978-1-940771-77-9

Printed in the United States of America
For more information, please visit: http://ung.edu/university-press
Or e-mail: ungpress@ung.edu

For Shannon
(pinky swear)

PART ONE

CLAUDE

Your wife dies and you buy an expensive foreign bicycle, and yes, you know how that sounds, how cold and borderline brutal, how it possesses not even the tiniest speck of compassion, but you have been lusting after a bicycle much longer than she has been dying, and the two events collide on a Thursday evening in late summer. Call it synchronicity. Call it whatever you want. Except don't call it unfeeling.

Because she isn't really your wife when she passes away. Okay, technically, maybe on paper Peg is. But she is a month and a day from becoming your *official* ex-wife, what with South Carolina's odd, year-long waiting (contemplating? second-guessing?) period after you separate. The two of you are, as they say, estranged. Add to that, you are completely out of shape, a physical wreck. Of all the things that flutter in and out of Peg's cloudy brain during these last cloudy weeks, you hope one scrap of information that lodges in her mind is the fact that you are going to buy a bike no matter what happens. And she is okay with it.

On that Thursday, you walk through the door of the only bicycle store you are familiar with, the one housed in a rusting Quonset hut on Pleasantburg Drive. The fact that it is on a *pleasant* drive you consider a good omen, though you are not a big believer in signs. You walk up to the first person you spot, a beanpole-thin young man, a kid, maybe twenty-five, tops. His back is to you, but you can tell everything about this kid screams aerodynamic. Hair buzzed to a bristled fuzz. T-shirt wrapping him like a second skin. Body fat of a splinter. And his legs shaved smooth like a runway model's.

"I'm here to buy a bike," you say, and he pulls his attention away from the display of rubber tire tubes and wheel rims to scan your worth, not as a consumer but as a potential cyclist.

What stands before him is a man rounding the horn into his fifties, a man with a wealth of questionable genetic bequests from both sides of his family: doughy love handles and moderate hypertension from his father, chronic creaky knees and slightly bowed legs from his mother. If the kid possesses the ability to look even further back, Aero Boy might discover the medical resumes of your grandparents and aunts and uncles, checkered with everything from childhood rickets to a third cousin on your father's side born with the four long fingers on each hand webbed tightly together, a cousin who, at a young, impressionable age, was given the unfortunate but apropos nickname of Mittens. You have seen black and white pictures of Cousin Mittens taped into dusty family albums, him smiling and waving at the camera with his botched hands. You have always worried when *that* strand of DNA would worm its way back onto the branches of the family tree.

"Looking for something easy to get around on, I'm guessing?" Aero Boy asks confidently, like some sort of bicycle profiler. His nasally voice is pitched high. You know you can't call him Aero Boy, so you ask his name. "TJ," he says, and you think, *Well, of course you're a TJ. Even your name is aerodynamic.*

You talk, and words pour out like desperate escapees. "Well, TJ, let me tell you what I want. I want a fast bike. I want a bike like I see on television, the Tour. That's what I want. Not walking out until I get it," and at that point you punctuate your speech with action: you lay your credit card on the glass-topped counter, above the electrolyte powders and the caffeine beans and the energy bars and the bullet-like canisters of compressed air. The card floats like magic on the glass. The scene is cinematic, one you scripted in your head that morning, even practiced—you, whipping out a credit card and tossing it on a counter like a poker shark flipping his final ace onto a giant pot.

"Whatever you say." TJ doesn't take his eyes off the credit card.

"TJ, this will be the easiest sale you make today," you say. "I hope you work on commission. Set me up," and the two of you stroll into the maze of wheels and spokes and carbon frames and naked handlebars hanging from the Quonset hut's rafters, TJ leading the way like a frontier guide into your brand-new wilderness.

CHERYL

Let me get on the record about this. My house started smelling different the day the hospice people hauled in those goddamn rolling stands and tubes and pumps and all those special square throw pillows I guess they thought were some kind of fucking miracle pillows that would cushion all the suffering and suffocate it amongst whatever the hell they were stuffed with. Feathers or nylon or little scribbled prayers from some monastery in Hospice World. I curse when I get frustrated. Fucking sue me.

The actual equipment, the hospice things, none of *that* stuff smelled. That was industrial stuff, metal and plastic and rough, not a scent on it. Where'd the smell come from? I'm pretty damn sure it came from the hospice workers who showed up at my door every few hours, clocking in for the latest shift of the Great Last Wait. They crossed from the front porch into the little foyer with a big dark cloud hitched to them. A goddamn odor. I tried to put my finger—my nose, I mean—on it for days and days. What did it smell like, exactly? It wasn't entirely unpleasant, but nothing sprang to mind. I didn't conjure up oatmeal cookies or lemony cleaner or dryer sheets. The smell was blunt. A fucking sucker punch of an odor. It smacked my nostrils the minute I came back inside the house after walking the dog or running to the grocery store.

I certainly had not planned on the smell of my house changing when I offered to move Peg here for the Great Last Wait. I know, I know, she's my sister, yadda yadda, but we could have hired the hospice people to come to *her* house. I could have visited her *there* every day, done the same freaking vigil under her roof. Shit, I could have moved in with *her*. But for some not-exactly-sane reason, I thought it would be easier for everybody if she lived in my house while the inevitable became the real. Patrick still hasn't forgiven me. He said, "We'll never sell this house if people find out somebody died in it," and before I could remind him that lots of people die very happily in their own goddamn homes in their own goddamn beds every day, we were off into another argument about something totally unrelated to my sister and the tumors doing a victory lap around her skull. For the record, I didn't much care what Patrick said. I rarely did anymore. The fact that I still possessed the innate ability to piss him off made my day.

If I were to go to confession—where I haven't been in years—and the priest asked me point blank why I did it, I think I would tell him the reason I wanted Peg to die in my house was so I could be there when it happened and usher her off and feel great about doing that deed. Maybe I was selfish.

But who wasn't? Sometimes I even think Peg was selfish, the way this went down. Yes, she was the sainted one, the sister that did all the right things. Preserved her virginity like a fucking holy grail until she was engaged to Claude. Didn't get drunk until our mother was dead and not around to frown at her. Only made one B in college and cried for days about it. Birthed Marlene in a bathtub full of water, without a drop of painkiller.

Well, she was making up for that now. She sucked away all our time. The damn morphine dripped like a clock-tick. When the morphine took over, Peg reminded me of a lazy surfer. She would drift away lost and unintelligible for hours, then suddenly catch a decent wave that nudged her back, back to the shore, back to where she could ask questions about the weather and the day of the week and Marlene, and yes, even Claude. After everything, she still asked about Claude, for fuck's sake.

But I thought, *okay, I'm going to do the damn good thing now. I'm going to sneak in there and be the good sister,* so I offered up my house, and I pulled one of the medium-sized, overstuffed chairs from the den and planted it beside the spare bed, and I watched Peg surf in and out, drifting away on waves that kept her out to sea most of the day.

One time, when she returned to the morphine shore, she opened her eyes and said, "I'm so glad you are here. I want you to be here when I'm not." So I figured we had an agreement—me and Peg and whoever sets the timing on this sort of thing, God or whoever. The Great Timekeeper for the Great Last Wait. It was a deal: *Peg would not die unless I sat there beside her.* With our agreement firmly in place, I could safely run to the store or walk around the block or go outside with a couple fingers of overpriced bourbon in a Solo cup and wander the edge of my goddamn yard and sniff the whiskey and flush the smell of the house completely from my nostrils.

I didn't know who to be mad at on that Thursday, when Peg broke the goddamn agreement. My first choice was Patrick. He saw me out there, Solo cup in hand, staring into the tops of the Leyland cypress we had planted when we moved in. They grew so fast, I hadn't noticed how much of the sky they blocked these days. The asshole saw me there and came and started another argument, this time about his missing credit card. "I know you did something with it," he said. "So what if your sister is in there dying. That doesn't mean you aren't still an irresponsible bitch. That hasn't changed."

The Leylands topped out over ten feet, higher than a basketball hoop now. They must have grown, like, a foot and a half a year, if I did my math right. They grew fast because of the direct sun they soaked up all day long. Constant light.

"Where is the card?" he said, and I gave him my stock answer: "I wouldn't know."

He kept on and wouldn't let me leave the yard. He didn't hold me against my will, but he wouldn't let it all go. I quit staring at the Leylands and the sky and turned to look at the house. The back deck needed new stain. Patrick wanted to sell the house and downsize because I had quit working. He thought I left my job to piss him off. Nobody with half a freaking brain would buy this house with a deck looking that shabby.

"Did you steal my card?" he said. "I need it."

Before I could come up with a smartass answer—and like I was destined to see it—I detected movement behind the bay windows off the kitchen. I knew it wasn't Marlene sneaking back to her room. She never came home before dark. She was having trouble with a terminal illness down the hall, so she waited for the cover of goddamn darkness. It was the hospice worker. She flashed across the openings. She had never moved that quickly. I noted hospice people tended to move deliberately, almost in sync with the sadness and decay going on around them, slow and steady and awkward. *Elephantine.* Peg taught me that word once, doing one of her crossword puzzles. Patrick was still talking when I pushed by him and dropped the Solo cup at his feet. I moved fast too. That is the moment I knew. I goddamn knew.

When I ran into the kitchen, something odd hit my nose. What I mean to say is, *nothing* hit my nose. The funky, strange smell had disappeared. My house smelled like my house again. The hospice funk had magically evaporated. I realized at that second what the damn odor had been all along. That smell, the one that had changed my house, was the smell of patience, of people patiently waiting for something to happen. *So that is what patience smells like*, I thought. When there was no reason to be patient anymore, no reason to wait, like smoke through a thin crack in a door, the smell disappeared. That's when I absolutely knew Peg was gone.

I walked into the spare room, and she wasn't surfing anymore. She wasn't riding waves back and forth. She was gone. The hospice worker didn't speak a word. She looked at me and nodded. *Yes*, she was saying without moving her mouth, *yes*, but I already knew what the fuck she meant. I had not been there when it happened. This was not part of the agreement. There was nothing *yes* about Peg dying alone. Three minutes ago, I stood forty feet away, listening to a man trying to argue his way into a reason big enough to leave me, and I missed my sister's dying. I wanted to cry for all the goddamn things I missed.

For the record, do you remember the last fucking thing my sister said to me before she died?

Neither do I.

CLAUDE

L ittle do you know.

Your cell phone rings away in the cupholder of your hot truck while you slide thin, hard bike seats into your crotch and ride careful circles around the almost empty parking lot, trying to decide in a few uncertain laps if this bike or that bike is the bike for you, the one you will zip down streets and up mountains, the one that will melt away the twin ghosts of your father's inherited love handles that you lug around. You do not hear the ring tone, the special ring you programmed for calls from your sister-in-law, "Under Pressure" by Bowie and Queen. You have too much wind in your ears, and you swear, you are smiling. You think TJ smiles, too, as he watches from the square of shade beneath the green awning of the bike shop, yelling occasionally for you to shift into a lower gear or to stand up on the pedals and see how it feels. "What do you think?" he continually hollers from the shade, and you cannot answer him because you don't have thoughts at all. Your brain spends all its energy on balance and steering and how the chin strap on the blue and red helmet digs into your jawline and is in the process of rubbing your right earlobe raw. You cannot *think* of anything but staying upright as you sample bike after bike.

Confession: they all feel the same to you, even though TJ assures you each one varies in qualities that sound academic and formal, things like geometry and softness and flex.

What do you feel? The road coming right through the pedals, up the frame and straight into your ass, and there is nothing soft or flexible about it, but you nod back at him and never take your hands from the handlebars. You never hear your phone blaring "Under Pressure."

You roll to the front of the store, sweating and panting, on the sixth or eighth bike you sample.

"That's the one," TJ says, pointing between your legs.

"How do you know?" you ask.

"You finally looked like you were having some fun," he says, and you dismount and follow him back inside. Your credit card still sits there on the glass counter, glaring up at you. You didn't realize you'd left it out in the open. "Almost like it was waiting on us," TJ says and scoops up the card and tallies the damage. Bike, shorts, helmet, water bottle (which he tosses in for free), a jersey you're sure is too tight, but you are too tired to argue. "Shoes and clips are later. Get used to things first. You aren't a hammerhead," he says, and you have no idea what a hammerhead is, other than an odd type of shark and you don't believe TJ is talking about sharks.

You paid off the credit card a couple of years ago, before Peg got sick. She never knew about it—not that you kept many secrets, only the usual amount—but the card was always there for an emergency or a wild hair. The credit limit is $5,000 and TJ bites off a healthy chunk of that with the bill he hands you. You don't blink, because you don't care if the tab is $4,999.99. You suppose you could call this an emergency. Most definitely, it is a wild hair.

TJ helps you remove the front wheel and load the bike gently into the bed of your pickup. "You need a rack, man. You carry it around like this, you gonna get scratches. Could even crack the frame." You aren't listening. You are busy noticing that your truck and your new bike are the same color. Deep, dark blue. "We sell rack systems for pickups," TJ says. "You're probably done spending money today, huh?"

"Hey, you didn't tell me this bike was the one for me because it's blue, did you?" you ask him. "Blue truck, blue bike. This isn't a joke, right?"

TJ folds up the tail gate and eases it shut without slamming. He ignores your question. "When those cables loosen up, you'll feel it. The gears will slip a little. Brakes will be gummy. Bring it back in and I can adjust them while you wait. No charge," he says and waves and retreats into the store, his thin, sharp frame barely making a dent in the air.

You missed four calls from Cheryl, and that makes your stomach churn. The only reason Cheryl ever calls you is to get on the record about something you've done wrong. That is not an exaggeration. Almost every conversation the two of you have begins: "I have to get on the record about this," then she proceeds to tell you that she knew you would eventually leave her sister one day. Or that she disagrees with you giving Peg a dog on one of her birthdays. Or that *you* somehow convinced Peg to refuse that last round of chemo and go gently into that good night. That was her phrase, not yours. "How could you fucking let her go gently into that good night?" Cheryl likes to toss out snatches of poetry because she was an English major back in the day, but she's never done anything with that degree. You think it makes her sound like an unhappy middle school teacher. Which may be redundant.

Four missed calls and one short voicemail. You see in the queue that Cheryl only talked for twelve seconds, so if she rants, mercifully, it is brief, hardly enough time to say, "I have to get on the record about this."

In your ear, Cheryl murmurs quietly, barely above a whisper, and she speaks as if she's rehearsed her speech. "Dammit, I've been trying to get you," she says but doesn't sound that angry. "Peg is gone. A few minutes ago. I told Marlene of course. Goodbye."

The last few seconds of the message? Only the quiet hiss of someone who has forgotten she still has to hang up on you.

LeJeune

Windows so dirty, cut the sunshine, no matter what time of year. Hate the front windows at The Oorah. Stupid name for a bar. What happens when a Marine buys a bar. Should not allow Marines to own bars. Should not allow Marines to have daughters. Should not allow Marines to name daughters for the Marine base where they were conceived. Not *born*. Was born on Parris Island in dead of summer. So I can handle humidity and mosquitoes that would deck a man twice my size. Conceived at Camp LeJeune. My father? Dead and gone for years. Platoon buddy of his owns The Oorah. Tending bar is easier than working for a living. *Oorah*.

Don't wear a wristwatch, but knew it was after six-thirty. The dirty light got a little dirtier. Could tell that from where I stood behind the taps. Only three taps. Bud, Bud Light and Coors Regular. But nobody drinks draft beer at The Oorah. They want the cans and the bottles buried in the cooler. Like to see me sink my skinny arm in ice water to the arm pit, fishing for PBR and Coors Light and Miller High Life. Don't wear sleeves, even in winter. Got a tattoo down the backside of my right arm. *Suck it up, Buttercup*, it says. A thing my father always said. Funny. He died and left me a pair of dress blues, a marksmanship medal, and a phrase that banged around my head for years. Banging stopped when I moved the saying from my head to my arm. Green ink. Fancy old-school cursive writing. *Suck it up, Buttercup*.

Close to empty at six-thirty. Not a shocker. Thursday, always a late start. Thursday's the new Friday, even for drunks. Not expecting much of a happy hour and predicted correctly. Crowd coming later. Was on my own. Sgt. Emery wasn't coming in tonight. Nothing unusual about that either. Rarely stopped by anymore. Can do that when you own a bar that runs on its own. 1) Beer delivered Tuesday and Friday morning. 2) People drink the beer. 3) People pay for the beer. 4) Deliver more beer. Drink. Pay. Repeat.

Leaned on the taps because I was tired. Long night ahead. Thought of it made me even more tired. Made my feet ache ahead of time. Through the front window, saw Claude's truck. Looked like a bicycle in the back, same exact color as his truck. Color coordinated. Very boujee. But Claude is no wuss. This I know. If he is, puts on a good front. And a good back. Skinny girl like me likes a man with some meat on him, like Claude. Might be his daughter's bike or something.

Claude sat there. Listening to music, maybe? Playing with his phone, maybe? Playing with himself? Thought I saw a puff of exhaust from the tailpipe. Should mention that to him. Might be burning oil. Bad gasket. Loose seals. Truck didn't have enough years on it to be burning oil like that. Flash my tattoo at Claude a lot. *Suck it up, Buttercup.*

Because he will sit at the bar, same chair every time. If his chair is occupied, he stands and waits 'til it isn't. Drinks shots of Beam and PBR and tells me anything. Too much of everything. Know about the sick wife. Know about the bitchy sister. Sister-in-law, I mean. Know about the daughter. Know about the suck-ass job at the college. Know about how everybody in town with an opinion thinks he is a dick. *Suck it up, Buttercup.* Never *say* that to Claude. Instead flash the arm at him. Same difference.

Most nights, tells me everything 'til he can't tell anymore. Then he leaves. Sometimes in a cab. Sometimes in his truck. Every now and then in my Mustang. '67, 289 V8, two-door, Cherry Bomb glasspack muffler— sounds like a Harley with a bad attitude. Fenders with more rust than Pittsburgh. Springs squeak. Runs good, runs hot. It breaks down, I fix it. Okay, maybe Daddy Marine left me more than a tattoo. Taught me cars too.

Claude comes home with me, and nothing ever happens, him always too drunk at night, too guilty in the morning. Don't mind. Appreciate having somebody around worse off than me. Sometimes, sorry for him. Then I look down at my tattoo.

Swear he sat in that truck for fifteen minutes. Checked the mirror behind the bar. Make sure I was presentable for inspection. You never know. Maybe one day he will leave here with me—how to say?—uplifted. Won't have to flash the arm at him. Never known Claude to put off drinking to hang in the parking lot. Maybe a heart attack? I wondered. Then he moved, so no.

He climbed out, looked at the sky, toward the trees, the six-thirty sun long gone behind the old bleachery building across the road. He peeked into the bed of his truck at that bicycle. Peeked toward the bar, like he was making a plan. Took a first step across the lot, so I dove into the ice and fingered around. There it was, the shape of a PBR bottleneck. Cracked the cap. Five of Hearts.

Play this game, me and Claude. Under the caps of PBR bottles are cards. Not real cards. The card *writing*, the symbols—the hearts and spades and clubs and diamonds and all the numbers. Printed there. Give him a hint, and if Claude guesses the card-under-the-cap with a clue, gets the bottle for free. Five of Hearts. Poured a full snort of Beam in a little plastic cup, like the ones you piss in at the doctor. Sgt. Emery won't buy shot glasses. Told me once glasses were a poor bar investment.

Door opened and new light got in, brighter stuff. Saw dust where dust shouldn't be. Need to clean one day. Smiled at him, but Claude would not look up. That was different. He always looked at me first. Today, shuffled to his empty seat and settled down in front of the wet bottle of PBR and the specimen cup of Beam. Then sighed. Too loud.

I said, "Okay, pip card between two and eight, red." Stared at the bottom of the cap to make sure. Looked at him next.

He said, "Not today, LeJeune. Not today." Sounded like a man who lost a good bet.

Flashed my arm at him, but his head stayed down. Wasn't having any of it this afternoon.

Suck it up, Buttercup.

CLAUDE

You slouch behind the wheel of your blue truck, the AC blasting cold right in your face like an argument, and you detect the faint scent of burning oil. In the bed behind you, something else sits: the most bike you can buy with a high-APR, low-limit credit card. In your hand is the phone that announced, a few miles earlier, that your almost-ex-wife died. What do you do now?

Sure, you could see this whole thing coming, but frankly, no matter how long you straddle the tracks and study that odd light bearing down on you, the surprise is still loud and angry and aggressive when that train finally runs your ass over. You wonder if somebody watches in this minute, if somebody records your response right this very second, spying on you in the truck, wondering, *Will he cry? Will he hang his head? Will he shrug his shoulders like he usually does when the shit of the world hits the giant fan of the world?*

Because you know one thing beyond a shadow of any doubt: you have felt watched for a while now, under the social microscope since that afternoon you moved out of your house and left the wife, left the daughter, left the dog. When you moved out, you did not know—*you swear, did not know!*—that your wife was already sick, the thin, gray cloud already forming quickly in a far quadrant of her brain. Peg did not suspect she had a head full of impending doom. *Nobody* knew, least of all you. But when that diagnosis arrived months later—and yes, even though you were separated at that time, you sat right there with her when the doctor, a medical automaton with the personality of a soup ladle, reported the grim news—and people began to find out about her illness, they branded you, gave you a new identity. You were immediately The Man Who Cut and Ran When His Tiny Wife Got Sick.

She told you not to worry about it. "I know the situation, silly. The two of us know the timing. Don't worry about what the neighbors say," she said, and you felt so small and stupid and trivial, complaining about what the neighbors whispered behind their hands, while your soon-to-be-ex-dead-wife adjusted the bandana on her newly slick, newly sick head.

There are distinct categories for the troubles of this world. Some fall under the "petty" filing (like your current anxiety regarding how former friends view you), and other troubles can be found comfortably existing on the "serious shit" shelf. Apples and oranges. You know better than to compare them, but you cannot help yourself. Like those nights, in your small apartment, when you wandered onto your small balcony—a space barely large enough for a potted plant and a hibachi—and peered into the night, and you chanted a little prayer (god knows to whom) that your wife would get better, *not* so she could live out her life and be a constant mother to your daughter, but so you would not be blamed for bringing on the head-clouds that blanketed her brain. When you contemplated that sort of thing, the guilt pressed down on you like a cement vest and squeezed the air from your lungs.

And your daughter. You do not know what to think about her. She never liked you, right from the start, even when she was a tiny baby and you walked laps inside the house trying to calm her after-midnight colic. She stared up at you and screamed and squirted tears from her tiny eyes, but you knew what was going on behind those eyes. She was saying, *I want you to be miserable and never sleep again.* For six months, she got her tiny baby wish. You were the walking dead, stumbling through the days only to arrive at another night of laps and tears, you and your wife swapping shifts, passing the baby off in the hallway like a baton in a crappy, late-night relay race.

She grew up, and you didn't grow closer. You always imagine you will, however. You imagine one day Marlene will smile at you the way you see daughters smile at fathers they like, love. When Marlene was a freshly minted teenager, you wondered out loud to Peg—on a night outside under the umbrella where you swilled limoncello like lemonade yet amazingly could still form complete sentences—and asked if Marlene was definitely your child. You asked Peg if some possibility existed, however slim, that Marlene had been switched in the hospital for a random renegade infant in that busy nursery. "She doesn't look like either one of us," you said. "What if there is some sweet, laid-back kid out there who has my eyes and your nose?" You whined long into the lemony night about the difficulty of being a father to a daughter who didn't want to be around you, and you were on the cusp of commenting to Peg about what a good listener she was when you noticed she was fast asleep in the lawn chair, her head back, jaw open, like she waited to catch rain in her mouth.

Now that you think about it, you wonder if the clouds were gathering way back then.

Not that you and Marlene hate each other. It is something else. You knew it then and you know it now. It is this: you and Marlene simply don't *care* about each other. You aren't important to her and vice versa. Or quid pro quo. Or who the hell knows which one of those phrases to use? Peg kept you two together when you lived under the same roof. The tie that bound, the common thread. But the moment you left, the bind frayed a bit, the thread grew thin as spider webbing. Now, with the news that Peg is gone, you fear the thread has completely snapped.

From inside the cab of your truck, you glance over your shoulder, and yes, maybe you catch a glimpse of someone spying on you, the shadow of LeJeune in the front window of The Oorah. She is one of the few who has heard the whole story, the true story. She has told you what she thinks of you, usually when she deposits you on her couch and your drunken eyes are closed and she doesn't realize you are listening to every word she whispers in that funny, clipped way she says things. She does not think you cut and run.

You would never categorize yourself as an alcoholic because there have been times (many times!) in the past year when you go without bourbon or beer for days, long stretches when you stay away from The

Oorah or the beer coolers at the Food Lion or the QT station at the corner of Hollis Highway and Poinsett Street, and so far, you don't have any signs of withdrawal. Boredom, not beer, is the magnet that constantly draws you back to The Oorah, and even when times are tight, LeJeune lets you run a tab the length of a toilet paper roll because she knows you are good for it, knows you are a good person. Not a cutter-and-runner.

So that's why you left the bike store on that pleasant drive and drove—Cheryl's voicemail echoing in your head—down Broad Street where the aggressive potholes are strategically situated like land mines, over to Franklin past the pawn shop, then left onto Old Bleachery Road, where The Oorah sits in the skeletal shadow of the huge, abandoned bleachery, which has been closed for years, but in the decades before that dumped oceans of bleach and dye into the Reedy River, effectively killing the water for future generations. There are men who used to work in the bleachery, men who often camp out in The Oorah and tell stories of when they were kids, swimming in the Reedy and coming out purple from the dye, stained like grapes with legs. Most of them have a variety of different kinds of cancers, and they know it is the bleachery that kills them slowly today, but to a man, they think disease is reasonable compensation for forty years of a steady paycheck.

You wonder if it is safe to leave your brand-new bike out in the open in this neighborhood—a modern melting pot of clay-stained mobile homes and peeling mill houses filled with Hispanic families and white families and Black families and, you suspect, a meth head or two, so you park near the trees in front, where you can watch your truck from the bar and keep an eye on your new purchase. And not just the bike. On the seat sits a bag of expensive accessories. Everything in life comes with accessories. If you have an empty house, you must fill it. If you buy a car, you need floor mats. Purchase a bike, and you are required to wear tight shorts with the cushion in the crotch to guard vital elements and a helmet to protect your brain. You wish Peg had possessed a helmet that worked from the inside out, something hard and sturdy to keep the clouds from forming. You even bought a pair of fingerless gloves to improve your grip on the handlebars and, yes, protect your palms in case of a fall. Jesus, one requires a surprising amount of protection to ride a bike down the street, you think.

A Pabst Blue Ribbon and a shot of Beam wait on you like a pair of lazy friends, the beer already sweating a ring onto the bar. LeJeune starts with the bottle cap game, but you aren't playing today. When her eyes adjust after the sudden splash of sunshine that led you into the dark room, she notices something is different, probably something wrong, and like all the best bartenders the world over, she doesn't ask you about it. She knows you will spill the information sooner or later. LeJeune is a listener with instincts. With those skills, she could be making wheelbarrows of money as a counselor or a shrink, yet she ended up here, and on this afternoon, you're damn glad she did.

The Beam cuts a spicy path down your throat that you cool with a pull of the PBR. Though LeJeune openly hates the use of cells phones in her bar—she says it pisses her off to be forced to hear only half of what is going on—she doesn't so much as blink when you remove yours from your back pocket. She slides to the other end of the bar and pretends to wipe spills that have not occurred yet.

Cheryl answers on the first ring, as if she might be perched beside her phone. The topography of your relationship with Cheryl is lined with bumps and troughs. You have never been able to peer over the hills in time to see how she is going to treat you. When you married her sister, Cheryl thought you were perfect for Peg. Then she got to know you and decided you were absolutely wrong. "Let me get this on the record," she said once, "I was dead fucking mistaken about you." When her niece came along, Cheryl was the one who first noticed Marlene's complete disinterest with you, and thus began Cheryl's long, slick slide toward complete disdain. Unlike others, Cheryl does not think you ran out on a sick woman. She is more disappointed you did not flee years earlier. When she tells you this on various occasions, she is never mean or biting. She simply says, "Why were you around for so long? You wasted everyone's time."

"I got your message," you say when she picks up, and she doesn't respond, and you don't know if she has been muted by grief or simply has nothing to say. Of course, you didn't ask a question, so you aren't officially deserving of a response, you suppose. You are not comfortable with awkward silences—who is?—so you continue talking: "I don't know what to say." Which would suggest that you're going to stop talking, yet you ramble on. "And you told Marlene." You know that will get a response. Any mention of Marlene is a trigger for Cheryl.

"For the record, yes, I told her, but it turns out I didn't have to. She already knew somehow. She's like that, you know. She senses things before other people do." You have no idea what she's talking about. Marlene is psychic? Marlene, a soothsayer?

"If you were thinking of calling her, I wouldn't. Marlene is angry at the world now. And she's sad. The memorial service is Saturday. Peg already took care of the details. All you have to do is show up. You should be able to handle that. Three o'clock." Once Cheryl has that on the record, she hangs up without waiting for a response. You pocket your phone, and LeJeune sidles down the bar to refill your specimen cup.

"My wife died today," you say, then catch yourself. "Ex-wife."

"I know," LeJeune says, and you wonder how is it all these people in the world know things without being told, yet you get all your bad news delivered normally? "Phone is on speaker, dumbass. Couldn't you hear how loud it was?"

Of all the things LeJeune knows about you, you have one secret. You are almost deaf in your right ear. But for some unknown reason, you insist on holding the phone up to the bad side of your head. Force of habit for a right-handed person, maybe. You don't know why one side of your hearing went AWOL years ago. Perhaps you have a cloud over some part of your brain too. LeJeune probably thinks it is cute and urbane, the way you tilt the left side of your head toward her when she talks. You've always assumed you hear about half of what anybody says to you. You are a fifty-percent man. That might be one of your problems.

"You okay?" LeJeune says.

"I believe I should be sadder," you say, turning up your beer so you won't have to say anything else.

"You been sad for years, Claude," she says. "Just didn't know it." You peer through the window and make sure your new bicycle still lies in the bed of the truck, the bike that will always have a strange, memorable anniversary.

LeJeune lays down a fresh Beam because she knows what you need without asking. She's one of those people.

SAMUEL

When Claude called me from his barstool at The Oorah, it was still light out, but I guessed he needed a ride. On nights when I saw his name pop up on my phone—nights when I wasn't already perched beside him, playing PBR poker with LeJeune—I knew he was calling for a lift. Claude never knew when to quit, but he did have enough intelligence not to climb behind the wheel of his pickup after a lot of Jim Beam, and most of the time, I was happy to get out of the house and take him to his apartment. He always thanked me.

This call, however, was different. It was too early; the shank of the evening had not hit yet, and this wasn't a request for a ride. It was a slow, measured announcement, and while I was sad, I was not surprised Peg had passed; that news had been working its way to Claude for weeks. I'm almost ashamed to admit, but in the first minute I heard about Peg, my first thought wasn't about Claude's loss. It was about my mother. That shouldn't have surprised me either. I have always associated loss with my mother.

I truly have no vivid memories of her, no tiny snatches of images I can stitch together into a whole recollection. My mother left the house she grew up in before any of those could take root in my mind's eye. Everything I know about her was filtered through my grandmother, Esther. Esther was the one who repeated the anecdotes. The one who dealt out the photos of my mother on the dining room table like playing cards. Esther answered the questions I asked. Some of them, anyway. So many were left unanswered. Esther had a stock reply to anything she could not or would not to put into words. "God only knows," she'd say. "Ask him."

Esther was the one who told me about my mother's love of the Bible. Supposedly, she would bury herself in the pages and imagine the verses made sounds, talking to her as if they weren't simply words in a line but friends at a church social, gossiping with her, offering word-of-God advice about how to live and navigate in the world. And how to name a son she never expected. Hence, I am Samuel.

I won't go into all the scriptural details of the Biblical story of Samuel, because like most of those narratives, there are holes in the plot, but here's the short version: according to the Bible, a woman back in the ancient times, named Hannah, married this dude with whom she could never beget. One night, a local priest named Eli saw Hannah mumbling to herself, and he thought she'd perhaps had too much wine, so he said—since ancient priests gave unsolicited advice on this sort of thing, I presume—that she ought to keep a little distance from the bottle, and Hannah informed him she had *not* been drinking. She was only offering up prayers for a baby. Priest Eli encouraged her to keep her chin up, because sometimes, as he told her, you get what you ask for when you ask God the right way, and sure enough, that night Hannah and her husband canoodled, and little baby Samuel was begot a few prerequisite months later. Soon enough, folks recognized Samuel was special, because he was a prophet for God, handing out news people did not expect—and sometimes did not want to hear.

Not to say my mother spent *all* her time with scripture. "Your momma loved her music," Esther said. "She loved listening to all the Motown stuff and rhythm and blues on her little transistor radio, all the time, that radio stuck to her ear. Oh, and she was very popular. She never had any trouble with the young men, nice young men. No trouble at all."

She showed me photos of my mother at a school dance. One of them caught her in mid-twirl, dancing with a tall boy wearing a skinny tie, her expression flashing behind distinctive cat-eye glasses. (I always imagined they were dancing to something by the Four Tops, maybe.) Those eyes, always searching for the camera, and in some pictures, she leans against older, beat-up cars that appear to be held together with duct tape and baling wire. Perhaps she rode in them, but oddly, in those photo albums, I've never found a picture of her *inside* one of the cars. And I've never seen the drivers, only her in a tight-waisted skirt, cocking a hip against a fender, her brown skin shining in the sun, those cat-eyes glinting, daring the camera to snap her image.

According to Esther, my mother had her priorities. Bible first. Fun second. "She loved those Bible verses," Esther said. "She even made her dates bring her home early so she could get her reading done." So, connecting the dots, I suppose she *did* ride in strange cars at some point.

The one date that didn't bring her home early was my father. All Esther ever said was, "Your momma was late the one time." She never explained the difference with that one man, never revealed what made my mother forsake Bible time or transistor radio time, but in those couple of hours that she should have been reading scripture, she *may* have been in a back seat of his station wagon or in a back room, or if I get romantically fictional, in a hotel suite with robes and room service, conceiving me with a man she would never marry. Unlike Hannah in the book of Samuel— the woman who couldn't have a child until she had a heart-to-heart with a priest and the Lord—my mother conceived a child quickly. God was not involved, as far as anyone knows.

"One thing about your father," Esther told me when I was maybe ten, "he sold breeze box fans door to door. He must have been good at it. He always had plenty of walking-around money. His name was Zeb, short for Zebulon."

Selling fans in South Carolina in June—I was born the following March—couldn't have presented that much of a challenge. Where my mother grew up was far enough from the coast that any summer breezes petered out by the time they brushed the town limits. Beginning in late May or early June, people in the neighborhood pulled fans down from the attic and mounted them in windows until the end of September. Esther said that my father wandered from door to door—in a suit despite the heat—on the lookout for houses without fans in any of the windows, and when he found one, he would knock until someone answered, then he would make his pitch. His salesman secret? He would mount a fan in one of the front windows of the house and let it stay overnight, for free. "He told us, 'Folks, one night with a cool wind blowing through the house, you'll be reaching for your wallet,'" Esther said.

"But Zeb couldn't sell your granddaddy Thomas a fan, and I think that made him mad," Esther remembered. "He kept knocking on our door, kept telling Thomas that we could try a fan for a couple of days for free, and we could keep it overnight, and Thomas told him that he didn't need a fan to know what a breeze felt like, and if it wasn't wind made by God, he didn't want any part of it, then *your* father made a joke about God breaking wind, and I thought Thomas was going to punch him in the nose. You didn't joke about God under our roof. I am pretty sure that's the same night your momma came home late. She told me she lost of track of time at Martha's house, but I knew something was up. I saw the way they cut their eyes at each other every time that fan salesman came to the door. I will say, Zeb looked sharp in that suit. He never looked like he was sweating."

There was one other thing she said I should never forget. "Your father went off to war," she told me. "That's why you never met him." Her eyes tended to turn colder when she talked about how he made his exit, how when he sold the last fan he had stacked in his Ford Fairlane station wagon, he decided he should go to Vietnam. "Your momma had letters from him," she said, "boxes of them, and she had you. But the fan salesman never came back from over there."

In her version of the tale, Zeb wasn't drafted. He volunteered, something few Black men did during the early 1970s. She said maybe he wanted to be more than a fan salesman, more than somebody who walked through neighborhoods, making artificial, godless breezes that could never win battles against the thick summer heat. "Your daddy was almost a hero," she told me on more than one occasion. "When he didn't come back from that war, it broke your momma's heart. She couldn't stand to be here, where everything happened. I believe that's why she left us. Her heart broke in two. It's hard to raise a baby when something that keeps you alive is broke in half."

That was how Esther talked about my mother and her departure, as if it were simple cause and effect. A slick fan salesman named Zeb went off to war, was almost a hero, and died . . . and as a result my mother ran toward parts unknown before her son made any memories of her. But I never bought what Esther told me. As I got older, I questioned her more. Like with Hannah and Samuel in the Bible, there were holes in her story. I wanted to know how close he had come to being a real hero. I asked her why he never came back, how he died. What happened to the Ford Fairlane station wagon he must have left behind? Did he have any family that we could meet? "God only knows," Esther would say.

And of course, I wanted to know about my mother. For years, I peppered my grandmother with questions. Why would she leave me? What could make a mother run out on her boy? Is she alive?

"God only knows," she said. "Ask him." So I did.

I spent hours sitting between Esther and Thomas in the Gethsemane AME Church, staring at Brother Timmons. He preached, and I threw silent questions in the direction of heaven. I asked where she went. Why she went. How was she? I never received an answer. Esther would only tell me about her daughter in the time *before* I was born. How she grew big during the fall and early winter then stopped going out of the house at all when the chillier weather showed up around New Year's and stayed through February. It was as if time halted when my mother left her home, left her child.

When I got no answers, I set out to find my own. I left that hot house as soon as I could. I went to college. I kept my head down and shoved inside books. In my interview for a PhD program in mathematics, a man on the panel—a white man, they were all white men—asked me why I wanted to study math at this level, and I said, "I want to find my mother." He couldn't understand, of course. I didn't truly believe I would find her on a chalkboard. Yes, I still use chalkboards. I like making dust. I wanted some answers, some solutions God had nothing to do with.

So Claude called me just as the last of the afternoon melted away, and what he told me was slurred around the edges, but I recognized the sound of loss. I'd made the same noises.

CLAUDE

L ess than a day to recover. Not even a full spin of twenty-four hours, and at your age a completely inadequate time frame after an Oorah-kind-of-night. Less than a day for the news of Peg's death to waft through your head like thick fog, less than a day to begin cataloging the memories you want to keep and those you need to forget. You wonder if everyone does this sort of thing, if memory-scrapbooking is part of the grief process for those who have lost the ability to cry. Less than a day to think about riding your new, expensive bike for the first time. Not enough time to work yourself up to it. Laps in a parking lot are one thing. A road—and all the road brings—is another. So you decide to go. Take a flyer.

On Friday, you wrestle on the tight cycling shorts that squeeze your thighs like sausage casings and tuck your testicles against the soft foam pad between your legs. You dig your abandoned running shoes out of the closet. TJ said you weren't ready for real bike shoes, the kind that clip right onto the pedals and for better or worse adhere you to the bike, making you an intimate extension of the machine. When you were young—like ten or twelve—you ran around with a gang of neighborhood kids, and the bunch of you used to ride up and down the sandy roads near the river. Back then, if something went wrong, you could always bail off the bike: simply lay it down, let go, and hit the ground running. But as TJ said on Thursday, "Dude, with clips, if the bike takes a digger, so do you. Get used to riding, then we'll talk. Go with regular pedals right now." You strap on your helmet, tug the tight gloves up and push off from the street in front of your apartment.

The air is a wet, muggy curtain you ride through. *Muggy*, you think, *like your head*, the effects of Beam and PBR scratching like sandpaper between your ears and deep in your throat. It might help to throw up.

Speaking of memories, you should try to remember this ride, your first one, so you glance around you and take in some scenery, but as you pick up speed you quickly realize: You cannot take your eyes from the twenty feet of asphalt ahead of you. It's too dangerous to look away. So you miss how the oaks have leafed out thick this summer because of all the rain, miss that little girl hawking lemonade on the corner of your street and Berkley Ave.

This is so different than cutting little circles in the parking lot outside the bike store. In only a few pedal strokes, you feel as if you are breaking speed limits. The bike rolls faster than you ever wanted it to, faster than you ever imagined it could, but you cannot slow down. Slowing down feels like defeat. The way your head pounds, a wreck might not be the worst thing to happen.

Within a couple of speedy blocks, you learn how clearly the profile of the road translates directly off the asphalt and into your legs. You sense even the most minute changes in elevation. Any dip downward, and the bike takes off under you. Any rise, and you feel the elevation in your straining calves. *This*, you think, *is gravity, pure gravity*. Sure, back when you used to jog, you perceived when you were going uphill, but the pounding of running destroyed any detection of subtle changes in elevation. On this bike, you know the millisecond you violate complete horizontal, and you enjoy that sense of knowing precisely where you are. It is a new feeling.

You suddenly recall how pedaling a bike can aid the thought process. You knew this as a kid. The summer following the sixth grade, you had a paper route, and after your heart was flattened a couple of times, you rode through town, slinging papers, imaging exactly how each of those girls would mourn loudly when your lifeless body was discovered beneath a pile of undelivered *Evening Posts*.

You aren't delivering papers today, but you do some relatively serious thinking while your legs turn circles beneath you. You contemplate the memorial service you must attend the next day. That thought ping-pongs inside your aching head as you take a downhill and stop pedaling, letting gravity do all the work. The wind blows clearer in your left ear, the good one. The speed forces you to tighten the few things under your control: your death grip on the handlebars, your crotch packed around the tiny, thin seat. The downhill bottoms out, and you immediately dump your speed as the road inclines again. You aren't used to shifting yet. Perhaps you are thinking too much about funerals and paper routes, because in seconds you find yourself in the wrong gear—a gear too hard for the hill—and feel as though you are pedaling in a puddle of waist-deep mud. You are scared that in a few awkward seconds, you might tip over. You try to find an easier gear and jam the shifter, and the new, shiny chain clangs and grinds against itself, but finally catches the teeth of a higher gear, so you pedal a few desperate strokes to keep the bike moving forward and upright.

That's when you think hear a voice behind you, a man's voice, on the side with your good ear, but you cannot make out the words (something about a *theft*?) You turn slightly to look over your shoulder, toward the direction of the sound. You have already discovered the first law of bicycle physics, the one that dictates gravity always wins. However, you quickly learn the second law: lean to the left and the bike follows.

Which is why you veer—a quick, unexpected dodge—to the left as you glance over your shoulder. That is when the voice begins to yell things you hear all too well, words like *asshole*, *fuckhead*, and *dipshit*. Not one voice—it is a chorus now. You dip your bike back to its original line when a group of riders streams by you like you are standing still, four men decked out in what looks to be bright, wordy uniforms, all of them riding bikes that reek of dollar signs and technology and ego. They shake their heads as they cut by, none of them making eye contact. The last of the four in the line eases off his speed and pulls in beside you, so close your elbows could touch. He talks out of the side of his mouth, keeping his focus on the road ahead. "When somebody says 'on your left' that don't mean cause a wreck, fuckhead," and with that pronouncement, he stands up on his seat, pounds out a series of powerful pedal strokes and catches up with his friends, who climb this gentle, rolling hill like gravity is only a minor, passing annoyance.

When TJ said you weren't a hammerhead, you had no idea what he meant. You were too afraid to ask what a hammerhead is.

You think now, you know.

CHERYL

For the record, I did everything she asked, because what are you going to say to a dying person? You cannot *not* do what they request, you know what I mean? Because there's always this fear, this little voice inside your fucking head that says, *Don't fulfill her wishes and she might come back to haunt you.* Haunt can mean a lot of things. I don't believe in ghosts and things that open doors in the night, but you know what I'm saying? There are other things that freak you out. I didn't want Peg haunting me, all up in my head, running around until the end of fucking time.

She didn't want a religious funeral. Thank god for that. There'd been enough Bible thumping and dark clothes and gnashing of teeth in the weeks before she died, when hospice came to town with their towers of morphine and their strange odors and their pasted-on cheeriness, and Peg's friends followed. Peg wanted more of a wake-type thing—even though she isn't Irish, *wasn't* Irish—in this place downtown that she used to frequent when she was still able to frequent, before she was too sick to go to a happy hour.

Originally, Peg wanted her body donated to the medical school in Charleston. She filled out all the paperwork, signed all the forms, but they (I got no fucking idea who *they* is) informed her they couldn't take her body because of how sick she was. I'm guessing they needed *clean* cadavers to teach medical students about *sick* people. Peg decided on cremation and having her ashes on display in the middle of a long table in the party room at Dunean's.

Dunean's is this combo bookstore and bar, owned by twin brothers everybody assumes are gay, Wallace and Wade. Older guys, probably in their sixties, maybe early seventies. I suppose bookstores can't sell books only and stay alive these days, and I'm guessing the bookstore twins didn't know enough about running a bar to manage a freestanding watering hole. For fuck's sake, choose one or the other. Why does one thing have to be something else at the same time? Maybe the books propped up the bar or vice versa. Who knows? If brothers break even, maybe they are happy. They always appeared happy whenever I was in there, happy with what they had. I went with Peg every now and again. She used to like to go and pick out books then thumb through the first few pages of one while she sipped on tea, or if it was late enough in the afternoon, something a little stronger. I never could keep up with her reading habits. For a while, it was historical novels, real people doing imaginary things in places like India and shit. Then when she got sicker, she read books about miracles, then when her own personal miracle didn't happen, there were books about what to expect when you were preparing to do something unexpected, like dying. That's what she was doing—trying to get ready for the thing you can never be ready for, right up until the moment *the thing* arrives. She would sit in one of the chairs near the window and read about how to handle being gone. The chairs aren't fancy in Dunean's. Nothing is fancy. Wallace and Wade were very subdued to me. They don't appear to be the kind of men who care about an excess of anything, especially profits, judging from their store. But what the fuck do I know?

Anyway, Dunean's was a decent place to say goodbye to her. Good as any, I suppose.

CLAUDE

When you have had time to recover slightly from the hills and from the embarrassment, you call Samuel. Your legs burn because of the new miles in them, the aches firing up in foreign, unknown territories, pinpricks of pain that flash every time you shift in your chair. The slightest movement, the tiniest twitch, tweaks pain somewhere. You know you will need a ride to the memorial service tomorrow. You cannot be responsible for your legs. Or yourself.

"I wasn't planning on going," Samuel says, which surprises you. He has known Peg for years, for as long as the two of you have been teaching at the college. Samuel keeps talking: "C'mon, man, you know, it's that place. Those two."

You had forgotten about Samuel's ragged relationship with Dunean's. Samuel has been teaching mathematics at Addison College for a dozen years now. You still sometimes catch him in his classroom at the end of the day, filling his old-school chalkboards with formula after formula, all the numbers written in his tiny, perfect handwriting. From a distance, the writing on the board resembles an intricate map with hundreds of destinations. As an English professor, you find his fascination with math interesting, all of that searching for proofs and solutions, answers that float out there, waiting to be plucked from the air. The two of you began your teaching careers at Addison the same fall years ago, and while you might think an English person and a math person would not necessarily mesh, you have become close over the years. You've grown experienced and jaded and tenured together, the academic ties that bind.

But Dunean's, the story there . . . Once—you think it was two or three years ago—one of Samuel's graduate school friends published a thick biography of Dudley Weldon Woodard. Samuel had to explain who Woodard was and why you should know about him. Samuel is always patient with your lack of knowledge. He is patient with everybody, usually. That's why his classes are full every semester.

The Woodard biography received a lot of national attention, and Samuel convinced his department chair to part with some money to bring the writer to Addison for a lecture and a reading. Samuel thought it would be a nice idea to have the reading at Dunean's. "It makes sense, right? A writer, surrounded by books, talking about *her* book . . . even though it's about a math person?"

Samuel called Dunean's to ask if they would be interested in hosting a reading for a visiting writer. He thinks the twin he talked with was Wallace, and Wallace said that a reading with a guest writer sounded wonderful and simply drop by one afternoon and discuss the details. The older man on the other end of the phone even offered to print flyers to promote the reading, at no cost. A couple of weeks before the reading, Samuel walked in the front door of the store, the little bell tinkling above his head, and asked to speak with the owner, and Wade stared at him like a contestant on a game show who had been asked the million-dollar question—confused, possibly angry, but not without confidence.

"I'm the owner, one of them," he said without offering up a name, and Samuel flashed a smile at him. This was, of course, Samuel's retelling of the story, but he does indeed tend to flip the switch on his smile when he thinks it will help, so you doubt he was lying about that particular detail.

"I'm Samuel Jenkins, from the math department over at Addison," he said. "I called recently about you hosting a guest writer here. I may have talked to someone else. I'm sorry, I can't remember the name of the gentleman I spoke to."

Samuel told you about the expression on the man's face. "It's that white people look," he said, "the one you folks get when you're afraid I might sit on your furniture." Samuel said he knew what had happened; it was not the first time his voice had camouflaged his skin color. Whoever he'd talked to on the phone the first time thought he was a lily-white professor at Addison College, not a six-foot-three former basketball player with a Woodstock-era afro and a voice made for drive-time radio. "It was stupid of me, man," he said to you later. "I dropped my guard. I didn't have my radar up for a gay, racist bookseller. Rookie move." You don't know how Samuel realized Wade was gay. Maybe he sensed it.

As Samuel soon discovered, Dunean's is a sweet-smelling, chatchka-selling bastion of flamboyant, hard-boiled bigotry. Wallace and his brother, Wade, are the rarest of creatures: gay, Southern racists. When Wade told Samuel, in no uncertain terms, that Dunean's would have no interest in hosting a writer from the college—even when Samuel reminded him they had previously offered to print advertisements—Samuel realized pressing the issue would get him nowhere. Samuel is smart. He knows when to dial back his indignation.

Samuel shrugged his big shoulders and wandered through the bookstore section of Dunean's, searching for the African American writers' shelf, which of course, he never found. He perused the fiction section, looking for some Alice Walker or some Marlon James or Victor Lavalle. It did not take Samuel long to figure out that Dunean's was the whitest bookstore he had ever walked through. Not only were the shelves stripped bare of any Black writers, all the Hispanics authors had been exiled to some literary penal colony outside the walls of Dunean's. Wallace and Wade had no problems with white women writers or white gay writers. Samuel saw plenty of them—and the white queer writers (at least the ones Samuel recognized as out and publishing) were cover-forward on most of the shelves.

"I thought about pitching a fit of some kind," Samuel told you, "but you know." And you, indeed, know Samuel. He isn't the kind to pull down bookshelves or lead a loud protest on the sidewalk outside Dunean's. Instead, Samuel strolled into the Southern History section, opened every book he could find about the Civil War, and carefully, slowly tore out the last page. When he had a sheaf of final pages an inch or so thick, he walked to the counter, where the twin brothers stood side by side now, where they had been watching Samuel's every move.

"Funny," Samuel said, "they saw me the whole time, ripping out those pages, and they didn't say a word. They stood there like a creepy reflection of each other. But I could tell, one of them was more pissed than the other. I'm not sure which one."

Samuel tossed the pages into the air, and they rained down on the twins, like giant confetti, the conclusions of all that history floating down to the floor at Dunean's. Samuel looked at Wallace and Wade and said, "Now you'll never know how it turns out," and he left, the door tinkling behind him like a limp alarm.

Samuel told you he expected fall out of the worst kind—a bill for all of the books he destroyed or a reprimand from the college, maybe even a visit from the sheriff, but nothing came of it. "All that means is I should have done worse," he said. "It didn't even faze them."

Samuel's snub at Dunean's occurred years ago, but you'd forgotten it. The fact that Peg dragged you to the bookstore at least once a week wore the racist sheen off the place. Maybe cancer trumps racism, you think. You had to go with her. You had no choice. You pretended Wallace and Wade were gay and psychotic, not gay and racist. Samuel did not hold it against you that you added dollars to their till.

Now, you need Samuel's help, and you know from experience if you push hard enough, he'll give it to you. "Man, I don't want to go to Peg's wake by myself. I don't know what kind of shape I'll be in afterward," you say. "And there's the fact that I can barely walk."

"You drunk already?" Samuel says. You imagine him on the other end of the line, glancing at his wristwatch.

"No. It's a long story. Actually, it's not that long at all. I bought a bike. I rode it," you say.

"Which is what you do with a bike," Samuel says.

You whine. "And now I can't walk. Listen, up until a couple days ago, I had two real friends in the world. Now I'm down to one, and I'm asking *him* for a ride to the wake of the other one." You pause. You have been friends with Samuel long enough to know which buttons to push.

"Well then, I'm sitting my ass in the car the whole time while you go memorialize," Samuel says.

You knew he would ultimately give you a ride. He is one of those people who always does the right thing in the end, like not firebombing Dunean's and instead ripping pages out of books nobody reads anyway. Samuel understands better than anybody about the whole thing with Peg. He knows the two of you had been treading in water that grew deeper every month, that you left long before it finally flowed over you, before it turned you and your wife into awkward strangers, that you left weeks and weeks before Peg got sick then sicker. He understands. You stayed in Samuel's spare room for a few days after you left, while you looked for a new place, something you could afford. Samuel understands because he listened while you sat on his couch and drank his beer and told him why you had decided you weren't such a bad person. The only downside those nights was that Samuel played his Diana Ross albums while you talked, and he sort of weaved during your stories, a quiet little dance. Now, when you think about Peg, the memories that pop into your mind's eye carry a distinctly Motown soundtrack.

"I'll bring you beer," you say. A final bribe.

"I'm sorry about Peg. You sure you doing okay, man?" he asks you, and you say yes, and that is all the two of you need to say about Peg passing away. It's nice to have a friend who is patient with you.

WALLACE & WADE

What we do is, we sit and wait on the UPS man to deliver boxes chock full of white authors, and we put them on our shelves, and no one has ever raised a fuss except that Negro professor a few years ago, and for heaven's sake, tearing the final pages from a few insignificant history books was a small—and pitiful—cost to absorb for never having him breach our threshold again.

So simple . . . when the publishers distribute materials about their upcoming book lists for a particular season—with descriptions and author photos and what not—and they ask us what we want to stock, we simply do not order any books by Black authors, no matter how supposedly *renown* they are. We own this store, and we can carry exactly what we want to sell because we own the shelves too. There is no legitimate law requiring us to carry every shade of author. We have extended this practice to Hispanic writers as well—men and women. This has nothing to do with hate. It has more to do with a particular type of palate. We simply have no *taste* for that sort of thing, much in the same way we don't care for, say, olives. You will never find tapenade on our bar food menu. And you won't find Toni Morrison on the shelves.

You think we don't know hate? Try being us. In the South. Especially in the sixties and seventies. It was akin to belonging to a club possessing dozens of members, yet you could not mingle with any of them in the harsh light of day. It wasn't simply that someone might back you against a wall and call you a fag and punch you in the nose. Oh, those were the minor irritants. And common. No, belonging to this Southern fraternity could get you killed. There were no *hate crimes* in those days. There was hate. And there was crime. And rarely the twain met in the halls of justice. Justice? Oh, for heaven's sake.

That same Negro professor who scattered those pages across our counter probably assumed our attitude toward people of color was a cry for revenge because of our own coming-of-age persecutions. Some sort of cultural tit for tat. To which we would say to him: *You never heard the story of our father. That tells you everything.*

We will relate it as economically as possible. It would make a wonderful libretto. What we mean to say is: the tale contains drama heightened to the point of gothic, which we would agree is a staple of the opera *and* the South, wouldn't you?

Back in the day, our father owned the icehouse in town. This was, obviously, during the time when people would still pull their cars and delivery trucks to the lip of the loading dock behind the icehouse and roll away with solid blocks of clear, wonderful ice. A time when people still had iceboxes in their houses, when grocery stores required boulders of ice. He spent most of his daylight hours sequestered in his tiny office inside the icehouse, in the dark and cool, sipping bourbon, emerging only to shave fresh ice into his whiskey with his pocketknife or to load blocks of ice for customers with a pair of rusty, iron tongs or to run off nosy children—mostly Black ones—who wanted to scoop stray chunks of ice from the ground and suck on them in the hot sun. Our father felt that nothing in the world existed for free, even frozen water.

The only time the two of us breached the inside of the icehouse was during our summer vacations. Our mother—and she is another story, God rest her soul—would drive our powder blue Plymouth Fury to Claussen's dusty roadside fruit-and-vegetable stand on Highway 25 and thump several watermelons until she found one in tune. We then carried the melon to the icehouse, where our father would *harrumph* at us from the office door like we had intruded upon his day. We toted said watermelon to the far, dark reaches of the icehouse, our PF Flyers crackling on the frozen cement floor, and wedged it softly in a cold crevasse where we would leave it to thoroughly chill overnight. The next afternoon, we would return and retrieve the frozen watermelon. In all those trips, ferrying watermelons back and forth from the icehouse, we don't recollect our father ever saying a word to our mother. To be honest, we don't recall her ever venturing inside with us.

Back at our house, we would scurry around the yard half naked in order to work up a sweat while our mother cracked the watermelon in half on the edge of our picnic table. With a steak knife, she carved tiny chunks of frozen red meat. She removed the seeds and fed the fruit to us like we were the twin kings of Egypt.

Our father habitually returned home minutes before dark, no matter what season, no matter how long the afternoon light wore on, like some sort of human alarm clock set for dusk, his still-wet, salt-caked boots announcing his appearance and serving as a prelude for the silence that settled over the house for the rest of the night. We do not remember our parents ever looking at each other. We are pained today to recall how our dear mother was, for all intents and purposes, two different women—the laughing, handsome lady brandishing a watermelon-tipped knife *and* the quiet servant who stared at her feet while she walked through the house, ferrying a fresh toddy or an empty dinner plate for our silent father. Our poor mother.

Anyway, one particular August morning, we made the pilgrimage to Claussen's and mother must have thumped two dozen melons before she found one that would suffice. We recall her smiling at Mr. Claussen, teasing that he must be hiding the truly good ones at the bottom of the stack. He smiled back at her and watched her walk away. Oh, we noticed him leering. Our mother was thin and perfect, her off-the-rack dress swaddling her like a runway model, her blond hair shining.

As per usual, we found a niche for the watermelon far in the rear of the icehouse. We placed it there and watched our father watch us as we made our way back into the sunlight. His expression never altered while he sipped whiskey from one of his paper Dixie cups. Mother left the air conditioning running in the Fury, and we slid into the chilly back seat, like normal. Except this time, mother decided she wanted a lunch date with her little boys, and she aimed the Fury downtown instead of toward our neighborhood.

Like it was meant to be, an open parking space revealed itself right in front of Brown's Diner. Miracle of miracles, as we walked in, three stools freed themselves at the counter. We sat and devoured hotdogs and relish and Coleslaw, mother between the two of us, smiling as she cut her hotdog into bites small enough for her fork. Mother never believed in eating with her fingers if she could possibly avoid it.

After lunch, the way home took us by Claussen's once again, and instead of waving and roaring by, Mother whipped into the small dirt turnaround in front of the stand. Mr. Claussen looked happily surprised, and she told us to remain in the car, that she had a feeling about something. From what we could discern from the back seat, she told Mr. Claussen she felt as though she hadn't done a good job picking a melon that morning, and could she try some others? Before long, she'd found a new one, so new it was still dirt-covered. Mr. Claussen pulled out a hose and washed it bright green. We headed toward the icehouse for the second time that day.

Mother was oddly engaged, in a rare mood, singing along with the radio and driving faster than usual. She pulled the Fury up to the loading dock and told us to put this new melon by the other. She said she would wait for us at the car. "Don't worry," she said, "I'll be right here. I'll always be waiting for you." Together, we carried the melon inside, and it felt heavier than the one from the morning. Perhaps we were tired after lunch, in need of our nap.

The door of the icehouse office was cracked slightly. In past summers, we'd only seen the door closed and locked, or seen our father filling the doorway with his scowling figure. We shuffled slowly toward the darkness at the rear of the icehouse but felt ourselves magnetically drawn by the shaft of light emanating from his office, the melon like a divining rod between us, pushing us in a common direction. Maybe we were attracted by the sounds we heard behind the office door where the light originated—a scrape and a moan and the smack of a meaty hand on a tabletop perhaps, all the noises connected, woven together like several bars of dissonant music—and we must have grown bold because we peered through that slim crack. In that slice of vision, we could see a tower of paper Dixie cups and a bottle on a small table. A woman's shoe, not a man's boot, lay on the floor near some shiny, bunched-up garment. Above that, we saw the faded bottom of a small, dark, delicate foot cocked toward us at an odd angle, as if someone were sitting slightly out of sight in a chair, pointing their toes. Whoever was attached to that foot must have sensed us peering through the door, because a woman suddenly whispered loudly, *hey!*, or it could have been *help!*, but before we could translate her hiss, our father stepped into our view, blocking the view behind him. We have no memory of the expression on his face at that moment. We can only imagine the rage rising like heat waves from his dark eyes. Our attention was more on the fact that he stood not five feet from us, facing us, his pants bunched below his knees, his—and how to put this delicately?—loins in full, unobstructed view.

The watermelon suddenly became too heavy to hold or too slick or too unimportant, and we dropped it. The rind cracked and broke, splattering on the threshold—a terrible red, seedy, sloppy mess somebody would have to clean up.

And we ran. One of us slid on the wet, cold icehouse floor and landed on our knees, the salt water on the floor instantly intensifying the new scrape. We burst into the sunlight and were blinded for a moment, scurrying like puppies that had yet to open their eyes. When we finally adjusted to the light, we saw the look on our mother's face, and she was not at all surprised to see us. In fact, as we've deconstructed that precise moment over the years, we've come to realize her expression was perhaps one of relief, relief that her boys had finally seen something she had been living with for years. She leaned casually against the Fury, and she seemed to be saying, *I couldn't tell you about this before, but now we have something we can share when we need to.*

We didn't wait to see if our father appeared on the loading dock. Our mother herded us into the car and said absolutely nothing, and we took our cue from her, which was not an unusual thing. She sang to the radio the entire ride home.

SCOTT GOULD

Later that afternoon, as the sun disappeared, we heard our father's customary footsteps on the porch, and to be honest, we didn't think much of it. Though only a few short hours had passed since our father stood naked in a room with a whispering, shoeless woman, it felt like days, months. Mother wasn't concerned, so why should we worry? At that time, we had no idea what our father was doing with that woman. We were too young and uninitiated. We were our mother's boys. We know better now.

He stalked into the house with a paper cup in his hand, sipping as he moved. We remember so much of those seconds, even now—the crunch of his damp boots on the pinewood floors, the dank smell of him, the sandpaper calluses of his grip, calluses turned red by the rust of the iron ice tongs—as he grabbed us by the necks and herded us into his bedroom. That was where he beat us.

The buckle on his belt, the same belt that we had seen hanging loose and at his thighs earlier that very same day, whipped around and caught us on our legs and arms. The brass brought blood. He bent us over the edge of the bed, and he dared us to run as we heard the wind-sound of the belt followed a millisecond later by the arrival of the metallic sting. He talked as he beat us, never yelling, calmly asking us questions. "What did you see?" he said between strokes with the belt. "Who did you see?" And when we answered again and again that we only saw *him*, he called us liars, which spurred him on. Once, our mother tried to enter the room, and he screamed at her, "Get the hell outta here. You know what I'll do to you," then he returned to his calmer voice. He asked us if we were learning anything, and we screamed each time the wind-sound came because we knew what followed. "Are you learning anything?" he repeated loudly and calmly. He said, "Do you know what people will do for a little ice?" We screamed for our mother, but she did not make her way to the bedroom again. It took so long for those belt buckle marks to heal properly.

We never again drove to the icehouse. We wondered what happened to the watermelon left hidden in the dark. We imagined how many other women sat in that chair and pointed their feet toward the ceiling. We wondered if our mother had ever looked through that crack in the door. We thought these things, but we never said a word. None of us

44

ever said a word. Our mother's silence made her crazy eventually, but that is another story.

As for us? We grew relatively thick scar tissue thanks to our father's belt buckle. Women and icehouse offices grew synonymous with pain. The belt ultimately cinched our silence. We searched for new people to love and new people to hate and learned when to be quiet about the whole of it.

Enough with the family tale of woe. Seconds ago, the UPS driver stuck his head in the front door and said he left two new boxes of books on the loading dock at the rear. He said we might need a broom, that some creature left a mess on the platform.

What in the world?

PEG

Weather does not happen here.

I'm not sure where *here* is, but yes, I was missing weather. Humid breezes and falling leaves and humidity and the bite of cold on the end of your nose. All of that.

Here, I didn't feel a thing, and now that I thought about it, I'd felt that before. Well, for an hour at a time. When I was in college—my sophomore year, I think—I considered myself curious and intellectual. One afternoon, I saw a new flyer on the door of the psychology building. A professor named Dr. Seegars needed volunteers for some experiments on sensory deprivation. If you lasted through the whole series of tests—I think there were a half dozen—you could make a hundred dollars. A hundred dollars was a lot of ramen. I signed up. Because I was a curious intellectual.

Dr. Seegars was one of those young men whose hair probably turned gray when he was fifteen. His boyish, doughy face was framed by shaggy, gray hair. A sheepdog with glasses. He told me every little thing that would happen to me. If I'm remembering correctly—and I think I am—he read from a checklist of items so he wouldn't forget to mention something. I wondered if an experiment of his had gone horribly wrong in the past and this was some new safety requirement leveled on him by the school or the school's lawyers, or maybe he was always this cut-and-dried and list-driven. I almost ran out at that point, and I tried to recall if I had seen any maimed psychology majors walking around the building, victims of Dr. Seegars's latest battery of crazy tests.

Here was the deal: Dr. Seegars was going to hook my head to a bunch of electrodes and close me up in a sensory deprivation tank. He said I could wear a bathing suit if I wanted to but that he'd prefer I was clothes-less. That was what he said: *clothes-less*. Not naked or nude. He appeared embarrassed to say it, hiding his eyes behind that mop of hair. He said I would float on my back in some salt water in complete darkness. I'd use ear plugs to block sounds and keep water out. I was supposed to try and not move a muscle, but if I did, the tank utilized some sort of wave reduction system that would keep me from bobbing in the water. Dr. Seegars would chart my brain during all of the sessions and see what happened with my waves, the ones in my brain, not in the water. He started talking beta and theta, and I zoned out. I didn't need the details. The way I saw it, I was going to get a hundred dollars for taking a soggy nap once a week.

After that first session, I would have done it for free. The feeling was so wonderful. I don't know how to explain the lack of *any* sensation tweaking my body. No sounds, no touches, no smells. I couldn't tell if my eyes were open or shut, the darkness was so complete, so total. The one sense I couldn't turn off was taste. I kept imagining tastes. My mother's lemon pound cake and the way the bites of it would crumble on my tongue and dissolve. The sting of Texas Pete I drizzled on the fish tacos I ordered from Paco's on the corner across from the football stadium, on cold days when games were going on, but I didn't attend because I cared a lot more about tacos than football. I pretended that when I took a bite and heard the roar from the stadium, the people were cheering for my taco. They were that good.

When I didn't have sensations sneaking in from the outside, the *inside* of my head caught fire. Anything that flickered across my mind's eye appeared in Technicolor. The real world was cut off, and the world that *wasn't* real suddenly became more intense, more important. During one of the sessions, I imagined having crazy-loud sex with this cute, tall, stupid frat boy named Carson. I had an orgasm in my head. I'm not sure what happened in the salt water where I was "clothes-less."

When I dried off and dressed after that session, Dr. Seegars asked me what had been going through my brain. He said some irregular activity showed up on the graphs. I told him he had no idea how irregular it was. I never spoke to Carson again. It was too embarrassing to recall his sensory-deprived performance.

But now, here in this place, where I landed or settled or whatever the hell it was, the sensations around me, or the lack of them, reminded me of the tank. Here, it was dark, totally black, the dark before the world began. I couldn't feel anything pressing against my skin. I wasn't even sure I had skin. I floated and waited and watched what happened back there, in the place that wasn't *here*. I could see it all, but I couldn't touch any of it. I could see it, and I had this sensation that I should laugh or cry or scream, but of course I couldn't do anything because, well, I was *here*, a long way from there.

For instance, from here, I saw the front door of Dunean's. A cute little sign hung from a cute little hook. Wallace hand-lettered the sign. I recognized his precise, loopy handwriting. The sign said, *We are closed for a private party*, and I thought to myself (or imagined to myself or talked to myself, I couldn't tell which), what a funny way of telling people that in the back bar beyond the bookshelves sat an urn full of ashes and a bar full of people waiting to say goodbye, and the ones who weren't crying laughed quietly. That was not a *private party*. I mean, I wasn't so dead that I couldn't tell the difference between a party and a wake. You'd think Wallace or Wade had a better handle on the decorum required.

Then it occurred to me: that was not a new sign. That was the sign they hung for *every* private affair. Bachelorette parties, birthday celebrations, business happy hours, readings. And wakes, quasi-funerals. I'd been lumped in with everything else. I was an event now. A party. I didn't know whether to be happy about it or angry or sad. I didn't even know if I was allowed to have a range of emotions. I floated and watched.

People walked up to the door of Dunean's, read the sign. Some walked right in, and others peered through the windows and shook their heads, making new plans because they knew they weren't invited to the super special private party. They sweated in the sun. I saw them glistening. Some fanned themselves, their hands like fluttering wings in front of their faces. They were such beautiful people, every one of them, even the ones who didn't realize I was gone.

I missed weather so much.

CLAUDE

On the ride to Dunean's in his cranberry-colored Lincoln Continental, Samuel asks you two questions and nothing else. He says, "Are you sad?" and "Why are you walking like that?"

The sidewinder walk is, of course, a result of the bike. Earlier that morning, when your feet hit the floor, you entertained thoughts of amputation. You wanted your legs removed at the source of their pain. You admit you went too hard for your first ride, but it is a bike, for god's sake. An expensive one. A fast one, sure. But it is *not* designed to inflict immeasurable pain and suffering. You have a burning desire to get in shape. You want to forsake your love handles and expand the capacity of your lungs. You don't want to die in the process, so you tell Samuel, "I cooked my legs on my new bike. I don't want to talk about it."

As far as being sad? You are, but you have yet to cry, and you can't escape all the death clichés zipping through your head. *She is in a better place. She is not in pain anymore. Etc. Etc.* You do not believe any of them. You're sad because the two of you will no longer have those small talks about things that on the surface were not vitally important but made all the difference in your tiny world, like unusual weather or the length of Marlene's hair. You're sad because your daughter is motherless now with a fair-to-middling chance of being fatherless, if the pain in your legs is any indication. You are sad because the world, your world, is lighter by the weight of one soul.

But when Samuel asks about sadness, you simply reply, "What do you think?" and you pry yourself out of the car then attempt to quiet your screaming legs by walking like a man who has recently discovered he owns feet.

"I'm going to park over there in that shade, and I'm going to listen to music. Bring me a light beer when you can. Oh, and a copy of something by Colson Whitehead," Samuel says, smiling, easing the Lincoln away, its tires crunching in the gravel parking lot.

You have no expectations in terms of a crowd. You know there will be that awkward second early on when the low murmur of people mingling goes quiet as you walk—lurch/gimp/short-step—into the room, not because you are unwelcome, but because you are not to be trusted. ("I mean, he left a sick woman, you know . . . ")

Sure enough, there it is—an unmistakable lull when you break out of the bookshelves and enter the back bar. You scan the crowd like it doesn't bother you. You spot neighbors you lost in the divorce—the ones who live on either side of your old house—and the crotchety, bent woman from across the street who year-round throws sticks from her yard into the street. You see Peg's running buddies, the group of women with tanned legs and faces that glow with health and toothy condescension, and you think they could at least tone down their preening for one day. A quiet cadre of people, men and women, sit at tables on the outskirts of the room. They wear bandanas around their bald heads. You imagine them taking mental notes, wondering, *How long before . . . ?* or *But for the current grace of God.*

You don't see Wade slide in beside you but feel his hand come to rest on your forearm. "No formal ceremony, of course. She wanted people to talk and reminisce. A few might choose to speak. I'm not sure. There's an open bar. I'm sorry for your loss," he says, waving in the general direction of the beer taps and racks of liquor. Wade is one of those guys who's always talking as he leaves. Or leaving as he talks. At the bar, you spy a tall man who strikes you as familiar for some reason, but you can't place him. You stare, trying to make a connection, and somebody else eases up on your left, and you think, *I have to be more alert. People are sneaking up on me too easily.*

It is Marlene.

"I had a bet with Cheryl about whether or not you'd show up," she says. You want to ask her which side of that bet she laid her money. Marlene often opens conversations in strange, off-putting ways. Even when she was a little kid, she did that. And it was not reserved for the rare times she chose to talk to you. Anyone she speaks with, she enjoys starting them off imbalanced. "Hey, but you need to be here. I totally get it," she says.

"Are you okay?" you ask her, not because it's completely appropriate for the circumstances, but because you do, indeed, wonder how she is getting along. Marlene's eyes lock on yours, brown eyes, her mother's, but you cannot help glancing over her shoulder, maintaining a lookout. She notices your nervousness.

"Yes, Claude, they are all watching us, wondering what will happen, wondering if one of us will gnash our teeth or pull hair or fall to our knees. You should probably hug me. That will fuck with their heads. They won't know what to do with that," she says and suddenly her arms are around your waist, her head tucking sharply under your chin. With your nose in her hair, you smell places she's been. You wish she would call you dad. Your daughter feels wonderful. When she squeezes, you put your own arms around her and lose your balance a bit—your real balance, not the kind that Marlene toppled with during her opening conversational salvo—and stumble slightly.

She hisses at you when you weave in her grasp. "Already drunk. Shocking," she says, and she is wrong. Sure, you had a quick belt before Samuel picked you up—a tweak of the old courage and an homage to the pain in your legs—but hardly enough Jim Beam to create instability. Also, you found an out-of-date bottle of muscle relaxers hiding in the medicine cabinet and gobbled two, maybe three, to take the edge off the bite in your legs. (Confession: has not worked.) In any event, certainly not enough narcotic to make you wobble.

"No," you say, "it's my legs. I bought a bike. It's a long story. I'm very, very sore right now. Walking is a challenge."

Marlene breaks her grip. "You and exercise? You *do* need a drink," she says and spins you in the direction of the open bar. You grimace when your legs are forced to operate, and you track Marlene as you follow her toward the drinks. From the outside, she appears to be the normal seventeen-almost-eighteen-year-old girl, with the clothes that suggest she is far, far beyond the braces-and-zits middle school phase. She wears make-up now—too much for your taste, but that is not your wheelhouse. *Those brown eyes do not need anything to bring them out*, you think. She has yet to master walking in shoes with heels, but you have no room to talk about anyone's gait at this point. On the inside, Marlene is one of those kids who houses a soul four times her age, like some cranky AARP member has taken up squatter's rights beneath her high school skin.

"I need to go think about what I'm going to say about mom," Marlene tells you as she veers away from the bar. "We can talk later, Claude, you know, about things."

You know what she means. When Peg was alive, but convinced the end was ultimate and soon, she, Cheryl, and Marlene worked out a type of unofficial custody agreement for Marlene to live with her aunt until high school graduation. You were not brought in on the discussion, only informed of the ad hoc committee's decision, but you can't blame them. You gave up voting rights the minute you moved out. You guess Marlene wants to relate the details of her continued residence with Cheryl, now that Peg is gone. When the bartender hands you a bourbon—light ice—you wonder what Cheryl's husband thinks of his additional boarder. You wonder if Cheryl let him get anything "on the record" about the arrangement.

The interruption comes from a man on your left, the tall guy you spotted earlier. "How far did you pedal yesterday?" he asks, and something clicks in your brain. He was in the group that you almost ran off the road. He is not the guy who hung back and scolded you, but this guy was definitely there, hammering out a rhythm on his pedals, like pistons firing beneath a car hood. "Hal Sloan," he says, sticking out his hand. "Sorry about Larry and the language. He likes to think he is the king of the road, the local Lance Armstrong or something. Don't worry about him. He has a lot more anger than sense."

Hal stands a good four inches taller than you and many pounds lighter. He is a truly skinny man. You can't help but notice his thin, delicate wrists that look too weak to anchor his large hands. You should have immediately marked him as a cyclist who spends hours perched on his bike: the tanned face and pale outline around his eyes where sunglasses usually rest, the hands white from wearing fingerless cycling gloves in the sun.

"Sorry about swerving. I'm new," you confess.

"Everybody was new at one time," he says. "You need clips. You'll go faster."

You do not *want* to go faster. Every step you take that morning causes you to write classified ads in your imagination, advertising the sale of your bike.

"Yeah, right," you say, "clips." You down the bourbon and ask for a repeat.

Across the room, Cheryl grabs attention by clanging on an empty glass. Marlene stands beside her. They resemble an organized team, the team that eased Peg as gently as they could through her final days. At least that is what everyone thinks. Nobody in the room—other than Cheryl and Marlene—knows about the novels you read aloud to Peg when she wanted a story she could fall asleep to. They do not know about the feet you rubbed with peppermint lotion or the dog you took to the vet to be put down because you were the only one who could handle something else in the house dying. All this *after* you left your wife. No one knows. In their minds, you abandoned a sick woman when you had the chance. The second bourbon scuttles down easily.

"You rehydrating there, sport?" Hal says, chuckling, and you decide to hate him. Because you hate any man who calls another man *sport*. This is not *The Great Gatsby*. You hate that he can pedal up mountains, that he wears clips, that he can laugh at someone who wants a couple of belts on the day of his wife's wake. Ex-wife's wake. Almost ex-wife's wake. You glance toward the urn on the table full of flowers. *Why* is *Hal Sloan here?* you wonder, and you start to ask him, but the first word emerges from your mouth like a soap bubble and turns into several wet, slurried syllables. You shake your head, because a couple of bourbons—no matter how speedy—never leaves you with speech impediments. You should have read the label closer on that pill bottle. Your legs don't hurt nearly as much because you cannot, for sure, confirm they exist. You count this as a good thing. Hal laughs again, and you want to hit him in his perfect teeth, but you know better than to start a bar fight at a bookstore/bar wake. Cheryl motions at one of the bandana-wearing women and asks her to say a few words, and you are certain if you are asked later to analyze your actions, this moment will be identified as the tipping point: the split-second Bandana Woman takes the stage.

You lean against the bar, trying to relieve some pressure on your legs, which have begun to burn again, right there in the glow of Hal and his perfectly fit smile. You can maintain a sense of decorum with all the little storms around you. But when the cancer patient—one of Peg's chemo friends who, unlike Peg, still exists in the strange limbo between dead and almost dead—asks the crowd to bow its collective head in prayer, you transform into a man possessed. Possessed by what, you cannot truly confess. Your action is not an anti-religious one. You have no problem with prayer. And though Peg had never been a churchgoer, this request for prayer doesn't float in the air like a violation or an insult. However, when you see Bandana Woman dip her head and ask everyone there to do the same, you suddenly have a plan, as if you are an intrepid explorer and the hidden pass through the mountains suddenly reveals itself to you. *Perhaps* that *is a religious sensation*, you think, *an epiphany that comes from the inside or above or from wherever epiphanies originate.*

Bandana Woman has a voice suited for the pulpit or a yoga class—a strong, hypnotic rhythm that lulls all who dare to listen into a semi-sleep. As she talks about the fight in which Peg no longer has to throw punches, you feel the air in the room stop moving. Next to you, Hal still has that smile fixed to his face, but his eyes are squeezed into tight, physically-fit slits.

This thing you do next, it is very simple. And it makes perfect, wonderful sense at the moment.

Peg

In the eleventh grade, our English teacher, Miss Sharper, had us read *Huck Finn*. She made a big deal about the scene when Huck snuck into the church to watch his own funeral proceedings. I remember her telling us this was something every human being desired to do, to be able to see how people acted when you were dead and gone, to hear what they said about you when you couldn't talk back, couldn't defend yourself. I always thought Miss Sharper was a shade melodramatic about that scene and, well, about the whole book, for that matter. I thought it a bit bold to draw conclusions about the desires of the entire human race. Turns out, Miss Sharper was spot on.

I was very excited about my memorial service at Dunean's, more than I should have been. Even though I no longer possessed the ability to react to anything that happened, I wanted to simply listen and observe, to be a fly on the wall, you could say. A dead fly on the wall. The ultimate eavesdropper.

Full confession: I wasn't completely sure of the logistics about how to put an ear to the wall of one's own funeral. Here, there were no instructions, only silence and that monotonous floating sensation, which sounds airy and comfortable but quickly turned irritating, like all things that begin slowly and beautifully but soon become a pebble in your proverbial shoe, e.g., train rides, a child's questions, sitcoms, long vacations, sex.

And it's not your body that floats. That fleshy bag of bones no longer exists. What floats in the dark silence is simply the *idea* of you, more like a cloud of vapor that still possesses enough electrical spark to create thought and memory and the ability to keep a naked eye on the world you left behind. I don't wish for more, because that is another thing that no longer exists: wishing for something else. Because there is nothing else. Here, I don't desire more because *more* is not a concept. That, I think, is the only valuable attribute of where I am currently making residence— the fact that I no longer have to worry about longing for more, about wishing for things I don't possess. I never realized how much time and energy I'd spent wishing and desiring and, ultimately, being disappointed. None of that wasted time and energy now.

The first thing I noticed after the attendees filed into the bar at Dunean's, was who didn't bother to come to my memorial. I'm glad I didn't lay odds and money on who would show up. I thought for sure my Aunt Lois from Florida would make the trip, but no sight of her. I have cousins scattered across the South, all of whom knew my death was imminent, and none of them bothered to attend. I thought maybe old boyfriends and ex-teachers might want to pay some sort of final respects. Was Miss Sharper still alive? That would have been interesting to see her there, while I watched Huck Finn–style from the great, wispy beyond.

On the other hand, the people that showed up, god. I mean, who would have thought my mailman would be shuffling from one foot to the other at the back of the room, in his uniform because he dropped by in the middle of his Saturday route to say goodbye? His name was Randy, and I cannot forget the day he found out I was sick and knocked on my door and said that I didn't have to worry about walking the sixty feet down to the street to get my mail anymore because he was going to bring it to the porch and lay my magazines and bills on the cushion of the wicker glider. "I don't care what the federal government says about having to put mail in an official mailbox, I don't want you walking down that sidewalk. Screw the government. You could trip or something . . . " His voice trailed off. Randy came to say goodbye.

There was Marlene's tutor from the seventh grade, back when we thought she had some sort of learning disability with math. Turns out Lauren the tutor was right: Marlene's only problem was she hated math, which isn't so much a disability as an inalienable right. I hadn't seen Lauren in years, yet there she was, a glass of wine in her hand, wandering around the table where my urn of ashes sat, surrounded by wonderful, colorful tiger lilies and hydrangea.

Of course, the expected were scattered among the unexpected. All the girls from the hospital where I went for my chemo, Rhonda and Tiff and Ginny, who always pulled their chairs and their IV stands into a sad little semicircle while we talked about anything but the future and stared at anything but that steady drip making its way down the tube and into our veins. It was good to see them walking around, still able to sit in the chairs lining the wall of the bar. I realized I had never seen them sitting down *without* an IV trailing from their arms. And the others. The women I used to run with in the mornings, when I could still jog. Friends from the neighborhood.

Marlene never stopped walking, as if her constant pacing would burn off the energy required for grieving or crying, but I knew she wouldn't shed tears. I saw her sneak behind the bar when she thought no one looked and down a quick, sneaky shot of Fireball from a paper cup. I was more proud than disappointed when I saw that. Cheryl was Cheryl, trying to keep everything on the record, maintaining control of everything except, of course, her husband, who spent his time wandering aimlessly among the bookstore shelves, sending texts, then receiving replies that made him smile, then sending more. I assume the texts were headed toward that woman, Louise. Patrick is the worst kind of adulterer, the kind that thinks he is clever and clandestine and flying invisible under the radar, when in reality, everyone knows what he's doing and who he's doing—and everybody simply doesn't care. When he dies, it might be a very small memorial. One attendee. *Hi, I'm Louise, chair for one, please.*

Wallace and Wade fluttered in and out, and I don't mean that as a slur. They actually beat the air with their hands like tiny funeral parlor fans as they moved. When I was still alive—in the bookstore reading and drinking tea and trying to decide if I had enough life left in me to finish the thick novel I bought—I studied the two of them. They've always walked that way, moving the air out of their way, the two of them side by side through the shelves, around the bar, into that locked back room where I assumed they had their office.

And speaking of walking. Poor Claude. I guessed he was already drunk, with the walk he walked, as if he were in pain. Plus, he had Samuel drive him. Samuel served as Claude's default transportation when drinking was involved. He had ferried Claude from any number of watering holes or faculty receptions or happy hours. Claude was always very slick and practiced about covering up the extent of his buzzes. You could never tell by looking at him or watching him maneuver around furniture or through crowds. Once, Claude passed a field sobriety test after a full day of drinking. The highway patrolman admitted defeat when Claude recited the alphabet backwards while tight rope walking a yellow line in the highway. But something was wrong. Claude's walk wasn't the usual drunken shuffle. He gingerly put one foot in front of the other, like the floor was made of thin glass and he was afraid of breaking right through it, fearful of snapping a bone. I'd never seen him walk that way, at least not from this point of view.

He looked sad, but that was not a news flash. Claude had never been the happiest of people. When I first met and married him, I mistook his demeanor for academic seriousness. You know the type, the brooding English professor. It took me a few years to realize that he would have been a depressive person no matter what the occupation. He could have been a circus clown and still glower about everything. For Claude, the world was a series of constant mazes, and his only option was to constantly bang his head against the dead ends he encountered.

I know what people think. In fact, one clique of women rudely talked about nothing else during my memorial at Dunean's. I could hear them. When Claude, on his way to the bar, soft-shoed by the women I used to jog with, they launched into a none-too-quiet reexamination of his leaving me and how they *find it so hard to believe that a man would abandon a dying woman* and how for all they knew *he basically killed her, what with the added anxiety and stress of a divorce for god's sake he might as well be sent away for murder.*

Those gossipy witches could not be further from the truth. I hoped Claude wouldn't hear them, but it wouldn't have been a shock to him. He knew what people said. We talked about it after he moved out. People didn't understand the timing, the fact that the process of him leaving had started years before, long before I was sick, long before the cells—the bad ones—multiplied at horrifyingly deadly rates. Honestly, I simply tired of being married to a sad man, a man who got up every morning wondering what dastardly things life was going to toss in his path that day. He wasn't a mean man. He wasn't loud and abusive. He was the unhappiest man I knew, and the damn problem was I happened to marry him. The first day I started calling him Eeyore, I thought it was a joke. I was trying to be being funny. A new nickname. Lighten things up. Maybe that would make a difference.

All he said was, "Well, now you got me figured out. Happy?"

I mean, that's why Marlene wouldn't pay much attention to him. She figured out early on, even before she was potty trained, that her father was the worst kind of ballast. He weighed down the entire family, and she would have no part of it. You can see the irony, right? This made him even *more* depressed as the years went by. Sure, those girls in the running group asked me all the right questions as the years ticked by. They suggested all the right things. *He should see a shrink.* Well, Danielle, he went, and it didn't work. I think Claude ended up depressing Dr. Gayle with the clouds he brought into his office each week. *Is he on any medications for that?* Yes, Margo, he has tried a number of things, and nothing brightened him up. He actually liked most of the pills because, he said, they made him have vivid, amazing dreams. "Little full-color movies in my head at night," he said. During the day, things stayed black and white for Claude, I suppose. *You two should see a counselor. And take Marlene with you.* Well, Susan, you're an idiot. We all trudged into Dr. Freidman's office like a good little troop, and we talked and talked, and Claude always said something nice afterward, like, "Well, I think that was helpful, don't you, Marlene?" and the next morning he would wake up, and I saw that overcast look behind his eyes, and I knew we were still spinning our back wheels and the mud hole wasn't getting any drier.

I suppose you get to a point where you decide this is the way the world turns, and it won't ever change until something knocks it off its axis, which is my way of saying I told Claude to leave. Yes, I was the one who suggested it, the one who made all of the plans, who created an actual timetable for his departure. Yes, there was a spreadsheet of major events and how we would handle them and when we would tell Marlene. I like spreadsheets. I can't help it. And Runner Girls, if I showed you this spreadsheet—which I assume is still folded up in the hall closet, under the shoebox full of Marlene's baby photos—you would not be able to find a column for THIS IS WHEN SHE GETS CANCER because it happened long after his drawers were empty and only naked wire hangers and dust bunnies cluttered his side of the closet.

So, a sad Claude that day in Dunean's? Not exactly a news flash. I was happy he was there, that he had perhaps reached a point where the loud whispers of running groups and assorted neighbors no longer bothered him. Maybe he was numb to it all. I'm only guessing. That's one of the great pastimes in the airy afterlife: you keep guessing.

What I didn't expect was Claude taking action. He is not an action man. I saw him talking to Margo's husband, Hal, at the bar. They only spoke for a second. My attention was drawn away from Claude when Tiff began to speak, so I never saw Claude's epiphany. Oh yes, there had to be a moment of revelation. Claude would not have come into the Dunean's with a distinct plan. He was not a planner. He did not create spreadsheets. All I saw was a flicker of movement at the back of the crowd—a crowd focused on what Tiff was saying about me, a crowd that did not see Claude scoop me up, so to speak, and make a break for the door, his gingerly walk suddenly transformed into a painful half trot that resembled a man with a stroke trying to stay upright. Only this man was carrying an urn of his ex-wife's ashes.

Why Claude suddenly thought that was a good idea, I'll never know. I suppose I should be angry that he disrupted my memorial service and turned it into a Keystone Cops caper, the angry mob filing toward the door in pursuit while Claude screamed at Samuel to start the car. But if you could have seen me at that moment, you would have seen me light up (if I had the ability to light up, here in the dark), not because I was happy about being stolen. I mean, I wasn't literally stolen. Only my earthly remains were snagged. I lit up because when Claude turned around to see how close his pursuers were, I saw something sparkling and rare on his face: a giant, face-splitting smile. Hell, he was almost laughing.

For the first time in years, I saw my husband—my ex-husband—happy. Good for him. It was the closest we'd been in months.

SAMUEL

Why the hell does Claude do the things he does? In the years I have known him—and there have been quite a few of those—I have developed various theories and hypotheticals. *He has a chemical imbalance. He is an amateur psychopath. He can't handle the brown liquors. He wasn't hugged enough as a child. He was hugged too much.* But the fact of the matter is, I know better. The way somebody acts is—usually—never about chemicals or hugs. Our lives are all about timing.

That is my theorem: timing is the key that unlocks every door life tries to keep locked. I have often wondered if there is some math behind the timing in the world. I once proposed teaching a class about it at dear old Addison College. Advanced Timing Theory, maybe a mathematics 300-level course. Could we actually calculate timing, find a formula for it? I couldn't get approval by the dean. Yet the more I watch the world around me, the more I am convinced that it spins on the axis of timing. What I mean is the entire world turns on the phrase *if it were not for . . .*

Let's say you are filling your car with gas at the local QuikStop and a convertible pulls out of the lot, and you catch a glimpse of a shock of beautiful hair, and you see the quick profile of a perfect nose, and you sense this is more than likely a gorgeous woman. When she glances for some reason—oh, I don't know, call it *timing*—in your direction, the pillar holding up the huge metal awning blocks your gaze and hers, and the two of you never make eye contact, never exchange looks. What if she was the perfect woman for you, the one you were meant to be with for the remainder of your life, before the split second a piece of steel and concrete gets in the way of fate? That, my friend, is timing. *If not for that support beam . . .*

Or the less dramatic: the fact that you would have never been in that fender bender near campus if you'd caught one less light, or one more. Or how you stood in line for tickets to the Motor City Revue and nabbed the last two before the box office hung the *sold out* sign in the window. Timing. It's everything. If not for this. If not for that. I can't believe they didn't let me teach that class.

I knew the Advanced Timing Theory had something to do with the fact that Claude suddenly appeared, yelling, in the parking lot, an urn tucked under his arm like a shiny football. A smile split his face, even though he was chased by what looked to be an angry mob of memorial attendees. Bourbon was involved. I guessed that immediately. I did *not* know about pain pills. (I found that out later, when Claude attempted to explain the whole incident.) I didn't know the other factors either, until Claude confessed that everything happened at once: the haughty laugh of a man who called Claude a sport; the hypnotic prayers of a sick woman sporting a bandana; the side-glances of women who ran marathons. Again, you see, all about timing. And for god's sake, don't try to call all of that shit that happened in Dunean's a coincidence. Coincidence is another subject, another field of study. Timing is *not* synonymous with coincidence. Timing is the internal master gear of the world. Coincidence is simply God scratching his itchy New Testament sense of humor.

The mob gained on Claude because he couldn't summon a full-fledged sprint, but he finally half limped into my car with his wife's ashes. It was all about timing, but it was about this too: he missed his wife, and he wanted to be close to her one more time. That's my theory. He, no doubt, felt a sharp pang of guilt running through him like a hot sword, a heated feeling quite different than the burn of bourbon he was experiencing. He looked sorry when he begged me to start the Lincoln and get the hell out of there. He looked apologetic, but you see, he knew *the timing was right* to be with her one last time. I did not for a second think Claude came to Dunean's, to the wake, intent on stealing his ex-wife's ashes, but there were, of course, those scenarios when you couldn't be responsible for your actions. Why? The vice grip of timing.

I confess, I had been asleep in the shade, lulled to a nap by the Temptations' *Greatest Hits* and the slight breeze blowing through the open windows. It was a confusing awakening—Claude smiling despite the pain, clutching the urn like a new puppy, the angry village mob streaming and screaming out of Dunean's, a cadre of cancer patients leading the charge as if all they needed was a shot of pissed-off adrenaline to bring them back to something resembling life. When Claude hollered that he had Peg's ashes and these people were going to kill him, my first thought was: under what category of larceny does ash-theft fall? And who would press charges? More existentially, to whom do the ashes of a deceased, nearly ex-wife belong? I wanted to tell Claude he had rights, by god. Instead, I started the car, punched the gas, and left several weeks' worth of tire tread among the gravel on Dunean's parking lot.

When Claude caught his breath, he demanded that I take him to The Oorah. I kept offering alternative options, like his apartment or another town or the sheriff's office or "Why don't we pull a U-turn and return the ashes to Dunean's?" He wouldn't hear of it. The thing I recall most was him saying, "Get me to The Oorah and turn off that fucking music," which I found a little mean-spirited. Claude kept pointing the way, telling me to turn left or right or stay straight, until I finally hit the brakes and skidded to a stop and reminded him that I knew the way to The Oorah. It must have been the way I said it, sitting there in the middle of road, the Lincoln rumbling under us, humming on top of the sticky pavement, because he shut his mouth.

Admittedly, The Oorah may not appear to be the kind of bar I frequent, that the country juke box and mostly white clientele would keep me out, but you would be mistaken. I always have a seat at the bar. Nobody looks at me twice. The people in The Oorah are not angry rednecks. They are drunks, plain and simple, and in my experience, serious drunks don't care who sits next to them when a beer and a shot sits in front of them. I will *never* set foot in Dunean's again. But I'm at The Oorah a couple of times a week.

On this occasion, Claude didn't want a drinking companion, or in this case, a partner in crime. He asked me to pull up to the door of The Oorah and let him out. He groaned in pain as he unfolded from the front seat and said, "I hope we aren't in trouble. I mean, I hope I didn't get you in trouble," to which I replied, "No problem, nobody in that mob will remember that a cranberry Lincoln Continental was your getaway car and your wheel man has an afro."

Claude's smile returned. He glanced down at the urn in his arms and said, "I need a shot and a chaser. Goodnight, Samuel." I shook my head at him and watched him ferry his wife's ashes into the bar.

I'll never figure out that friend of mine.

LeJeune

Fired off questions quick, didn't wait on answers. *What you sweating for? Why you in a suit on a Saturday afternoon? What you doing, bringing pottery in my bar, don't you know somebody will break it with a pool cue?*

Hugging that big pot like a naked prom date. Got no answers from him but still put the PBR and shot of Beam in front of his barstool. Tongue-relaxing tonic. Empty bar for the most part. Couple of guys shooting nine-ball. That was it. No reason *not* to talk, and he piped up soon as bourbon crossed his tongue and bottomed out in his belly. Professional opinion? Claude didn't need another drink, but I will not be anybody's momma while they run a tab. Worst thing in the world for a bartender to do, count somebody's drinks.

Told me it was an urn, told me what was inside. Never been that close to a dead person, no matter what their final state of being. Do not like funerals. Don't ever go. Said to Claude, "Goddamit, can't bring a dead person into a bar. That's probably illegal." Thought the nine-ballers might hear me, but they too busy talking about what they couldn't afford, like good-looking women and big pickup trucks.

Claude smiled at me, said "the nooks and crannies of The Oorah are no strangers to malfeasance." For real, that's what he said. Hate it when he talks like a professor. You so smart, why you running around with a pot full of ex-wife ashes? Asked for another beer from the bottom of the cooler where the cold ones swim. Never saw him finish the first one. Claude, man on a mission to touch down fast in some goddamn LZ I didn't know about.

From behind the bar, saw Claude grow fuzzy around the edges. Happens a lot to folks who sit here. It's a thing. Memory starts to sour, tongue starts to wag. Claude went all bobblehead. Began to chase words he couldn't catch in his mouth. Wouldn't let go of that pot.

Ortiz stocking beer in the walk-in near the bathrooms. Not sure if he'd ever tended a bar, but now was his chance. Told him the boys at the pool table already closed out. If they wanted more, had to pay cash as they go. *Dinero, Ortiz!* Told him to sell beers and not worry about liquor drinks. Told him I'd be back in a half hour. His eyes got big. Not sure he understood. All he does is stack cerveza and mop out bathrooms. This was new for him. Told him to wash his hands before he touched a tap. *Lavos tus manos, Ortiz.*

Poured Claude in the front seat of my Mustang and said, "Don't spill no dead ashes on my seats," and took off. Heard some spark knock. May need a tune up. All the way there, he kept singing parts of some song, something about sunshine on a cloudy day. Made no sense to me. Wouldn't shut the hell up.

Walked in my place and he said, "What are we doing here?"

I said, "Shut up and lay down on the couch. I have to go back to the bar. Don't choke on yourself."

"Oorah!" he said and smiled that smile. Kills me, that smile. Every time. Damn him. But got him all tucked in.

Pulled back into the lot twenty minutes later and already a cop car idling there. Saw it wasn't a real cop but a campus cruiser. Rental cop. Plastic Badge. The Addison patrol. Fucking Ortiz. Probably sold a beer to a frat boy. Even worse, a frat girl. Why else would the college Barney Fife be here?

Got inside and thought, *Yep, frat groupie caught drinking.* Standing at the bar was a young kid and the cop from Addison. Him, a fat guy, belt full of pepper spray and taser guns and Boy Scout handcuffs dragging his pants down below a respectable beer belly. Didn't know him. Thought I knew all local enforcement, rental cops and all. Seen plenty of beer bellies in my day. And cops.

Ortiz spit-firing Español at the cop. All the cop could say was "Hablamos Inglesias?" Ortiz kept shaking his head, but the cop kept asking. Determined sumbitch, give him that. Girl turned toward me, then I knew. Not a frat girl flashing a fake ID, looking for a Long Island Iced. Nope, Claude's kid, the daughter. Knew right away what she was looking for. Tiny girl, standing next to that mound of law enforcement material. Saw me out the corner of her eye. The boys at the pool table had hauled ass. Probably hauled ass out the back when the cop hit the front. Probably carrying a bag of weed in their pants pockets or something.

Walked up to the bar. Ortiz looking like a man saved from the hanging tree. Total relief. Ran toward the back where he could stock beer in peace and quiet. Cop didn't know whether or not to reach for his taser when Ortiz ran. Saw me and said, "Ma'am, are you the proprietor?" Before I told him to define *proprietor*, the girl spoke up. Big voice. Bigger than it oughta be. Older than it ought to be.

"Where the fuck is my mother?" she said. Big pipes on that girl. Big words. Good for her. She didn't wait for an answer. "I checked Claude's place, his office at Addison, Samuel's house."

When she said "Addison," the cop sucked up his stomach and nodded. "Ma'am," he said to me, like he'd been introduced.

The girl said, "Samuel sent us here." She noticed the bar then. Dammit, Ortiz. Hadn't even cleared off the empty plastic cup and two dead PBR soldiers. She pointed at the bottles. The girl knew her daddy's footprints. "Where is he? What has he done?" she said.

Stared at her. Had Claude's nose. Unfortunate. But the eyes must have come from momma. Looked hard at those eyes, and they softened. She was through cussing at me. Done yelling. Before she even whispered it, heard it in my head. Read her mind. Knew it before it happened. She was about to say, *Please give her back. I need to say goodbye. That's all I want.*

Bar got quiet. Only sound that big cop shifting on his feet, the leather on his useless Batman belt squeaking. Heard her say it out loud: "All I want is a goodbye."

PEG

For some time after the cremation, I kept hearing urn jokes in my head. *I died the old-fashioned way . . . I urned it.* Or *What's a Grecian urn? About six-fifty an hour.*

I know, I know. Very corny stuff. *She was* thinking *about jokes? Thinking? How did one think when one was dead, as dead as dead can get?* Punch line—I haven't thought about it much.

The end of things began when Claude and I sat in a little beige room that smelled like new carpet and the doctor didn't say a word because there was nothing left to say—no encouragement, no verbal tap dancing, no cautionary tales. Only lead-heavy silence.

I thought death would offer the same thing—complete and utter silence. Not in a beige room, of course, but in a dark one, not even a hint of light from around a door jamb or through a window sash. Darkness and quiet, which, I thought, might not be a bad way to spend whatever time turned into once you passed away. Well, I got the dark part right.

I was not religious and never had been. I went to church when I was a kid, but once I hit college and discovered I would rather spend Sunday mornings recovering from Saturday nights, I categorized religion as something I might pick up as an interest later in my life, like Crock-Pot cooking or bridge. *Maybe when I had children,* I thought, *that's when I might return to the church.* Well, I had one child and never again set foot inside the doors of a house of worship.

During chemo, I met people in the midst of their mad scrambles back toward God, the panic behind their eyes not a result of their illness but of their fear that they would indeed be cast into some new kind of hell. I always wondered what in the world these people had done to possess such fear. Embezzle money? Cheat ȯn their spouses? Drown kittens?

I had other worries about being gone. About Marlene and what would happen to that sharp anger that boiled inside her. About Claude and what would happen with all that Pabst Blue Ribbon that boiled inside him. Most of all about Cheryl, who was always a disappointed person. When I told her I was sick, I could tell her first (silent) reaction was *so how is this going to further fuck up* my *life?* Cheryl isn't selfish. She craves layers of disappointment like an expensive drug. And she constantly roams her personal streets, looking for the easiest, darkest fix.

But I didn't worry about any bad behavior that might translate into a painful afterlife. I didn't fret about my afterlife, period. I figured on the scale of transgressions, I was at most a 3 or 3.5, which I didn't think was so bad. In my mind, you have to post a solid 6 or 7 to burn in hell. The afterlife I landed in wasn't a concern. It was the life I left behind that kept me up at night, so to speak.

But I don't sleep at all now. I sort of float perpetually, which you think would be a wonderful sensation, yet it's discomfiting. Correction, I don't *float* through space. I don't get anywhere. I am destination-less. I hover, I guess you'd say, like a quiet blimp on a leash, wrapped in blackness, and the scenes flicker through my mind's eye like a never-ending selection of movie trailers. The scenes are the things I left behind and can't do anything about. I saw Marlene in her little bedroom at Cheryl's house, staring at the chest of drawers, wondering what she should pack when she ran away, *if* she ran away. I saw Cheryl sneaking around while her husband showered, trying to find his cell phone so she could check his text messages. I saw Claude take me to The Oorah for the second time in my life, only this time I was dead and gone to ashes. Oh, and I saw Claude buying things he didn't need with money he didn't have. Bicycles, for christ's sake.

I couldn't do anything about anything. I floated and watched those scenes and cringed when somebody screwed up down below. At least I think I cringed. I couldn't tell.

This dead eavesdropping. It was like being a substitute God, and I have to say, it was absolute hell sometimes.

MARLENE

I wanted to be mad at him for stealing my mother, but if you thought about it long enough, it was a little romantic, as far as ashes go.

PART TWO

CLAUDE

You ride a regular route because, well, you're a human, and humans so love their habits. Habits are comfortable things to have at your disposal. Plus, you can easily chart your success on the bike (how much faster you pedal your good old comfortable, familiar route) or your decline (how much slower you drag your fat ass around the same old asphalt). You don't need spreadsheets and statistics. Peg would definitely have made a spreadsheet for your rides if she was around to see this. You only need a decent watch.

Your progress can slide either way, depending on whether you spent the night before anchored to the bar at The Oorah, lubricating your cycling stories with Pabst Blue Ribbon. Stories about the speed you hit flying down Roe Ford Hill near the country club or about the beige Oldsmobile— driven by a little old lady peering between her steering wheel and the dash—that drifted left, right into your path, and you did not have time to flip the little old lady the bird because you were busy looking for a soft landing site on the grassy shoulder. LeJeune listens to your stories, and you wonder if she is really that bored or truly that interested. You don't worry about the answer to that question. You keep talking.

One story LeJeune won't let you repeat under the roof of The Oorah is the one about the urn, about how you woke up in her apartment the morning after the wake, your arms wrapped around your nearly-ex-wife's ashes—weirdly spooning with an urn—the pounding of your head concerning you greatly until your feet hit the floor and your legs screamed for equal time.

LeJeune is not pleased that she was, as she calls it, "a damn accomplice in a damn crime," but *crime* is too melodramatic for what you did, you think. *Crime* suggests that justice will, at some point, prevail, yet in this case, justice is never a factor. At least, not the *official* justice system. It never comes to bear. No charges pressed, no rights read, no mug shots taken. You simply return the urn to Cheryl the afternoon after the wake and wait for the looming legalities to land on your head, for the police to show up at your door. That knock never comes.

Cheryl told you at the time that you would—how did she put it?— "catch enough shit from everybody who was at the wake that you'll be a dickhead forever. You'll never not be a dickhead. Why waste taxpayer money when you're a forever dickhead?" She smiled when she said it, happy that in addition to being the guy-who-cut-and-ran, you were now the guy-who-stole-ex-wife-ashes-from-a-wake-and-ran. A social hole out of which you could never dig.

You can learn to live with that.

But that's not the only story you keep under beer-soaked wraps at The Oorah. You suspect LeJeune would not like to hear the one about the woman either. The Woman. On your regular afternoon ride, the one you take after your last class in the afternoon—American Poetry: WWII to Vietnam—there is always a woman, her hair pulled back into a tight auburnish ponytail that dangles from her helmet, her legs spinning manic, perfect circles; a woman who blows by you like you're tied to the dock, leaves you panting and standing up on your pedals while you watch her fade over the next hill. You wonder what she looks like behind all that cycling camouflage.

Anonymity is part and parcel of the official cycling uniform, with a helmet and glasses and chinstrap and clothes that fit like a second skin. Everybody looks the same. You consider it very socialistic attire. But you think/imagine/fantasize this woman is different. You feel it in the whisk of wind she trails behind her when she passes you.

Each time she pedals past—warning you loudly on every occasion that she is *on your left!* so you don't veer into her blazing path—you catalog something different, something new and wonderful. The flex of her calf, the cut of her straining thigh, the tiny tattoo that peeks out of her right sock, the curves of her backside that balance so proportionately on each side of the tiny saddle of her bike, a bike which, you have also noticed, is one of the expensive brands, the kind of bike you do not dare waste money on unless you know what the hell you are doing with it.

Sure, it depresses you, the fact that she dusts you off with a few pedal strokes. She must surely notice that you sit on a bike that costs a fraction of hers and weighs pounds more. She cannot miss the fact that you still press against shameful, flat pedals, that you haven't found the courage to chance clips and official cycling shoes. You think this makes you invisible to her, weak and inconsequential, something in the road to avoid, like a pothole or fresh roadkill. The fact that you're nothing to her makes you momentarily happy during your rides. Hell, you have nothing to prove. Well, not yet anyway.

You can't put your finger on the exact moment you make the decision, but there is one gorgeous bright fall afternoon when you pedal along, listening to your tires sing on the warm asphalt, not daring to glance behind you, waiting to hear her warning. You've guessed her routine. She more than likely takes her bike to work and changes into her cycling kit in some company bathroom at the end of the day then walks into the parking lot where her bike sits locked on a roof rack, looming over the rest of the slacker-owned cars driven by people who never sweat, who never grind up a hill on a bicycle, people who trudge off to happy hour instead of toward the road. She carries her helmet and shoes in her hand, tosses her flip-flops into the car. She spins a couple laps around the lot to loosen those legs—ah, those legs!—and heads for the country. A half hour later, she is on the outskirts of town, where the traffic thins and the hills begin to roll. This is former farm land, ex-pastures, now filled with houses and pools and golf courses, but gentrification cannot remove slopes. There's that one section where the oaks and sycamores grow thin on the shoulders of the road, so the pavement sits in direct sunshine all day. A hot section of cycling. This is where she usually puts you in her sights—her fast bike, her expensive bike, eating up the space between you.

You've learned to look for her in this sun-splotched part of your ride, but the day you make the decision, she surprises you in another section. Suddenly, she hollers she is *on your left*, and you turn quickly and feel the bike veer slightly, and you try to look her in the eyes, but the both of you are wearing sunglasses so dark, you can't tell where either of you stares. When she passes, you give her a little nod, as if to say, *Well, here we are again, you passing me. Have a safe ride.* Before the last hint of her blows away in the air that rushes around your bike, you finally make the decision.

Actually, you make more than one.

Samuel

I was never sure of the recipe for revenge. I was never sure I desired anything approaching revenge. You could say I'd had my dramatic moment when I ripped the pages out of those books; however, on the revenge meter, that probably didn't move the needle. Oh, and I had served as the wheel man for an ashes theft, leaving a few new ruts in the gravel on the Dunean parking lot. Again, pretty benign. I knew it was not enough, would perhaps never be enough, and I was nagged by this frustrating, anxious (perhaps, obligatory?) feeling that I needed to do more to disrupt the lives of those twins. They, no doubt, had it coming. I just didn't know how to deliver it

Please note, this was not an obsession. I did not waste hours examining my shortcomings as some sort of cultural avenging angel. It was more of an itch I couldn't reach, and it kept me from falling asleep some nights, me staring at the ceiling, trying to calculate the precise formula for revenge— at least the brand of revenge a man like me could reasonably unleash in the world.

I had no solutions until the night I heard the sound.

It was late, one of those mild fall midnights when the air conditioner wasn't needed and neither was the heat, a night when I had all but convinced myself I was too smart and too busy to worry about a pair of aging racists. In the stillness, I heard something in the ceiling above me, a scratching loud enough to sit me up in bed.

I don't believe in signs. I place my faith in research and rationale and numbers that ultimately add up. But I will swear a hundred times—a thousand times—the sound called to me. It *had* to be a sign, created especially for me. I cocked my head in the dark, shut my eyes, and listened harder.

There it was again. Louder this time, above my head. My sign.

I live in an old, old house on a run-down street. Not to say that I live in a poverty-stricken neighborhood. I'm surrounded by people like me, people associated with the college—professors and adjuncts and the few graduate students who can afford to lease an entire house. The majority of us have enough money to own or rent but never enough left over to fix the problems that accompany occupancy. I haven't used my broken dishwasher in two years. My porch cants to the east. My gutters don't steer the water; they sift it through the rusty holes in the aluminum. In twenty years, my neighborhood will be a hip, shady enclave on the outskirts of campus. But first, those of us living here must give up. And we have not yet reached the point of surrender.

I was already aware the attic of my somewhat dilapidated house served as a halfway home for a variety of creatures. I saw the occasional field mouse or squirrel disappear into the eaves. Once, when I worked up the nerve to poke my head into the attic and shine a flashlight into all the corners of the dark space up there, I didn't see destruction. Mostly I saw the remnants of nests or dens or whatever they called their homes. I rarely saw a living and moving creature. Once, I caught the tiny, yellow dots of a herd of something gathered against a far joist in the northwest corner, pin-prick eyes shining like a constellation in my bright beam. I let the attic door flop into place, and I said something to the effect of "live and let live." Plywood and plaster kept our two worlds safely divided. That was enough for me.

But that night, the borders between those worlds erased themselves. I told myself I was out of ideas, out of energy, ready to let those twins have their snow-white shelves, when something walked loudly above my head as if to say, *Have you considered us?*

I had not. And a new plan popped into my head.

The next morning, I drove to Simmon's, one of those old school hardware stores. You know the kind I mean—the messy, unorganized, magical kind. You might discover a toilet plunger next to the displays of S-hooks next to a selection of quasi-illegal herbicides. I assumed Simmon's Hardware would stock a selection of animal traps, and I was right. Nothing that would harm an animal, but something that would allow me to capture it and keep it in one, healthy piece. I would become a trapper. I felt very eighteenth century.

There was a predominant brand, Havahart. I bought two different sizes: the #1025, to accommodate smaller creatures, and the #1083, to tackle the thing that stalked above my head in what sounded like animal clogs. When whatever it was walked above me and gave me a sign, the signal possessed some audio heft.

First, I had to conquer my fear of setting foot in the attic. I had lived in the house for six years, and the last time I walked—not simply shined a light, actually *walked*—along the rickety pieces of plywood that spanned the attic space was the week I bought the house. After that, I left the attic and its inhabitants alone. Like I said, live and let live. Luckily for me, there had been no reason to visit the attic—no leaks, no branches puncturing the roof.

I decided broad daylight would be the best time to set my traps, even though the attic had no dormer windows and stayed nearly midnight-black 'round the clock. What did I know? I assumed the animals left during the day, hunting food or whatever animals do when they weren't pirouetting above me. However, when I cracked the attic door, I swore I heard scurrying somewhere in the dark, and I chased the sound with the beam of my flashlight but saw nothing at the edges of the attic.

I climbed the ladder and eased into the musty, dank space, and I could immediately tell I had entered animal territory. The smell of feces and fur singed the linings of my nose. Though it was mid-fall, inside the attic was still summer-humid and thick and warm. Once inside, I scanned with my light and spotted scat scattered across the plywood flooring. The more I looked, in the nooks and niches of the roof joists, I discovered more evidence that my attic was indeed some sort of animal condominium complex. Hopefully, all the tenants were away for the afternoon.

On one end of the attic, I set up the Havahart #1025, the small one with two tiny doors, so small it was hard to bait the little seesaw tray in the center of the trap. I brought a jar of peanut butter with me, along with a sleeve of crackers. I was no experienced trapper, but I guessed any animal possessing taste buds and a nose would crawl into a Havahart for Skippy on a Ritz. At the other end, I baited the larger #1083 with the same menu.

I was smarter than I thought when it came to luring rodents. I folded up the attic steps and levered the door closed, and before I walked to the other end of my house, I heard a distinctive metal clank over my head. Then, after a pause of a few seconds while I stared at the ceiling, I heard the arrhythmic scraping of metal across the ceiling, more of a banging than anything else. As if that wasn't enough, I heard another clank, a bigger one, maybe, in the pause between the scrapes.

This was the moment I realized I had not planned what to do if I trapped something in the Havaharts. I knew I needed to capture these things, and I knew what I wanted to do with them. But I'd neglected the middle act, the part that required me to go into the dark attic, among the rodent scat, and retrieve what I trapped.

I waited until the metallic scraping traveled to the point farthest away from the attic door before I opened it and climbed up. I had my flashlight and a broom and no plan. I stuck my head into the opening and aimed the beam into the corner where I'd last heard the banging and scraping. The second the light entered the space, the noise silenced. I searched for my Havaharts with the beam. A little farther right than I'd aimed, I saw the indirect glimmer of a pair of eyes, and I pointed the light that way. There, in the larger of the two traps, the #1083, crouched one of the biggest rats I had ever seen, larger than the ones I've watched dive into dumpsters behind my office building on campus. He appeared to be the size of a Chihuahua. Oddly, he was content behind bars, munching on peanut butter and crackers. He wasn't panicked a bit. He was biding his time. And that scared the breath out of my chest.

While I stared at him, the now familiar metallic scrape began again, a few feet to my left, and I threw the beam in the direction of the noise. This was the smaller trap, the one I imagined would be perfect for squirrels or some such. The opening was probably six inches tall. In this Havahart, the #1025, no squirrel peered out. Rather, stuffed inside was another rat, maybe a bit smaller than the first one but too large to be in the #1025. His fur pushed through the tiny metal mesh, and enough of his feet extended through the bottom that he could drag himself around the plywood floor. Both doors on the end of the #1025 had somehow—miraculously—closed and latched. His face was pushed against one of them, and I could see his yellow teeth working against the metal as he banged closer to me. He was not a happy rat. There were sounds. Not the squeaks you would expect but more like pissed off grunts and rumbles, the low, brassy notes you might hear from a something bigger and more dangerous.

I was thankful I had the broom with me. The rat squeezed inside the #1025 appeared ready to attack, to exact his revenge on me. He couldn't maneuver in a straight line, the way he was crammed into the cage, but he managed to weave a drunken path toward the attic door, close enough that I defended myself with the broom. The second I made contact with the metal ribs of the cage, the larger rat, the one that was content to eat and watch, began to rumble as well.

The two of them are communicating, I thought. One was cheering the other on, and I suddenly felt outnumbered by the rats in my attic.

Another thought came to me. I was a full-grown man. I could look dangerous if I wanted to, and *I wasn't in a cage*! I had a broom. I controlled the light. I owned the goddamn house. I was the rat landlord. I pulled myself into the attic and did something that embarrasses me now, but at the moment made perfect sense: I yelled at a pair of trapped rats.

I screamed at them. I called them names. My voice echoed beneath the low roof of the house and bounced back to me, growing louder on its return. I swear, dust sprinkled down on my head when I hollered and rattled the eaves. Both rats froze where they were, one in the middle of a Ritz Cracker and the other concocting a meandering escape/attack attempt.

After my outburst, I felt more in control. Handling my rats became an easier task. With the one jammed in the cage, I simply picked up the Havahart by the handle and carried him down the attic stairs, careful to keep him away from my body. He caused no trouble. He looked almost excited, like someone who had packed for a vacation and was seated happily on the plane. The other situation proved more delicate. He had some room to move in the cage. I was afraid of those teeth, especially on the attic stairs. So, in the dark, I found a thick cardboard box big enough to cover the cage. Once it was safely over the box, I took a piece of equally thick cardboard and slid it under cage and turned the box upside down. Before I folded the box tops over him, he made one last attempt to free himself from his tiny cage, but all he could manage to do was flip the #1083 again and again, smearing Skippy peanut butter all over the bars of his little Havahart prison.

He emptied his tank with that spurt of energy. He eventually quieted, and the expression on his face was complete and utter rat resignation, which amazingly didn't look all that different from a human being throwing in the towel.

THE HAMMERHEAD CHRONICLES

CHERYL

An item for the record: Patrick walked in one day and said, somewhat out of the blue, "You know what your problem is? You think the world owes you something. You think you're so downtrodden and so put-upon and entitled to some prize, like the world is a game at the fair and it's your turn to win the big fuzzy bear. You're an idiot."

That was the day I knew he was sleeping with someone.

He wasn't off base. I *do* feel like I am owed something from the world at large. I don't think that is so unusual. I am a nice person. I do nice things for people. I feel like I should be properly compensated in some way for my goddamn efforts.

Such as being Peg's nursemaid. You might say that as her sister, I had a duty to care for my sibling in the event of catastrophic illness, and I wouldn't argue with you about that. I was happy to ferry my sister to her freaking chemo treatments. I certainly couldn't depend on Claude. No one could. Okay, right, he gets an A for effort. He *tried* to be the Chemo Taxi Driver for a few sessions, but he couldn't keep it up. So I stepped in. Fine. Not a problem. I even moved my sister and her moody-ass daughter into my home. No simple task, that. I wanted an easier way to keep an eye on her. Okay, so I've said it. It was easier for me, ultimately, but that was not my priority. I don't have priorities. That might be part of my problem, a lack of priorities. Maybe if I had some priorities, I wouldn't be staring fucking divorce in the face.

Peg didn't like the idea at all, at least not at first. She did not want

Marlene uprooted to my house. She didn't consider how it might be possible Marlene would be more comfortable in the privacy of *my* home. Hey, impending death doesn't mean someone can't be bitchy. But I knew she didn't have much fight left, and finally, one afternoon on the way back from chemo, I pulled into my driveway and that was the last morning Peg saw her own house. Marlene was my co-conspirator. She brought over everything the two of them might need. I told Peg, "Listen, this is so much better for you." That was a lie, but I'll own up to it, no problem. I've always said that. *Own up to what you say and what you do.* I ought to put that fucking bumper sticker on Patrick's car.

I even tried to give Claude some direction, tried to tell him to stop worrying about other people. I realized that he had been looked down upon by most people because he left his soon-to-be-sick wife—not the kind of action that wins a big payoff—however, he was not a bad man. He was mostly lost and wandering, and Peg was never, ever the type to provide a proper compass heading. Peg was a live-and-let-live type of person, yet as I say that, I realize how terrible that sounds, what with her being dead. I am not trying to be funny. That is not in my goddamn nature.

Back to Claude and direction. His life is so simple. He goes to the college. He teaches his little classes. He drives to that bar that smells like the inside of a wet boot. He plays tennis sometimes with Samuel. Oh, and now he rides a bicycle for miles and miles. What kind of life is that? He isn't doing anything for anybody that will result in—when the final tallying is tallied—what one might call *a good life*. I am working on a good life. Is it too much to think that I might be fucking rewarded for it?

I knew the minute that Patrick confronted me with his new Theory of the Fuzzy Bear that something was up. Shit, I figured that man out a few minutes after I met him, admittedly not a difficult task. He was the kind of man who could never admit anything about himself if it happened to put him in a darker-than-usual light. He was scared of the consequences of confession, a strange trait for a semi-Catholic to have. So when he accused me of requiring compensation for done-deeds, he was of course talking about himself. *He* was the one begging for payment.

There is a proper name for that sort of behavior, but it escapes me right now. From psychology. Something about transferring or ricocheting or boomeranging.

Obviously, Patrick felt as though he had earned a respite from the hard life he had been living under our roof. He wanted payback. Again, he was not incorrect about me. I felt the same thing. As he blustered, I almost felt sorry for him. I felt his pain. However, I saw nothing in my immediate future that would come close to balancing my books. I was keeping the world around me in good working condition. Peg was in a better place. Marlene was living with me like a daughter. Claude and I met for coffee on mornings when he wasn't out riding that bike. Like I said, Claude was not a bad man. And Patrick? If I was reading the tea leaves correctly, had found some relief.

And relief went by the name of Louise. That, I was sure of.

CLAUDE

You cut your ride short and make a U-turn toward home, miles before your usual turnaround. Instead of pedaling the rolling hills out beyond the country club, you swing into the BP station at the intersection of Roe Ford and Old White Horse Road then beat a path back the way you came. You haven't yet begun a good lather yet, probably because it's one of those fall days when you can feel winter lurking out there somewhere. You always wonder where the mystery woman's halfway point is. Maybe she has a loop she follows and never retreats down the same path that got her there. You wonder.

You pedal hard for home, harder than ever before, not because the road and the low hills have defeated you but because you're running out of time and for some reason—some inexplicable, mysterious reason—you *have* to do this today. You need get there before they close. Back at your apartment, you hang your bike on the big industrial hooks mounted to the wall and dash out, still wearing your bike clothes.

You barely make it. Maybe twenty minutes to spare. You fast-walk through the door, and TJ is a little disappointed that you might delay him going home, and his expression lengthens even more when you tell him you want to look at cycling shoes and buy some new pedals.

"Is something wrong?" you say.

TJ shakes his head and tells you that he had *the over*.

"The what?" you say.

"Yeah, all of us here always do a little over-and-under bet on how long it will take a newbie to come back and get real pedals. We set the over-and-under for you at six months. I took the over. Hell, personally, I didn't think you'd *ever* come back for pedals. I think Al won the big money. He was the only one who took the under." You think about asking to meet Al so you can thank him for his blind faith in you. You want to tell TJ about the woman responsible for his loss, but you decide to stick to business and follow TJ to the shoe display.

You have watched the Tour de France on television. You've seen the posters in the store. You know the pros wear wildly colored shoes—oranges and bright yellows and reds. You're not sure if you are ready for the loud colors. You don't want to appear like you know what you're doing when you are still relatively clueless on a bicycle. You don't want the mystery woman on the expensive bike to think you are impulsive enough to buy lemon-tinted shoes on an afternoon whim. You decide to stick with basic white. Probably because black feels too somber for you and maybe too hot to be spinning over the top of sticky asphalt during hotter days.

"I guess you must be riding a lot," TJ says.

You tell him that you're spinning around a hundred miles a week. Which is a borderline lie. Only during the last two weeks have you figured out a schedule that allows you a hundred miles every seven days. Actually, it is not as hard as you imagined. You don't need Samuel's help for this math. A touch shy of fifteen miles a day. Barely a warm-up ride for true hammerheads.

"You look like you've dropped some pounds, man. That will help in the mountains," he says, which you think is a compliment, but you aren't sure.

He is correct, however. The afternoon rides in the last of the day's heat have melted off a good ten pounds, mostly from your waist. Your love handles are shrinking. This is now a happy by-product, because you've discovered something: you don't ride to burn calories. You ride for the therapeutic benefits. And for the now regular appearance of the mystery female cyclist on the road, of course.

You mumble a type of thank-you, but you don't tell TJ that you haven't dared tackle anything more than a mediocre hill yet. Mountains scare you because you're smart enough to know (and appreciate) how gravity works. You are not one of those little water bugs of a cyclist—like TJ—who might tip the scales at a buck thirty-five sopping wet and who can churn up mountains with a speed that makes a mockery of modern physics. That is not you. From the tiny, nearly imperceptible slopes on your route, you realize that an honest-to-god mountain would bring about pain and suffering, and that's not why you bought a bicycle. You did not purchase a pain machine. You bought a bicycle. Mountains are for cyclists who have forsaken pleasure. You're a fan of pleasure.

TJ finds a pair of white Specialized shoes in your size. You put them on and suddenly you have two pieces of plywood fastened beneath your feet. You ask TJ if cycling shoes are supposed to be this stiff, and he says that cycling shoes are made for pedaling, not walking.

"They make you walk like you've had a stroke," he says.

You find a pair that fits, a pair not too expensive, though the fact of the matter is, your new cycling shoes will be the costliest footwear you own.

TJ asks what style of pedals you want, and the expression on your face betrays your lack of knowledge. You know him well enough to say, "Do I look like somebody who knows about pedals? Hook me up, TJ," and he does, with a set of Speedplay pedals costing almost as much as the shoes.

"Did you bring your bike?" he says, glancing out the window of the store toward your truck.

You didn't think about the bike. That's stupid. You need more than your feet when you buy pedals. You're embarrassed by your cluelessness.

"Not at problem," he says. "Bring the bike by whenever. I'll go ahead and screw the cleats on your shoes. I can put on the Speedplays later, while you wait. But bring some shorts so we can sit you on the trainer and let you pedal. I can tell you some things about using clips while you're on the trainer." TJ's tone softens now, as if you are the uncle he's suddenly decided is cool. You elevate to a new, nicer level of cycling. Maybe the fact that you came back so quickly for pedals helps. You and TJ appear to be on the same wavelength because as he rings up your total, he says, "Tell me something. What was it? What brought you back so soon? I mean, I'm never wrong about these things. *Never.* I figured more than six months was a sure bet." You wonder how much this mysterious Al won betting on you. TJ doesn't give you an opportunity to answer.

"I'm figuring it was one of two things," he says. "You either got embarrassed by somebody on the road. Like, when you know you're faster than the other guy, but he's got a lighter bike and a better gear set and real pedals. Or it's a girl. Some hammerhead girl torched you, and you want to chase her down. It's usually one of those two that bring people back for pedals."

You wonder if this skinny bike shop employee is some sort of amateur fortune teller.

He keeps talking: "We do a shop ride every Saturday morning starting at seven thirty," he says. "Get used to these clips some and come with us. All levels. We don't leave anybody behind on the road."

You almost want to hug TJ, even though he is speaking a foreign tongue. *Shop ride?*

"I'm betting it's a girl," he says, handing over the receipt. "You don't look like the kind of guy who gives a shit about being embarrassed by another guy. Yeah, I'd put money on a girl."

You want to tell him that it's not a *girl*. It's a woman. A mystery woman, an obsession. TJ is not old enough to know the difference. You feel good about yourself, good enough to mess with your newest pal, the skinny kid in the bike shop.

You say, "Haven't you lost enough money on me for one day, brother?"

TJ is still laughing when the door of the shop closes behind you, and you walk into the cooling air of the evening.

Wallace & Wade

One quick anecdote regarding our birth, before we talk about Confederate retail:

As the story goes, our poor mother had no idea she was expecting— or should we say, *unexpecting*—twins. The night we arrived, the doctor on call at Kelly Memorial Hospital, not our mother's regular physician but a newly arrived, sleep-deprived young man from New England, was not surprised when a bald head crowned between our mother's thighs. Though young, he had delivered a good number of babies in his short obstetrics career. No, the appearance of the head did not startle him. That sight was normal. What gave him pause was the odd appearance of the feet, one on either side of the head, almost like bizarre alien ears. He may have assumed a number of things in those first few confused seconds: that this child was a contortionist prodigy already bending into inhuman shapes in the womb or perhaps this baby was badly broken in half and would never survive the world outside of its watery safety. But of course, the young doctor quickly came to his senses and realized two babies were racing to make their escape, albeit simultaneously. One headfirst, the other feetfirst.

Which is all to say, the two of us entered this world in lockstep, so to speak, one of us slightly leading the way and maintaining a gaze forward while the other had his back, again so to speak. This is how we run our business, one a visionary and one a rearguard. For example, one of us strongly recommended turning our unused back room at Dunean's into the current treasure trove, but we assure you, it was ultimately a unanimous brotherly decision.

Onward to the Confederacy. Naturally, the tchotchke treasures of which we are about to speak could not be sold in our main retail area. That would have been an insane business model. Keeping our shelves free of ethnic authors is one thing. As we mentioned, that is a simple ordering and inventory issue and does not loudly announce itself to our white patrons, many of whom make regular contributions to our cash flow but may not possess our passion for states' rights sensibilities. To each his own. We certainly don't want to wave the Confederate flag in their faces.

Hence, we opted to create a new space. We spent a couple of weekends painting the large spare back room and ordering thousands of dollars' worth of merchandise from a number of like-minded wholesalers we vetted. Discreet purveyors of Southern pride. A modern underground mercantile railway.

You might say it was a razor-thin niche opportunity, but we saw enormous potential in our decision. As well, we saw an intelligent investment in our futures *and* our pasts. You see? One of us looking forward, one looking back!

Over the course of a month, merchandise arrived in nondescript parcels and boxes, nothing that would arouse suspicion. We received the deliveries from UPS at our rear loading dock in the alleyway. We ferried the merchandise to its new secret room, where we inventoried it, set up separate accounting, and arranged the items tastefully on the wooden shelves.

Certainly, many of the items could be purchased at any of a number of locations in the area, such as truck stops or that gaudy fireworks stand on the outskirts of town. We stocked some of what you would suspect. We dislike the expected, the clichéd, but what are you going to do? One must know one's marketplace. We bought Confederate flags of various sizes. Cigarette lighters adorned with the Confederate flag. Dish towels, napkin rings, oven mitts, light switch covers, baby mobiles, flashlights, cell phone covers, thumb drives, trucker hats for men *and* women, Frisbees, urinal cakes, belt buckles, women's thongs/men's briefs, children's composition books—all decorated with the spangled symbol of our collective Southern pride.

Of course, these were typical, and frankly, we like to think at Dunean's we are far beyond typical. Which was why a large slice of our financial investment in the back room consisted of Confederate-themed merchandise that one could *not* possibly find at Billy's Poinsett Truck Stop or the Pump 'n Go on Highway 25. These unique items came packed and bubble-wrapped in the same brown boxes as the others, but inside were—and we don't think this is hyperbole—Confederate gems. We now stocked an array of flavored lubricants with the bottles' labels displaying the flag of the South. Handcuffs and fuzzy, furry shackles and stilettos and anus plugs and dildos adorned with the distinctive stripes and bars and stars of the Confederate states. Several of the dildos were black, a mistake on the sender's part. We called the supplier and shipped them back immediately and were rewarded with several additional imitation Caucasian penises at no extra cost. (We appreciated high-level customer service.) We ordered a case of ball gags, the bright red ball decorated, of course, with the rebel flag. There were several devices with which we were not familiar that resembled gynecological instruments. Each of them screamed torture to us, yet the scream was somewhat softened by the appearance of the Confederate flag wrapped around the metal bars. Perhaps the most impressive of the collection was the variety of vibrators featuring the flag, naturally, but with an added musical feature. One flip of the switch and the vibrator began to whir excitedly, then the distinctive, tinkling tune of "Dixie" emerged from the device. Southern women—and adventurous Southern men—could now enjoy themselves and hum along with the classic refrains of the Confederate anthem.

We could not have been happier, and we could hardly wait to begin to market our newest wares through a careful, quiet, below-the-radar word-of-mouth campaign. And the markups? The margins, especially for the vibrators and lubricants, were beyond economic belief.

To make money *and* feed our pride? In a word, a Southern retailer's dream.

CHERYL

Yes, for the record—a cryptic, scribbled note on the back of a crumpled-up receipt. That's all. Damned funny how the biggest things come tumbling down because of the tiniest discoveries. One short note: *We shall return here for sure. Kisses, L.*

I also ran across a very business-like email about expanding Patrick's brand awareness and product exposure and "more eyeballs on the content" from a woman named Louise Alberts, Director of Marketing Strategies and New Business Development at the idiotically named company IdeaSparks, but honestly, the email dripped with so much sexual subtext, damned thing had to be a code. A too-cute code. For god's sake, Patrick is a chiropractor. His *brand* is all about hiding his embarrassment of being a not-quite-real doctor, and everybody knows that already. I started connecting the dots, which didn't take a rocket scientist, and I came up with the fact that Louise was getting her eyeballs' worth of looks at Patrick's product. If I'm telling the truth here, I wasn't all that goddamn torn up about it.

I honestly didn't have the energy to confront Patrick, at least not right away. Actually, I didn't even want to. This sounds borderline insane, but as long as Patrick was happy, life flowed smoothly, so why rock this goddamn rowboat we were all drifting in? He had Louise, the eyeball strategist. Let him build up his brand a couple of nights a week. What did I care? But fuck me, I'm human. I acted like every scorned woman in history: I checked out the competition. I wanted to see who bested me.

I wanted to see who Patrick ran toward when he decided to haul ass in a new direction.

I know, I know. I've read all the magazine articles, thumbed through the books in the self-help section at Dunean's. They told me deconstructing the other woman wouldn't make me *feel* any better. They said it wasn't *healthy*. They said it would only cloud my judgment at a time when I needed crystal clear thinking and laser-sharp reasoning. What they don't tell you is that when something like this happens, your first thought is that you are going through a situation unique in the known world. And your second thought is, or should be, *au contraire, lady, you are a walking/ talking cliché*, that everybody everywhere acts the same way when their spouse is banging somebody else. So why fight it? You're kind of following the pack, right?

Tracking down Louise wasn't difficult. I had her name and her place of business on the email. I started to look her up on Facebook, but I said to myself, *Nope, I want to see this person in the flesh. I want to see her breathe. Social media is for pussies. Go old school.* I decided to stalk her office building downtown and watch the people coming and going and guess which one was Louise, the new business guru, owner of eyeballs. I nixed that idea because I was afraid it would ultimately be a waste of time, and while you couldn't say I was the busiest person in the world, I didn't enjoy burning what time I had to myself. A stakeout would probably be boring anyway. I've seen goddamn cop movies.

I could call her up and tell her I had a great new business concept that could use a few of her ideasparks, but of course she would want to know my name and the concept. Thinking up believable lies? Not my wheelhouse. I could send her an email from Patrick's computer one morning when I knew he busy untangling patients' vertebras. *Had a cancellation, baby! Meet you in twenty min for coffee?* But she might be suspicious if that wasn't the way they communicated on the run, wasn't their usual hook-up email. Maybe he didn't call her baby. If she was like Patrick (if she *liked* Patrick) texting would be the way to go, and there was no way to get close to Patrick's phone. He basically slept with the thing tucked up his ass like a suppository.

I was about to give up on getting a real, live look at her and opt for a normal Facebook stalk or a picture on the company website, but something stopped me. People edit out the real, raw parts of their lives on Facebook (like the sister-in-law that wasted away in your house, the philandering husband, etc.) Company photos are professionally taken, airbrushed into fantasy. Still, it *would* be the easiest route.

Then one afternoon, I happened to be downtown, and I walked by her building on my way to somewhere else, CVS, maybe, or the coffee shop, I can't remember. There, plain as day in the small parking lot, was a reserved sign on one of the slots with L. Alberts's name on it. I can't believe I'd never noticed it. In that parking space sat a small, sleek Mercedes sedan, a black one that oozed speed and money and success and an expensive lease agreement. My heart sank for the first time in months. Patrick had traded up. I still drove the goddamn Honda Accord his father had given us a couple years earlier.

Louise came into focus. The woman who drove that black Mercedes was confident and cocky. She wore clothes tailored to her body. Oh, and that body. Legs toned by professionals in a private gym, perfect thighs and calves that feared no steps. No cankles like me. Her shoulders hinted at a swimming background somewhere in her past, back when she perfected the butterfly and made precise flip-turns, shoulders tapering into a waist bordered by visible abs that shunned fat. Not chiseled, just *there*, you know? Her two-hundred-dollar haircut framed her face like a blond, glowing frame. She never looked people in the eye because she didn't need to. She never talked to anyone unless she absolutely wanted to. *That* was the woman who drove that car. I was freaking sure of it.

But the world. Goddamn, the things it does to you. The timing it throws at you. I stood there, constructing that fem-bot in my head when the front door of the building opened—no big deal, that door probably opened hundreds of times a day. A woman walked out and across the parking lot toward the sidewalk where I stood. Again, not a news flash. I didn't even notice her at first, so I'm sure she didn't notice me. Things got interesting when she pointed a key fob at the black Mercedes, made the car chirp, then opened the passenger side door. She tossed in a plastic bag, locked the door with another chirp and made her way down the sidewalk, the opposite direction from me. Did I follow her? What the fuck do you think?

One other thing: this woman had never, *never* been a swimmer.

LeJeune

Guy hunkered down in the corner, dirty Carolina Panthers t-shirt? Jack and Diet. Old-looking man but probably not as old as I thought slumped at the end of the bar in a suit that had never fit? Vodka and ginger ale. (Asked for a lime. Limes here? Seriously, dude?) Pair of dusty construction workers in thick brown boots—started early because the city shut down their project because they didn't have permits for plumbing and electric? Pyramid of empty Coors light cans they started stacking late morning. Only thing they built today. Skinny woman, about ninety pounds and smelling like a mixture of, hell, maybe curry and White Shoulders and meth? Tall boy Buds with Old Crow chaser. Took her credit card early. Could be a runner and didn't want her bugging out, shorting my drawer at the end of the night, not that a short drawer matters when you the only one who does the counting.

Door opened, a couple walked in. Made a bet with myself. Her, Corona-no-lime, and him, probably something you wouldn't expect. Probably ask if we have a damn blender. Almost as funny as asking for limes. Was half wrong. Her, a Corona. Could tell Corona folks by the way they sniffed the air in the bar the minute they walked in. Coronas are bar sniffers. Him, more hard core than I figured. Ordered a Cutty neat. Not surprised about being wrong. Usually bat around .500.

The early drinkers, drinkers on a mission. Out of the bright sun and through the door with something specific in mind to drown or lubricate. A pain here, a loss there. Bellied up to the sticky bar or grabbed one of a half dozen tables on the way to the pool table. Didn't like to make a big distinction between regulars and those only wandering in. Gotta say though, always curious: how do strangers find us? People didn't arrive here by accident. Not anywhere near a beaten path, not a place you pass by and go, *Well, what a nice little establishment, honey. We should try that out.* Ending up here meant you had to want to be here. Don't know. Maybe word of mouth brought in strangers. Can't imagine the word or the mouth that would do that. Maybe some sort of secret agent tracking device the sad and thirsty carry around. Same thing that makes birds fly a thousand miles every year without a compass to a familiar pond the size of a mud puddle somewhere in Minnesota. Maybe was what I had here—a mud puddle with a happy hour.

Only thing these folks brought in the door? The baggage between their damn ears. Most of that wasn't all that interesting. All they ever wanted to talk about. Things they didn't do and regret. Things they did do and regret. The regret they couldn't shed. Or the other things they couldn't shed—wives, boyfriends, belly fat, bills, guilt. Wanted to yell at them, *Hey, you ain't all that special, Buttercup.* Of course, I didn't. Need to keep them sad. Happy people have small bar tabs. Happy people don't know how to treat a bartender. That was why I liked Claude. Didn't treat me like a bartender.

Other guys, they think every bartender wants to stop slinging beers and get a real job. Men sit at my bar, stare at their drink or at what little chest I have, and think they could be the Chosen One. Could drive me away from this shit storm of a dive in his nice car. Could set me on a bright, happy path toward freaking righteousness and regular daylight hours. All I had to do? Pour him drinks inside the friendly confines of his own house, get naked on occasions when he still had the energy and wherewithal.

News flash, Buttercup: leaving was not an option. The Oorah was always my plan, what I was always running to. I been out there in the world where people wake up in the morning, drive home in the afternoon. Meals at regular shifts. Did my time there. Didn't get all these tattoos until I showed up here. This was my uniform. Claude knew that somehow.

Knew I'd found my best life. Got everything I needed right here on this desert island.

But Claude was doing battle with that bicycle now, though. Used to come in four, five afternoons a week. Sat down with his Beam and PBRs, asked me how I was doing. Folks don't realize how little bartenders get asked that. No worries. In bar world, things revolve around the drinker, not the pourer. Whatever. But a handful of times a week, Claude saved me from the bad suits and bar sniffers. Asked if I was getting new ink. *You got any skin left to draw on?* he said once. I laughed. He could know answer to that question if he wanted it.

Maybe once every other week Claude used to get too shitfaced to drive. Poured him into my Mustang then in my door. Let him blind-walk to the couch then push him face down. Might say, *Drop and give me twenty, soldier.* If he wasn't passed out, he'd laugh. Sure, could get naked and slide beside him if I wanted. But I don't. Not that I'm shy. Been known to wake up and play Twenty Questions before I figured out who that guy—or once, that girl—was snoring on my shoulder. *Where is my Mustang parked? Where'd my panties get to? Which door is the bathroom?* But never did that with Claude. Like I was saving him. Like he was a good bottle of Scotch I wanted to crack open further on down the road. In a different time, different place.

Didn't know I'd have to deal with a bicycle. Now he might come in once a week. Maybe only on a weekend night. Spent a lot of his happy hour time riding around on those skinny wheels. Told me about it. Told me about the speed. Told me going downhill was butt-tightening. His word, not mine. *Butt-tightening.*

He was getting skinnier too. One afternoon, didn't even recognize his silhouette in the doorway, in the blast of light. I never minded his softness. Enjoy a man with meat on his bones. Skinny men remind me of me. *Me?* Thin like a damn rail. Can bend like a Gumby doll, heels in my ears. But cannot compete with a bicycle. Don't know the rules. Make a rule book for everything and nobody would fuck up. But how much fun would that be? *Suck it up, Buttercup.*

So yeah, got distracted thinking about bicycles and Claude and didn't notice a guy slide into end of the bar, nearest the door. Eyes adjusted to the light and there he was, still blurry from being backlit. Had on a sweater, not odd for late October, except it was still seventy degrees out. People might say it was fall. They'd be wrong. You're still sweating and the leaves were all down. Love weather in the South, by god. Man waved like he wanted something. Never wave at fucking a bartender. We all know what you want, Buttercup. You in a bar, not Home Depot.

Usually ignored waves. Did not run like a dog after a tennis ball. "What," I called from my end of the bar. Sweater man wanted to know if we had a beer list. "Yeah," I said, "we got cheap and cheaper. There's your list." Guy in the no-fit suit cracked up. Make a drunk laugh, get a tip. Sweater wanted to know if we had an IPA. That cracked up the suit guy again. "You pee what?" I said back. An old joke in this bar. We don't sell beer you can chew on. Told this to the guy, started walking toward him.

Normally, IPA drinkers would leave about now. Realized they landed in the wrong beer universe, where smart ass bartenders sell cheap beer. Got to the end of the bar, let my eyes try to gather some light. Saw the smile on his face. "Same old same old, I suppose," he said. "Some things never change." Smiled like a man who laid money down on a sure thing.

Knew what he wanted. Wanted me to place him. Wanted me to remember something important. Important to him, at least. Stupid ass look smeared across his face. The look said, *I'll give you a minute to come up with the details, honey. No way you could forget me, sweetie.* But swear to god, didn't recognize him. Went through the catalog in my brain. Could see him better now. Beginning of a mustache on his lip. Or maybe the end of one. Too much slick stuff in his hair. But was expensive slick stuff. Could smell it where I stood. Smelled like a beauty parlor. That thing I thought was a sweater wasn't. Was a sport jacket. Nice fit, cut close to the shoulders. A shirt with starched collars. No tie. Looked like he came from a talk show. And he was the guest. I came up blank.

"Sorry, Buttercup," I said. "You a wanted man or something? You a movie star? You both?" He laughed again. Nothing bothered him. Couldn't rattle him.

"Aw, come on, Junie," he said. "You can't forget me."

Junie. Heart leaped up in my throat like a bad meal. *Junie.* Hadn't heard that name in years. Too many years. Not enough years. Only two people in the world ever called me Junie. One of them a dead Marine. And this douche across the bar was still alive and grinning.

"Give me one of those cheap beers," he said. "It'll come to you."

But was not hearing things because of the ringing in my ears. Not ringing. More like screaming. Felt like all the air been sucked out of the bar. Ringing/screaming stopped for a second.

"I'll bet it all comes back to you before you get me my beer," he said.

Thought about running out the door.

But to tell the truth, got no other place to go.

SAMUEL

I would call the experiment moderately successful but somewhat lower than my expectations. Isn't this normal? This falling short? I would also call it a learning experience. I definitely discovered a new fold in my brain when I started carting my captured rodents from the attic to the back door of Dunean's. I learned to adapt quickly, to evolve.

After my first round with the rats in the attic, I gave up on the tiny cage and replaced it with an additional model #1083. The only variety I attracted with my peanut-butter-Ritz recipe were the rather husky rats. I never saw any mice. Maybe the rats ate them. Or intimidated them. I had no idea how territorial these monsters were. That may not be entirely true. I suppose I could conclude that rats were amazingly territorial sons of bitches. In this case, their territory was my attic, and they were not at all pleased that I had crossed the border and become the newest stranger in their strange land.

With two Havaharts, I was capturing a pair of rats every three or four days. The more I caught, the more arrived on the shores of the attic. When I closed my eyes to go to sleep, I tried to avoid doing the math in my head, a difficult task for a mathematician. Consider this: if I was catching four or five of the damn things a week, how many more of them balanced *uncaptured* along the joists above my head as I slept? I concluded that for every rodent I saw, there were another three or four I didn't. Where did these things go in the daytime? Why could I not hear them at night, little armies of rats goose-stepping in a military parade across the plywood? Ultimately, I decided I was doing the best thing for all of us, this thinning of the ranks. Better for the rats, better for my state of mind on a number of levels.

The first time I transported a pair of rodents to Dunean's, I waited until well after midnight, when I knew the small back alley behind the store would be completely empty. I was not used to this sort of sneaking around. I only knew what I had seen on television and in the movies, so I put on some dark clothes and a black watch cap and loaded the Havaharts into the trunk of the car.

Without planning to, I named the pair of rats that first night. One was Wallace and the other, Wade, and each time I ferried a new pair across town, I kept the names the same. The rats were always Wallaces and Wades. That first night, Wallace filled the small cage and Wade sat quietly in the large one, both awaiting their fate. They gnawed at the tiny metal bars that held them, their teeth yellow like butter. When I picked them up and carried them to the car, they shit through the bottom of the cage, another sign I suppose, a signal meant for me.

At the front of Dunean's, the soft glow of a security light bloomed somewhere inside the store, near the cash registers, I believe. I drove to the rear of the store and turned off my headlights as I rolled to a stop next to a couple of large metal dumpsters. The alley behind the store was barely wide enough for two cars to pass, dark and nearly shadowless except for an oval of dirty, brown light beside the tiny excuse of a loading dock, enough dingy light that anybody walking by either end of the block-long alley would have no trouble spotting me. Of course, I didn't expect anyone to be strolling around at one in the morning. And that, it turns out, was the problem.

You see, at that time of the night, I was in sharp focus, because I was the *only* one in sight. Even with my black t-shirt and black jeans and black skin, I was basically naked in a spotlight. I felt sure the Klan Twins didn't have security cameras or such—they were too old-school for that kind of technology—but the sensation of being exposed flowed over me like a cold wave. What if a cop drove by? A Black man dressed like a ninja carrying a couple of pissed-off rats? I could almost hear the tasers zipping through the air. I had no real plan. That was stupid.

So that first night, I stayed on the edges. I listened for cars, for voices. Paranoia welled up in my chest. Something padded to safety around the back of the rusty dumpsters, a dog or feral cat. Maybe rat brethren. I knelt in one of the few shadows I could find. I jostled Wade to the end of the cage and opened the door. He stared at me, confused. If he could talk, he would have asked, *Why here? Why now?* Finally, he ambled into the darkness and without a look back dashed into the thin, dark spaces between the dumpsters. Wallace was more problematic. After several shakes and prodding with a ruler I inexplicably found in my trunk, I eventually persuaded him to back out of his tight confines, and he ran in the opposite direction from Wade, toward the light at the loading dock. There, sweating in the alley, I felt the night was a failure.

Later, home in my bed after I'd reset the traps, I realized my mistake. I had not controlled their escape. And I was too exposed at night. I hated the nakedness of the alley way and the way I had to release Wallace and Wade in the darkness.

I thought, *Would anybody expect a math professor to be releasing rats at ten in the morning? Or three in the afternoon? Nobody does that kind of thing, right?*

Then it struck me: I should hide in plain sight. I should act like it's the most normal thing in the world for a man to saunter up to the loading dock behind the bookstore and make a delivery. Calm and natural and confident. From that moment on, I took my pairs of rats and pulled behind the store in broad daylight. I always had a fake bag of trash with me that I tossed into the dumpster, for camouflage. I checked the traffic at both ends of the alley then watched the back door for a minute or so to make sure those twins didn't appear on the dock. With a couple of quick motions that became more practiced with time, I put the cages on the lip of the loading dock, their escape hatches aimed directly at the back door of Dunean's, and opened the latches. The furry Wallace and Wade invariably glanced at me or at each other then scampered onto the loading dock, disappearing into whatever crevice they quickly discovered.

I often recited little chants. You could dub them prayers. I hoped all the Wallaces and Wades that I repatriated ultimately found each other. I hoped they gathered and talked. I hoped they found their way above and below and into the store. I hoped they screwed like, well, rats.

I had such high hopes for my Wallaces and Wades.

CLAUDE

Your father pops into your head, and you wonder: *what would he think of you now?* You don't know what triggers these moments that ultimately degrade into self-loathing and sadness, a lethal combination. You want to blame him for the way you feel after he appears in that tiny fold of your brain where memory of him took root years ago.

Sometimes he appears while you sit on your usual stool at The Oorah, because that's where you tend to recall the only two pieces of decent advice he gave you. One was don't ever get backed into a corner. He meant this literally, as in, when you get in a fight ("And you *will* get in fights," he said), don't get pushed into a place where you can't maneuver, where you can't stick-and-move or where there isn't enough space to wind up to throw a big right cross. A corner, your old man told you, is only good for the guy who isn't in it.

In the decade since his death, you've turned that piece of literal advice into more of a metaphor, a thing that your father would laugh at. You can't help yourself. You teach English. You adore metaphors. Hence, a *corner* could represent any number of metaphorical things: a dissolving marriage, leaky plumbing that you never get fixed, a tiff with your department chair about your class schedule. You wander into situations with an ex-wife/ leak/asshole, and you can't maneuver, can't use your usual footwork, and every time that happens, you sense your father peering over the top of his Schlitz can, hissing at you, "Got backed into a corner, didn't you? I tried to tell your ass."

The second piece of advice? Always keep pissing and you'll never be too drunk to function fully. For your father, fully functioning meant the ability to drive, dance, or fuck. If he could accomplish that trifecta, he was *fully* functioning. This proclamation was his drinking advice to you, because your old man was a true believer in hydraulics when it came to defining a man. "Hydraulics is the difference between a man and a woman," he often said, fueled by Schiltz. "A man," he said, "ain't nothing but one giant hydraulic engineering project. The raising and lowering, the ebb and flow. A woman never has to worry about hydraulics. You keep pissing, son, and you'll be fine."

You try to spin this one into a metaphor as well. You wonder if your father was, in his crude, loud way, trying to give you something bigger, more metaphorical than how to remain upright during a night of drinking. Or dancing. Or fornication. Was he speaking in code? Did he mean that you should constantly rid yourself of the bad things in your life, the toxins, because if you accomplish that—if you continually piss away the bad elements—you'll always be ready to accept the good things that come your way, like driving and dancing and doing it?

In other words, the longer your father—your Schiltz-swilling, loud-mouthed, blue-collared father—is dead, the more philosophical he becomes. In another five years, you think, you'll turn him into a goddamned Nietzsche.

But here he is again today, popping into your head when you are, of all places, on your bicycle. You know why he's here. He's here because the condition of your pelvic region has you worried. You've heard of this, read about it, but you never thought the sensation would happen to you. In a nutshell, bottom line, the thing is: your penis is asleep. The hydraulics have checked out. And you are frightened. You're more scared than you have been in years.

The feeling when you fall asleep atop your arm then wake up and the arm feels as though it doesn't belong to you anymore? Numb to the point of complete and utter uselessness, and it flops there? That's how your penis feels down there, between your bike saddle and your pelvis. Useless and bloodless and asleep. Your first fear is that something has gone terribly, tragically wrong, and feeling will *never* return to your penis. You will never again have normal relations with a woman or your right hand, and you've lost one third of the drive + dance + fuck equation that defines a man, according to your father. Okay, you tell yourself, you can live with that. Your life might actually be more manageable, more sane if the feeling never returns to your penis. It could be the dark secret you walk around with, one that ironically takes some pressure off you and the search for companionship. (A pressure release. Hydraulics again!) You wonder, as you pedal up a slight slope, if the pills advertised on television, where the good-looking man can't get it up until the woman smiles at him and reminds him that a prescription bottle with *both* their names on it sits in the medicine cabinet, will help you, in this case. Do doctors prescribe Viagra for Cycle Dick Dysfunction? Is CDD a thing or did you make it up?

You realize your panic is irrational, that you cannot, *cannot* be the only one this has happened to. But how would you know? This isn't the sort of condition that male cyclists confess to other male cyclists over their hoppy brown beers. This isn't the sort of thing about which hammerheads compare sweaty notes following a long ride.

You shift on your bike seat, trying a new position, but that only intensifies the numbness. Now you're worried. You begin planning for a life without feeling in your penis, without erections. Erections do not make the man, despite what your father said, you think to yourself, breathing hard as you continue to work uphill. You pause mentally, feeling the degree of elevation change slightly under you, become steeper. Bullshit, you think when you top the hill, erections totally make the man. Your father was right.

You'll have to cut off all contact with the outside world. No more Samuel. No more visits to The Oorah. Or to LeJeune's condo, where you have never once needed or attempted to summon an erection but have occasionally considered it. Become a hermit. Have everything, any and all provisions, left at your door after a quick ring of the doorbell.

You're having the wrong kind of thoughts.

And you're having them because you haven't been drinking enough water, because you've been worrying and panicking and reaching down occasionally and poking at the outside of your bike shorts, trying to conjure up contact with the inner sanctum of your pelvis. You hear your father in your ear, louder than even your heavy, labored breathing. *You haven't been pissing enough, idiot. And you don't piss if you don't drink.* You want to tell him to shut up.

Here is something interesting: your father, for all his bluster about hydraulics and the intricate systems that make a man a man, died because his avocado-sized prostate choked his urethra like an anaconda around a drinking straw. Actually, that didn't kill him, only made him unbearable to be around. He would rise seven or eight times a night to pee. Or not pee, depending on what kind of mood his prostate was in. He refused to seek any treatment, only whined constantly about his condition. He thought increasing the flow of Schlitz would aid matters, but that only further confused the ebb and flow through his manhood. Finally, when he realized he was getting little to no sleep every night, your father went to a urologist who made one digital prod in the back door and said, "Wow."

Wow is not the word you or your father or anyone wants to hear whilst a physician is two and a half knuckles deep in the rectum.

When the doctor proposed trimming some of the over-reaching prostate away from the channel that runs from the bladder to the outside world, your father said, "I don't like the word trim when it concerns that general vicinity." But he relented nonetheless, and it was during that procedure that the doctor discovered, peering at the screen while he steered a tiny scope into the tangled world of male hydraulics, that your father more than likely had cancer in that enlarged prostate, and it was currently in the very active process of killing him. His hydraulics let him down completely less than a year later.

So, you never could decide whether to take him and his theories seriously. But now, with your penis as unfeeling and useless as a . . . as a . . . you can't even think up a simile (which is not a metaphor but rather a metaphor's less attractive second cousin.) Is there some way to prime the pump, to reboot the hydraulics that have obviously let you down on the ride? How do those Tour de France guys do it, ride for so many hours and so many miles in the saddle? Do they even remember what an erection is after years of professional bike riding? You're sure some of them have children. You know you've seen pictures of them with actual families, but for god's sake, that could be obtained through any number of modern methods. Lance Armstrong was missing a testicle, you recall. Did that make him a better bike rider because of the less-than-complete hydraulics system?

You ask yourself so many questions and don't concentrate on the road like you should, and you slam right across a pothole, one large enough to dislodge your molars. The pothole jolts you back to the here-and-now. You're lucky you didn't rupture a tube, in the tire or your pelvis. You've ridden this route a dozen times and never noticed that hole, and you wonder if it's new. There your mind goes again, contemplating the trivial, deflecting the task at hand. You don't hear the bike approaching behind your left shoulder, the snuffling whisk of the wheels as the rider rocks the bike to gain some speed for the pass. Suddenly, there she is again, that woman with the legs chiseled into rises and dips of muscle.

Since the day you had TJ install your cleats and pedals, you've been waiting for this moment. In fact, you took a week away from your favorite route so you wouldn't run into her. Or more precisely, so she wouldn't pass you. You practiced clipping in and unclipping from the pedals until the motions felt natural. You rode dozens and dozens of miles during that week, practicing all the things you would have to do on your regular route: the downhills, the climbs, the intersections where you might have to come to a complete stop and unclip your right leg, because like TJ told you, one leg is always the go-to unclipper. You chose the right. You fell twice during your practice week, which TJ also said was no big deal. "Everybody dumps when they first get pedals," he said. You pedaled up to a stop sign. Slowed down. And forget to uncleat your right shoe. In a slow-motion fall, you and the bike dumped right there at the curb. No harm, no foul. Nobody bleeding. Only cheek-burning embarrassment as you untangled yourself from your machine and hoped none of the cars at the intersection were paying attention. Today is your first day back on the old route, and normally, you would have been dreaming of her potential appearance. She should have been dominating your thoughts. That is, had your penis not fallen asleep and taken precedence.

You snap back the minute she hammers by, gives you a little smile, and says, "On your left!" She has that familiar smug expression across her lips, as if to say, *Well, it's you again and I am dusting you off, sucker. Again.* Today, however, you do something different. You smile right back at her.

When her bike clears the front of yours, you stand up on your pedals, out of the saddle, and rock the bike back and forth with the rhythm of your feet. You feel your chain dig into the teeth of the gears. In the past, she would have been yards and yards ahead of you in seconds. In a couple of minutes, she would be a tenth of a mile in the distance, leaving you pressing on your old, flat pedals. But this is a new day, and a new plan is in the works. You operate the bike now like it's a part of you, because, well, it sort of is. You are attached, clipped in. You aren't separated from the machine that you provide the power for. You've never had this feeling before, even during your week of practice. You almost stomp on the pedals, almost dance on top of them, because hell, your feet have to go in the same circles the pedals travel. In a dozen strokes, you are stuck to her back wheel, staring directly into that ass you've been thinking about for so long. Then a couple of things happen.

First, your penis comes to life. A hydraulic miracle! Maybe because you stood up on the pedals and suddenly had to work hard on the bike. Whatever it is, you sense blood returning to places where blood should always flow freely, and frankly, it hurts, like when blood flows back into a sleeping arm, an intense twinge for a few seconds. If you could rejoice, you would, as you feel hydraulics begin to take effect once again.

Second, you think about your father. Perhaps he was correct. Maybe life is *all* about hydraulics. Maybe the ebb and flow of bodily fluids and bodily events is a comfortable metaphor for the way life pans out. And to think you were contemplating a life without hydraulics only minutes before, and now, with her appearance, you suddenly function fully, inches from her back tire, screaming down the road at twenty-plus miles an hour.

You wonder if she notices you're wearing cycling shoes. Real cycling shoes. She glances over her shoulder and catches sight of you in her peripheral vision. Her smile goes away when she realizes she has been challenged, and she stands on her own expensive pedals. You know she's going to try and dust you off, teach you a lesson. She gears down and somehow manages to increase her rhythm. In a few yards, you've lost her wheel. Space begins to open up, and it grows a little wider each couple of seconds. You quickly learn a new cycling lesson: lose the back wheel, and you are fucked.

You try to stay hitched to her, but it's no use. You're quickly cooked. Your legs turn thick, and you feel as though you're rolling through deep, deep mud. That ass fades into the distance. The last thing you would have expected at that point is your father's voice, but there it is, clanging in your head: *Don't get backed in a corner, son.*

He wasn't a stupid man, you think.

MARLENE

People say I'm an old soul. I don't even know what that is supposed to mean. Who tells a seventeen-year-old girl she has an old soul? What the eff is a soul anyway?

People say you have an old soul when they cannot figure out what to make of you, when they can't think of anything else to say. Sort of like when somebody walks in wearing an ugly ass dress, and in your head, you're thinking, *Oh my god, that sucks*, and you cannot *not* say something, so you say, "Where did you find that dress? Oh my god, I love it!"

People don't know what to make of me, so they say I'm an old soul. Whatever. Maybe that's not bad. I mean, I'd rather be called an old soul than melodramatic. That's what Cheryl calls me. She says I revel in melodrama. That's exactly what she said once. "For the record, you revel in melodrama." Who says revel?

Maybe I was a touch melodramatic. Could you blame me? Dying then dead mother. Father who could not get out of his own way. At least not enough to find his way over to Cheryl's house to say hello to his daughter. And the name. Who names their kid Marlene? It sounds like a movie star name from the forties or something. It sounds like I'm *supposed* to be melodramatic. I'm ready for my close up, Mr. DeMille. My father used sit me in front of old movies when I was a kid and he was trying to be a father. No wonder I'm melodramatic. Have you seen Bette Davis? Have you seen Gloria Swanson?

I was named after a song. *A song.* The first time my parents laid eyes on each other was at a bar where a band was playing. That was the first domino that started the whole thing tumbling forward. They laid eyes on each other while this band called the Killer Whales was onstage playing a song called—wait for it—"Marlene." Melodrama must be genetic.

I was not conceived that night. I was not even thought about. But that was the night when the effing stars aligned or something like that. A bar, a song, Killer Whales? When I was eight or nine or somewhere around then, Claude told me the whole story about seeing my mom on the other side of the bar and staring at her while the Killer Whales played "Marlene." He said the sound quality was crappy in the bar and you could barely make out the lyrics. The only word he understood was *Marlene*, over and over in the chorus. "I knew," he said. "Knew I would have babies with that woman, and I would name them all Marlene." He laughed when he made that little joke. Joke is on you, Claude. You had one baby. Your wife died. Bar band karma. That would be a good band name. Ladies and gentlemen, please welcome to the stage BAR BAND KARMA!

Eff yeah, I get bitter. Marlene? Who wants to go through life with a name like Marlene? Who wants to go through high school with a name like Marlene? You can't turn it into a nickname. You can't be Marl. Or Lene. And Marley is the name of that movie dog that died. You cannot be a dead movie dog. *Dead movie dog.* Band name.

Claude bought a bicycle to take his mind off of this life. He asked me if I wanted to learn to cycle. Like I needed that. I told him, "Only if it can get me the hell out of town." I wouldn't call that a melodramatic answer. More like funny. And true. He did look better though. Thinner, and he looked younger. That wasn't supposed to happen when Mom died. He was supposed to be devastated and start blimping out from grief.

I was not the only one who thought he looked better. Cheryl noticed too. She didn't say anything, but I knew. I was in her house all the time, and let me tell you, she was not, repeat, *not* looking across the dinner table at Patrick the husband. They were done. Somebody ought to have balls enough to throw in the towel. Or the dinner napkin.

But I saw Cheryl looking at Claude every now and then, still trying to act like she usually did, which was a mixture of pissed off and disappointed and angry at him. But lately, like a few weeks after he got that bicycle and a few months after Mom died, well, she still said the same things to Claude—the pissed off, disappointed, angry things—but they sounded different. Now, she sounded like she didn't mean them. Like they were simply things to say while she looked at him, like she was *supposed* to say them. I saw all this, and I am not being melodramatic. What I'm saying is I knew she had a thing for Claude. I wondered what my mother would say about that. My mother and Claude had changed from married to used-to-be-married-but-still-friends before she got sick. Time had passed. Things had happened. Maybe mom would be happy about it. It was her sister. Keep it in the family? Maybe if Claude and Cheryl went to a bar and saw each other across the room and made goo-goo eyes at each other, they'd feel better. I should see if the Killer Whales still tour. Maybe they are old souls like me.

Sometimes I wondered where all of this was going to lead. I worried about it. I couldn't see the future, but I could feel it out there. What can I say? I'm an old soul.

CLAUDE

You get frisky. That's what you tell yourself.

You load your bike and head to the bike store one Saturday morning because TJ keeps telling you need to go on the shop ride. While you don't normally trust someone like TJ (young, cocky, athletic) to give you advice, you've come to discover that TJ is right more often than he is wrong, excepting of course, the time he bet against you and the real pedals. He mentions the shop ride each time you are in the store buying chain cleaner or new gloves or air cannisters, but you shake your head and say something like, "Saturday morning is when I recover from Friday night," because you think it sounds cool and hip to suggest to a young guy that you are a party animal, that you still get in the cups on a Friday night. You never ask him what *exactly* a shop ride is.

Then one afternoon, you catch sight of the flyer in the store, thumb tacked to the wall near the bathroom door. *Shop Ride Saturday Morning! We'll roll out at 7am sharp. Two groups . . . A Group 18–20 mph avg and B Group 12–16 mph avg. Nobody gets dropped! A Group 25 miles, some climbing. B Group 15 miles, rolling hills.*

Because you think about the wrong things most of the time, your first question is What happens to the people who average 17 miles an hour? Where do they go? If you are a seventeen-mile-an-hour person, are you an outcast, a pariah? Second, you are positive you are a B Group guy, no doubt about it. You've done fifteen miles time after time, and it's no big deal. You do not have a computer on your bicycle. More accessories. The need for accessories still amazes you. Since you don't have a computer, you aren't completely sure how fast you ride your bike. You know that the other day you did a twelve-mile loop in right at fifty minutes. Simple math says that comes out to somewhere around fourteen miles an hour, squarely in the B group.

You've lied to TJ. You don't spend Friday nights at The Oorah anymore, at least not long, drawn-out sessions with LeJeune and Beam and PBR. You like getting up on a Saturday and being able to ambulate without your head splitting in two. And you enjoy riding on Saturdays, but always by yourself. No people. You've never ridden with a pack of people. You aren't sure about the rules for riding in a group, but if you know one thing about yourself, it is this: you're a master at keeping your mouth shut and watching and imitating what the smart people do. And you're pretty practiced at picking out the smart people in a group. They always stand out.

That Saturday morning, you arrive right on time. You park in the lot near the little covey of cars and remove your bike from the rack (another accessory!), and you gear up. Air in the tires, gloves on the hands, glasses on the eyes. The cyclists gather at the far end of the lot, near the exit onto Pleasantburg Drive. You see men and women, all sorts of shapes, some of them a great deal larger and plumper than you. You witness some of the etiquette happening, even from a distance, and you make a mental note: Cyclists do not stand beside their bikes. No, they straddle them when they're at a standstill. They slip their butt forward and sit gently on the top tube of the bike. This could possibly cause pain if you're not practiced in the art of sitting gingerly. But still, you make a note. You're happy because your radar is up and working. You're sharp, even at this hour. You are noticing things.

You clip in carefully and pedal toward the crowd. That's a lie. You don't attach your right cleat to the pedal. You keep it resting light, unfettered, so you don't make the rookie mistake of falling in front of the gathering throng. As you approach, a few cyclists nod in your direction. These, you realize, are the people who look mostly like you—a little apprehensive, a little out of shape, their bikes a lot less expensive than the fifteen or twenty riders to your left, who nuzzle thousands of dollars' worth of carbon and titanium with their crotch. The expensive-bike-owners don't even give you the time of day, which is now a couple of minutes before seven.

From behind, you hear TJ holler, "Alright, fresh meat!" and you don't realize he means you. He rolls up on your right. "You going with A Group, right?" Before you can protest, he cuts you off and jumps into his instructional talk. He reminds the crowd that they have to ride no more than two abreast. (You know what the words mean, but you don't know what that means in the cycling world. This is a large group. You can hang toward the back and watch and learn.) TJ says to use hand signals. (You have no clue what hand signals he talks about. You have hands. You know what signaling means. You'll keep your eyes open.) TJ tells everyone to call out potholes and road furniture. (Road furniture?) Everyone nods. They understand. But you are the new kid in school all over again. The class is so far ahead of you. You tell yourself to stay alert. TJ reminds everyone that the combined group will remain together for the first five miles until the intersection of McIlhaney and Buncombe Road. "Then A Group will head toward Paris Mountain and B Group will go left toward Green Valley." Good, you think, at the five-mile mark, things will thin out. You'll be safe after that.

You aren't prepared for the sound, the commotion, when TJ finishes his comments and tells everyone to roll out, the sound of three dozen people clipping into their pedals simultaneously. It is loud and medieval, as if a strange, metallic animal has woken up and is hungry, snapping its jaws, sharpening its teeth. You feel your adrenaline spike in your ears. You wished you'd skipped the coffee. You suddenly need to pee. You're smart enough to realize that the most important thing to do is watch the guy in front of you. Don't nick his wheel. Don't weave and take out the person on your right or left. Keep your line. You have never been this close to other people on your bike, other than that first day when you got yelled at. You hope the guy behind you is as cautious as you are. You hope *everyone* is. You've never had to trust so many people you've never met. Who knows where the guy behind you was last night? He might have taken over ownership of your Saturday hangover. The guy to your left might be blind in his right eye. Who are these people?! Why did you do this? Why couldn't you have been content to take your safe little rides all by yourself?

At the half-mile mark, the group strings out into a long serpentine of riders, two abreast. (Ah ha!) The faster riders move to the front, but other than that, it's a mixed bag. The guy beside you, who grunts a *good morning*, is an experienced cyclist. You can tell by the way he isn't a man-on-a-bike. He is part of the machine, connected by more than the pair of pedals. You know he won't bowl you over as you head down the road at a reasonable pace, one that you could maintain for a couple of hours, at least.

You are pondering why you subjected yourself to this when you notice the rider directly in front of you. You recognize the ponytail and the rear end cranked aerodynamically in the air. You recognize the kit and the shoes. You recognize the legs. It's the woman from your route. The mystery woman. You have never been this close to her for this long. You've only seen her in passing, then that one time that you latched onto her wheel before she ditched you on an upgrade. Now you can watch her pedal and see the strain of her calves. She has a visible vein that runs vertically down the right one. You imagine that gives her superpowers. She is close enough to touch.

This, you say to yourself, *is why I came this morning. This is a sign. I'm supposed to be here. I was lured here without even knowing it.*

You spend the next couple of miles locked on her wheel. Even when the entire group stops for the big intersection at Parker Road and the serpentine reforms and you have a new guy beside you, she is still right in front, mere inches away. She is starting to warm up. You think you detect a little perspiration on her neck inches below her hairline, where the ponytail is pulled away from her skin.

Word passes its way down the long line of riders—the jumping off point for the B Group is the next intersection. Everyone begins to slow down and maneuver one way or the other. But the woman, she stands on her pedals for a couple of strokes and moves away from you then angles to the right. She is going with the A Group. Panic and indecision swordfight in your head. The B Group enters the intersection and turns left toward Green Valley where the rolling hills are not painful, only minor rises you are familiar with. Ponytail Woman melds in with the A Group. You don't know what to do. You know what you are *supposed* to do. You're supposed to be sensible and rational and stay with the group of people who ride like you. They're the smart, reasonable people. The others, the A Group, have crazy eyes, eyes that don't care about anything in the world except going fast. These are the ones you've heard about, you think. These are the hammerheads of the world. You wonder if Ponytail Woman is a hammerhead. You think you would have picked up on that.

But of course she is, you think. Look at her. She slides her bike beside a fellow hammerhead. They nod to each other as if they are friends. She pedals away, leaves you like every time before. But today? Today is different. Today, you follow her. Who are you to screw with signs and portents? You're supposed to be here. Act like it.

Keep up with the group, you say to yourself, but the speed rises, and before you even crest the top of the first rise on Poinsett Road, you realize you're in way over your head. Way over.

WALLACE & WADE

We are constantly amazed at the utter confusion of the younger generations flocking around us. Had we the ability, we would ban anyone below the age of twenty-one from the bookstore side of Dunean's because, frankly, youngsters of that age are far too immature to be trusted with the written word. Too immature, in fact, to be trusted with much of anything, including but not limited to money and their own genitalia. We see this daily among the shelves. Young people can't keep their hands off themselves. We discuss these sorts of things on our porch while we partake of our late-afternoon cocktails and talk about our day. Our beverage of choice is a Dark 'n Stormy—rum and ginger beer with a healthy squeeze of lime. The darker and stormier it gets, the higher the porch swing arcs and the more we make fun of things in the world, like young people with brains the consistency of cottage cheese. We were never that silly. Honestly, we were never that young.

And we were never like Colt Thomasson. He is the reason that the meetings take place in the special room every other Tuesday evening. We are not sure if Colt is his given name or a nickname, but it certainly suits him. He either grew into the label he was bequeathed at birth or he looked in the mirror one day and realized that he was, indeed, somewhat coltish. Gangly and awkward, Colt Thomasson could not walk down the aisles of Dunean's without knocking into shelves. One evening, an uncontrolled bump of his wayward hip took out an entire display of recent science fiction we had spent hours arranging, but it was only science fiction, which was no great loss in our opinion. From the few times we saw him, it appeared Colt's clothes only fit properly for a day or two before his wrists or shinbones magically extended and there, suddenly, was *more* of Colt Thomasson, dangling from his too-short shirts and pants. His large head balanced precariously atop his blade-thin shoulders as though it might topple off at any moment. And Colt Thomasson had never learned the secrets of proper skin care. What wasn't covered by flaming acne was decorated with the scars acne left in its wake. We often thought of telling him there were cures for that sort of ailment, but we realized Colt didn't care about his face or his thin wrists or his high-water trousers. Colt was angry about other aspects of the modern world, and ultimately, we found that endearing. Hence, the rental agreement.

The first time Colt Thomasson appeared in our store, he lingered at the register nearest the front door. We say lingered. More like he loomed, waiting for a customer or two to chat and pay for their books or magazines. Oh yes, we saw him there, even while we talked to people with money in their hands. We thought for a moment that he might be waiting for the optimum moment to rob us, so we fingered the little derringer that we carry in the side pocket of our sport jacket, a tiny nine-millimeter Cobra over-and-under we like to call our Little Persuader.

When the register was free of paying customers, he walked unsteadily toward the counter, clipping the *Staff Picks!* display with a renegade hip, nearly toppling the entire rack. He said, "Sorry," and we knew then that he was not there to rob us. Thieves never apologize during the commission of a crime, at least not in our experience. He leaned in toward us, and we noticed he was in dire need of orthodontic care. His picket-fence arrangement of teeth—upper and lower—had never been tended by a professional. "Can I ask you two something?" he said.

His voice was not what we expected. From his look, you would have anticipated something Southern and nasal, an accent with its origins in the mountains a few hours north of here, something whiny that dragged out syllables into tinny, echoey twangs. We expected a country dialect, yet what we heard was gravelly and measured, as if someone much older and scarier had taken over his vocal chords. His voice, which should have been possessed by a bourbon-drinking, Camel-smoking construction worker, was alien inside of this scarecrow of a boy. His voice was middle-aged, and we could not help but listen to it. We forgot our manners and neglected to answer his question. Fortunately, he asked again.

"Well, of course," we finally said.

"Not out here," he said, surveying the room quickly with his dark eyes. "Maybe in the flag room."

Now, that took us a bit by surprise. We had never called the room that housed the Confederate accessories the "flag room." He had obviously taken the liberty to name it himself. One requirement of our regular customers in that room was heightened discretion. If, for example, there was a person who might benefit from any of our wares, then please, we asked, exercise word-of-mouth. However, we also requested our customers not spread information willy-nilly. Not that we sold anything illegal. Basically, we wanted to segregate our customer base. The young hipster who buys the latest issue of *The Nation* from the periodical display is probably not going to purchase a set of Stonewall Jackson poker chips. The woman who rushes to grab the latest Jodi Picoult novel is rarely in the market for a Rabbit Vibrator emblazoned with Robert E. Lee's profile. (One caveat: lately, we've seen a marked increase in women who have been making purchases in the regular shelves *and* behind our closed door.)

We wondered how this young man, who couldn't have been more than eighteen or twenty, could have known about the room. Maybe a relative clued him in. In any event, we relaxed our fingers from around the Little Persuader and walked toward the door that led to what had moments before been dubbed the Flag Room. We didn't mind the name. When things have names, they tend to become more substantial. The Flag Room sounded fine by us. In fact, we were smiling as we led the young man through the shelves. Behind us, we heard the near-disasters as he bumped and banged his awkward way, following us much too closely, we thought to ourselves.

Inside the newly christened Flag Room, Colt Thomasson assaulted us again with that wonderful voice and said, "You might ought to close that door." Well, we thought, we must be distracted. Normally, we *never* forget to close that door behind us, lest some customer wandered beyond the *Employees Only After This Point* sign and peered into the assortment of Confederate-tagged memorabilia. As we paused, we noticed the way the Flag Room smelled, the brisk odor of brand-new things, as though a hundred new cars had parked in the room and swung all of their doors open. Colt took note of it as well, glancing around and taking a deep inhale, like a man ashore in a friendly new country.

"Well, anyway," he began, "I guess I ought to jump in. You see, I belong to this group. Well, in other words, I am the leader of this group. We are the WLF. You heard of us?" he said in his gravel-silk voice.

We turned to each other. The WLF? There was a time, in our much younger days, when we watched wrestling on television. The showmanship, the theater, the costumes. The strapping men. We fondly recalled the days of Johnny Weaver and Wahoo McDaniel and the Anderson Brothers, who sadly weren't actually brothers, we came to discover. Our wrestling infatuation was merely a phase, but naturally when we heard of an organization called the W-Whatever, we immediately thought of the ring. We ventured a guess.

"Does this have anything to do with wrestling?" Colt Thomasson chuckled at us, a chuckle as beguiling as his voice.

"Man, got nothing to do with wrestling. We are the White Liberation Front," he said, his eyes narrowing. "It's a fight we got going on, but it for damn sure ain't wrestling."

We were immediately suspicious, and he could no doubt see the reaction plastered across our faces. He rushed to fill in the awkward silence. "Here's what I figured," he said. "It ain't no secret that you two have this room and you support the Confederate cause."

We wanted to interrupt and suggest that the Flag Room may be more of a secret than he assumed. Yet, he was correct on our support of all things Dixieland, excluding jazz, which we found monotonous and derivative. We decided to zip our lips and be attentive listeners.

"We are sorta on the same page, is what I'm saying. You ever use Ivory soap?" he continued. We paused in thought again. We were sure that at some point in our past we had bathed or been bathed with Ivory soap, but for the life of us, we couldn't remember. Colt continued, "Well, Ivory soap says right on the package that it's 99 and 44/100 percent pure. White and pure. That's us. Our sort of secret name is the Ivory Boys. We can't walk around talking about the WLF. People would wonder."

We, of course, *wondered* about a group calling itself the Ivory Boys, which to our ears sounded like a pop singing group, but no matter. Still, not a very ferocious nickname for a white supremist organization. We kept our ears at attention.

"We need a place to meet that has the right feel, you know what I mean? We can't meet at anybody's house. We can't meet outside because it's gonna get cold soon. We'd like to meet here," Colt Thomasson said, waving his arm in the general direction of the Battle of Shiloh feather-tipped riding crops display. "We meet once every two weeks. We can pass the hat. I'm thinking fifty bucks a meeting to rent the room." Colt's voice drifted into silence, and he drew another deep breath, not to speak but rather to signify that his speech was over, that his work here was almost done.

We should have retired to the other room at the rear of the store, our actual office, and privately discuss the proposition Colt Thomasson had laid on our table, but we didn't. (Later, we would wonder why we didn't follow our normal procedure and talk things through on the porch swing that evening with a Dark 'n Stormy sweating gently in our hands.) Truth be told, we were instantly excited and agreed on the spot to let Colt and the Ivory Boys—or the WLF or whatever they wanted to call themselves— use our Flag Room for their little club meetings. Let the Ivory Boys sow some wild Confederate oats.

There was something else too. We may have seen something of ourselves in Colt Thomasson. He was different, not only physically, but different in the way he looked at the world and awkwardly plodded through it. And we knew that type of awkwardness. Colt Thomasson had given up trying to find existing roadmaps for his path through adolescence and young manhood and had decided to become his own cartographer. And we were intimately familiar with that feeling of being lost in the social wilderness. The expression that occasionally flitted across Colt Thomasson's face was one we had long ago seen in our own mirror, that mixture of pleading and defiance and anger and out-and-out confusion. No, he wasn't an Ivory Boy. He was another Lost Boy, and if we could help him—if we could help a whole roomful of them—than we, by god, we would.

We stuck out our hands, and Colt could not decide which to shake first, so he gave each of us one of his thin-fingered, gawky hands. From an outsider's perspective, the gesture might have looked like the most fumbling social custom in history, but we smiled at each other and thought it was about the cutest thing we had seen all day. A little prayer circle of sorts. A pimply-faced white revolutionary who couldn't figure out how to shake hands. We would remember this moment.

We lingered in the doorway of the Flag Room and watched Colt Thomasson retreat into the store, grazing bookshelves and display racks with his mutineering hips and shoulders. We sighed, remembering those days, those wonderful, halcyon days when we thought we could actually change the world around us. We felt good about ourselves for the first time in weeks, but the spell was broken from behind. We heard quick shuffling in the display of Andersonville Prison jigsaw puzzles—a quick movement, low to the ground, a scuffling if you will, but we blamed it on our overtaxed imaginations or the weary settling of an extremely old building on its aged foundations.

Nothing to worry about, we were sure.

PEG

When I was a freshman in college, I drove home from school one Friday afternoon, heading back to see the parents for the weekend. I skirted the edge of this little town called Newberry, past the fast-food joints and cheap hotels and tanning shops. Not only do I remember the disc I had in the CD player, *Creedence Clearwater Revival's Greatest Hits,* I even remember the specific song that was playing, "Run Through the Jungle." Beyond that junky strip-mall section of Newberry, beyond the Walmart and the fire station, where the country begins again, a large cemetery sits on the left-hand side of the road.

By large, I mean acres and acres of grass and gravestones and only a pair of large oak trees on the whole plot of land. I always wondered why those two trees were there. As I came around the curve, I saw a couple of cars stopped where they shouldn't be stopped, their fenders sticking out too far in the road. Another car faced the wrong way, turned away from me at a strange angle like it had been placed there by a giant hand. When I touched the brake and looked a little closer and saw a pickup in the cemetery—not on the road that wound between all the plots and around the oaks, but in the grass, on its side, in front of the broken and battered head stones—I knew what had happened. I saw the bodies, all men, that had been flung out of the pickup when it went sliding toward the graves. They lay like toy soldiers in a kid's game, but they weren't soldiers. They were dark-skinned men, Hispanic men, scattered and unmoving among the markers. I saw blood when I looked a second time. It had happened only minutes before; there were no sirens yet and no blue lights, only a couple of passersby who happened to stop.

I don't know why the brain works the way it does, but the voice inside my head told me not to look. The voice said, *You know what happened and you already know it's bad, so don't look. You don't have to confirm anything.*

But I had to look, didn't I? There was no way to keep from staring at the men who were—what is the word? littering? decorating?—the cemetery grass. I longed to see movement. Honestly, I glanced around, looking for a camera because I thought this might be some movie scene being filmed on the outskirts of Newberry. I ignored the voice that said *don't*, and now I can never unsee that afternoon, can't unsee the men arranged in the grass like pick-up sticks.

It was like that for me now. I knew what was happening in the life I left behind. I could sort of predict how it might play out, and *I couldn't keep from watching.*

I want to think it was all about love, that I couldn't tear my eyes away from Marlene and Claude because of my deep feelings for the two of them, but that would be a lie. Love had taken on a whole new meaning. Now, love no longer meant commitment or devotion or sex or joy or rejection or compromise or loyalty or take-your-pick-of-words. When you reached this point, love was exactly like the feeling you get when you order a wonderful meal and eat the perfect amount. Now, love was a feeling of being completely satiated and guilt-free about it. And that feeling never went away and it never changed. So no, I didn't watch the ones I left behind for the sake of love. I would still have that wonderfully full feeling about the people I cared for whether I kept an eye on things or not.

I couldn't turn away because *I didn't want to miss anything.* The glances that Cheryl and Claude exchanged over the table in the coffee shop. How Claude kept adjusting the crotch of his bike shorts while he pedaled. The way Marlene no longer looked Colt Thomasson in the eye. Or how Samuel stared and stared at that dusty page from that dusty book.

I lived to spy on those little things.

SAMUEL

I could navigate my attic with my eyes shut. I didn't mean to become so proficient in balancing on joists in the dark, but now when I made the trips above my ceiling, I didn't pull the hank of string that hung from the bare light bulb. I didn't need to. And I certainly didn't want to have a hand preoccupied with a flashlight. Yes, I did consider a headlamp, but that felt . . . I don't know, obsessive or something. Too precious, maybe.

With only a few pinpricks of light escaping from the outdoors into the musty air of the attic, I could find my way fine. Sturdy pieces of three-fourths-inch plywood spanned the joists, but most of my careful steps were spent cradling a jar of Skippy and a sleeve of Ritz in my arm, a kitchen knife in my back pocket. I have no doubt they knew I was coming. The Havaharts filled so quickly, I deluded myself into thinking that the rats looked forward to my visits, anxious for me to slather some peanut butter on a cracker and give them an excuse to join their friends on the loading dock at Dunean's. It was as if I conducted some sort of military draft, and they waited in my attic for their furry little lottery numbers to come up.

Enough trips, and the map of the attic became imprinted in my mind. I could shut my eyes and visualize the tricky corner around the now-defunct chimney. If I stopped long enough, I felt cold air escaping from inside my house through the sloppy, uninsulated space between the bricks and the sheetrock of the ceiling. Money flowed through that chilly slit, wasted energy. I knew how many steps I could take until the angled pitch of the roofline caused me to squat and duck-waddle to the far corner of the space. I loved the geometry of the attic. It tweaked my mathematics soul. I knew which end of the attic to avoid, the social area, the place where all of my future Wallaces and Wades huddled, standing by for me to bait the traps that would eventually take them away. I had no idea exactly *how many* rats I wanted to expatriate, no idea how many it would take to accomplish my ultimate goal. And what was that, I wondered, as I picked my way through the dark? Did I have an end game? You have become more interested in the *means* than the *end*, I thought.

I looked forward to my trips to the attic, the smell of fresh peanut butter mixing with the dust and heat, the bitter sting of old fiberglass insulation in the air. Once they were captured, I had become a master at cruising to the far end of the loading dock in broad daylight, popping my trunk and dumping two new warriors into the bigoted confines of Dunean's. I had borrowed a little prayer, a rat mantra that I recited as they scurried into the openings around the loading dock. *Go forth and multiply*, I said, recalling some snatch of a Bible verse from my Sunday school days.

But what did I want my little band of beady-eyed counter-insurgents to accomplish? I asked myself.

I sometimes imagined a horror movie of epic proportions: thousands of angry, yellow-fanged rats pouring through the doors of Dunean's during a busy weekend afternoon, nipping everyone in their path, knocking over shelves, crawling up the wildly Madras-colored pant legs of the owners. It could happen; I'd done the math. From my research, I calculated a single pair of mating Wallaces and Wades could grow to more than a thousand in a year if they all put their minds to it.

But was I still putting *my* mind to it? Truthfully, in the past few weeks, I'd felt a change come over me. I believed I'd lost some focus, some purpose. Now I was simply going through sticky, sweaty motions. Maybe I was getting bored, and one Tuesday, I was on the verge of ditching the whole forced-rat-migration scheme, or at least curtailing it, and rethinking my options.

Oh, one more trip, I thought, one more run with a Wallace and a Wade, and I'll lie awake tonight and reassess my priorities.

As usual, the Havaharts sprung loudly, though I rarely noticed the metallic clang of success anymore while I rambled around my house during the mornings. I had grown numb to the sounds of capture. I carried the traps one by one down the attic stairs and into my trunk, then headed for Dunean's. I remember on that Tuesday I had turned the radio up loudly to mask the terrified/pissed/confused squeaks coming from the trunk. The local classic rock station was very proud of their Two-for-Tuesday promotion, but before the first half of "Freebird" finished, I punched the cassette player and smiled when Smokey Robinson and the Miracles emerged from the speakers.

I turned from Mills Avenue onto the narrow alley that ran behind Dunean's, checking nonchalantly in the mirrors for anything that might be wrong with the usual picture. No one followed me. No police to be seen. Everything as it should be. I turned the volume down on Smokey. Wallace and Wade grew quiet in the trunk. I glanced toward the rear of my car, maybe to assure them, and something suddenly registered with me. A warning flag popped up in my brain, and I jerked my sight back toward the loading dock.

Everything was *not* as it should be. (Like I mentioned, my focus was fuzzy. I hadn't checked carefully enough.) A bright, lime-colored panel van was parked in my usual point of rat deportation. A bright, lime-colored van with huge block printing running the length of the vehicle, all caps, as if it was screaming at me: PETE'S PEST CONTROL!! CALL THE DEATH PATROL!!

With his blazing lime vans that patrolled the streets, Pete's was the most visible pest control company in town. I sometimes thought Pete put several empty vans on the road simply to drive around, giving people the illusion that he and his death patrol were constantly on their way to a new pest battle. Here he was, bringing his lime-tinged extermination to Dunean's. I smiled.

Correction: I laughed. At first only a giggle, a little eruption I tried to capture in my mouth, but then it became too much for me, quickly escalating into a full-on howl. I suddenly knew what Ecstatics meant when they said their mystical experiences caused them to break into uncontrollable frenzies. I danced a little ecstatic dance in my front seat. *Because the plan was working!* Dunean's was having a serious problem. I guessed their problem possessed four legs and a squeak. The experts had been summoned. Chemicals were being spread. And it was too late. Even Pete and his Lime Death couldn't stop the onslaught. The Wallaces and Wades had been following my preachings. They had, no doubt, gone forth and multiplied. The furry things were out of control.

I could not contain myself. I rocked in my seat. I turned Smokey Robinson and his Miracles up as loud as I could stand, celebrating my own little miracle. I pulled close beside Pete's van and turned my face to the bright green glow. I noticed that the windows of the van were open, a futile attempt to keep the cab cool while parked. I laughed even harder as I popped my trunk lid. The squeaking inside the Havaharts grew frantic, but I loved the noise. For me, this was a moment of unexpected joy. The right music, the right alignment of the stars, the right van in the alleyway.

The new pair of inductees stared up at me, plotting how to sink their jaundiced teeth into my arms. "Patience, boys," I said. "Or girls."

I checked the door at the loading dock. No movement. That gave me time to quickly open the driver's door of the van and roll up the windows in the cab. Thank god the van had old-school cranks on the doors. Another quick movement, and I grabbed one of the Havaharts, settled it on the seat, and unlatched the gate. The rat saw his chance and launched himself into the rear of Pete's van, into the most convenient darkness he detected. I did the same with the other trap then slammed the door shut on the van. I thought I heard things being turned over in the back, and I imagined boxes being ravaged, bottles being tipped, cords being gnawed. I was still laughing.

Twenty minutes later, when I pulled into my driveway, I heard the two empty Havaharts clanging in the backseat, the scent of old peanut butter filling the air in the Lincoln. Maybe it was the smell, perhaps the comic adrenaline still pumping through me, but thanks to the appearance of Pete's Pest Control, I decided then and there: *I would redouble my efforts in the attic.*

I had no clue how many more rats colonized in the darkness there, but I would trap until I could trap no more. Wallace and Wade—the real ones, not their rat doppelgangers—had enlisted Pete's Pest Control. The twins were becoming desperate, so as I yanked the cord and dropped the attic stairs, I decided I would keep going; I would not sleep until I no longer heard the pitter-pat of rat feet above my head.

I had developed an alternating system for laying my traps—a method to my madness—and the time had arrived to place them on the south wall, which meant I had to tiptoe across a couple of sagging joists, dodge the bricks of the useless chimney, and load my Ritz-and-Skippy in the dusty gray light that trickled in from a minute crack in a soffit. I didn't need the light. I could set the Havaharts in a sensory deprivation tank if need be.

I heard a shuffling behind me, and I smiled, imagining who might be lined up for the next shipment to Dunean's. In retrospect, the smile and the mood I was in contributed to my misstep. It wasn't a bad one; I didn't punch a leg through the bathroom ceiling or anything that dramatic. Simply, as I made my way toward the attic door, I glanced over my shoulder to see if I could spot the traps in the dark. That slight turn caused me to lose my footing on the joist, and I banged against the rough cull brick of the chimney. To avoid going completely down, I spun and wrapped myself around the chimney, hugging the bricks like long lost friends. At least that's what I think happened. All I know is that I ultimately ended up with my forehead planted against a collapsing cardboard box.

I knew the contents of that box. One of Esther's relatives had shipped it to me years back, months after her funeral. The afternoon it arrived on my porch, I sifted through it: some old letters I had mailed her from college, books Esther read the last few months of her life, a couple of photos of people I didn't recognize, some table linens. I don't know why my grandmother wanted me to have table linens. I still didn't believe in omens, but as I lay there, I thought there must be some reason I fell face-first into *this* box on *this* afternoon.

I lugged the box across the joists and balanced it on my shoulder when I climbed down the attic stairs. I cleared space on the dining room table I never actually dined on and opened the box. Most of the books had been gnawed on by my future Wallaces and Wades. The linens were yellow and soiled. The corners of the box were lined with rat droppings. I sifted through all the trash and remains and discovered the only thing still more or less intact in the box, the only thing that rats and heat and humidity hadn't completely fouled: a large leather-bound Bible zipped tight against the evils of the attic.

I didn't remember the Bible being in the box the first time I had inspected the contents. I must have missed it or ignored it, but here it was, the leather cracked and molded on one corner. The zipper was rusted, destroyed to the point that when I tugged on it, the teeth ripped away in a little puff of musty dust.

I had no need for a Bible. I'd spent enough time climbing in and out of its pages as a boy, looking for clues, looking, I suppose, for my mother. Back then, I searched for answers everywhere I could. Once I unzipped the cover, I recognized this Bible. Esther carried it around the last few years of her life like it contained a valuable map, which of course, in her mind, it did. Her guide to the next life.

I opened it, and my breath caught when I saw the tiny, precise, curly cursive on the inside cover. It was Esther's handwriting, and in the thick flyleaves before Genesis, she had continued the tradition of recording the family tree in the family Bible. Esther's mother had also written in some of the space, writing that had all but faded to hieroglyphics. Perhaps a woman even before that had made notations.

I sat in my old overstuffed chair and pulled the chain on the lamp. The Bible smelled like old age, and I sneezed at the dust rising from the pages. I studied the roadmap of births and deaths and marriages and relations recorded in ink that, in most cases, was miraculously still legible. The best parts were the comments.

Esther called my uncle Jonathan the *ugliest baby I ever saw.* And when my great aunt June Nell died, someone, maybe my great grandmother, said the day of her funeral *was so hot six peeple faynted.*

I needed to find my mother's place on the page. Maybe I could finally say, *At least I know one place she exists.* And I wanted to see my name as well. I wasn't overcome by waves of nostalgic grief or anything. This was a ledger of who was born and who died. I wasn't expecting answers to any of the questions I had stopped asking years before. I wanted to see our place on the family tree, on the Bible's page. This was simply information, facts. Tools, at best, perhaps something I could use one day. Who doesn't look at something written in the past and think it might offer some launching pad into the future? I followed my finger as it dragged the page. There were the names of both sets of my grandparents. Thomas had died long before Esther. He had not received a comment, only a date.

There, in ink that looked fairly recent, was the birth of my mother. And there was her death. My breath caught in my throat like a shard of bone. Twenty years earlier. A year with no month, no day. In an instant, in a couple of scratches from a pen, she was gone. And no one bothered to tell me. I wasn't sure who to be angry with, so for some time—maybe fifteen minutes or so—I stared at the wall, trying to decide if I felt any different knowing that she was no longer out there working her way back to me somehow.

When I looked down at the page again, there I was, my birth. I didn't expect the name of my father to appear anywhere. I didn't believe I would see a solid line between my mother and That Fan Salesman Who Went Off to A War. I didn't see the name Zeb in the vicinity of me or my mother. But lines trailed off in strange directions. The page reminded me of a kid's connect-the-dots game. Among of all the lines, I saw a notation, a carefully scribbled comment from Esther's pen, sitting adjacent to my birth date. Again, this appeared to be newer ink, as if Esther added it much later, like she meant for me to discover it one day. Today was that day. The words hadn't faded over the years. I read them out loud, and they echoed in my little dining room, flew right up to the ceiling. I didn't know whether to cover my eyes and sob or begin howling with laughter for the second time that day or be angry at the world or my mother. Because what I read felt like the punch line of a giant genealogical joke.

I sat there for a while in my dining room and didn't make any more noise and wondered why this particular day had decided to become so odd and important and confusing.

Wallace & Wade

Pete was rumored to be the best. At least our friends, the ones we prize as trustworthy, said as much. If a pest was to be had, they all said, Pete was the one to ferret out the vermin. (Which we thought was a very interesting turn of a phrase, since ferrets are vermin, aren't they?)

He was truly unique in the pest control world, which is to say, he read a great deal of heady material. We had waited on him in the store while he picked up something on physics or—what was it that one time?—oh yes, he purchased that nonfiction volume about the creation of the Oxford English Dictionary. Who would have thought that a pest control man cared about etymology? His father, now long dead, had been a Baptist minister and was still remembered and renowned as a pastor who could orate with a vocabulary that would impress any linguist. Perhaps pest control and the ministry do not exist far from each other on the occupational flow chart; ridding the world of unwanted rodents and bugs is somewhat akin to making the world safe from sin. Also, Pete had always been rather vocal about his politics. His bright lime-green vans sported bumper stickers promoting his left-leaning opinions. He was an enlightened Democrat pest control expert. We hired him anyway.

While we did not think Pete's left-of-center politics or his religious upbringing would ever taint his ability to objectively do his job, we felt it our right and obligation to keep him away from the Confederate/Flag Room. We couldn't take a chance that while he searched for rats, he might be distracted by *States' Rights!* dildos and Jeff Davis Joy lubricant. We did not need the wrong people making incorrect assumptions, and by wrong, we meant people who had no idea about the good, solid intentions behind our secret room and its exclusive inventory.

So when Pete pointed at the locked door and said, "What's behind there?" we answered, perhaps too quickly and too in tune, "Nothing to worry about."

"For me to make a complete examination, I need to see all the heated space. Pests like warm places, you know." We did not, but that was beside the point. He put his hand on the knob and tried to turn.

"It's locked," we said.

"Obviously," Pete said back. "Okay, maybe I could look at it from above. In that little crawlspace in the attic."

For a second, we considered letting Pete commando-crawl to the far corner of the attic above the Flag Room but decided against it. He could, with the simple removal of a ceiling panel, gain a bird's eye view of the room in all its antebellum glory. We were very careful about who was allowed inside the room. Pete did not pass our vetting procedures. He was a liberal risk.

"Suit yourself. With the little bit of scat I have seen and what not, I think you got yourself a garden variety rodent problem, which is to say, not that bad of one," Pete said. "But from what you two were telling me on the phone, you had yourself quite an event this morning. Rats on top of rats." He paused briefly, then rubbed his chin. "You think you might've been overreacting a bit? You know, getting dramatic?"

This may have been a subtle homophobic slur, which surprised us coming from Pete. He realized it, too.

"What I mean," he said, retreating a bit, "is that you may have seen a single big rat and figured where there is one, there are a few dozen more hiding out somewhere. That's not unusual."

That was when we repeated the story we had told him earlier that day over the phone, how we had come to the store that morning and turned on the lights to the stampede of small feet and scuffling toward the rear. We asked each other what we had heard. We knew from where the sound emanated: in the direction of the Confederate Room. Yet when we turned on the hall light and expected to see the owners of the tiny footsteps, we saw an empty corridor.

We stood there and shared a guilty, caffeinated grin and asked ourselves if we had consumed perhaps too much coffee. When we opened the door to the room, we were admittedly a little off-balance, not as sharp as we should have been, because we did not *immediately* notice, in the dim glow from the hallway light, that the floor of the Confederate Room appeared to be moving.

Moving was perhaps an incorrect word. Undulating? Flowing? We should have asked Pete if the Oxford English Dictionary would help us in this instance. Whatever the case, we stared at what we assumed was an optical illusion—a floor that rocked with waves here and there. And the waves made noises—tiny, orchestrated squeaks and peeps. We wanted, again, to blame the coffee, but in our heart of hearts, we knew that an extra cup of Americano would never cause this.

We reached for the light switch and missed, and we will swear until our last breath that something ran between our legs, which caused us to squeal not unlike middle school cheerleaders. We finally located the light and flooded the room, and we can only say that the sight before us was so surreal—well, we are sure that our hearts are healthy, because the shock of seeing scores of large, gray, toothy rats huddling en masse on the floor of the Confederate Room is the recipe for cardiac arrest.

We were unsure what to do. Shut the door, trap them all inside the room? Or push the door wide open to facilitate their escape? We did neither. All we did was run. And scream more. And retreat as quickly as we could to the front of the store, where we hid behind the *New and Noteworthy* section.

We watched the short hallway that led to the Confederate Room, waiting on the parade of vermin to follow us down the passage. The door behind us, which led to the outside, was closed. "For heaven's sake, we should give them an escape route," we yelled to no one in particular, and thank god we weren't officially open. This sort of gossip would spread wildfire-like and infect business to the point that . . . Well, we didn't want to consider that possibility. Honestly, what we had seen was far, far beyond gossip. It was a stomach-churning reality. We opened the door halfway, offering a clear path to the sidewalk and street outside of Dunean's.

We waited to the point of distraction, looking around the shelves for other unseen exits the rats might have taken. "Do you see them?" we wondered aloud. Behind us, a woman approached the door and hesitated before walking in. We checked our watch, a quarter of the hour. "Fifteen more minutes, ma'am," we said, reaching back to shove the door closed. Lord, we almost hit the poor woman in the nose. She huffed down the street. Better a single annoyed soul than an entire regional customer base that had heard the story of the Dunean Rat Swarm.

Speaking of swarm, we had waited long enough for them to appear. We knew what had to be done, but neither of us relished venturing again down the hall to assess the status of the floor full of rats. Especially when we had shown our true colors by fleeing and screaming only ten minutes earlier.

Once more, to no one in particular, we raised our voices. "Oh, for god's sake, they are more scared of us than we are of them," but we didn't believe that cliché. There were so many of them. They had numbers and speed, and they were sly, we thought, but we didn't know that for sure. Our experience with rodents was limited.

We had no choice. We needed to know what had happened. For all we knew, the rats had begun eating everything on the shelves of the Confederate Room, which would be a financial disaster. Yes, we were curious, and curiosity killed the cat, which was a strange thing to think at that moment. If, a year ago, we had adopted the feral tabby that loitered by the dumpster in the back alley, this problem may have been avoided. Spilled milk and all of that. Much too late to think about prevention when the disease was—quite literally—running rampant.

We crept down the dim hallway toward the Confederate Room, keeping our profile low, as if being closer to the floor would provide immunity against a stampede of rats. We are unafraid to confess that we held each other's hand. We think the last time we did that was the eighth grade, when Rollie Turpin decided to take out his latent yet smoldering homophobia on us in the boys' bathroom. We accepted our lumps together then. And we would now, if lumps were to be had.

Steadily slinking—that was us, all the way to the opening of the Confederate Room. By now, our eyes adjusted to the lack of light, recalibrating the shapes we expected to see in front of us. But we heard nothing like before, no peeps or squeaks from inside the room. We made our way closer until we were almost in reach of the bank of light switches. A swipe of our free hand, the one not tightly grasping another, and we flooded the room with light.

There in front of us was something completely unexpected. In front of us was . . . absolutely nothing! Not a single rodent. In fact, the only thing amiss was an overturned box of John Wilkes Booth ribbed condoms, unopened and undamaged, lying in the middle of the floor.

Since we had spent the better part of the morning talking to empty space, we saw no reason to discontinue that idiosyncrasy. "What the hell?" we wondered. "Where the hell?"

We cocked our head to listen for any evidence of what we had seen. Or did we see it? Had it been some sort of illusion or psychotic episode? Had we been working too hard for too long? If we were to mention this to our therapist, our twice-monthly confidant, what would she say about us conjuring up a pack of illusory, mystical rats?

"No!" we said loudly and confidently. We knew what we had seen. We were sure of it. We were not a couple of aging hippies whose pasts were laced with psychotropic drugs. Our nightly Dark 'n Stormies were our only vice, and as far as we knew, the beverages packed no lasting side effects. No, we had witnessed the rat hoard, and now it had vanished. That led us to call the lime Death Patrol.

Pete's somewhat tactless suggestion that we had overblown the immensity of the swarm caused a bit of doubt to boil up in our minds, which we quickly dismissed. We were sure, and we told him so, right there to his face, when we finished our story. We did *not* tell him that the packs of rats had manifested in the room he wasn't allowed to enter. We edited as we went. A sin of omission, but a necessary evil.

"Okay, fellows, if you say you got rats—lots of them—I'll take your word for it. I'll keep looking. But like I said, I'm not seeing anything out of the ordinary. I mean, I can put out some traps, if that'd make you feel better. I'll look around some more too."

We stood there in the hallway, outside the locked door to the Confederate Room as Pete made his promise to continue his quest for renegade vermin. As if on cue, something happened in the wall beside us, the wall nearest the alley entrance to our loading dock. By *happened*, we mean noise, an audio clamor somewhat akin to marching. It was rhythmic, almost festive, we thought. We had never heard it before inside our walls.

"Holy shit," Pete said, a phrase that sounded very non–Oxford English Dictionary. He appeared to recognize the sound. Nevertheless, it embarrassed us a tad, so we may have said something to the effect that our pipes are old. *Water must be rattling on its way through the building.* Something like that. What luck we have. Rats on the Confederate Room floor and ancient water pipes in the walls.

"You're right," he said, "probably pipes," but we could tell he was trying to convince himself. Pete put his ear to the wall. His eyes widened, then he fought to gain control of himself. He heard something back there, and it was clear he wanted nothing to do with it. "Yep, exactly what it sounds like. Pipes going bad. Absolutely nothing I can do here."

He quickly packed up his tools and his tanks, hitched the belt that nestled beneath his middle-aged midsection and bid us a hasty adieu, with no mention of a bill for services rendered.

That, as we say, was that. We never saw Pete again. He never called us, and we are not ones to chase. We know when we're not wanted. We decided to look for other death patrols when we had the time. Who knows? Maybe the rats had their fun and left the building never to return. If not, perhaps if we ignored them, they would go away and leave us in peace.

We could make a gentlemen's agreement with a pack of rats.

Peg

I remember the seesaw on the playground of my middle school. An unpainted wood plank and a rickety metal base, it was a dinosaur among the more modern, padded equipment. The seesaw even sounded like an ancient creature, the way it creaked and squealed when the plank teetered and tottered. I remember riding it with my friend Ellen after school. I was a skinny sixth grader. Ellen wasn't, and I recall how she would launch me into the sky, and I spent those amazing few seconds at the top of the arc, pressing for all I was worth against that metal handle, fighting the suck of gravity that threatened to pull me down the board. Those few seconds, Jesus, they were fantastic. From that perch, you could see more than you ever had, if you took the time to look.

But I knew it would never last, because Ellen would shove with those big legs of hers, and I would find myself slammed back to the ground, suddenly looking up at her hovering above me, like she might tumble down the plank and flatten me for good. We would go like that for a half hour. The ups and the downs, the highs and the lows. A view from the top, a view from the bottom. Never was there a time when things balanced perfectly. The sixth-grade seesaw is a symbol for how the world works. Or maybe it's a metaphor. Claude would know the difference.

I have no idea about the equipment on Samuel Tisdale's sixth-grade playground, but here is what he did not realize: slouched there in his reading chair, studying his family Bible, he was riding the seesaw of his world. He was getting the highs and lows, and whoever was sitting on the other end of the plank was tiny as a bird, because when Samuel slammed down to the ground, it hurt.

But not at first. Because, you see, Samuel was all about facts. That's why he taught mathematics. For him, facts were tools. They were benign, and they couldn't harm him. They were to be collected and studied. He sat there, studying. He saw his name in the Bible, right under his mother's. Such a beautiful name. *Carlotta*. A short, dark line of ink connected Samuel and Carlotta. So much hidden inside that short line: all those photographs, all that R&B music, all those questions he asked his grandmother again and again . . . all those answers he never heard. All those facts Samuel couldn't find about why Carlotta left and never returned. All those stories he was told about a father who sold breeze box fans and never returned from a war. The only true fact he had on that page right now was that his mother was gone, for a second time.

I watched Samuel gather those memories from that little line and spread them out in him mind and arrange them as he saw fit. That was when Samuel sat at the tip-top of the arc, the seesaw at its zenith, and if he wanted to, Samuel could look out and see the whole world. But like I said, Samuel adored facts, and I'm not sure he was seeing all of the facts on that page in the right order, because he finally discovered another line, this one longer, extending from his mother's name across the width of the page to a man. And the man's name was Hixson Hance.

Samuel had heard of Hixson Hance. Everyone had heard something about him. Hance owned the icehouse, and he was attached to all the stories that still floated around, stories about what went on inside those cold walls with women he wasn't married to. The icehouse burned down the summer Hance got too sick to run the business anymore. We all heard the story about people lining the street to watch the old icehouse—which had been so full of cold for so many years—go up in hot flames. People cheered, according to the story. No one knew how the fire started among all that ice, if it was an accident or arson. Now the only thing left of Hixson Hance was his twin boys. Wallace and Wade inherited the property where the icehouse once stood, but they refused to do anything with it, so these days, kudzu choked out the cement foundation and pulled down the walls. These days, most people don't know what an icehouse used to be, back when folks had to work to keep things frozen.

I watched Samuel study the lines, watched him try and connect the dots. The line from Carlotta to Hance—Samuel knew it couldn't mean Carlotta was the mother of those twins. No, that was impossible. Hixson Hance's wife, a thin, quiet woman, gave birth to those two boys. She'd been seen, big-bellied and haggard, carrying around those twins.

Samuel said out loud, "What the hell?" and I must believe that he still didn't know at that point, because he ran his finger along the line again. He shook his head. When his hand moved out of the way, I believe that was when he saw the little note his grandmother wrote farther down the page. The seesaw came crashing down.

Samuel
i'm sorry
he is your father

He read it several times. He even recited it out loud, tracking the words in the air. Samuel, the math professor, was trying to add up the words Esther wrote and see what they equaled. Was she sorry that Hixson Hance was her grandson's father? *I'm sorry he is your father*. Or was she sorry, as if she had done something wrong? *I'm sorry. He is your father*. The lack of a period was troubling for Samuel. I could tell from where I watched. It's often the little things—or lack of them—that hide the bigger ones.

Slammed to the ground by the seesaw, Samuel looked up and realized Esther had told him a lifetime of lies about his father. Suddenly, all those warmer memories disappeared and were replaced with blank spaces. Was there ever a fan salesman named Zeb? Was the weather ever that hot? Were all those rumors true about Hixson Hance? Was she trying to protect him?

Samuel, if you were to ask me, I could tell you—that's what grandmothers do when their daughters run away. They protect the babies they leave behind, and sometimes protection isn't the prettiest thing. Something else, Samuel. Sometimes you are forced to tell the people you love anything but the truth. Maybe Esther *wouldn't* tell you, Samuel, because she *couldn't*. That is a fact. That is something for you to think about.

More questions flooded over Samuel as he sat there, staring at the page. Did his mother walk into the icehouse because she wanted to? Or needed to? Did she have a choice? He wanted to think his mother had been trapped—a scared, young Black woman with nowhere to run. But maybe she knew exactly what she was doing, surrounded by blocks and blocks of ice. Maybe she had desires no one knew about, not her own mother, not God. Samuel wanted to feel sorry for her. I could see that. But he stopped short. He couldn't do it. She'd left so long ago, his mother had never been more than a ghost. Now she was even less.

Then I spied something curious, something unexpected: a smile crept across Samuel's lips. Not a full-blown grin, but the subtle, definite hint of a smile. That surprised me. I would not have expected him to be feeling anything close to happiness at that point. When he let that smile peek out, the seesaw started to move toward the sky again.

Samuel suddenly realized he was half-brother to the most flamboyant racists in the county. Samuel was blood kin to the men who banned Black writers from their shelves. No wonder Samuel smiled. All that time he spent capturing rats, and the only thing he had to do to torment those twins was look in the pages of his grandmother's family Bible.

Samuel Tisdale was no longer an only child. The seesaw lifted him high again, and he thought about Esther, and he wished he could thank her and tell her she didn't have to be sorry, that everything has a way of finding its balance.

CHERYL

Louise did not walk like a woman with a destination. For the record, she meandered. She stared into windows, she hesitated at corners deciding on a direction, she was overly attentive to the sidewalk under her feet. She even backtracked unexpectedly once, and when I couldn't avoid her, she passed right by me, heading the opposite direction. I mean, she wasn't *going* anywhere. Even from the distance I kept, I could see Louise was a practical woman. She wore sensible, flat shoes. Her brown hair was cut short and blunt, so it never got in the way of her face, a face that was oval-shaped and wide open to the world. I didn't worry about her breaking into a fast-walk; she didn't appear to be in terrific shape. Her figure was . . . I don't know, like I said, pragmatic. It worked perfectly, for her.

She, pragmatically, checked her goddamn watch every forty-five seconds or so, and it finally struck me: she was in the process of wasting time, burning minutes until she reached some sort of witching hour when she had to be somewhere, and that deadline must have been the top of the hour, because at five 'til, she became a woman with a purpose. She picked up her pace and beelined it for The Stratford School. Louise could move when she wanted to.

The Stratford School stood out in the downtown landscape. While most of our city blocks had been knocked down and renovated in the last fifteen or twenty years, the school was the one thing that hadn't changed, an enigma in the downtown architecture. An old bluish Victorian house with gingerbread molding and a long porch that ran the length of the front and cupolas sticking out like lighthouses, The Stratford School was given a pass from destruction, probably because nobody wanted to sign off on bulldozing a school for special students.

You couldn't help but notice how the place stuck out, and its students were the same way. If you walked by the school, you saw them sometimes, wandering in the yard, their teachers shepherding them one way or the other. They couldn't attend a regular school, so they attended The Stratford School, where they had their own safe little world.

Louise marched up the steps of The Stratford School with a bouncy familiarity. Have to say, the woman knew where the hell she was going *now*. I waited across the street, in the doorway of a florist shop where I'd bought flowers a bunch of times. I even waved to the man inside, behind the counter. When I had been there long enough to feel uncomfortable and awkward, I moved a couple of doors down and put a telephone pole between me and The Stratford School. Louise reappeared on the steps, holding hands with a boy that, from where I stalked, looked too old to be holding hands with her.

Physically, he was way different from Louise. None of her pragmatic, pear-shaped body, none of her short limbs. He was tall and thin, almost too thin. *With arms that long, his wingspan must be enormous*, I thought. And his pants were too short for his legs, as if someone had let out all the hem that remained and had finally given up finding a good fit. From my hiding spot, I couldn't tell how old he was. He could have been fifteen or thirty. He lifted one leg at a time, like the surface of the porch was too hot to stand on. Louise led him down the stairs, and I heard them counting together as they hit the steps. *One and two and three and . . .* I know now there are seven steps between the sidewalk and the porch of The Stratford House.

They crossed the street toward me, and he suddenly wanted to go left. I heard Louise say, "Now, Willie, you know it's this way. Don't you want some? You've earned it, buddy." She tugged him to the right, back toward the middle of downtown and her office. He grunted a disagreement at her, but as thin as he was, he didn't stand a chance against Louise. She steered him away from where I stood. She leaned over and whispered something to him, and Willie batted at his ear like a bug had suddenly flown into it. He shook his hair out of his face. The kid needed a haircut. His dark bangs fell into his eyes.

Louise walked as fast as Willie would let her. She never looked anywhere but straight ahead. Willie, on the other hand, was distracted by every unexpected, shiny thing. He craned his head at the passing cars. He wanted to follow the pigeons that gathered around the trashcans. A dog on a leash was a new discovery. Louise steered him around other folks on the sidewalk, but that was unnecessary. People got out of Willie's way.

At Hite's Dairy Bar, Louise pushed open the door and ushered Willie ahead of her, and the two of them disappeared behind the glass. I hesitated for a minute, deciding whether or not to follow them inside. Here, on the sidewalk, I could spy on Louise safely, but inside, I would be hemmed in. For the record, she obviously had no idea who the fuck I was. I could get right behind her in line, order a Rocky Road, and she wouldn't have a clue. Unless, of course, Patrick had shown her pictures of me. Did she even know I existed? No way. Patrick would never tell her anything about me. He didn't have the balls.

I had never been inside Hite's. Dairy doesn't agree with me. I hung near the door for a couple of seconds and watched the two of them order. The girl behind the counter, who could have been the same age as Willie, recognized Louise and her son. She greeted them by name. *Miss Alberts.* Or maybe *Mrs.* It was hard to tell. But she was a friend. Willie's face lit up when he saw her, when she spoke to him. He had a crush on her. Or maybe he liked the ice cream more. He couldn't make up his mind on a flavor.

"Oh, Willie," the girl said, "you do this every time, and you always end up picking orange sherbet." Willie ran his fingers across the glass cooler.

"I'm sorry," Louise said. "I'll wipe off his fingerprints." She started to rummage in her purse until the girl told her not to worry about it.

"Don't be silly," she said.

"That one," Willie said, and the girl scooped up some orange sherbet.

When they sat down, I slid into the booth nearest the bathroom, where I had a straight-on view of Willie and the back of his mother's head. At least, I assumed it was his mother. He had barely said a word to her, and now all he could concentrate on was the double scoop of orange sherbet melting down his wrist.

"Willie, come here," she said, plucking napkins from the holder. "Let me clean you up."

All of us turned our heads toward the door when the lightning first flashed, and the crack of thunder right on its heels rattled the windows of Hite's.

"Hello, God," Willie said, looking in the direction of the thunder.

"It's a storm, Willie," his mother answered. "We need the rain."

"God," he repeated.

I heard the rain making its way down the street in rattling sheets that drummed against the buildings. When the shit finally hit us, the wind blew the loud drops sideways into the glass. Louise kept her eye on the door, expecting something. Was she worried about rain through the door? A tornado? Willie didn't care that a monsoon had sprung up outside. He raced orange trails of sherbet around his wrist with his tongue.

"Willie," his mother said again, but before she could finish her sentence, the tiny bell above Hite's door tinkled, and the door swept open. In from the rain came a man with a sopping newspaper over his head like a makeshift hat. He turned his back to us to take the newspaper off his head and shake like a dog fresh out of water. That motion looked familiar, and a wave somewhere between panic and nausea rose in my goddamn throat. Patrick turned around and spied Louise and Willie in the booth. Willie looked up from his cone and smiled.

"Go ahead and order something," Louise called out, "when you quit dripping."

Patrick laughed and walked toward the counter, and I was trapped in Hite's, with the people I was spying on (including one who could ID me) sitting between me and a wet getaway.

With Patrick concentrating on which flavor to choose, I moved quickly toward the bathroom, the only place I could think of to stay out of sight. Luckily, the women's restroom was in a small hallway near the booths, and if I cracked the door, I could continue to watch the three of them. Couldn't hear them but could still see their booth.

Patrick walked up to their table with a cup of something and leaned over to Louise and kissed her on the top of her sensibly shorn head. Willie slid over in his seat and hugged Patrick around one leg. Patrick laughed while Willie shook a little, still wrapped around his thigh. From where I watched, Patrick looked different. He wasn't thinner or tanner or any different than that very morning, when he left for work. He was *lighter*, like the world didn't sit as heavy on him inside Hite's. He moved with less effort, like an athlete—something he had never been—light on his feet, bouncing a bit.

He slid into the booth beside Willie, so I could see the two of them clearly. Louise still had the back of her dowdy head toward me. That wasn't fair. I had no idea whether or not she was dowdy, but I was beginning to fucking hate her, her and her pragmatism. Patrick smiled around the spoon when he slid ice cream in his mouth. When his spoon was empty, he waved it, an orchestra director leading the conversation. Something he did or said made Willie laugh, and Louise shook her head. The boys were ganging up on her. She loved it. I could tell that, even from the back.

The rain continued to beat against the glass, but the thunder and lightning had moved on. I was sure the streets were flooded by now, from a rain this hard and sudden. It didn't matter. I had nowhere to go. Or did I? What if I walked right by them? Maybe nodded at Patrick and said something like, "You think this shit is ever going to let up?" then walked away and left him to explain to Louise and her sticky-mouthed son who I was. And why I was.

It would make for a wonderful movie scene, but in real life, it wouldn't accomplish much. Might even make things better between them, bond them somehow, because of my—I don't know—arrogance or whatever. What I needed was time to think, and to think without spying, without peering through a narrow slit in the door to a bathroom that was beginning to smell like bread or dough. At least, that's what I detected from somewhere behind me.

I could outlast them, if they could outlast the storm. An observant person, maybe the girl behind the counter, might begin to wonder what happened to the woman who went to the bathroom fifteen minutes ago, but it dawned on me that I was, as usual, not very noticeable. I tended to blend into everything. That made me smile and turn my face away from the door in the same instant as Louise slid out of her seat and walked toward the bathroom. I saw her when she was only about five steps away, so I dashed for one of the two stalls behind me, almost knocking over the stack of waffle cone cartons inside the door.

That's the smell, I thought. Waffle cones stored in a goddamn bathroom? I threw the latch on the stall as Louise walked in.

She obviously didn't need to use the bathroom, which was a relief because, for some reason, I didn't want to hear her pee. From what I could tell, she stood at the sink and washed her hands. She was probably sticky from cleaning her son's messes. I thought about how she left Willie with Patrick, how easy that was for her, how natural the three of them were with each other. There was too much crap banging in my head, too much about our long-gone past and the more recent history between Patrick and me. Bits and pieces of scenes flipped through my mind. He and I talking about children. About Marlene moving in. Peg dying. Patrick always fighting about money, fighting about a lost credit card, fighting about fucking nothing. And this new history: the way he smiled as he levitated around the booth in Hite's.

Louise turned off the water and racked a couple of towels from the dispenser, and I would have been fine, would have been able to keep it together, if she hadn't started humming. I didn't even know what the song was. But she *hummed*, and her voice sounded so sweet and so content. People who are happy with their lives hum, and they don't even realize it.

Louise hummed all the way out the door, and left me there, crying in the goddamn stall, breathing in the smell of fresh waffle cones until it stopped raining and their booth was empty and I could finally escape.

CLAUDE

You haven't taken your eyes off the mystery woman ahead of you, more specifically, off the mystery woman's ass, as you try to match her pedal cadence, wondering what her voice sounds like, what she likes to eat, what she does for a living. You think it must be something that requires speed, movement. She is a woman who thrives on motion, which, of course, makes you wonder about her in bed. You are bombarding yourself with stupid thoughts. You hear a song in your head. "The Things We Do for Love," a cheesy one-hit wonder by some band back in the . . . when? The eighties, maybe? Maybe the seventies. What was the name of that band? You begin to feel the ache of too much speed in your legs, the little twinge that comes from going beyond what you would call your personal limits. Going too far, another thing we do for love. You have to laugh at yourself. Love. *What the fuck is love?* you almost say out loud. That would be funny, spouting out a question like that to a peloton of strangers on your first shop ride.

Love used to be a thing you could wrap your head around, something to grab for. These days, you aren't so sure. Love has become something for display, a museum artifact that you gather around and take pictures of and say things like, *Once upon a time, love roamed the earth, then the giant meteor struck, and love was suddenly extinct.* You are too old for love. You are too old to be tailing (literally) an unnamed woman on a bike, too old to be spying on the rigid cut of her calves as she attacks the pedals. A stinging fire lights in both your quads. Love must be pain, you think now.

THE HAMMERHEAD CHRONICLES

The speed begins to drop, and your little thought-bubble of love pops. That's when you think of Mr. Blevins, your physics teacher in the eleventh grade.

Mr. Blevins was a round man with a giant head. He resembled a cartoon. He didn't so much as walk as waddle from points A to B, but you liked him because he didn't care how he looked. He used his appearance as a method of teaching physics, especially when he tackled the subjects of mass and gravity. "Look at me," he would say. "I defy gravity daily with this body. I'm supposed to fall over, but I don't, thanks to Isaac Newton."

Mr. Blevins loved the concept of gravity, the idea that something bigger would attract something smaller with an invisible, undeniable force. "Physics is about explaining something you see with something that you can't," he said. And gazing at that woman's backside with your pedal rate dropping, you think, *you have never been more correct, Mr. B.*

Because you see why the speed has decreased. The head of the long snake of riders makes a right turn seventy-five yards ahead. You touch your brakes slightly to match the speed of the mystery woman in front of you and wait for the turn. You match her line, follow her path. The things you do for love.

When you make the turn, you wonder what Mr. Blevins would say at this moment, because you glance ahead and see that the road is no longer a road. It has morphed into a wall, rising in front of you. The road points up now. *Gravity is about to kick your ass*, you think. Dammit.

You realize the hills bring out the hammerheads. Earlier on the ride, you tried to pick them out. Your conclusion is that most of the Group A riders are hammerheads, jockeying for position, looking a little disturbed when someone doesn't shift correctly or when someone's wheel noses slightly ahead of theirs. They are the ones who scowl at drivers when their cars pass too closely on their left shoulders. One of them flips off an older woman who peers through her steering wheel at the shop-ride peloton, and the rest of the hammerheads laugh like a spandex Greek chorus.

Hammerheads whine—the pace is too slow, the road is too rough, the heat isn't hot enough for them. This early in the morning, they are not happy people because they haven't been allowed to exercise their legs or their egos properly yet, tucked away in a long line of two-by-two riders with those peasant B Group people.

That all changes when A Group makes a right turn and hits the bottom of Paris Mountain, turns up Altamont Drive, and greets the grade. The hammerheads scatter. The line breaks up. People sprint to the front of the group and begin climbing the slope, standing on the pedals, wagging their bikes back and forth beneath them. The effect of gravity is immediate and drastic. Mr. Blevins would be smiling, especially at the effect gravity has on your bicycle. On you.

You are not extremely proficient at standing up on your bike—or *out of the saddle,* as the hammerheads would say—and running in place with the bike between your legs because, frankly, you've never had to perform that trick too much. You can do it, but not all that well. Sure, you've been up and down hills, but you've never ridden an honest-to-god mountain. There is a sudden sound, the frantic *chink* of gears being changed, of the hammerheads pushing their derailleurs to bigger, easier rings. You notice they know exactly where to stop shifting. You also notice that you have waited too late to shift, and you are pedaling in very, very slow circles. Gravity, again. Mr. Blevins is in your ear, telling you the effects gravity has on velocity when the mass spent too many happy hours at The Oorah. *But Mr. B, I've cut way, way back.* The song is gone from your head because the girl is gone from sight. She knew which gear to find.

When the hill arrives, you creep so slowly, you are dangerously close to moving backwards. In fact, two cyclists, who are still laughing and chatting like gravity doesn't affect them, come by either side of you at the same exact speed, giving you the stressful illusion they are standing still and you are actually rolling downhill.

You glance ahead and spy a sweeping curve to the left, and like tiny, gravity-defying water bugs, the pair of hammerheads sprint around the bend and launch themselves onto the next grade. You know there are almost three miles of this torture left before the top of the mountain, and you recall what TJ said to you, that "nobody gets left behind." TJ is a liar.

Like you conjured him up, TJ appears at your side, the last of the riders, the final hammerhead.

"You doing okay, man?" he asks, smiling. You notice how pencil-thin he looks in his riding kit. A gravity-defying sliver. You smile back because you can't talk.

"I'll turn back with you, you know, if you don't wanna do the whole mountain. No shame," he says. You think, *Ah, what a compassionate hammerhead.*

"Seriously, man, it gets a little steeper as you go up," he says.

Ahead, you see the mystery woman make the turn and crank up the next switchback. Your legs are beginning to give out, give up.

You muster up enough breath to say a few words. "Nah, I got it," you huff, and he doesn't know if you mean you can climb the rest of the mountain or you can find your own way home.

"Okay, man, be safe. Head on a swivel," he says and stands up on his bike, digging into the grade of the hill, and you wait until he's out of sight, until *everyone* is out of sight, before you actually throw in the towel. You quit. Gravity pulls you to a stop in a split second. You unclip your right foot and lean on the bike, trying to suck whatever air you can into your mouth. You can't believe how much a few hundred yards of a hill destroyed you. You are light-headed. You wonder what Mr. Blevins is up to these days, if he's still alive. You're ready to go downhill now, let gravity do the work for a change, because in that direction, gravity is your pal. You remount the bike, which now feels like gravity's evil sidekick, and push off without checking for cars coming down the mountain. You don't follow TJ's advice. You don't keep your head on a swivel, and the last thing that you recall is that obnoxious song playing once again in your head.

The things we do for love.

SAMUEL

I found that note in the family Bible and subsequently spent days worrying about so many things. So many of the *wrong* things. I worried about my mother and how much more I suddenly didn't know of her life. I worried that carrying around the deadweight of her own heavy history shortened her life, that if she had only returned home and told me and lightened that load, she might still be around. Why was her leaving the answer to everything?

But Samuel, I told myself, she made those decisions by herself, the bad ones and the good ones. And Esther made decisions too. (For all you know, Esther and Thomas may have chased her away.) Samuel, you can't be held responsible for the cards someone keeps close to her vest.

Did I want to be mad at Esther and my mother? Damn right, I did. I wanted to be mad at everybody. Here I was again, where I always ended up, forced to make educated guesses. Something happened to her in that icehouse. Or in a car or in a field or in a motel. Or I don't know where, because NO ONE TOLD ME. All I got was a scribbled note in a Bible, and the scribbler was gone.

I spent several nights lying in my bed while I rifled through the catalog of memories, trying to put my finger a time when Esther tipped her hand, let her guard down and did something, said something that was a clue about what happened to her daughter. But I found nothing. Those cards pressed against Esther's vest were a second skin.

There was my sudden, inherited hatred for Hixson Hance, this man

I had heard of but never met, a man who treated ice like it was some valuable spice for sale. I knew the irrationality of hating something or somebody who wasn't standing right in front of you, and I had never met Hixson Hance when he was alive, so I couldn't put a face on that particular villain, but I despised him just the same. Whatever happened between Hance and my mother could not have been good or sweet or wonderful. It had to be brutal and dark, dark enough to cause her to flee her life and her son. There was the chance I was completely wrong. I never knew my mother. Maybe she was the kind of person who ran when the door opened. I wish I could ask Esther.

I needed to temper this debate inside my head. I could already feel it eating a hole somewhere deep inside, far beyond blood and bone. The only thing that helped was the occasional scrapes and thuds over my head, and I began to listen more to them than the worries in my brain. I had to stop fretting about things that happened before I was born, even if I was born because of those things. Maybe there are facts we are never meant to know.

But those twins. They loomed right in front of me, in a manner of speaking. They represented the one pen-drawn line I could not erase. I had business with them. *Facts* to share. The question was: how to break the revelation to them? I didn't have to be in a hurry. Nobody was going anywhere. Those two would still be running that bookstore and shunning Black writers and Hispanic writers and most women writers until the day they died, which—barring some cataclysmic event—was years down the road. I would certainly be at the college as far into the future as I could see. The bottom line? No deadline existed, and I am at my worst when I operate without deadlines. I can be a world-class procrastinator; that is, until you give me a time and date to have all my work done and handed in. Then I button it up.

My immediate concern involved whether to cease and desist with the forced rat migration. Trapping and transporting the rats represented an act of revenge that might, when all was said and done, pale in comparison to what I'd seen in that dusty Bible.

Maybe I should sit down in front of Wallace and Wade and say something like, "Hello, brother," and they would think I was coding, falling into some sort of clichéd vocabulary, until I followed up with: "And by brother, what I mean to say is . . ." Then I would tell them the story about finding the Bible and connecting the dots from their father to my mother. But how to tell them that story? How to tell them and make it hurt? How to make them believe it? Because I sure as hell believed it. I'd seen it written in a Bible. That is the one place where Esther would not tolerate a lie.

After a few nights of bourbon and a few more nights of not trapping rats, I concluded I had reached a point in my life when the next chapter in the story was more important that any of the previous ones. I realize that sounds, well, stupid. What I mean is this: I had begun to look at my life like the world's largest domino exhibit. Sometime, those many years in the past, perhaps my mother kicked the first domino over, and the succession began, one after another, one domino ticking down the next.

If that was the case, looking back was supremely useless. Easy, but useless. A glance backward, and all you would see was a line of toppled dominoes. The only direction worth focusing upon was dead ahead, upon what might come tumbling down next. And here we were.

With that sort of half-baked, bourbon-fueled rationale, I was excited by the prospects of wrecking the lily-white fields of Wallace and Wade's existence, not so much for revenge but more to see what would happen next. Honestly, I already had a measure of revenge. They had called an exterminator. If I was a betting man, I would lay decent odds that Pete had not been parked behind Dunean's that afternoon checking for termites.

The rats had pushed that domino over. Now, it was my turn.

PEG

Claude will say that he was close to dying. He will tell you, or anyone who will listen, that he rolled within an eyelash of his demise. Or maybe he won't mention it to anyone, because to tell the truth, the whole event was—and should continue to be—pretty embarrassing. It's one thing to confront a debilitating disease and fight and scrap and watch your body waste away and finally, *finally* have some peace. But good lord, to plant the front wheel of your bicycle—and for all intents and purposes, your nose—up the well-sculpted ass of a woman you don't even know and have *that* be the reason you end up in a strange limbo between near-dead and dead? That's stupid.

You could say the woman was not the cause, but think about it: the only reason Claude was on that mountain in the first place was that he wheeled in behind that woman. And don't think I haven't seen her before, zipping by him on the road like some sort of two-wheeled nymphet. He thinks she doesn't have a clue who he is, but trust me, she knows. She sees everything. I mean, she doesn't see everything like me, but she knows, she watches. She's seen Claude out there struggling on his bike. She's watched him get better, faster. She even smiles a little when she buzzes by and leaves him in the dust. Claude never catches sight of those little smiles, and if he did, he would probably misinterpret them. He would probably think she was making fun of him, taunting him, but that's Claude being Claude. He never did understand women and the things they do—the smiles, the touches, the words. I had seen that woman smiling, and I knew exactly what she meant by that little upturn of her mouth. It meant she was momentarily happy. And she wanted a more long-term dose of it.

No doubt in my mind, she noticed Claude getting thinner and sleeker over the weeks. Who couldn't? It wasn't like he was obese or anything before he started riding that silly bike, but once he began pedaling, especially in those hot months, Claude's excesses began to melt away. I'm sure that morning, he thought he could follow that woman straight up that mountain. From where I observed, the whole thing was becoming somewhat metaphorical. The girl you chase but have never seen. The new speeds you are attaining. The mountain you've never even considered climbing before, but now it looms before you. *And the mysterious girl you chase is already on that mountain!*

I felt sorry for Claude when I saw what the slopes did to him, how quickly his pedals slowed to painful circles, how longingly he looked ahead, where the girl reversed onto that switchback and was suddenly gone. I hated watching Claude give up. I knew that feeling, when you tell yourself that calling a halt is worth more than forging ahead. Of course, when I quit, I died. Claude wasn't going to die on that hill that morning, no matter what he tells you. He was going to fail, and he would have to live with that for a while. Maybe that was worse, in some way. When I gave up, I was happy. Claude certainly didn't look happy when he turned that bike around and decided to let the slope of the mountain do some work for him.

Claude did not die when he gave up, but he gave his death the old college try. One of the frustrating things about being here is that I can watch but cannot warn. I cannot nudge anyone or tap on a shoulder or whisper in an ear. I couldn't tell Claude about the car behind him. Maybe that's an additional metaphor at work, something about how you can always see the world in front of you, like the sculpted-assed girl or the road ahead that rises up, but you'd better keep your eyes behind too. If Claude had looked behind, he would have seen a small BMW, one of those roadsters, a Z-something, z-ooming around the switchback above him. He should have heard it, the downshift of the engine and the way the tires bit into the bank of the curve. I imagine Claude was breathing hard from his effort, the drumbeat of his pulse pounding in his ears, so perhaps he couldn't detect the little convertible bearing down on him. And who knows why the couple in the Beemer didn't catch sight of Claude in his bright cycling clothes? My guess is they had passed a large group of hammerheads and figured they were all clear. They didn't account for the lone, lonely straggler.

Honestly, I don't think the guy driving even worried about at the road. With a car like that, you sort of throw it into the curve, and if the men who engineered the road did their math correctly, the slope and the bank do the work for you. Hold on for dear life, right? They weren't looking ahead so much as enjoying the ride, which was what Claude should have been doing. Instead, he was bemoaning his fate. Licking his emotional, invisible wounds, thinking that he would never see the woman again, that he had punctured his last chance to chase the girl, to climb the mountain. I could have told him that he was wrong. There's always another girl, another mountain. Unless, of course, you die.

And he wasn't going to die. Don't let him tell you that. Claude's legs were done. I could see that. He had trouble clipping one of his cycling shoes back onto the pedal, and while he worked on that, he wavered. The bicycle wavered, I mean, and he wandered across the double yellow lines. The BMW wrapped around the curve, the top down, the music on. I think there's a club whose members take their little sport roadsters out on mountains roads on Saturday mornings so they can test the curves. When this club member glanced ahead, he caught sight of Claude fumbling with his pedal, and he had a split second to go for the BMW's brake pedal, but he fumbled as well. Something about pedals and fumbling was afoot that morning. Pun intended.

He was able to jerk the wheel slightly to the left, and that may have saved Claude, because instead of the Z-something catching Claude full-force, he was hit with a glancing blow. The right fender of the red roadster caught the bicycle's back wheel and spun Claude, launching him into the air. I have never seen Claude look more surprised than that moment he became airborne. Or embarrassed, and that surprised me. I wouldn't imagine someone who'd been struck by a car while messing with his pedal would have time to feel embarrassment, but it was there. Learn something new every day.

Claude elevated across the opposite lane and in midair became separated from his bike somehow, man and machine both spinning through the air. The BMW driver finally found the brake and jammed it much too late, bringing the car to a quick, albeit too late, stop. Gravity took over at that point, and Claude struck the ground first. The lighter bike landed twenty feet beyond him. Claude met the ground on his head and his shoulder and his hip, and he rolled. Then he stopped rolling and slid across the pavement and onto the shoulder. He rolled again, over the top of the bike and into a drainage ditch of some kind, and he rolled right through the ditch and into the trees, and those trees were the only things that kept him from rolling all the way down that mountain he couldn't climb.

When Claude came to rest, he was humming. I swear to you. Amid all the pain and possible broken bones and wracked body parts, he hummed a little tune. Something from back before high school, I think. I believe it was that song by 10cc called "The Things We Do For Love." Which struck me as stupid on several levels.

But he wasn't going to die, so I thought, *Who am I to judge?*

Wallace & Wade

We slipped in the door at the inaugural meeting of the White Liberation Front in the somewhat secret room of Confederate geegaws at the rear of Dunean's—the Flag Room!—and we realized, simply by scanning the room of attendees, that we may have made a terrible mistake allowing them to congregate anywhere in our store.

We know, better than most, that you can *indeed* judge a book by its cover, and judging from the collection of humanity, these were all the lost and angry boys from every nook and cranny of the county. And girls, as well. Who knew the Ivory Boys included girls? A small gaggle of females sat on the fringes of the room, near the display of Antietam Nipple Clips, chattering about nothing. We kept our eyes on them and their potentially sticky fingers, but as far as we could discern, no one had pocketed any of the merchandise. But there were too many of them to monitor, and hence, our anxiety increased.

There appeared to be an alpha female among the girls in the room, a tall blond with a strikingly realistic tattoo of Robert E. Lee on the slope of her exposed shoulder. The other girls formed a covey around her and hung on her words. They looked only where she looked and didn't dare laugh until they first heard a chortle emerge from her mouth. We discerned a stolen look or two between Alpha Female and Colt, who appeared to be the leader of the pack overall. He made his way around the room like a grimy, bean-pole politician, doing that ridiculous fist-bumping ritual and slapping other WLFers on their backs, people mostly clad in threadbare tank tops.

The preponderance of those t-shirts and the accompanying halter tops on the females allowed us a grand view of the tattoos, which were, without question, de rigueur for WLF. We could not tear our eyes away from them, probably because we've never understood the need for second rate art on the largest organ of the body. Of course, there was an artistic theme at play here. Southern Heritage. White Supremacy. States' Rights. These people—these young people—did not wear their politics on their sleeves. They wore them, quite literally, on their skin.

Our favorite was splayed across the upper back of a young lady. The scene depicted a magnificent horse, which we came to understand later was Robert E. Lee's horse, Traveler, rearing wildly above a meek and downed Union officer, hooves about to crash upon him. The caption read, *Ain't skeered never*. We could have done without the caption, but the depiction of the horse was anatomically amazing. No second-rate art here. We could almost sense the equine muscles popping to life on the young girl's back.

They were rag tag and unkempt, all shapes and sizes, yet a commonality existed among them. They all occupied a shared demographic of age, all in their late teens or early twenties, probably in the gray area between the end of high school and the end of college. And no, we didn't think any of these young people had matriculated to a post-secondary degree. We say this simply as a way of marking their age.

Each member of the WLF possessed dull eyes that constantly blinked against what we could only guess was an intense, unquenchable boredom. Their eyes were resigned to the fact that they had nothing else to do in the world but despise anyone who was not Caucasian, yet it wasn't hate that came from the eyes. Hate emerged from the sneer plastered across all of the faces. The eyes were simply tired, much too tired for people that age. Their eyes were the eyes of the elderly. But their sneers boiled youthfully.

Colt did not officially call the meeting to order. Rather, he walked to the front of the room and help up his hand for silence in a salute that appeared somewhat Hitlerian. We had never previously noticed the roughly sketched map of the Confederate states tattooed on the underside of his emaciated bicep. The crowd grew collectively quiet as Colt stood in front of the display of Confederate unisex cotton onesies. Very steady sellers, we might add.

"Stripey was supposed to bring the beer, but he's running late, so don't blame me," Colt said, and we looked at each other.

Beer? we thought. Nobody told us there would be alcohol at these meetings. Is anyone here over twenty-one? Alcohol tends to fortify one's courage and cause one's inhibitions to diminish, which in the retail business inevitably leads to theft of merchandise. We acknowledged that we should talk to Colt about beer at future meetings, but we had never planned on being regular attendees. We could not be expected to keep our eyes on everything, all the time. These people did not look like activists. They looked like high school detention veterans, a Confederate Breakfast Club. We decided we would figure this out later, on the porch, perhaps with a Dark 'n Stormy in our hands.

We huddled by the door, our lame attempt to remain inconspicuous. We were not wearing tank tops on our shoulders and chain link on our wallets, so we were afraid we stood like brightly colored weeds against the rear wall. But because we sat nearest the closed door, we were the first to hear the rapping behind us. Not a demanding knock, but a confident, soft one, that no one else noticed.

We peered through the small spyhole in the door. On the other side was a somewhat familiar face, so we opened the door and ushered a young girl in, immediately recognizing her. Her mother had died several few months ago. We'd seen her inside the store a few times with her withering mother prior to the wake that had deteriorated into a minor, memorial felony. Her name was Marlene, and when she crossed the threshold, she said nothing and wove her way between the WLF members and the displays of edible Fort Sumter panties and First Battle of Manassas plastic, insulated tumblers, finally alighting in an empty chair almost within reach of Colt. And he wanted to reach for her. We could tell. Young love bears very flimsy camouflage. We remember.

Because we are constantly on the lookout for potential, interesting conflicts in the world, we glanced toward the Alpha Female with the Lee tattoo and saw her set her jaw so severely, we imagined the grinding of molars. We do love drama.

With Marlene's entrance, Colt's shoulders squared a bit, and he threw his chest forward, such as it was. Truth be told, he absolutely preened. Marlene didn't see him, or if she did, she didn't acknowledge it. We were familiar with this no-nonsense behavior of hers, having witnessed it in other occurrences, most recently when she all but took over the coordination of her mother's memorial service. It was lovely to see youth at its fullest flower.

Suddenly, we heard ourselves being introduced. "We're getting a pretty good deal on this meeting place, you know, and I wanted you to meet these guys who give it to us so you'd know who they are."

Colt pointed our way, and having never experienced a spotlight we did not relish, we began making our way through the crowd toward the front, where Colt stood. In retrospect, we're not sure he *wanted* us to step forward, but it felt the thing to do at the moment. Normally, we would have expected polite applause to accompany us, but the room was uncomfortably quiet, only an occasional shuffle of a jackboot on the floor. It was as though we had not been noticed until Colt pointed in our direction.

We stood beside Colt and looked out. The ill-clad and the bored stared back at us. Several—including one of the females!—had dips of smokeless tobacco protruding in their lower lips, their spit cups between their feet, and our breath caught at the possibility of the mess this might create. But we weren't there to scold or housekeep. We were there to welcome and support, which is what we did.

We told them how happy we were to provide an apropos environment for their little activities, and we think it may have been the use of the word *apropos* that triggered them, but in the seconds after we said it, most of the heads in the room examined us carefully for the first time. Their heads cocked in unison like a pack of dogs that picked up a train whistle blowing miles down the track. We kept talking, yet we could tell no one listened, or at least no one listened with the same intensity as they stared. We felt like zoo animals.

"Hey, Colt," one of the boys said from the right rear, near the display of nylon Confederate flags folded with a military neatness into small, wooden cubbyholes. The interruption was rude, yes, but it intrigued us nonetheless—why would someone call out for Colt amid such a nice, warm Southern welcome?

We gestured at the interrupter then looked to Colt, who didn't appear as though he understood any of what was happening.

"Huh?" he uttered.

The boy in the back looked absolutely astonished, which made us smile. Perhaps we had, without knowing it, become unofficial members of their little gang. We had brought something new to their band of the disgruntled and disenchanted. Some warmth and civility. If possible, our smiles grew even broader. At our age, helping youth is an elixir, a tonic against aging.

"Damn, Colt," the boy said again then paused as he raised a plastic cup to his bottom lip and spat, leaving a slight, brown dribble on his chin, which he quickly wiped with the back of a hand. "You got a couple of identical twinks there." The crowd giggled collectively.

Not like we haven't heard that before. We realize we tend to stick out in a crowd. We'd been called worse, of course. However, the comment was ill-timed, as we were about to announce that we would not be charging the WLF a cent for the use of our space. We had, nights ago, decided that we would allow their group to meet in the Flag Room gratis in the hopes that their membership might purchase items they caught sight of during their meetings. And, hopefully, there would be word-of-mouth sales, as well. We sensed a good return on our investment.

Colt was at a loss, which we found endearing in that split second, and so were we. We were not accustomed to being called names in our own building.

"What the hell you thinking, man?" the boy said, and another rumble flowed through the small contingent.

At that precise moment, the eyes changed. The group that was so bored and lacking a collective pulse only minutes before suddenly energized and came alive. Their eyes positively glowed with an excitement usually reserved for bright Christmas mornings. For a split-second, we wondered if this happened on a regular basis within these types of groups, if—in this case—tossing a pair of Southern white homosexuals to the crowd was akin to holding a steak through the bars toward a hungry lion. We wondered silently if this was Colt's intention all along, if we were part of the menu for the evening. Had we been set up?

No, we decided. Colt didn't have a brain capable of that complex a plotline. Set up or no, we felt it our responsibility to say something, especially with Colt beside us, him choking on any sort of comeback to the brazen fellow who brought up our orientation. And we would have said something too. Something witty and calming. Something that spun the attention off us and into a new direction. Because that is what we do, isn't it? Use our charm and humor and misdirection to defuse confrontations like this one?

However, as we all know, timing is the mother of us all, isn't she? Thinking back, that is what we should have said at that precise moment. *Timing is the mother of us all, is she not? Who agrees with us?* But the timing was suddenly off, and we couldn't get a word out of our mouths, because atop the display of flags, atop all those cubbyholes, a few feet above the heckler's head, sat two of the largest rats we think we had ever seen to that point in our lives. The pair squatted on their furry haunches, two sets of beady eyes bearing down as if they recognized us. Perhaps they had been in attendance that morning, when the floor was made of rats. In their fearlessness, they were calm and waiting. For what, we didn't know. We thought about trying to ignore them and simply retreating out of the room and back to our office, out of sight, out of mind.

However, because all eyes were on us—two well-groomed men in their pressed shirts and seersucker trousers—and our eyes were locked on the rats, the room turned to see what we saw. When they did, a scream arose. From where it originated, we did not know, but suffice it to say, the boys in their skimpy t-shirts and the tattooed girls scrambled like children on a playground, which of course startled the rats. Which of course caused the aforementioned rats to leap like cliff divers onto the floor, pinballing between the feet of the retreating White Liberation Front. Which caused us to think that perhaps there was a good, sane reason Pete never made a second reconnoiter inside the walls of Dunean's. These were rats of a different kind.

LeJeune

My memory? Racked it while I reached in for this guy's beer and slid it across the bar and came up with nothing. Looked for the clues: pretty nice clothes, cared-about hair, decent teeth. Not the kind of person I hang with.

"You don't have any idea, do you?" he said, sticking the beer bottle toward his smile, not actually taking a sip.

Had no clue. Don't like feeling stupid, left out of the loop. "Meet lots of people doing what I do," I said, stalling, doing the brain rack again.

He laughed. "Oh, yeah, folks are lining up to get in this place." Waved his bottle in the general direction of the pool room, where George and David were having their daily game. "I'll bet you get totally swamped here." Waved the bottle again.

"Tell you what," he said. "I'll give you a clue. We met for a short, short period of time. Quick as a minute, then I was gone. But you had to know I was out there somewhere." Smiled that mother effing smile again, the I-know-something-you-don't-know grin.

"Last time I played twenty questions? Second grade, Sparky. Got no time for this sort of shit," I said back, shutting it all down.

"Funny you should say that. Let me see," he said, letting his gaze slide to the ceiling, doing some deep thinking all of a sudden. "Second grade..." Trailed off again. Toying with me. I knew it and he knew it. Him, enjoying it. Me, not so much. Waited a damn long time, doing that stare at the ceiling. Started to walk off and find something to do.

Rearrange bottles in the cooler or pretend like I was counting change. Anything but watch him do his little dance.

"You were at the base in Georgia then, I believe. Living in base housing, if I'm not mistaken. You had a stray cat that followed you around. The house was—let me see—sort of this baby shit yellow. White gravel covering all the flower beds. Am I close?" Looked real proud of himself. Lucky guesses.

Had me enough of that. "Listen," I said, "Don't know who you are or why you hosting this game show, but I got things to do." Trying to get him mad. Trying to break that smile up. Negatory.

"Oh, Junie, don't get your shorts in a bundle. I'm having some fun. I'm a little disappointed you don't recognize your own kin," he said.

Hit me like a bolt out of the blue. Maybe because he said that name again. Maybe because the past finally ran down the present. But there he was. Dammit, there he was.

He could see that I finally remembered. Funny thing, memory. Never understood why some folks only remember the really good stuff and really bad stuff and none of the in-betweens. Me? Tend to forget everything that makes no freaking sense. And when I was eight years old, it made no sense that I had this cousin show up one afternoon, leave the next morning. So I forgot him. Wilton. Cousin Wilton.

Back then, wanted cats. Wanted dogs. Never got any of my own. Mother said wouldn't be fair, having something in the house that eventually got left behind. Never understood why a dog and cat couldn't move with us. Always had strays around at a Marine base. Never took them to the next base. Had moving down to a science. Two boxes. Permission to fill them up, sir? Anything didn't fit in those boxes didn't make the move. Life was two boxes. Never asked if I could put an animal in the box. Gunny Sergeant didn't appreciate a smart ass.

Do remember packing up. Moving back to LeJeune. Another lateral move by dear old dad. Yep, would get teased big time there about my name. Was used to it, though. Marine kids laughing at my Marine name. Life in two boxes and a funny name.

Remember hearing a car on the gravel driveway the day before the move. Cousin Wilton was right. Flower beds lined with bright white rocks, so bright they glared in the sunshine. Driveway was white gravel too. Heard a car but didn't look, didn't care. You don't care about looking when you are leaving. Like I said, had it down to a science.

Next thing I know, my old man, Gunny Sergeant, stood in my doorway with a kid. Hair too long for a Marine kid. Clothes too sloppy for a base rat. Looked to be ten or twelve years old. Older than me for sure.

"Junie, meet Wilton," my father said, like he was addressing his men. "He's your cousin. Converse while I update your mother."

Said nothing to each other at first. Watched me pack, that's all he did. Sat on the edge of my bed and watched me fill a box.

Heard the screen door slam when my father took my mother into the back yard, in more white-rock glare. Talking way too loud. Remember that, all right. Big, loud stuff. When my father argued with my mother, didn't use his Gunny voice, the Marine instructor voice. He had another voice for arguing. Higher pitched.

My new cousin stared at the wall, in the direction of the arguing. "That ain't going too good," he finally said. "Could be better."

"Cousin?" I said finally. He nodded his head and shrugged his shoulders. Like he was saying, *Whatever . . .*

"Why you here?" I asked him, and he said, "I don't know, Junie." Remember thinking he didn't have a reason to call me that. Only Gunny called me that. Stole that from Gunny.

That was all I got. No more memories. Next morning, left for Camp LeJeune and Cuz Wilton was nowhere to be seen. All packed up and not a boy shoved in a box anywhere. Big blank spot in my brain for anything else that happened that night.

Now, grown up, sitting right in front of me. Wilton leaned across the bar. "You remember, don't you?" he said. "You'd think with the Internet and social media, it would've been easier to find you. You'd be wrong about that. I was about ready to hire some professional, but I decided to give it a couple more months of hunting and poking."

Not a new thing, men hunting and poking around me. I get it. I'm a bartender. Got lots of body ink. Cuss like a sailor. Certain kind of men like a certain kind of me.

"Wilton," I said.

"Yep, in the flesh," he said. "You don't have to hug me or anything."

"Don't worry," I said.

He didn't look disappointed. Noticed he hadn't taken a sip of his beer. Sitting there, sweating. The bottle, that is. Not him. He pushed the bottle away.

"I don't want this," he said. "You got a club soda with a little lime or something?"

What the hell with people wanting limes today? Jesus H. Christ. Did they look around? Ain't a lime kind of place. "I don't actually drink any more. I ordered the beer to start the conversation going. I didn't want you judging right off the bat," he said.

Only alcoholics we get in The Oorah were the ones still drinking. "Well," I said, pouring his club soda into a plastic cup. "Good to see you, I suppose. How are you?"

"You aren't surprised," he said.

"Takes more than a long-lost cousin only met once to surprise me." Kind of a lie.

"Cousin," he said. "Hmmm." Not a question. He took a sip of his club soda.

In the pool room, George and David yelled at each other, but wasn't anything that was going to elevate into fists and bone. I could tell.

"That's funny. That's not making this any easier." He smiled across his cup.

Had me interested then. What exactly *this* was, didn't know. Didn't know if I wanted to know. Not much on family relations, honestly. Not my thing. Didn't know this guy, this Wilton, enough to care much one way or the other.

"You lost me, cowboy," I said and bent toward the cooler. The front door opened, spilling sunlight into the room like a wave, dust swirling everywhere.

"So here's the deal," he said, but my attention was on the door. Samuel. Walked in with the light. Got close enough to see he brought trouble with him.

Wilton didn't stop. Kept on talking. "That's why I'm here, I guess. You probably already know something, what with the club soda and me not drinking and all," he said. "I'm here to make amends. Part of my recovery stuff. Step number eight. Eight outta twelve."

Heard him, but wasn't looking at him. Samuel sat down a few stools away, stared ahead at the bottles. Nobody was watching what they were doing, me included. I reached into empty space in the cooler.

"Somebody shoot your dog?" I asked, knowing all along what he would order.

"I hate hospitals," Samuel said. "I need something to accompany that beer."

Wilton going on and on. Like a tape recorder somebody left running. "First, I want to tell you I am not your cousin," he said.

Turned toward Wilton a bit. Samuel said, "There's been a bicycling accident," and turned back toward him. Sumbitches about gave me whiplash.

"I'm your brother," Wilton said. "Well, half-brother. I wouldn't lie about that. I'm here for step number eight."

"He's in a damn hospital," Samuel said.

Between the two of them, not sure which one made my head spin more. But my head did. Started spinning and spinning like it might all but screw itself off and fly across the bar.

CHERYL

For the record, I'm in Claude's records. In his cell phone, I am listed as his ICE, his In Case of Emergency contact. I never thought Claude was the kind of man to have an emergency contact. Then again, all those nights at The Oorah, he probably could have used somebody to pick him up and get him home. I know. Those are not emergencies. Those are excesses. This was an honest-to-god emergency. And for the record, it could have been worse. Isn't that what you say anytime somebody gets that hurt and doesn't die. *It could have been fucking worse.*

An EMS driver called me and asked in a monotone that didn't sound human, "Is this the emergency contact for Claude Lander?" and I immediately thought of Peg and how she would have occupied the ICE slot if she hadn't died of cancer, and oddly, I was sadder in those few seconds that I had been the entire eleven months since she passed. Weird, right? An EMS guy says nothing about Peg, yet she pops into my head, grief tagging right along with her.

"I suppose," I said. "What's wrong?"

He proceeded to tell me that there had been an accident, and they were transporting Claude to the hospital, the one on the far west side of town. I wondered why in the world they were going to that tiny hospital, but I didn't say a word. I thought to myself, *They are the professionals. And professionals never get shit wrong, do they?* Of course not.

The EMS person said that they would carry what was left of the bicycle with them in the ambulance, but somebody would have to, as he said, "Pick up the pieces." I wondered how many pieces Claude was in. I felt like I was picking up enough pieces as it was. They wouldn't tell me any details about his condition except that he was alive and heading to the hospital. For the record, I don't like half stories. I like having all the information available, right at hand. Why do you think I followed a dumpy woman to an ice cream parlor in the rain? And I shouldn't say *dumpy*. That's not fair.

I suppose I should have called Patrick and told him where I was headed, but I had pretty much shut down communication with him, other than the most vital need-to-know-things. Like, where is the toothpaste? And did you lock the back door? I was afraid if I began opening my mouth too much, I would start asking about the woman and her Stratford son and Hite's ice cream, and yes, I wanted to talk. I wanted to yell and scream and tell him how I watched through a slice of space in a goddamn bathroom doorway, but I wasn't sure what I wanted to say. I needed some time to plan. I felt like a speechwriter, and the state of the union address was around the corner. I mean, I knew I needed words to say what I felt. I wasn't sure which ones. Or what order to put them in. I shut up, for now.

So Claude had been on his bicycle, I thought. My personal jury was still out on the bicycle. It was obviously doing him some good. Okay, a lot of good. Being on that bike had trimmed his belly, and when that went away, so did some years. I wanted to feel bad that a) I noticed and b) he didn't start looking better until *after* his wife died, but I wasn't sure that this was classic cause and effect. It was more like, Claude decided to start pedaling fast because something was gaining on him. I wasn't sure what that *something* was. The bike was working. Nothing had caught him yet. Correction. Sounds like something may have fucking caught him or pulled in his way or whatever. The paramedics don't call if *nothing* has caught up with you, right?

I knew Claude was spending less and less time at The Oorah. That had to be healthy. I had been inside that place once, with Peg, when she went to look for Claude. I wasn't a fan of that kind of bar. There was never enough light to see what you didn't want to see.

The whole drive to the hospital, I thought about Claude and how he looked so much better and smiled more these days, even when he dropped by the house to see Marlene. I had even started calling him and suggesting times to come over and visit his daughter. Yes, and looking back on it now, I confess: I was doing it more for me than anyone. Is there a problem with that? I liked seeing him walk through the door. His appearance always made me think of Peg and made me remember that people can get over things and people can find new ways to be happy. For the record, I needed some new happy right about now.

All in fucking all, I was in a weirdly hopeful mood when I pulled into the hospital parking lot, and you normally don't see a lot of people in cheery moods around hospitals. Before I got out of my car, I texted Samuel and told him, in a few short, clipped, unpunctuated words, what happened and where I was. I would call Marlene from inside, when I knew more. I didn't want to give her half a story. She hated half stories as much as I did. I was almost humming when the automatic doors parted and ushered me into that acrid, cleansed hospital air.

I know. It's borderline sinful to be happy while entering a hospital to visit an accident victim, but I was handling something on my own. And it involved Claude. What I mean to say is I was in the exact wrong frame of mind to see what waited in his room. An entire side of his body was scraped raw—from the road, I guess. I suppose they had to leave it exposed to start healing, but there it was—raw flesh looking like it had been turned to hamburger. A thick bandage wound around his head, and both of his eyes were black like he'd been beaten up by goddamn Joe Frazier. And they were squeezed shut, not like he was asleep and calm, but like he was trying to keep every tiny bit of the world out of his head. He looked like he was in pain, even though you couldn't see into his eyes. That's where you normally detect real pain. I knew *that* after months with Peg. She would always say she was fine and didn't hurt. But one look into her eyes, and you could see she was lying. Pain lurks in the eyes.

A male nurse was slathering some sort of ointment on Claude's deep scrapes. He didn't notice me for maybe half a minute. He startled when he turned, and there I was. Everything happy had run from my head. I had some sort of terrified look on my face, I'm sure.

"Are you the wife?" he asked me, then added, "This road rash looks worse than it feels."

I wanted to ask him how the fuck he knew what it felt like, but I didn't.

I said, "Yes, I'm the wife," and I swear I saw Claude's eyes relax a bit. From that moment on, at the hospital, I was the wife. The nurse called me Mrs. Lander. The name had a certain ring to it. I didn't stop him. Why should I? Who did it hurt? To be honest, I sort of enjoyed it. I felt like I was in a play, and I had been typecast as the concerned wife. The real wife was permanently indisposed. Time for the stand-in to have some spotlight, I thought to myself.

When the nurse left for a few seconds, I walked to the edge of Claude's bed and leaned toward him, his eyes still squeezed shut. "I'll bet you twenty bucks you can goddamn hear me," I said, but didn't get an answer. I waited for something—an eye twitch or a smile or anything—but the expression on his face never changed. I sat in an uncomfortable chair against the wall. The nurse breezed back into the room.

"What should we do with your husband's bike?" he said. "It's pretty much totaled. The frame is cracked in three or four places. You might be able to salvage some of the gear set, but most of the rest of it is scrap. Sorry."

That was when I noticed the nurse was thin and athletic, with a tanned face except for pale sunglasses-circles around his eyes.

"I'm guessing you . . ." I said.

"Yes, ma'am, I cycle. I heard they were bringing in a cyclist, so I asked for this patient. I've been there, let me tell you. It's no fun munching asphalt."

I played with the phrase *munching asphalt* in my head for a couple of seconds.

"It's funny," he said, "you never asked what was wrong with your husband, if he's going to be okay." The nurse suddenly sounded like a cop.

"Big head banger," the nurse said. "Rattled his brain. The doctor can tell you more, but I think he's going to be fine. The worst part will be trying to wear clothes over all that road rash. That hurts. Trust me. Go buy some baggy shorts. The doctor is on her way down to fill you in."

The doctor is a she. Perfect, I thought. And we both stood there looking at Claude when he began to hum. Claude, that is, not the nurse. At first, I thought he was moaning, like he was in pain. The nurse thought the same thing. He immediately began checking the numbers on a monitor near the IV pump, like something medical was happening. But then the moan turned into a tune of some kind.

"Claude," I said. "What are you doing?"

I didn't recognize the tune. I don't think the nurse did either.

"Mr. Lander?" the nurse said, hovering over the bed.

But Claude didn't answer. He kept humming, his eyes squinted like something sharp was on the other side of them, poking to get out. I grabbed his hand and squeezed it.

That's the kind of things us wives do when our man hums in pain.

CLAUDE

There is a reason you decide not to open your eyes right away: you are not sure you are prepared to see the world. That makes sense to you at that moment, and the realization that you are making sense—thinking rationally, connecting dots—is comforting for some reason you can't put your finger on. In fact, comfort surrounds you. You lie somewhere warm, but there's a niggling feeling you are a bit exposed to the world. A little naked, maybe. With your eyes closed, you detect odors that might be floor cleanser. Could be hand sanitizer. Lurking behind those smells is the distinct odor of something antiseptic, like the Merthiolate your mother used to drip into any cut and scratch you came home with when you were a kid.

You still have a song in your head. You woke up with it. That stupid song that you hummed when you were on the bike. The bike. Your bike. *What happened to the bike?* you wonder. The things we do for biking.

You remember the bike and you remember the song (because it still loops in your brain, which, thank god, is in working order), but you don't recall anything else other than the bike might be in trouble. Why would a bike be in trouble? And what was the name of that goddamn band that sang that goddamn song?

You should wiggle your toes, because something in your brain—another dot to connect—tells you to check if that simple function is available to you. You try the right foot first, and all is good with the toe world. You feel them push against whatever is draped loosely across your feet. A sheet, maybe. On a bed? And you have something stuck in your right arm that is not so much painful as annoying, and there might possibly be something connected to your penis, which is not so much annoying as it is terrifying. But at least your penis is covered. You detect something draped across your waist and your crotch. Another sheet, maybe? You think about your penis.

Which makes you consider the bike again. Your bicycling has some connection to all of this. When you ride your bike for a couple of hours, your penis falls asleep. You remember how much you worried about that when you first began cycling. Now, for some mysterious reason, you lie semi-exposed on a bed or a cot, and something has been threaded up your penis. At least you think this is what is happening, but hell if you are going to open your eyes and find out. You know that a quick peek from behind your eyelids might clear up a number of things, but you sense it isn't safe right now. You sense people in the room, and they are probably waiting for you to open your eyes so they can ask you questions. Maybe about your penis. You do not want to answer questions about your penis.

You want to know who recorded "The Things We Do for Love," the song that *still* bangs against the inside of your skull, currently a very painful part of your body. A headache like you've never experienced before pulses both sides of your skull with tiny bolts of constant lightning. Somehow the bike and the headache are related. And connected to the song. And to the sheet across your waist. And to your penis.

You hear a shuffle of feet, soft soles on a hard floor. A rustle of papers. A door opening, releasing a murmur of voices into wherever it is you lie, voices that go mute when the door eases shut again. *Open your eyes*, says a voice in your head, then the voice gets obliterated by one of the lightning bolts and another voice says, *If you open your eyes all this light will pour in, and you and your penis will die a horrible death.*

You again contemplate the fate of your penis when the murmur of voices returns. A door must have reopened. Probably not more than six or eight feet from you, two people begin talking, a man and a woman. She asks questions, and he answers them quickly, without hesitation. The smell of hand sanitizer grows stronger, and you strain to hear them. They talk low, like they don't want anyone to hear. You could open your eyes and see these people with their secrets, but you keep them squeezed shut. For a few seconds, they don't speak English. At least, that's what you think until you realize that they are talking in code. Numbers and gibberish. The papers rustle again. She asks about something that sounds like *lactate* or *ringers*, and the man answers back: "Eighty cee cees."

In your brain, a tiny electrical charge fires. Then more lightning. And there it is, all of a sudden. The name of the band. 10cc. Their one and only hit, "The Things We Do for Love." Thank god for that. Like magic, the song disappears from your head, vanquished for good. That particular dot is connected, and you feel suddenly energized. You are ecstatic. You believe you are smiling. The lightning bolts in your head die down for a moment, and you think you should thank the man for helping you come up with the name of the band. You want to shake his hand. So you make the mistake of opening your eyes.

You should have listened to the voice that told you not to because when you do, you stare straight up at the ceiling, and the ceiling is filled with brilliant, sharp lights, and the lights pound your head. So you blink and try to fend off the light, but it's too late. The world, indeed, rushes in and begins filling all the blank spaces in your skull.

You are in a typical hospital room. That you recognize immediately. The smells make sense now. The two voices in front of you belong to a doctor and a nurse. The nurse is the man. The doctor is the woman. You can tell this by the way they are dressed and how they stand with one another. They finally notice you.

"Look who's awake," the man says, and the woman smiles.

"I'm Dr. Hughes," she says. "I stopped by to see how things are progressing."

Ah, there is progress to be made, you think. This is a test. I wasn't told I had to progress. The only thing you've done to this point is move your toes and chase a song around your head.

"I wiggled my toes," you say, "and the things we do for love is ten cee cees." You wonder if this is an exhibition of progress. You hope so. You don't want to fail the test. You notice your legs and torso and arms are bare to the world. The only things covered are your feet and the heretofore mentioned penis.

The two of them stare at you as if you've lost your mind then exchange a wry smile with each other.

You wonder what their smiles are all about. Well, you *think* you are wondering to yourself, thinking it, until you hear someone say, "What's so funny?" and that someone is you. And the tone with which you say it contains a bit of an edge. Snarky would be a fine word to describe it.

The man says, "We weren't—" but the doctor cuts him off.

"You've had a traumatic brain injury. You banged your head pretty badly," she says. "Your helmet saved you, but you might be a little rattled for a while. We'll do another CT in the morning, but other than a severe concussion that will bring on a heckuva of a headache, you should be fine. I mean, other than the road rash and the separated shoulder." She smiles again.

"My helmet?" you want to know.

"Your cycling helmet," the man answers and reaches into the small closet to the right of a sink and pulls out a bright green and blue helmet from one of the shelves. Two cracks run across the top of the helmet, and the way the male nurse cradles it, you can see that it has basically separated into three useless chunks. The paint job is marred and scratched.

Yes, you wore a helmet, and you were on a bike. From the fog inside your skull, a memory or two breaks into the clear. You remember being on a bike. Another dot connected.

"This is progress, right?" and the two of them nod at you, even though they have no idea what you're talking about. The doctor glances back at the clipboard in her hand, and the nurse returns the helmet to its resting place, and you hear the scrape of a chair to your left, out of your line of sight. You turn you head to look, and that cranks up the lightning bolts in your head, sudden nails of pain accompanied by intense brightness that flashes in your eyes. You must remember not to move your head if you can help it, at least not for a few years. Your brain feels unhinged. You squeeze your eyes shut, and when you open them again, the chair scraper has moved to the foot of your bed. The chair scraper is Cheryl.

"For the record, they called me," she says right off the bat. "It wasn't like I showed up out of the blue or anything. How is your head?"

You want to ask why, of all people, Cheryl sits in your hospital room, but the lightning is too much right now. And you suddenly remember your penis is connected to something alien and uncomfortable, but why in the world do you think about the state of your penis while Cheryl stands in front of you, her arms crossed and that scowl/smile hybrid of hers plastered across her face. Why her?

"I don't remember much," you say, then add, "but I'm making progress." You want to look down at your crotch and see what your penis is hotwired to, but that would require head movement. Bad idea.

"I hope you remember not to ever get on that goddamn bicycle again," she says. "That would be some goddamn progress."

You squeeze your eyes shut and try as hard as you can to remember what this mysterious missing bike looks like, what color it is, anything. You come up empty, and you do not feel like opening your eyes again. Cheryl still talks.

"I called Marlene and told her what's going on. I'll bring her up here this evening. Samuel too. I'll get the word out." Though you listen to her talk—her voice coming through like a poorly tuned AM station—that goddamn song cranks up again in your head and drowns Cheryl out. That 10cc song.

You wonder if "The Things We Do for Love" will be stuck in your head forever. You decide to keep your eyes in the dark a little longer and bring a halt to the current progress.

SAMUEL

Confession: I did not go to the hospital straightaway for the simple reason I do not like hospitals. Never have I witnessed anything good happen in a hospital. A hospital is a poorly sanitized receptacle for pain and misery. You might say: *What about childbirth, Samuel? That is a happy occurrence at a hospital.* And I would answer: *Have you ever heard a birth taking place?*

Suffice it to say, I go to great lengths to avoid setting foot inside hospitals, so when I received the message from Cheryl that Claude had been in an accident, my second thought was, *Oh, god, I hope he is all right.* Because my first thought was, *Oh, god, I hope I don't have to go to the hospital to see him.*

Hence, my quick stop by The Oorah for hospital fortification tonic. I must have looked like something was seriously wrong because LeJeune immediately dipped into her batch of colloquial homespunisms.

"Somebody shoot your dog?" she said.

As she put my beer and shot in front of me, I mumbled something about a bike accident and a hospital, but I didn't use a name. I wasn't sure who knew what, or who was supposed to know what, and I don't enjoy delivering bad news unless it's to twin racists. But LeJeune is no fool. She connected the dots. I possessed only one friend in the world, and that friend happened to be a recent convert to the cult of cycling. LeJeune knew immediately what had happened.

Her cheeks drained and her eyes widened, so in my attempt to keep things from becoming too dark too quickly, I said, "What? Somebody shoot your dog?" I don't believe she enjoyed that humorous pivot.

She began screaming at me, which did not help my current state of mind. She slapped my hand away from the plastic shot cup she had seconds before laid in front of me. "WHAT?" she roared, so I tried to tell her as quickly and calmly as I could that Claude had been in a bicycle accident and was currently lying in state at the satellite hospital on the west side of town.

"But that's all I know," I said.

"Get up," she yelled at me. "You're driving."

I told her that I did not do hospitals well. "That's why I'm here instead of already there," I said, finally getting my fingers around what remained of the shot and throwing the dribble of cheap bourbon down my throat.

"Suck it up, Buttercup," she said, coming from behind the bar. It always surprised me how tiny she was when she left her post. "Chug that chaser and grab your keys. Take me to Claude."

The man sitting at the bar didn't know what to do. I sensed I had interrupted a serious discussion. He reached for his back pocket, to pay his tab, I guessed. LeJeune was beginning to breathe heavily.

"I have trouble with hospitals," I said. "You don't understand. I have to work up to it."

She walked to my barstool and put one of her tiny feet on a rung below me. "Get up, get into your car, or I kick this goddamn stool out from under you."

"What about the bar? The customers?" I said, standing up. "Why don't you drive yourself?"

"Too upset to drive. And nobody cares about this place," she yelled, moving toward the door. I grabbed my nearly full beer and trailed her outside like bird dog on a scent. She was already seated when I made my way around the Lincoln and turned the key. The engine lumbered to life.

"And turn off that Detroit shit," she said.

By the time we pulled into the small lot at the hospital, I had finished my beer. The bourbon (what little there was) settled warmly in my stomach and my brain. I was about to tell LeJeune I was ready for anything the hospital had to throw at me, but she was halfway across the lot, half walking, half running, a white bar towel fluttering from her back pocket like a tiny flag of surrender.

MARLENE

I was the last one they called. Whatever. I saw Cheryl's name on my cell phone, and I thought, *What the hell does she want to complain about now?* That was all she did lately. I think the deal was she wasn't talking to her husband, so she saved up all her conversational crap for me. They passed each other in the hallway, like co-workers on the way to their cubicles. They nodded. Maybe a little grunt. And here's the thing: they were perfectly happy with it. Someday, I am going to be in therapy because of all this shit. I'd seen my parents split up, and then one of them died. I'd seen my aunt and uncle stay together and be all happy with their unhappiness. I got no roadmaps here.

Colt was fine, as far as a boyfriend was concerned. If I thought about it for long, I only hung around him because we were the same person, sort of. We didn't look anything alike, but we were in the same club, a club for people young enough to be bored as shit but not old enough to give up. Cheryl was in the give-up club. I wasn't there yet. So I hung out with a guy with ceramic spacers in his earlobes and lots of extra energy that he released on anybody who wasn't white. Personally, I don't think Colt hated Black people or Mexicans or Asians or anything else. I think Colt hated Colt more than anybody else.

I almost didn't answer Cheryl's call. I enjoyed not talking to anyone except myself, which I tended to do a lot lately. I was beginning to find myself interesting. I wonder if that was what Cheryl meant when she said I needed to grow up. I forgot *why* she said that or what I had done to bring it on. But she popped it out on me one day. "Grow up, okay, Marlene. Grow the fuck up." I had no idea what she meant or how the hell I was supposed to do that, but maybe this was the beginning, me realizing the most interesting person in my world was me.

I decided to answer my phone, and I could tell in the first sentence something was wrong. Cheryl's voice was softer, calmer. She didn't ask to put something on the record. It sounded like she was getting ready to tell me a story that would last a long time. You know, settling me into something.

"Marlene, honey, where are you?" I had no idea why that piece of information was important, but I gave her a straight answer. Why not?

"The kitchen," I said.

"That's good," she said. Even though we weren't on FaceTime, I could picture her, somewhere, thinking hard. I could hear her thinking. I wondered if that was my special power, to be able to *hear* someone thinking.

"Why is that good?"

"Listen," she said, "There's been an accident." She paused, to let that sink in, I guess. "But, but everything is going to be fine. He's going to be okay. He's a little banged up. He's lucky. We're all lucky." I heard her sigh, then the breath caught in her throat, and I thought she might cry.

"What? I saw Patrick a half hour ago," I said, as if accidents punched a time clock.

"No, honey," Cheryl said, "it was your father. He was hit on his bike. We're at the hospital, the Westside one. He's almost awake." She never called me honey.

I was still confused. Who was the *we* at the hospital? And how could someone be *almost* awake? But I didn't have this rush of panic. I didn't feel any waves of concern wash over me. Like I said, I was confused. Nothing fit. Cheryl sounded motherly.

"You should get down here. You should be here for your father," she said, and I couldn't begin to tell you why Colt thought that was a good time to start biting my ear, the one not against my phone. He made this slurping sound, and Cheryl heard it.

"What is *that*?" she asked.

"What?" I said. "What is what?"

"That fucking noise." She was beginning to sound like herself again. I felt comforted in a way.

"I swallowed funny," I said, which was the first thing I could think of. I punched Colt in the side, and he grunted and laughed at the same time.

"Where did you say you were?" Cheryl asked me again. "Where are you?"

I had not lied. I *was* in a kitchen, or at least the thing Colt used for a kitchen. It had an ancient table, something yellow and faded from the fifties or sixties, and a couple of chairs he got from Goodwill. Colt found this tiny little apartment on the cheap side of town and moved out of his old man's place. One bedroom, one bathroom, and a kitchen you could barely turn around in. He called it a one-butt kitchen because that's about all you could fit into it. Somehow, we'd ended up on the table. I had a blanket wrapped around me, but Colt paraded around naked like a starved show pony, happy, I guess, that he could walk around without clothes in a place he paid the rent on.

Colt was not a looker with his clothes off. Rail skinny and decorated with tattoos. He dyed his hair yesterday, so the dark black was back again. He looked like a prisoner of war with good hair. One of the tattoos was my name. I asked him not to do it. I didn't think there was anything you could ultimately change *Marlene* into, because I was pretty sure that the tattoo would be around a lot longer than I would. Colt was a perfectly fine way to waste some time. Like I said, I hadn't totally given up yet.

"Kitchen," I said, and Colt laughed too loud. "Did you say you were at the hospital on the west side?" Cheryl didn't know about Colt's place. She didn't need to. She wasn't my mother, no matter how hard she tried when she broke news she thought might upset me.

"Yes," she said, and I felt the new tone through the phone.

"I can be there in five minutes," I said, slipping off the table and retrieving my clothes as I walked through the room.

"*Where* are you?" she said again. "Five minutes? That's all?"

"On the way," I said and hung up. I could walk to the hospital from

Colt's apartment. Why do crappy places to live always pop up within walking distance of a hospital? What the hell is up with that? Colt said he didn't feel like going to a hospital, and I thought, *Whatever. I don't care.*

"Suit yourself," I said instead, hoping he'd get dressed soon. He looked much better when he had clothes covering his bones.

PEG

I saw it all coming together, and it made me think of this class I took in college a couple of years after the whole sensory deprivation incident. The class, if I remember correctly, was drama *something*, like Drama 201 or Advanced Theater Studies, but I'm not sure what the name of it was. No matter. The white-headed professor had yellow teeth and nicotine stains on his fingers, and this was long ago, back when smoking was allowed in class, so this guy sucked on unfiltered Camels the entire time. Drama Something was a seminar course. We met one night a week for three hours. He sometimes went through a whole pack of Camels by the end of the class. Most weeks I left through a haze of unfiltered cigarette smoke, like walking through a smelly cloud.

I remember us talking about plays and playwrights, only the ones the yellow-toothed professor liked. I don't recall any educational rhyme or reason for his selections, but one night we ended up talking about farces. I sat beside a girl on the softball team. She had asked me out the first night of the drama seminar, and I felt bad telling her I didn't go out with females or softball players. On the night we talked about farces, she leaned over and asked, "Did he say farts?" then she giggled.

The plays he wanted to talk about were sex farces from back in the 1600s or 1700s, where somebody is always hiding behind something, overhearing somebody say something or do somebody. They featured emotionally bruised cuckolds and randy women and dandies in tights, and the professor loved to squeeze those words between his smoke-tinged teeth as if they were rare and wonderful pieces of hard candy.

The sex farces we read were pretty funny. They reminded me of episodes of *Frasier*, when people *just* missed out on finding the boyfriend or girlfriend or mistress hiding in the pantry or sneaking up the stairs. I know, I know. I'm mixing genres. I'll probably end up confusing myself.

Anyway, what I'm saying is that in these *sex farces* (picture that phrase being smiled around with a set of yellow teeth), at some point, all the characters have a stake in the outcome of the plot and end up uncomfortably in the same room. The awkwardness is funny. Again, picture the teeth framing a moist, tubercular laugh. That guy is probably dead by now. If not, he's an academic-slash-medical miracle.

I thought about farces when I saw all those folks come together in Claude's hospital room, all the characters in all the current dramas. They were all connected, whether they realized it or not, and while it may not have qualified as a full-fledged farce, I found it interesting, if not giggle-worthy.

The funniest thing was Claude pretending to be unconscious and out of it, with his eyes squeezed shut, eavesdropping in plain sight. The nurse, the guy, was in love with the doctor. I could see that clearly, the way he watched her work, and I don't mean to say he leered or stared at her butt or tried to catch the front of her lab coat falling open. Rather, he looked at her more like she was a saint doing her saintly job. A saint he could worship. And she could not have cared less about the nurse. She was all business. I appreciate that. Claude was in good hands.

When LeJeune hit the door, with Samuel reluctantly trailing in her wake, I knew things were about to liven up. Samuel looked everywhere but directly at Claude, as if he were expecting attack from above or behind. Paranoia wafted off him like a bad odor.

LeJeune did not care who was in the room other than Claude. She took the three or four steps toward the edge of his bed and stood there, rocking ever so slightly side to side, as if to the rhythm of a song only she could hear. Samuel, I suppose, decided that he should remain a moving target for potential germs, so he paced at the foot of Claude's bed. From my vantage point, there was an odd kinetic energy in the room—people rocking and pacing. And Cheryl seated unmoving, statue-like in the corner chair. I wasn't sure anyone noticed her until LeJeune said, without turning around to Cheryl, "Has he been awake at all? Has he said anything?"

I knew Claude heard her because a slight flutter rippled behind his eyes, so subtle I'm sure none of the people in the room noticed. It wasn't a happy signal to anyone. Claude had already heard Cheryl claim to be his wife, to be me, which didn't sit him upright in the bed. So now, with his personal bartender and sometime chauffeur in the room, he, like me, could probably see the farce beginning to bubble to the surface of the room. Or maybe his brain was too scrambled to worry about melodrama, farce or otherwise.

Samuel spied the wall dispenser of hand sanitizer and began to wring his hands clean. Cheryl started to speak then decided standing would be better. She walked to the edge of the bed and stood beside LeJeune. Cheryl is a tall woman and LeJeune is the size of a middle schooler.

Here we go, I thought. Let the farce begin.

"You're the bartender," Cheryl said, and it wasn't a question.

"I'm the friend," LeJeune said. "You're the sister, right?"

Cheryl was about to add the *in-law*, and maybe Samuel was going to as well, but like it was scripted, at that precise moment, the nurse burst through the door. Farce in full swing.

"Oh!" he said, "we've got a crowd. Some folks to keep you company, Mrs. Lander?"

If I had been directing this farce, I wouldn't have changed a thing about the reactions of our main players. The second the male nurse dropped Claude's last name into the room, Samuel stopped pacing and immediately looked to Claude. LeJeune snatched her head to the left and glared up at Cheryl. And Cheryl? She bent down toward LeJeune like she was talking to a kindergarten child who had spilled a juice box.

"Yeah, names got misunderstood and it was too much trouble to correct them," Cheryl said. "But it's nothing for you to worry about. I'm sure you have other things on your mind, like empty kegs or clogged toilets or something of that ilk." Cheryl tossed that word in to try and batter LeJeune. A little mean-spirited, I thought. Hitting her with *ilk*.

Like the farces we read during that seminar so many years ago, one actor played the overly confused character whose job was to continuously cause the dramatic beans to spill. The male nurse filled that role admirably. "Are you the daughter?" he said to LeJeune.

Now, two things happened at once, which, of course, is not good for stage drama. The audience can only follow so many simultaneous actions. I'm not sure who saw what, but a split second before Claude opened his eyes, LeJeune punched the male nurse in the throat. She couldn't quite reach his face, so she opted for the most damaging area available. A lightning-fast jab, right in his Adam's apple.

I don't know why Claude chose that moment to open his eyes. What did he see? A male nurse, hand to his throat, suddenly dropping to his knees to try and recapture his breath. LeJeune re-cocking her fist in case a follow-up strike was needed. Cheryl retreating, but smiling nonetheless, and Samuel wildly pumping the hand sanitizer for germ relief. Claude should have closed his eyes on the drama and gone back to a more comfortable place in the dark, behind his face. Instead, he watched the nurse recover enough to grab LeJeune by the back of her t-shirt and lift her onto her tiptoes, but LeJeune never got off a second punch because the doctor swept through the door, right on cue. And when a doctor comes in, everybody stops. I believe that is a rule.

"What is this?" she said in a controlled yell. The room was crowded now, bodies pressed into motion. "Why do you have that girl by the shirt?"

The nurse looked like he'd been discovered having an affair. He was embarrassed he'd been caught in mid-unprofessionalism by the doctor of his dreams. He didn't want her to think he had designs, or even thoughts, about another woman, even one who had punched him in his Adam's apple. Instead of letting her go, he tossed LeJeune aside, physically and emotionally, which, of course, a woman like LeJeune would never appreciate.

The play came to a screeching halt. All the actors stood together in the room, waiting. The discomfort was thick enough to spread with a butter knife. Nothing—not the plot, not even the air—moved.

That is, until Claude screamed at the top of his lungs. Banshee-like, he opened his mouth and hollered like he had lopped off a body part. High-pitched and shrill, not unlike some sort of jungle creature, he screamed, and it wasn't a word. It was pure noise, unadulterated emotion embedded inside of it. And the emotion was not so much pain as it was disgust. Or angst perhaps. In the years we had been married, I never heard Claude make a sound like that. I studied the people in the room. They flinched against the wave of sound, and the room went silent again.

Claude studied the scene in front of him. The nurse massaging his own throat. His sister-in-law—and current wife, according to false reports—looming over the bartender, who bobbed and weaved as if to land another punch. His best friend pacing and wringing his hands around another dose of sanitizer. Claude had no idea where he was or why he was where he didn't know he was, but it didn't bother him. In fact, he smiled at the group.

He said, "I'm so glad you all came," then he added, "Marlene," because no one noticed that in the current excitement, our daughter had strolled into the eye of the farce. Claude peered beyond his friends, through them, toward his daughter, the one person he longed to see when he awoke from his haze. "Marlene, you came," he said. "Why is everyone here? This is awkward, but wonderful."

Claude closed his eyes again. I could tell he was tired.

PART THREE

CHERYL

For the record, I wasn't going to say anything to Patrick about Claude's accident and why I spent an entire day and part of a night at the hospital, but he had to go ahead and open his mouth. "Where have you been?"

Before you accuse me of misreading his tone, there wasn't a hint of worry or concern in it. He was pissed that there was missing information in the world—in his world, I mean.

Still, I hadn't planned to get into anything with him. Had I been thinking about Willie and Louise and the ice cream store? Sure, I won't deny that. But I didn't have a strategy to let him know that I'd seen it all, that little slice of Patrick's brave new world through the bathroom door. I wasn't ready for that fight yet. I was getting old enough and smart enough to time my battles. The ones I could win, anyway.

Not to mention, I was fucking tired. Bone-dragging, ass-dragging tired. Hospitals did that to me. There's nothing to do for hours on end except sit and worry, and those two activities (sitting and fretting), suck every ounce of energy out of you. I'm not sure how that happens, but it does. I was an empty well, and he should have been smart enough to see it, recognize it, and give me some room to refill. Instead, he doubled down. "I asked where you'd been."

I was so exhausted. I couldn't dredge up anything close to anger or sadness, but I wanted to, swear to god, I wanted to. He wouldn't let it go. I had enough left in the tank to muster up a thimble full of sarcasm, and for that, I was proud.

"I was at Hite's, getting some ice cream. Great people watching there. You see the most fucked up stuff, right?" I said.

I hadn't planned on springing it on him. I wanted to be able to enjoy it more. I wanted time to prepare. Now, I was tired. I felt heavy, like I was anchored to the hardwood floor.

"Have you been drinking? What does that even mean? You were getting ice cream? For thirty-six hours?" He was pacing too fast, as if to put some distance between himself and the truth. Men will do that. Bob and weave so the truth can't draw a bead on them.

"How many flavors do they have?" I said. "I'm a big fan of the orange sherbet. I get it every week." I was rambling. I needed to pump the brakes a little. "It's mostly kids in there, though, with their moms. Some of them walking down from Stratford."

He stared at me, trying to decide if I was completely insane or maybe too smart for him. Maybe I was a little of both at that moment. Or maybe those two states of mind are the same fucking thing. And tired. Don't forget the tired part. But I wasn't too tired to notice that flicker in his eyes. You know the one? That ever-so-slight glint that was a mixture of confusion and recognition and—what else?—fear, maybe? That hesitant way the eyes glanced down slightly, a pause so he could think. He suspected or believed or imagined that I knew something he didn't know I knew. That made no sense. I was tired.

Patrick's brain was whirring; I could almost hear it. I had too much information. Why would I bring up, out of nowhere and apropos of nothing, the name of an ice cream parlor where he meets his Love Louise and her cuddly-cute son? Why would I mention the name of the school the aforementioned cuddly-cute son attends? Why, oh, why?

I love but also hate this thing men do. I love it because it makes them human and stupid. Hate it because they are not smart enough to realize the appearance of a no-win situation. It's when they try to make that decision: *Do I stick to my guns and refuse to fess up with the truth? Or do I drop to my knees and beg forgiveness?* Right. Men don't beg for forgiveness until it is too late for anyone to offer up second/third/fourth chances. I love that moment when men are caught, when the hook has been set and all they can do is twist on the end of the line. And what does a good fisherman—excuse me, fisherwoman—do when the hook is set? That's right. Play the goddamn fish. Tire it out. I wished I had more energy.

"What are you talking about?" he said, shaking the fear and confusion from behind his eyes, hardening them. Again, typical. Ask an unanswerable question. Stall for time. See if another door opens. Or closes, as the case may be.

"What do you think I'm talking about?" Me, with my classic, tried-and-true strategy: answer a question with a question.

"I have no idea," he said. "You're crazy." He huffed a little, thinking he had turned the argumental worm back on me. We were both so old and tired with our little tricks. You'd think people with this much sense would come up with better ways to fight.

"I am," I said, which gave him pause—me agreeing that I'm nuts. But I had more. "I'm crazy to get caught out in the rain, the biggest rainstorm of the summer, and have to hide out in an ice cream store and wait for the deluge to end." Two things: I used an SAT-level word on his ass: *deluge*. It sounded Biblical and apocalyptic. But I always started pulling out big words when I argued. Little darts that I get to throw. And, number two, I didn't bring up the fact that I had tailed his girlfriend into Hite's when the rain hit.

I wanted to stop right there. I'd had my fun, and another wave of complete exhaustion washed over me. I was a little lightheaded, and my feet ached. How could my feet ache when I'd been sitting on my ass for a night and a day, watching nurses and doctors and families and dying people flow up and down and up a hospital hallway like tidal waves of hope and resignation? Claude was going to be all right, he was going home in a few days. I didn't know what I was going to do. Marlene was already planning to move back into her old house with her father. Peg was long gone. All I had was this confused boob standing in front of me, trying desperately to decide how much information I had in my brain.

"I'm tired," I said. "I'm way too tired to do this."

That was my mistake. I knew it the second it rattled out of my mouth.

The mistake wasn't saying I was tired. He already knew that. He could see it on my face. The mistake was using the word *this*. That meant there was something specific, something I had in my head. He knew I wasn't crazy-talking in tongues. He knew something tangible existed. *This*. Dammit, that was a rookie mistake.

He jumped on it. It wasn't his first rodeo either. "Any of this? What's *this*, Cheryl?" He hit the word hard, a hammer blow. "What do you think you know? Tell me so I can let you know how wrong you are," he said. "Go ahead."

"I want to walk through the shower and rinse the last day off and crawl into bed. Whether you are there or not makes absolutely no difference to me. And when I said 'this,' I meant fighting, arguing. I didn't mean anything by it." I started to walk by him.

"You've got some issues, you know," he said barely above a whisper. That wasn't fair at all. I knew he was trying to get in the last word so he could strut around and grab his testicles and be the fucking cock of the walk who got in the last punch in a fight. But come on, that was so goddamn uncalled for, I thought.

When I was about to let it go and head to the shower, a song entered my head, a song I had not thought of, much less heard, in years. I didn't even like the song. It wasn't on my iPod. Wasn't even on some cassette tape tucked away in a shoebox somewhere. At that moment, somebody gave me that song, sent it to me, the God of Arguments Between Wives and Husbands, maybe. The tune, the lyrics—it all popped into my head. If I were to tell you the title, you'd remember it right away. First clue: the band that recorded the song is Sweet. Isn't that so, well, sweet?

I pushed by Patrick in the hall, and when I was out of his reach, but not out of earshot, I started singing. "Little Willy Willy won't go home. But you can't push Willy 'round, Willy won't go . . ." I paused, then set up for a big finish. "Little Willy Willy won't, Willy won't, Willy won't."

Patrick stood there, bleeding panic from his eyes. Or maybe he was mad, since I was pointing a finger at somebody he knew. Was it a low blow? Of course. But we had reached that point.

You know what he said? (I have to admit, this was pretty good, considering he had to come up with it on the fly.) He said, "It's spelled different. My Willie spells his name different."

I was too tired to cry, but I wanted to, I wanted to so bad. *His* Willie.

I couldn't get that song out of my head, but, you know, that was my fault. I should own up to it.

PEG

Here, you are not permitted regret, not allowed to look back—or down as the case may be—and twiddle your thumbs and fret over what might have been. Because the fact shall always remain that you are here, and they are there, and never the twain shall ever meet again, amen. The death of you is the death of second chances.

I can talk about regret and examine it, but I cannot—can *never*—feel it, can never experience that thrumming pit in the stomach or the sweaty angst of an opportunity long gone.

So when I saw Marlene pack up at Cheryl's house and relocate to her father's after his accident, I did not, of course, feel that weight fall in my chest when she walked in her old room and studied the walls, or when Claude watched her place her things back into drawers that had grown musty-smelling waiting on her.

I was so pleased she came home to nurse her father back to health. Not that he needed it. Claude, from my rather lofty point of view, was milking this accident for all it was worth. A bit melodramatic for me, I have to say. But it was working. People were giving him a wide berth, especially Marlene. She was changed now, or at least it appeared that way from where I floated. And not only her behavior. She wore her hair in a new way. Her nails were absolutely clear of any of that dark polish she started wearing in the eighth grade. She found an old pair of sandals in her old closet and didn't even look in the mirror to see how they looked on her feet.

But here's the big one: she cooked for her father. I didn't even know Marlene could find her way around a kitchen. Maybe she watched me closer than I imagined when I was the one in front of the stove. She walked to the Food Lion one afternoon and came back, loaded down with vegetables and cartons of chicken broth and pasta and chicken breasts and proceeded to make chicken soup from scratch. I *never* made chicken soup like that in my life. Where did she learn that?

While the soup simmered, Marlene searched the kitchen cabinets and the drawers below the counter until she found the place mats. She tossed the nice ones to the side, the mats with the hand-stitching down the sides. She kept digging until, deep in recesses of a drawer, she found her favorite placemat from elementary school, the plastic map of the United States with a star designating each state capital. She had learned all fifty capital cities using that map. We practiced during every meal. I would silently choose a state and cover up its capital city with my finger. "Montana," I would say, and I'd whistle the *Jeopardy!* theme music while Marlene squinted her eyes and tried to squeeze the answer out of her brain. "Helena!" she squealed. "They named it after a girl. I like Montana."

Marlene set places for them, and when the soup was ready, she called her father into the little breakfast nook in front of the bay windows. The soup steamed in the soft sunlight. Claude walked in and smiled. He did a lot of that lately, since the accident, him and his milking of things. Then, Marlene threw a curve ball. She motioned for Claude to sit down at the plastic U.S. map placemat.

"You remember that one, don't you?" she said. "I can't believe we still have it." Claude continued to smile. I wish to god I could read minds from up here. I would love to know what he thought when he looked down at a bowl full of noodles and chicken and carrots sitting on top of what appeared to be Kansas and Missouri.

"I made soup," Marlene said, stating the achingly obvious. Claude's smile grew wider, if that was possible. "I found this recipe for it a while back, but I quit following it and started kind of going with whatever I felt. I can't follow recipes."

Claude balanced a spoonful in front of his face, studying the steam. "Careful," Marlene said, "I just took it off the eye." Claude blew on his spoon for a few seconds, tested the heat with his lips, then ate the entire bite.

Marlene was suddenly twelve years old again, sitting at our little table. Funny, Claude rattled his brain around, but Marlene was the one who'd become a completely different person, someone transformed by the accident. I suppose it made sense. Now she made soup. She wore old sandals. You can never predict where change will surface. Or resurface.

Claude put his spoon down and moved his bowl to the southeast. He stared down at the map.

Marlene said, "So what do you think?"

Claude smiled and said, "Montana?"

Marlene smiled back and said, "Named for a woman. Helena."

"That's very good," Claude said. "Very, very good."

The two of them sat there in the shafts of sunlight, staring at each other above a couple of bowls of steaming chicken soup. I wished I could smell what they smelled right at that moment. Wished I could have felt the clink of spoons against the bowls. Wished I could have tasted soup my daughter made with her own hands.

I can't truly feel regret. But that doesn't mean I can't imagine what it would be like to guess some state capitals right now. I can smile with them from a distance, and that's something, isn't it?

LeJeune

Surprises don't surprise me.

Could be a bumper sticker. Or a tattoo. Mean to say—can't usually pull one over on me. But Wilton showing up and out of the blue telling me he was a brother. Surprised me. Got to admit.

Got to admit something else. But need to go back a few weeks, back to that day I went to the hospital. See, forgot all about Wilton while I was there. Yep, shoved him right to the back of my brain, I suppose. Claude took over my head and not ashamed of that. Things got mashed together at The Oorah—Samuel trying to stoke up his courage, Wilton sitting there all I've-got-a-secret, me finding out Claude wrecked. Shook me up.

Saw Claude and that doctor said he was fine and should be a hundred percent soon—that's when I remembered: left Wilton at the bar. First thing my brain said was, *Don't go back there.* Fight or flight. Wasn't up for a fight. Strange for me. Usually enjoy a good dust-up.

At the hospital, Samuel went, "I can't take any more of this germ convention." Made his way to the door. He was my ride. Dropped me off at The Oorah. Didn't look like much happened while I was gone. Pool guys probably didn't notice I left. Maybe served themselves. Couldn't care less one way or the other. There he was. Two hours later, still sitting at the bar. Empty plastic cup in front of him. Brother Wilton. Didn't know if I was glad or mad.

"Can I get a refill on this club soda?" Asked me before I even got behind the bar. Hate that kind of thing, trying to make me work before I settle in. Him, family and all, still pissed me off. Saying it like no time had passed at all. Wait twenty plus years to show up, what's a few more hours?

"You still here." Wasn't asking a question. Stating fact.

"Everything okay with . . . ?" he trailed off.

"Nobody you know. Or hell, maybe you do. 'Cause you see, don't know a thing about you, right? You aren't even here," I said. Instantly proud of myself. Sounded like a movie line.

"Oh, I'm here alright, but I'm not here to cause anybody any trouble. Like I told you, making amends."

"Don't get it," I said.

"Amends, amends," he said. "It's part of my recovery."

"No, no," I said. "Don't get why you all the sudden show up. What you ever do to me? Don't need amends from you. Never did."

"That's the funny part," he said, taking a sip.

Nothing funny where I stood. Stuck my hand in the cooler. Felt a few beers light under the ice. Freaking pool boys stole beer. Needed to stock. Pool boys saw me fishing around in the cold water, felt their day-drunk guilt beaming all the way from the table.

Wilton whispered, "They only took a couple each, maybe three. They made me swear not to tell, but since we're kin and all."

"What's the funny part?" Get him back on track. He was easily distracted by goings on in the world.

"Oh that, well, you see, I made a promise, and I didn't come through on it." He stopped, and I said nothing, so he went, "I promised Gunny I would look after you if and when he went belly-up."

"Might need to make some amends for calling my daddy belly-up," I said.

"My daddy too."

"Don't see how that is. Don't see how any of this is. Gunny was a lot of things, and a lot of those things were bad, but wasn't a cheater. Didn't play around. Didn't have the time," I said.

"He played around at least once," Wilton said, "and that's all it took, I suppose, biology being what it is and all." Proceeded to launch into his version of the story of his life. Actually before his life. Way he heard it, my father the Gunnery Sergeant had a weakness for *Georgia girls with long legs and short skirts*. Wilton's words and not mine. A short-skirted, long-legged girl from Macon worked on base in the mess hall, and Daddy couldn't take his eyes off her, and soon he couldn't keep his hands off her, and that led to the small stockroom off the kitchen in the mess hall. "I was conceived on top of several large stacks of flour, according to my mother," he said. "If I was a girl, I'd've probably been named Martha White. She told me everything. I guess it felt good to confess a little."

Story turned darker. Saw Wilton flip his gaze to the regiment of liquor bottles on the shelf behind me. Swear he wet his lips. Wanted a drink bad. Felt a little sorry for him.

"Keep on with amends, Wilton," I said, trying to get his mind off the Beam or the Cutty.

He choked it down, wanting a drink. Got on with his story. Said his mother was feeling fine one day, next she comes back from the grocery store dog tired. Only a couple of blocks to the store and back, and she didn't have much to carry. Made no sense. Was even more tired the next week. Wouldn't go to the doctor until she couldn't avoid it. "She had something in the blood, something that wouldn't wash away," he said, his eyes welling. "She waited too long to do anything, and it was too dang late. Putting things off runs in the family, I think, at least on my side. Hell, it took me all these years to talk to you."

One of the last things his momma did? Get in touch with the Sergeant. Let him know he had a boy he never knew about. Messaged him a couple weeks before we left for LeJeune. Gunny was ready to take on the boy, bring him in the house and put a roof over him. Ready to man up. Ready to suck it up, Buttercup. That's why Wilton was there on packing day, looking lost and undone.

"Your mother was dead set against it," he said, "and I can't blame her. In one fell swoop, she finds out her husband has a girlfriend and a son from said girlfriend. That's a lot to digest in a single morning." Not worried about my mother. Never did worry, especially in the twenty-five years since she died. Was more curious about Brother Wilton.

"You're probably wondering what happened to me and all," he said, reading my mind. Maybe that was what brothers did with sisters. Mind reading. Wouldn't know. Never had a brother before. "You may not recall, you being so little back then and all, but there was a Methodist boy's home outside the base. You know, that always made me wonder—a home for boys, almost connected to a Marine base, almost like they were expecting people like me to show up and need a place to sleep. Anyway, Gunny took me there and set me up. He sent me an allowance every month. I had new jeans and shirts every fall when school started. I wasn't sad. You don't need to worry about that. I wasn't exactly happy, but I wasn't exactly sad."

Knew what he meant. Suddenly remembered his face that morning when I packed my two boxes. Look of complete and utter nothingness on his face. Same look today. Not happy, but not exactly down in the dumps depressed about things. I thought, *this guy has learned to roll with the world. No doubt we are related.*

"Gunny kept in touch with me through the years, even when I was drinking bad. He was a good man. He wrote me one time, couple of years before he passed. Damn, talking about all this makes me want a shot of something," he said.

"Not today," I said. "Not on my watch."

Big old sigh comes whisking out. Sucked it back in, kept talking. "Gunny said that there may come a time when I would need to check on you, and he made me promise to do such a thing. I have fallen down on that promise, which is what brought me here. From what I can see, I might be too late."

He looked around the bar, looked at my tattoos. Kind of waved his hand at my general overall situation, suggesting I was in need of rescue. Pissed me off. On the other hand—was always another hand—tried to wrap my head 'round it. How we could do something so cold, up and leave that little boy behind way back when. Ought to make an amend or two myself.

"I never kept that promise, you know, to look in on you and see if things were all right. Most of the time, I was a little busy arm wrestling my hangovers, but no more. So that is my amend. I am truly sorry for what I have not done."

Usually say something smart or snappy at times like that. This was different. Was something else. Took a good look at Wilton. Stared long. Stared hard enough and swear, saw my daddy staring right back.

Should have told him to suck it up, Buttercup, but couldn't. Felt something rising in my throat. Words too unfamiliar to be comfortable. "Same here, Wilton. Truly am," I said. "But here you are." He slid his plastic cup my way so I could refill his club soda. Was happy to.

Have to say I was surprised. Even more surprised when Wilton said he might stay around a bit. Catch up on things with me. Surprised again. And happy. Both at the same time. New combination for me, got to say.

WALLACE & WADE

O f course this had to happen now. Truly atrocious timing.
Despite an opinion from the local pest control expert to the contrary, Dunean's was overrun with vermin, no two ways about it. Yet we remained unsure what to do. So, we did nothing, and amid our conundrum, our stasis, that man requests to see us. We have always said this is the story of our lives: when it rains, it will more than likely pour. Right now, we were in the throes of a downpour without an umbrella in sight.

We hesitated to answer the phone when he called. Of course, we had no idea who was on the other end of the line, but we sensed—deep down, in places that stir at the worst of times—that the news behind that ring could only be bad, no matter who placed the call. And right we were.

"You probably don't remember me. Dr. Samuel Tisdale from Addison College? We spoke some time back, a couple of years now, about bringing a visiting writer in," he said on speaker phone.

Oh, we remembered him. How in heaven's name could we forget? Because of some crossed ethnic wires, we had come perilously close to having a Black author speak at a bookstore with shelves void of any color but white. There was that squall he tried to stir up in the aftermath, that ripping of pages. He never offered to pay us for those books.

"And what can we do for you today, Mr. Tisdale?" we said, mustering up hidden reserves of faux gentility, assuming he wanted something we were unprepared to give. Doctor, our eye. Men with PhDs wear their sheepskin like insufficient loin cloths, attempting to hide their shortcomings.

"You know, I think it's more of what I can do for you," he said, which was completely unexpected. We had no reply to that, but he didn't wait for any, which was not an issue. This was never intended to be a dialogue. We were simply an audience for his well-rehearsed speech.

"I have come across a volume that you might be interested in checking out. I don't recall a rare or antique section in your store, but this is one that would rate some space somewhere, I promise. I could run it by and let you take a look, if you'd like. Being lovers of books, you would—what's the word I'm looking for?—adore this one. Maybe I could stop by for a cup of coffee and let you check it out. What do you think? Sound like a plan?" he said and fell silent.

It sounded *nothing* like a plan to us! But what could we say? Over the course of many years, we had learned there are times one must grin and genuinely bear it. To hang up and ignore this request might serve as a catalyst for more difficulties down the road. We did not want to inadvertently light the fuses for a long line of annoying, possibly explosive situations, courtesy of one Mr. Samuel Tisdale. With the Flag Room performing so well, we did not want to draw new attention to ourselves. To simply meet with the professor and see his little book would cost us little more than a half hour of our time. We could keep our distance, mind our watch. We could meet at the rear of the store. No one would see. No one would be the wiser.

"That sounds intriguing," we said. We lied, but no matter. "When would be a convenient time for you?"

He was ready with an answer. "How about Thursday morning?"

"Oh, we're sorry. Thursday is simply packed to the gills." We lied again.

"How about Friday?" he countered.

"Friday is another busy day, all day," we said again. We were beginning to enjoy this.

"Of course," he said. "Maybe *you* should suggest a time?" He did not sound the least bit discouraged.

We thought back to our school days when we enjoyed saying things like, *How about the twelfth of Never?* or *Maybe when hell freezes solid?* We were more polished now. We were having fun. We threw out an option.

"Sunday at noon is free, before the store opens. Will that work?"

He said, "I'll make it work," and we glanced at each other. We had both noticed it. There was a new edge in his voice, perhaps the inklings of a growl.

We punched the button to disconnect and continued to stare at each other. What had we done? Had we opened the door to something we could not possibly keep out? Why would he want to show us a book? Why would he want anything to do with us? We were on the verge of hitting redial and canceling when our better senses—and better natures— thankfully took over. Of course, we overreacted. We owned a bookstore. He had a book. He wanted to come to common ground and show it to us. Perhaps this was the extension of an olive branch, after all this time. He was acquiescing to us, possibly even capitulating. Why, we had no idea! What makes a person suddenly come to his senses? Aloud, we said, "He wants to make amends for past transgressions."

We thrilled suddenly at the prospects of this meeting. This wasn't the world continuing to pummel us with sour karma. No, this was the bright, silver lining inside a rat-infested cloud, the glass half full of Dark 'n Stormy, a frown turned upside down. We suddenly felt very Machiavellian. Keep our enemies close! That's what we would do. Well, as close as was comfortable.

The realization was so warming and comforting that when we heard the tiny, muffled stampede of little rat feet in the wall next to us, we didn't shriek or cast aspersions at Pete, the frightened pest control man. We simply thought more existentially that all the occurrences in our little world had manifested themselves because they were *meant* to happen right now. The timing was not atrocious. It was exquisite, rats be damned.

CLAUDE

Things are changing.

First, Marlene moves back into your old house. And, importantly, so do you. You are still laid up in the hospital when she—and you guess Cheryl—make that decision, make it without asking you. But what could you say? Most of Marlene's decisions about where to live have been made without your consultation. You are confused but not unhappy when she gives you a ride after your discharge from the hospital, and instead of heading to your tiny apartment, she pulls into your old, familiar driveway and announces, "Your apartment is no place to try and recover, and there's not enough room for me there, anyway. I moved my stuff back into my old room, and we brought all the things we thought you'd want. This is a better place to get better, don't you think?"

A bump on the head and a few layers of skin are a fair trade for having your old roof over your head and your daughter back in her bedroom. You haven't spent a night in that house since the day you moved out. You wonder if there are any hints of Peg lingering in the drawers, in the closets. You don't say a word, but you're sure Marlene sees you smiling.

Which, by the way, has become the newest habit of yours: this smiling and not saying a word. It started when everyone crowded into your hospital room that day. When you sensed them, you screamed loud—louder than you've ever screamed—and that is the last sound of that type you ever want to make. Because now, instead of screaming at the world, you grin and keep your mouth shut. You have an excuse: your brain has been severely rattled; you are temporarily a crazy man. You can grin and say nothing and feel perfectly fine. And they let you. It feels so good, you decide to adopt that behavior as your default setting for any situation existing on the gamut between stressful and joyful. People don't know how to handle you when you smile like a happy idiot and refuse to engage in conversation. You've spent way too much of your life trying to fill gaps in silences. You, naturally, still talk. But you've learned when to shut up. When Marlene declares that she is once again a boarder at your address, you don't ask what brought on the change of heart. You don't ask if she did something wrong at Cheryl's house. You don't want to know any more information other than the fact that she reenacts the whole prodigal daughter thing and returns home. *So you smile. And shut your mouth.*

Other differences? The house is immaculate, cleaned to a shininess you've never seen before. The mildewed grout on the bathroom counter has been scrubbed white. Every corner is free of dust bunnies. The shower curtain that had evolved into a dark Rorschach of soap slime and more mildew has been replaced with something that actually has flowers on it. The bedspread has been laundered and now serves its original function of being spread across your bed. The books you left behind all those months ago, stacked ominously like several in-progress games of Jenga, are now corralled between a pair of antique bookends you don't recognize.

Marlene trails you through the house, taking note of your smiles and your silence. "I had some time on my hands," she says. "I'm good at cleaning things. Who knew?"

The time has come to speak. "Marlene, everything looks wonderful, absolutely wonderful." Then you smile.

"Are you tired from the ride home? Do you need to take a nap? The sheets are clean as of yesterday," she says.

You want to tell her you feel fine, that you feel close to one hundred percent, but you have fallen deeply in love with the idea of people caring about you. You do not want to stop what is going on and break your own heart. You'll let them all care a while longer. It is doing everyone some good.

"Maybe in a minute," you say, your grin still plastered on your face.

"Aren't you going to say something about us being back home?" Marlene asks. She sits down in a nice armchair that looks to be upholstered in corduroy. You have never seen that chair before. "Aren't you surprised?" she says.

You smile and say nothing. This is the best part of your new habit: when you stay quiet, other people scramble to fill in the silence. Of course, you have plenty you could say to Marlene about the homecoming. You want to know if Marlene came back out of pity, or was something else at play? You want to know if the move is semi-permanent or a momentary stopgap, or is it more long term? You want to ask her if Cheryl was okay with it, or if she put up some kind of protest. Sure, you have all sorts of questions, but with your new communication strategy, all your questions will be answered in due course, if you keep your mouth shut. As you predicted, Marlene is uncomfortable with the silence in the one-sided dialogue, but she isn't about to sneer at you—a newly released, newly brain-injured person—so she begins to talk, quickly, and fill in the spaces.

"I gotta tell you, when I saw you there in that hospital—and you know they didn't call me right away, right?—anyway, I saw you there with your eyes closed, and I thought, well, I already have one dead parent, and if you don't die, I'm going to make sure I spend as much time with you as I can. I know that sounds crazy and quick, but it's true. I think something happened to me while I was standing there. I didn't hear voices or anything, but something definitely happened. I felt older all of a sudden." Marlene talks until she is out of breath and waits for you to answer with more than a smile.

Maybe she *is* older, you think, wondering if you have pulled some sort of Rip Van Winkle episode and were a hospital resident for more than the week you spent there. Has it been months? But no, your wristwatch, which miraculously survived the crash, tells you the date. You were out of sorts and out of touch for seven days. Now you are home. Your daughter, your newly grown and matured daughter, stands in front of you, having a real live conversation. You aren't accustomed to being this happy, so that's exactly what you tell her.

"I'm unaccustomed to being this happy."

Marlene wraps her arms around herself. She has not evolved to the point of hugging you yet. "Well, we deserve it, don't you think?" she says, then answers her own question. "Damn right, we do."

Yes, everything is different. Your bathroom is clean. Your sheets will crackle with newness when you slide into them. You have not had the time to consider any downside of Marlene moving back into your house. Is there any downside? There may be more expense, but you can certainly shoulder that. The way you see it, the benefits of having two-thirds of your family—the only remaining two-thirds—together again under one roof outweighs any new expenses. Plus, Samuel has told you that his lawyer buddy is convinced you will get a rather hefty insurance settlement from the driver of the wayward BMW that clipped you on the road. You have not given much thought to money or insurance. You've been too busy smiling and not talking.

One thought does flash across your mind. "What about this Colt fellow?" you say, seasoning the word *fellow* with an extra emphasis, knowing full well that he has never been, nor will ever be, a fellow.

"Colt is fine with it," Marlene says, mistakenly thinking you are looking for her boyfriend's stamp of approval. "He thinks that spending more time with you is healthy."

You consider that. You are sure Colt is not the type of *fellow* that worries about the health of others. You smile at Marlene and say nothing. God, how many times in the past, how many *hundreds* of times did you tie yourself into knots trying to come up with the right thing to say, something with the right tone that wouldn't upset or offend or anger anybody. And all you had to do was smile and shut your mouth.

Marlene fills the silence-gap again, but this time, she knows what's bouncing around your head. "Colt isn't what you think he is," she says. "He's—I don't know—deeper, maybe, than you think? I don't know. Anyway, he's not what you think."

Here you could, maybe *should*, say something like, *Well, what do you think I think?* but you don't. You don't care, to be honest. You know you should say something. You look at Marlene. She is growing up, but if you look closely, stare right into her face, you still see the shadow of the sixth grader, the dorky kid with only a handful of dorky friends. Here she is, growing up, flashing the sixth-grade face, moving back in with her brain-banged father.

"I think this is all a very good thing," you say, and it is perfect. You realize it is perfect because Marlene smiles at you, unwraps her arms from herself and folds them around you. You can't remember the last time you hugged your daughter. Or she hugged you. Did the two of you hug at the wake?

No one, not Samuel or Marlene or Cheryl, can understand why you would ever consider getting back on a bicycle. They say things to you like, *Didn't you learn anything?* or *Why would you tempt fate again?* When they say these things, they end their question with *idiot*, even though they don't say the word aloud, but you can sense it there, dangling in the silence.

Of course, they don't understand. They don't ride a bike. They don't know how it feels. They don't realize what the bike has done for you. Everything that is happening, everything *good* that is beginning to unfold—each new hug you receive or conversation with Marlene—occurs because of the bike. While you were pedaling miles into your legs, the world spun in a new direction. The accident was all part of the design. It was supposed to happen. And if another wreck happens, you're all for it. You got a bump on the head . . . yet you woke up with so much more.

There is no way you can afford a new bike until the insurance check comes through. You are clueless about the way insurance works, but Samuel explains it to you. There's math involved. "They're going to look at your medical expenses, total that all up and then multiply it by some number. One point five or something like that. The extra point five is for pain and suffering. Then my lawyer buddy will tell the insurance company that you suffered a lot more than point five and ask for a shit ton more. And you'll get it, because that guy wiped you out," Samuel tells you. You wonder how he knows about insurance settlements.

"But I didn't suffer. It hasn't been that bad," you say.

"That's why *you* don't talk to the insurance people," Samuel says. "That's why you keep your trap shut and pay a lawyer." You can be quiet.

It's becoming a habit.

The educated guess is $60,000, arriving any day now. Sixty-grand for taking a flying leap off a bike and banging your head. Sixty gees for something you don't remember happening. When you don't remember how something happened, that cuts down on your suffering.

You know you will use a few thousand dollars to buy a new bike. You've already discussed it with TJ. You don't want to go crazy, but you and TJ have decided you are ready for something better and faster. Until the check comes through, though, you are without wheels. Plus, the doctor has to clear you to ride again. She thinks you are a little crazy too. Nobody understands the bike.

In lieu of actually being able to purchase a bike and start pedaling, you decide to shave your legs, which somehow seems perfectly natural to you. You noticed—the first time that group of men flew by you on the street—that cyclists' legs are bare as newborns' skin, not a hair on them. During your trips to the bike store, you watch men walk in and talk with the mechanics, their calves muscled and shiny. The men with hairless legs are the hammerheads, and they take a razor to their lower extremities on a regular basis. You do not believe you want to be a hammerhead, but by god, you want legs like that. Bare legs leave nothing but the outlines of the muscles for the eye. Shaved legs mean you are serious. And you *are* serious now. You have been in a cycling wreck. You have fresh pink scars where the pavement ate your skin away. You have that badge of honor. Now you deserve bare legs.

You aren't sure how far north to shave. The hammerheads you've seen, there is no way to tell how far up the leg they go with the razor. It's not the kind of thing you ask a stranger in a bike shop. "Hey, excuse me, when you shave your legs, do you stop at the crotch? Or do you go for total deforestation?"

One day, you finally ask TJ, whose legs are as slick as a baby's ass. He doesn't even blink. "Kind of up to you," he says. "I stop at the top of the thigh. I don't do any serious manscaping."

So you buy a decent razor at CVS, not your usual cheap Bic. These are your only legs. They deserve quality steel.

MARLENE

The last couple of years, I felt like I was running through a freaking maze, making turns without any kind of map, but now, I knew *this is the right direction*. I moved back in with my dad. I could watch him get better. Watching him get better would make me feel better. Not that I was sick. I was just—I don't know—tired of waiting for life to start up. Or more like, tired of waiting for me to catch up with life.

Colt didn't understand. When mom died and I moved to Cheryl's, I have to say, he had it pretty easy, and by *it*, I mean me. He'd sneak over after midnight, after Cheryl had her bourbon in the backyard and Patrick went to bed. Colt would climb on the back fence and tightrope walk the top of it to a place where he could grab this ledge under my window then pull himself up and in. I had to grab his wrists and help a little. He's not the strongest person I know. He needed a little boost. But he liked me, and he was quiet in my room, and he'd stay until an hour or so before dawn. *He liked me and he was quiet.* That sounds so freaking lame, like that's all it takes to get me naked. Jesus.

Now, Colt was pissed that he couldn't stroll on over to my father's house and do the same thing. It was my father, for god's sake. My dad had a head injury. *Still* had it, I should say. Once a head injury, always a head injury. And he was happy to have me around. I was doing something good for a change.

It didn't take a shrink to figure it all out. I'd lost one parent. I'd come close to losing another. I had to get closer to the one I almost lost, get to a place where I could hold on, where I could keep an eye on what was important to me. He was suddenly important to me. More important that Colt, for sure, and Colt couldn't take it.

One afternoon, Colt came to the door, and I saw him before he knocked, opened the door right on him. "Let's do something," he said, which was his way of telling me he wanted to go somewhere and get busy. *Something* for Colt always involved flesh and noise.

"I can't," I said. "I'm cooking soup."

"What the fuck?" he said. "Who cooks soup?'

"People who eat," I said right back, like I had that line loaded in the chamber and all I had to do was pull the trigger.

"There's a meeting tonight," he said. "We could go to the meeting first then do something."

Yes, I thought, that was exactly what I needed right now. Sitting in a roomful of pissed-off haters. The truth was all those Ivory Boys in the WLF were nothing but the geeks of the hater world. They were dorks with bad attitudes. The only way they could get laid was to tattoo a quote from *Mein Kampf* across their ass and loop a chain on their wallets. They weren't that different than the chess club geeks. Only these guys wore black, shaved their heads, and smelled like a wet barnyard.

"I don't have time for that, Colt," I said. "Those meetings are starting to sound a little silly." I probably shouldn't have said that.

"Oh," he said. "Silly."

Behind me, I heard my dad heading up the stairs toward his room. Sometimes he took naps at strange times of the day. Then again, I guess anytime for a nap was strange, if you thought about it.

"I don't mean anything, Colt. I don't find it all that interesting anymore. Things have changed," I said.

"Nothing has changed except you turning into a bitch," he said, which I didn't take as mean or dirty. That was actually a pretty deep thought for Colt. But he was all talk. I knew he wasn't going to go crazy and get rough or hit me or anything. He was probably scared I would hit back. I'm relatively sure I could kick his bony ass.

I have to say, he was half right. I was the one who had turned into a different person. Not a bitch, but I did feel older. Once I found out about Dad and how he'd been hit on his bike, I decided it was time to grow up at a faster rate. Hanging around Colt, I wasn't doing any kind of growing up. Probably the opposite. That bike accident was an excuse to get real. I heard the bathroom door close at the top of the stairs.

"I gotta go," I said, nodding toward the sound, which was not the truth in any way.

"This ain't fair," Colt said. "I didn't do nothing to you. This ain't fair at all, goddammit."

"Oh, Colt, you know fair hasn't got anything to do with it," I said. "It's what happens. Shit happens."

"It's happening 'cause you want it to. You're such a stuck-up bitch," he said, and this time, he said the word like he meant it. A dark look washed over his eyes, one I wasn't familiar with, and his hands curled into fists at his side. Still, I wasn't worried. Boys like Colt only did bad things when they knew they could get away with it.

From the top of the staircase, from behind the bathroom door, I heard my father singing that song he'd brought home from the hospital. He sang it all the time now. It was beginning to drive me a little crazy, all about the things we do for love. Colt glared at me. I smiled and said, "Go to your meeting. Start a revolution. It will do you some good." I sounded like I was a college graduate or something.

Colt stomped off the porch, and before he hit the sidewalk, he turned and flipped me bird. I started to tell him to quit acting like a skinny-ass sixth grader, but I thought, *Why waste good oxygen on him?* He climbed into his car and sped off, taking the far corner a little too fast. That was what he was doing for love, leaving some rubber in the neighborhood. I didn't know why Dad kept singing that song. I didn't know if he had a history with that tune. It was such a cheesy pop song, and since the accident, he never let up on it.

When I eased the door shut, I also heard what sounded like the water in the tub turning on and off then on again. I snuck up the stairs, being quiet so I could hear what he was doing. He sounded happy. All he'd been doing since he got back from the hospital was smiling and hugging people. He was a jolly damn patient.

"Dad?" I called out from the landing at the top of the stairs, outside his bathroom door. No answer. He couldn't hear me over the water running and the singing, and there was this swishing noise too. I knocked, and he didn't let up. The door wasn't locked, so I leaned against it. It took a couple of seconds before I realized what I was looking at.

My father, perched on the edge of the tub, in only a pair of shorts, like gym shorts or something. His iPod strapped to one arm, his ear buds going, him singing to that damn song. Both of his legs all lathered up with shaving cream. He'd run a couple of stripes down one leg with a nice, fancy razor he held in one hand. I saw a thin trail of blood where he'd nicked himself on his Achilles.

When the door opened, he looked right at me, but he wasn't embarrassed or shocked or anything. He smiled and said way too loud, "I DON'T KNOW HOW YOU GALS DO THIS. I MIGHT BLEED TO DEATH BEFORE I'M FINISHED!"

He was the happiest I'd seen him since the hospital, which is saying a lot. I mean, my dad was turning into a pretty content dude. We were all changing.

CHERYL

So Patrick knew that I knew. It was funny, in that weird, sad, tragic way. Funny in that we didn't have the classic final knock-down cage match. As it turned out, it was a fucking quiet parting. For the record, a burp rather than a roar.

It happened very quickly. That night, after I hit him with that song, I could barely keep my eyes open. You would think with all the adrenaline pumping through my veins, I'd be wide awake. You'd be wrong. I lay down on the bed after doing my rendition of "Little Willy," and my eyes slammed shut. Somewhere in the background noise of everything—of the room, of my life—Patrick walked in. I kept my eyes closed and heard him pull a suitcase from the bed beneath me. He packed in five minutes or so. It sounded like he was already a hundred miles away. The only thing he said was, "I'm not sure how fair this all is."

We were worth more than a quiet separation, I knew that. But I supposed this way was best—me there, exhausted, my eyes shut, him banging around, stuffing his underwear and his frustration into a too-big suitcase.

I lied. The other thing he said was, "That's all for now," which sounded like the end of a cartoon, and I smiled in my half sleep. I thought, *I've been hanging around Claude too much. All he does lately is smile and smile.* Maybe some of that had rubbed off on me. "That's all for now." A cryptic statement, if you think about it, especially the *for now* part. A teaser, sort of. I'm not sure Patrick realized how cryptic he was being. He was simply talking, trying to give himself an exit line. The best thing to do was say nothing. I'd already sung that song to him. That was all it took. He knew I knew.

For now. What, for now? Sleep, first, that was top of my list. I heard Patrick snap the lock on his suitcase and roll it down the hall. I was asleep before the front door closed. I dreamt almost instantly. At least that was how I remembered it later. Maybe it was one of those combinations of imagination and dreaming, a mixture of what you think is reality and what can never be real.

In my dream haze—that's what I'll call it—Patrick's car pulls away from the driveway, and before he makes his way out of the cul-de-sac, Claude rolls up on his bike. He doesn't have on those silly biking clothes, those lewd, second-skin shorts or the bright shirts two sizes too small. He wears hospital clothes, a loose flowing gown that ties in the back. Around his wrist dangles his hospital bracelet. He holds his arm up to me. "Hey, any way you could cut this off for me? I'm out of the woods," he says, then starts laughing. "Out of the woods. That's funny to me. What woods? Do all sick people go to the woods?" He laughs and balances on his bike, then behind me, Marlene walks out of my house, a giant apron wrapped around her body. She smells like cinnamon and fried egg rolls. (I knew where that last detail came from. Every morning, on my walk, I passed Happy China II, when they were already dunking eggs rolls in hot oil by eight a.m. The smell outside the Happy China II was always fried egg rolls.) Marlene asks us if we want anything special for dinner, and Claude says, "The usual, sweetie," and Marlene answers, "Chicken soup, it is, then!" She sounds like June Cleaver, the singsong in her voice more a whistle with words. Her apron swishes as she flows back into the house. Claude looks at me and says, still smiling, "Have you seen Peg? I can't find Peg," and my eyes begin to well up. I do my best not to blink. "Claude, you know Peg is gone, right?" I say, but my voice doesn't sound like me. The words are softer, younger. The sharp edge the years have honed onto it is gone. "Where did she go?" he says, still smiling like a third grader. "I can't remember. You know, bump on the head and all." I want to tell Claude that his wife has died, but I can't do it. The words won't take the right shape in my mouth. "She's on a trip," I say, and he says, "Oh, good. She needed a vacation. The last time I saw her, she looked so tired." He rides his bike into my house, right up the front steps and into the little foyer where I keep umbrellas and raincoats. I still stand on the steps, staring into the cul-de-sac when I hear Claude call from behind me. "Soup is on the table, Cher. While it's hot, come on," he says.

In the real world, Claude had never called me Cher. When I woke up from the dream an hour later—or five hours later, I had no idea—my cheek lay in a small circle of dampness, and in the air, I swear I smelled something cooking, something like egg rolls or soup, but maybe it was my imagination playing tricks with a leftover dream.

Peg

You know how the world works out? Exactly like it is supposed to, that's how.

I was supposed to be *here*, balanced in regretless darkness, watching the pieces of the game below me meander into their comfortable squares. They were supposed to be down *there*, doing all the things they did: letting their bicycles stray into a switchback, getting caught in ice cream parlors in the rain, relocating rodents, finding Bibles in the dark, finding brothers in the light. It was less complicated than it appeared on the surface. When people say, "shit happens," they are only half correct. Shit happens . . . *exactly the way it's supposed to.*

Ah, but most people want a plan, a path. They want something or someone to be waggling the joystick of their lives, leading them to a wonderful, tied-in-a-bow ending. That's a crock. The plan is, there is no plan. It's the longest running joke in history. We are controlled by nothing more than whims on a breeze.

This isn't a bad thing. It gives *surprise* a new, exciting meaning. In my own humble opinion, the most common expression in the world should be: *Who knew?*

Who knew Cheryl would begin to lose that rough edge in her voice the day she began spending hours at the hospital? Who knew my sweet, sweet Marlene would find her way back home? Who knew? I wish I could tell Cheryl it was okay, that her being pulled into Claude's brand-new orbit was unavoidable and perfectly fine by me.

All I could do was watch and wonder what would happen next. That was, indeed, a fun game to play. Try and predict the next meander, the next square to be occupied. I wished I could lay odds and take bets.

I don't think I've mentioned this, but the strangest, most bizarre fact up here is that once you're dead and gone, you begin to live totally in the present of others. I remember the past, but I cannot alter it—mine or anyone else's. And I don't have a window into the future. All I can do is enjoy the present of those I left behind. They would be so much better off if they could live like me—say, *Screw the past and the future*, and let the present play itself out.

All in all, not a bad way to be dead. Who knew?

Wallace & Wade

We lost track of the time. This was *not* a habit of ours. We were usually extremely aware of the movement of clock hands. Looking back, we can't believe on that morning, we became so carried away in our work that we failed to notice minutes ticking away, but we did. Hand to god, we thought we had more time to fill before that man arrived.

We worked in the small hallway outside of the Confederate Room, slicing open containers of new retail goods, new stock to line the shelves inside the room. We unwrapped intriguing, wonderful items, like Appomattox Body Oil or—and we found this super exciting!—a tiny toy soldier collection, both Union and Confederate regiments. But here lay the wonderfulness: the Union soldiers were unable to stand upright. They had no bases! They were designed and condemned to lay prostrate on the battlefield forever. Ingenious, we thought to ourselves. Great for the kiddies! We plucked the new merchandise directly from its wrapping and immediately found places for it inside the Confederate Room, which was nearing capacity.

But we were not worried. When word of our new treasures filtered through the twisting grapevine of our customer base, space would soon clear. We had crunched the numbers. We were making more profit from the Confederate Room than from our entire book stock. The margins for book sales were onionskin thin. Those for Confederate memorabilia, especially the sexually oriented merchandise, were astronomical, sometimes approaching a 300 percent markup. Can you blame us for losing track of the time in our Christmas-morning–like excitement?

Though the store was not officially open, we left the front door unlatched for our noon appointment, thinking, of course, that we would hear the ceramic tinkling of the door chimes, giving us plenty of time to shove the boxes into the Confederate Room and lock everything safely away. We had no idea Mr. Samuel Tisdale would enter the rear, via our unlocked loading dock. We were doubly surprised, you might say. Surprised that the time had slipped away so quickly *and* surprised when in front of us loomed our guest. We use the term *guest* as loosely as possible. Odd, he was extremely comfortable using the loading dock entrance.

We were caught, so to speak, with our Madras pants down. Here was the Confederate Room, glowing in front of the three of us in all its stars-and-bars glory. Here was a Black man, staring into it as if viewing displays of the rarest of artifacts. Maybe in a way, he was.

"Well, isn't this some crazy shit?" he said. He was not angry, only mystified, not unlike a child at a circus. Perhaps a little amused. We preferred to view his reaction that way.

Why didn't we panic? Maybe in days past, we would have stammered and stuttered and slammed the door and made some sort of flimsy excuse for the room of Confederate memorabilia. *But why?* we thought. We were resolute in a strategy to keep enemies close. And how much closer could they get, hmmm? We suddenly felt more evolved, wiser and more conniving. Having a Black man looming at the threshold of our Confederate Room was downright operatic.

We waved away his opening gambit. "Oh, a little regional hobby of ours." There was no chit-chat. We could tell he was interested. We have always felt that most conversations require some verbal calisthenics to warm up the dialogue, but Mr. Tisdale was having none of that. He was all business.

We had not anticipated his next question, as we rose to leave for a different, safer area of the store. "Can we sit in here?" he asked, pointing into the Confederate Room. We noticed the moldy volume tucked under his opposite arm. Before we could answer, he said, "Actually, in a weird way, sitting in here might be perfect," and he strolled straightaway into the Confederate Room, the two of us parting and making room for his entrance.

Crossing the threshold, he paused, taking it all in. We gazed with him. We had not looked at the room that way in such a long while. We were always in too much of a hurry to truly notice it. The scene was quite impressive—a sea of Confederate flags of all sizes emblazoned on hundreds of products, shelves literally sagging with merchandise. He did a slow turn, almost 360 degrees of discovery. His eyes came to rest on the faux phallus collection. Most people did when they first saw the room.

"Black dildos?" he said, amusement once again buoying his words. We did not tell him about the mistaken shipment we had returned oh so many weeks ago. And we certainly did not confess *these* particular products were special orders for several ladies—and one gentleman—in the community, citizens who possessed, we suspected, deep-seated, unresolved issues about emancipation. We made it our policy to never question a purchase with anything but a smile and a cheery attitude. That was our business credo.

"Man, I have never seen anything like this in my life. I'm not sure how to feel about it," he said.

"Well, we may be biased," we said, "but we believe this represents the most extensive offering of memorabilia for sale anywhere. We can say that with a bit of confidence." We don't know why we felt the sudden urge to brag. We don't believe it helped with his mixed feelings.

He noticed several empty chairs leftover from the last WLF meeting and began to walk toward them, shaking his head the whole time. He sat and motioned for us to join him, which was troubling. He was suddenly in charge of the meeting! We had made a blunder, we thought, a subtle, tactical blunder, but a blunder, nonetheless. We had ceded authority without realizing it.

"I don't know, man," he said, while we pulled a pair of chairs directly in front of him. Our backdrop was a giant Confederate flag, suspended from the far corners of the room. "I'm not sure if all these decorations make this whole thing weirder," he said, gesturing to the book clasped under his arm. "On the other hand . . ."

We were interested, and yes, a bit fearful of what he had brought with him, especially since we were on our heels a bit beneath the umbrella of the Confederate flag.

"When you say *whole thing*, we assume you mean what?" we said.

He appeared a bit confused for a split second then recalled the volume he held under his arm. "Oh, yes," he said, flopping the book into one of his large hands. "This is a family Bible. My family." He stressed *family* as if it were a foreign word. He held the Bible forward like an artifact, and we reached for it, of course. We were, after all, booksellers. A typical reaction, we'd say, but not the one he wanted. He quickly jerked the book toward his chest protectively and smiled. "Not yet," he said, which we found infuriating. "I need to explain a few things first." Ah, the sales pitch, we thought. Perhaps he needed money. God knows what they pay professors these days.

We could see the Bible clearly. The cover was a faded brown—water-spotted and tattered on the edges. The remnants of a zipper hung on bravely. One of the corners may have been gnawed on by a creature. As if on cue, the moment the word *creature* popped into our heads, above us, the dance of the rodents began. (We had begun to imagine our rats as refugees from *The Nutcracker*, nightmarish creatures who pranced to some unheard Tchaikovsky above our heads several times a day.)

"I wonder what that is?" Tisdale said, but to be frank, he didn't sound extremely concerned. He smiled at the ceiling. "Sounds like something big. And a lot of it. I wonder . . ." His deep voice tailed away.

The activity above our head ceased, at least for the moment, like the mere sound of his voice had stilled them.

"We're checking into it. There may be a rodent afoot," we told him.

"Sounds like more than one foot," he said, proud of his little wordplay. We disliked punsters.

"You realize, we don't deal in antique or rare books. Mostly contemporary works," we said, steering this attention back to the Bible.

"I didn't bring it to sell. I brought it to show. I mean, it isn't for sale. This Bible has a lot of sentimental value, you see." He held it up like a preacher in full throat from his pulpit. His voice, we must say, was buttery smooth. "I have to say, it's intriguing."

"We can't remember the last time we looked through our Bibles," we said.

"This is one is pretty standard King James." Tisdale paused, gathering breath for the next part of his sermon.

Then something happened, a feeling came over the Flag Room, that kind of feeling when a breeze picks up and changes the flavor of the air. Tisdale lay the Bible on his knees and stared directly at us, like he was trying to see into some place far beyond our eyes. We knew we should look away, but we couldn't, our attention cemented in place by his large, wondering eyes that continued to study us, searching for something. The awkward silence made us squirm a bit in our seats, waiting for something to save us.

Finally, after several seconds, Tisdale broke his gaze and shook his head. "I don't see it," he said, "not a bit."

"What are we looking for?" we asked him, the only thing we could think of to say as we sat in our confusion. We thought we heard him say something under his breath about a person named Esther. He didn't appear pleased with her.

"Esther?" we said.

Tisdale took in a deep breath and let his exhale out slowly. "Listen, I can't kid around anymore. Some of this is fun—or could be fun—but I'm not sure where the fun is right now. I was going to come in here all high and mighty and pull the pin on this explosive and toss it into your little bookstore, but I have to tell you, that's not me. You don't know me, but that's not me. I don't do loud things. I'd rather let things happen on their own. Some people might call that lazy. I even considered doing nothing when I came across this Bible. I thought about calling and cancelling on you fellows. But I didn't because there's something you need to see, something I *need* you to see." He stopped and raised the Bible again, this time simply for drama's sake, we thought, until we realized he was waiting for us to lift the weight on our end of the conversation. We had no idea where to start.

"We don't know what to say." That wasn't a lie.

"Let's begin with this: you don't like Black people," he said and waved his free arm in the general direction of the shelves in the bookstore. "You don't have any Black writers in the stacks. You wouldn't let me bring a Black writer in as a guest. And there's all this . . . stuff, which I must say, as much as I hate to admit, is pretty damn impressive." He chuckled at this admission.

Well, we were not about to sit there and defend our deep-seated convictions to him. "We don't know what to say," we said again, thinking that feigning confusion was wise camouflage.

"To be straight up with you, I thought I had reached a point where I didn't give a shit about people like you anymore. I didn't have the energy. It takes too much damn effort to hate you from a distance, I can't imagine what it would take face to face. I thought I'd found a way to live my life and let people like you live yours. That might be lazy too," he said, glancing again toward the ceiling and cracked a smile. Again, as if on cue, something scurried above us. "You might want to get that checked out," he said.

We began to think Tisdale was insane, and we were not in the mood for a lecture. Were we curious about his Bible? Not at all. It was time for us to cut this meeting short, and that was what we were about to propose when for the second time in less than a half hour, we failed to detect another person in our store.

We should pay more attention to our surroundings.

SAMUEL

From behind, in the doorway, I heard a guy yell, "What the fuck?" The way he said it, you knew instantly he was both pissed off and surprised. I couldn't tell you which reaction was more important to him in that moment.

I'd seen the kid before, or maybe only seen others like him. He was the poster boy for disenchanted youth, the demographic that packed my intro math classes every semester. Constant pout, sleepy-eyed indifference, ever-expanding gauges in the ears, which for the life of me, I cannot understand. Trust me, one day they will grow tired of peering through the portholes in their earlobes. I wasn't completely sure, but I had some vague memory of Claude being associated with him. *Whoever* he was, he was not the kind of person that would frequent a bookstore. He was not a happy camper, either, judging from his tone.

Wallace and Wade jumped to their feet the second the voice cut across the room. They obviously knew the kid. "Well, well," one of them, Wallace, I think, said, "what a surprise, what a *complete* surprise," like he was talking to a long lost relative. The two of them began backing away from me. I still wasn't sure which twin was which. I forgot about the rats doing laps in the attic. I had been on the verge of telling these twins that had a new relative when this underfed punk interrupted my joy.

"The fuck?" he said again.

"Now, Colt, we were discussing a book sale," Wade, I think, said. "This gentleman, Mr. Tisdale, said it was important. He asked if we could meet.

You're welcome to join us. It's the Holy Bible!"

Wallace, I believe, said, "You have no problem with another guest, do you, Mr. Tisdale?" I most certainly did, but I didn't give him an answer. I stayed focused on this Colt fellow. I didn't want to drop my guard.

He was not listening to a thing either of the twins said. His eyes were locked tightly on me, and he would not turn away.

"What are *you* doing in here?" he said. I wasn't going to answer that question either, but he didn't give me a chance one way or the other. He immediately turned on Wallace and Wade and advanced. He reminded me of an animal—a skinny, feral cat, maybe—skulking forward with attack on its mind.

"What you let one of them in here for?" he said.

Here was the thing: I was not in the mood to get mad about what he said. I was going to let it pass. Not worth the energy required to push back. Probably not the best time for my laziness to kick in.

He had his eyes on the twins. Silly, I figured he'd want to keep tabs on me. You know, since I was *one of them.* Instead, he slinked toward Wallace and Wade, his hands balled up at his side, squinting like a man staring into the noonday sun. His face was flushed as well. In my opinion, he was a little overwrought for the situation. For all he knew, I *could* have been there to have the twins buy a book or appraise a book or simply peruse a book. I *could* be there to purchase something from the back room. He drew his hands back, like a boxer cocking his fists and charging his opponent's corner. Wallace and Wade shrank suddenly, grabbing for each other without taking their eyes off on Colt. They were *too* scared, I thought, especially when the guy in front of them couldn't weigh more than one-thirty, one-thirty-five. Maybe they couldn't figure out anything else to do.

"Why are you here?!" one of them yelled. "There's no meeting today!"

Meeting? I thought.

The kid was probably just out of high school, but his anger suddenly made him appear older. Anger can age you. And make you stupid.

"Hey, man," I started, but I did not get the rest of the sentence out of my mouth, because he said, "You shut up, nigger," and did not even turn toward me when he spoke. I have to say, being ignored bothered more than what he said, but still, I was not going to go after the kid. Because that's all he was, a snot-nosed, punk-ass kid. I decided to head toward the loading dock. While I could not put my finger on it, it was obvious this kid was pissed at something other than the twins. The steam in his pressure-cooker of a head came from somewhere else, and it was all about to blow, and I did not plan to be anywhere around when that happened. Like I said, I am not a fan of loud things.

The kid's wild eyes remained fixed on Wallace and Wade, and one of the twins, again I don't know which one, watched me leaving. The scene slowed for a second. The twin said nothing out loud, but I could read his face. I could tell he wanted my help. Using only his eyes, he pleaded with me for something. He was silently saying, *I shouldn't be here either.* I paused long enough to hear the kid hiss at the two of them, "You let a nigger in my room? What the hell is wrong with you faggots? That's fucked up."

The kid grabbed the twin that wasn't looking at me by the throat and lifted him a few inches off the ground. I think it was Wade, and Wade started digging frantically in his coat pocket for something, and he finally pulled out a tiny, toy-sized pistol. He tried to aim it in the kid's direction, but his hand shook wildly. The kid laughed and snatched it away from Wade and pitched the pistol in the direction of some Confederate Generals bobbleheads. Wade threw a weak-ass jab—more of a half slap— at the kid and missed then sort of went limp and gave up. The kid tossed him into one of the chairs we had been sitting in then snatched the other twin by his collar and headbutted him square in the nose. Blood spurted out through the fingers that twin threw up to his face. Around his fingers, I could still see his eyes. He had given up, too, given up on getting any help from me.

But hell, I couldn't leave. Of course I couldn't. The first thing I did was put the Bible down somewhere where it would not get caught in any of the crossfire. I wasn't about to predict what that crossfire might be, but I had to be cautious all the same. I did not want anyone spilling strange blood on the family Bible.

The kid didn't see me coming. I guess he thought I was going to be on my way and let him bang the twins' heads together. He was wrong about all of that, and he was wrong about me. I was not mad at him throwing the word *nigger* across the room like a dart. No, he had barged in and made someone bleed, someone who didn't deserve it. When I saw that, he crossed a brand-new line I didn't even realize had been drawn. Something inside me stirred, I admit, and I almost smiled at the new feeling in my gut. It was the opposite of lazy.

He wasn't facing me, so I could have sucker punched the kid, but I held back. I actually tapped him on the shoulder. When I got that close, I could see I had a good four inches and a hundred pounds on him. I tapped again, and he barely reacted, still ignoring me. Then he turned slowly. He smiled through those damn crooked teeth and gave me the look, the one I'd seen way too many times before, when white boys think you are too slow or too stupid or too scared to fight back.

"What the fuck you want?" he said.

"Not much," I said, snatching him under his armpits, and lifting him in the air. If he had stayed that way and not twisted, I could have simply shoved him against the wall and brought a knee up in his skinny balls, and that would have been that. But he went all gymnastics on me and did a half gainer in my grip, and suddenly he laid out flat like a missile, me holding him around the waist with his arms pinned to his sides, and I thought, *Oh well, Samuel, go with it.*

I did a little half jog forward a few steps, him poised like a battering ram, and ran his head right into the sheetrock. It crossed my mind that I might break his neck, but when his skull hit the sheetrock, the wall disintegrated like old chalk. I think I stunned him, because for a few seconds, we remained there, me still holding him around the middle, and him with his head buried inside the wall.

There was a second of dusty silence, then the kid screamed from the other side of the wall. I expected a reaction, but this was not the kind of scream you hear when someone is in pain. This scream had something else mixed into it. Sheer terror. That was what I heard coming out of the wall, muffled of course, but terror nonetheless.

As long as he kept yelling, I knew the kid was not dead and his neck was intact. He felt light in my hands, his bones hollow like a bird's. I was not sure I could pull him out of the same hole he went in, especially the way he started squirming.

His voice hit a new, higher octave. "Get me the fuck outta here," he shrieked, and I thought to myself, *No, man, this is what you deserve.* He tried to corkscrew in my grip.

"You stop moving and I'll think about it," I said, locking down my grip. Behind me, Wallace and Wade huddled together like a pair of first graders watching a scary movie.

The kid yelled again, his movements even more violent. "Stay still," I yelled back.

"I can't," he screamed. "THEY ARE ALL OVER ME!"

They? His arms, which worked their way loose from my grip, windmilling on my side of the wall, clawing at the sheetrock around the hole where his head was planted, scratching at the wall, punching it. In a few seconds, he left streaks of red on the sheetrock, and I could see that he was in the process of ripping his nails away from his fingers. I thought, *That has got to hurt, and I did not cause that. That's on you, kid.* The sound I could not place was the thin sort of rumble inside the wall, like a tiny motor humming away.

"Please, please. They bite!" he yelled from inside the wall. "For god's fucking sake!"

That's when the squeaking began, a high-pitched chorus. I gave a hard tug on his belt, and nothing happened; he screamed more. I tugged again, and his head popped from inside the wall like a cork exiting a champagne bottle. When the wall released him, the two of us fell backward onto the floor, but I still had a good grip on the kid. He turned toward me, and I saw the tiny cuts all over his face, all of them oozing a little blood. One cut was centered right on the end of his nose. He shook like a frozen man, and though he tried to speak, I couldn't understand a thing he tried to say.

The hole in the wall was above me now, since I sat upright on the floor. Something stared out from the head-sized opening. Actually, a few things. A lot of tiny heads. And a lot of beady, wild eyes. Then, without a second of caution, the Dunean rats began to leap and flow out of their new escape hatch, a narrow river of fur and yellow teeth. All my Wallaces and Wades.

"Fucking rats?" the kid yelled and promptly fainted in my arms like an overtired baby. I suppose the thought of those creatures munching on his face was too much for his consciousness to handle. I could see where one of them had bitten halfway through the kid's lower ear lobe. One ceramic gauge had disappeared, dropped, I guessed, into the insulation and darkness among the studs.

The rats kept coming—out of the wall, through the door, and down the hallway. I would like to think that some of them recognized me, although none paused to get reacquainted. Some smaller ones emerged, babies I imagined, new members of the crew. Over the many weeks, I had calculated that I had resettled maybe sixty or so rats. No telling how their numbers had multiplied. When they got to the end of the hall, they disappeared among the shelves. I had to smile. I couldn't help myself.

Wallace and Wade crept to my side. "I thought he was going to kill us," one of them, the one who had pleaded with his eyes, said. "We can't thank you enough." His nose was purple and already swollen twice its size. He stared down at the unconscious kid then backed off a bit.

He said, "Are all those rat bites? Won't he get rabies or something disgusting like that?"

I said, "Some of that damage might be from going through the sheetrock. But yeah, I see a tooth mark here or there. I can take him to the hospital. I guess I can tell them what happened, like anybody'd believe it. I hate hospitals."

Swollen Nose said, "Maybe you should let us take him. I mean, a large Black man carrying in a thin, bleeding white boy? You know how people are." He had a point, and I appreciated it. He kept talking. "I'm sure he'll be calmer when he wakes up."

"I would not lay money on that," I said.

He put his fingers to his nose carefully and felt the tip. "I think this is broken. I've never broken anything before. This might be interesting."

"You ought to see about that," I said, and at the same time, a scream ripped down the hallway from the front of the store. A woman's high, high shrill.

The other one, the twin without the recent nose job, said, "Oh my, a customer. And those vermin," and he took off for the front. "I'll take care of it." First, he looked at the hole in the wall. The rat deluge had ceased. He peered into the hall, took a deep breath, and charged toward the business part of Dunean's, closing the door behind him.

"He'll handle it. My brother is good at that sort of thing," he said. "I don't know why Colt was here. He was so angry. He's never been that angry. Everything is so confusing. Everything feels to be coming apart."

In my lap, the kid stirred. "You can always get rid of rats. You can always patch the holes," I said. I made a note to ask the twin later how he was acquainted with the kid I punched through the wall. Now wasn't the time.

He touched his nose again. "How does it look?" he said.

"Not pretty," I told him. "But when the swelling goes down, I think it will be a great conversation piece."

He laughed. We both did. "I want to thank you again. The look in Colt's eyes was—I don't know—it was the shade of something bad. When he saw us talking to you, he went crazy."

"My guess is he has always been a little crazy. He must have a lot on his plate right now. He sort of snapped," I said.

"Again, thank you for taking control. You may have saved us," he said. The kid shivered in my arms. Maybe he was dreaming about rodents in the dark places behind walls. "We appreciate it," he said, and he did not cut his eyes away. He meant it.

"Hell, that's what you do for family," I said.

That got his attention.

CLAUDE

The only thing that Marlene cooks, or wants to cook for that matter, is chicken soup, so after a couple weeks of hanging around inside your house and eating gallons of the stuff, you need to stretch your legs, need to get out, so you suggest a trip to The Oorah. Marlene says, "Well, I think I should drive. Remember what the doctor said. I'll take you."

Being chauffeured to a bar by your daughter is new for you, perhaps a bit emasculating, but you want a beer. Nothing drastic, only a couple of PBRs. You won't go near a shot of Beam.

You know you sound like an alcoholic in the throes of withdrawal, but it isn't so much the beer you crave. You miss The Oorah. Miss the stools at the bar with the ancient padding in the seats that bunches under your ass, the stools that rock on the uneven floors. Miss the light in the place. You've heard photographers talk about certain kinds of light. Well, The Oorah has its own glow, the way the sunlight from across Old Bleachery Road is filtered by the dust on the windows and turns a brown-orange on its way through the glass. Miss the way the place smells, like a frat house with smoke damage. Miss the sound of LeJeune's arm paddling the water, the rattle of ice cubes bouncing off the metal sides of the cooler. And you miss her, too, how she automatically knows whether you want to talk or sit in your little cone of silence. LeJeune always knows.

You haven't laid eyes on her since that day in the hospital. You recall vividly seeing her there—and hearing her—when you finally came out of the fog. You wanted to ask her who was watching the bar, but at that point, you didn't know what day it was, much less the time. Samuel was with her. You remember that. You thought, *Man, they make a right nice couple. The skinny tattooed bartender and the Black professor.* That sounds like the title of a television show. You can't help what pops into your head when you've banged it too hard.

You don't mention any of this to Marlene. You keep your mouth shut and smile and slide into the passenger seat of your pickup. Your knees are in your face, and the new skin tugs against your scars, but you don't feel like adjusting anything. It isn't that far to The Oorah.

"This is weird," Marlene says after a few blocks of nothing but music and commercials from the radio filling the air. "Taking you to a bar after a head injury. I feel like I'm doing something illegal and unhealthy."

She would understand if you told her about the chairs and the smells and the light, but that feels like too much of an effort, so you take the easy way out.

"We won't stay long," you say. "Only a beer or two."

She drums her fingers on the steering wheel, hands at ten and two. (That's your girl—safety first with her brain-injured dad.) "Colt came by. Did I mention that?" she says. "While I was cooking soup."

That doesn't narrow down the time frame. Marlene is always cooking chicken soup. "When?" you say.

"Oh, this morning. Sorry. Yeah, he came by this morning. I don't think he is happy with me moving back into your house. Actually, I know he's not happy about it. He left in a bad way. He flipped me off," she says, and she isn't so much as informing you as she is trying out the words. She wants to hear aloud the story of what happened so she can figure out what to do about it, about Colt.

"I know you don't care," she says.

"It's more like I don't actually know him," you say. "All I know is that he wears those things in his ears. Doesn't that hurt?"

"You *would* focus on that," Marlene says, but she isn't annoyed. She drove the most direct route to The Oorah. You thought you might have to tell her to cut down Townes Street to avoid the lights on Main, but she knows where she is headed. You are impressed and oddly happy about her sense of direction, and it makes you smile.

"What I'm saying is I don't know the boy. He happened when I wasn't around. I wasn't even riding the bike yet when you started going out with him, right?" A few weeks ago, you were time-stamping everything BB and AB, Before you bought the Bike and After. Now, you need a new time frame: Before the Accident and After. BA and AA. You're afraid if you start using AA, you'll be mocking all those people who go to meetings and make amends for things. You don't want to make fun of anybody.

"It's weird. You and I have these gaps in time, don't we? Colt started coming around and you started riding a bike and getting thinner," she says. She grins, so you know the two of you are on a good path.

"You were living with Cheryl and . . ." You pause. One of the lingering effects of the bang on the head is that you occasionally can't remember the smallest of details. You have identified a pattern in this ailment, however. Most things you forget, you don't *want* to remember. Like Cheryl's husband's name.

"Patrick," she says, helping you out.

"Patrick," you say back, "right. That guy."

"He is forgettable," she says. "You know, he moved out too."

Well, *that* is a significant bombshell. You had no idea Patrick left. You mask your surprise. That is another way you're positive you're recovering. You can throw up emotional camouflage. "Oh, really," you say casually, as if you're commenting on the weather or the price of unleaded gas.

Marlene enjoys being a newscaster. "Oh yeah, he's gone. I'm not sure of the details, but Cheryl says he's definitely gone. We talk every couple of days."

You love the word *kismet*, the idea that some sort of power out there brings things together or tears them apart. Kismet isn't always positive. But today, you feel kismet working for you, sliding good things across your plate. Or maybe it's timing. Kismet *and* timing! For instance, why do you decide you need to head to The Oorah today of all days? Why does Marlene drive at the precise speed that puts you at this precise corner when she tells you about Patrick and Cheryl, the corner where a simple right turn will lead you the four blocks, directly to her house. And today, a Sunday, so Cheryl will more than likely be at home? Kismet is in the air.

"Have you talked to her today?" you ask. "If she's home, we should swing by and take her with us. It sounds like she could use an outing too." You are a half second behind, because Marlene is already reaching for her cell phone while at the same time, making the turn. You don't think this is a particularly safe maneuver, but who are you to say? You are the one who wrecked a bike.

PEG

You've heard that phrase, *the perfect storm?*

Personally, I am not a fan of that pedestrian phrase. *Nothing* exists perfectly. We all know that. No matter how perfect you think something is, you will eventually discover a rough edge or an out-of-place piece. So even when the storm is supposedly *perfect*, something can always make it even better. Or worse, depending on your point of view.

What I mean to say is don't call it a perfect storm. Just call it a storm.

Oh, and the most interesting thing about a storm is watching it brew. Granted, not everyone has that opportunity. Sure, sure, when you're talking about a literal storm, weather forecasters study their maps and listen to their computers and observe all the elements—all the low pressure and high pressure and jet streams and whatnot—barreling toward an eventual confluence. They are the lucky ones, the ones who get to observe.

But when you're talking about people and not barometric pressure, now *that* is harder to witness. If you were to ask me what is perhaps the most advantageous thing about being where I am, it's simply this: I get to see all the elements brewing toward a big storm. No, I can't *predict* the future. I can't tell you how strong the metaphorical winds might blow or how deeply the trees will bend (again with the metaphors), but I can sure as hell tell you that a hard rain is going to fall.

I can't do anything to stop it. Not that I would. You don't want to screw with fate or the natural order of the universe. It is a little frustrating when you see the potential for a big storm and you are unable to sound the warning siren, but that's the curse of limited omniscience, and by limited, I mean I can't do a damn thing. I can only witness. Can I avert my sight? I'm not sure. I've never asked. Because I've never looked away. What fun is that?

Like the weather, sometimes the personal storms below peter out and all potential cataclysms evaporate. Suddenly, the sun appears when you least expect it, but when I glanced at this horizon, I didn't see much good rising with the clouds.

The Oorah was always open on Sunday afternoons. That was part of the problem. Sunday is the best day for the worst things to happen. Why? Because *nobody expects it*. The day of rest. The day of worship. The catch-your-breath-before-the-week-begins day. Nobody expects anything bad on a Sunday.

The Oorah welcomed its hard-core patrons—a short list, to be sure—on the off-day of the week. They opened at one o'clock, perhaps a passing nod to the church going crowd. They had always opened on Sundays, even before drinking was a legality on the Lord's Day. Before the overwhelming vote to allow Sunday bar business, The Oorah skirted the issue by claiming to be a private establishment, which meant the first time you came to the bar, you signed a filthy ledger and became a Member for Life. One perk of membership? Sunday Funday.

If you examined the place carefully, you'd see that The Oorah was perfect for Sunday drinking. The decades of dirt on the windows cut most of the sun's ray, so inside it was always dusk, no matter what the clock said. Time warped when the door closed. The weather inside never changed. It would be a clever idea for the management to collect all watches upon entry. You could lose track of the present in The Oorah, which meant you could dwell on the past or worry about the future, which is, of course, the curse of the drinking class.

Marlene (sweet Marlene) and Claude did not care about time. They didn't care that they called Cheryl minutes from her home to invite her to accompany them to The Oorah. She wasn't dressed for the occasion, even by The Oorah's standards, wrapped as she was in a bathrobe and planted in front of the television that wasn't even turned on. She stared at it, but whatever show was playing, only she could see.

She didn't want to go, kept backing away from the invitation until Marlene told her that Claude was in the truck, that he felt the need to get out for a bit. Claude yelped from the passenger seat, the loudest sound he'd made since returning from the hospital, as if to say, *Yeah, I'm here and I'm seconding the invitation.*

I couldn't help but notice the way Cheryl perked up at the mention of Claude's name. She tightened the terrycloth belt on her robe, as if he might be able to see down the front of it through the cellular connection. A small gesture, but revealing body language nonetheless: she heard his name and immediately thought of her body. I'd been seeing a lot of that with her the past few weeks.

Cheryl told them the front door was open, and she would be ready in three minutes, but Claude and Marlene decided to sit in the pickup with the air conditioning blasting and listen to music. Cheryl took more like ten minutes, spending extra time brushing powder around her cheekbones and checking to be sure she didn't have any renegade hairs twisting out of her eyebrows. Cheryl had always been self-conscious about them, since the day she learned how to operate tweezers. She had recently discovered a gray hair invading her left brow.

She didn't even let them out of the truck to greet her, just slid quickly into the small, back seat, into the bank of cold air, and I could tell she was instantly worried the bra beneath her t-shirt wasn't enough to hide the sudden appearance of her nipples. When Claude turned to ask her how she was doing, she folded her arms casually across her chest. We've all used that move, haven't we? The nipple concealer. Claude noticed too, because it was something we used to joke about every time I walked into an aggressively air-conditioned restaurant or department store. He recognized the signal of arms folded a bit too high on the chest, and he said, "Little too chilly for you, Cheryl?" and laughed. Maybe he didn't notice the leftover memory of his wife reflected on the façade of her sister. I was a little disappointed. Perhaps the thump on his head left him with fewer inhibitions and less nostalgia. He covered up his eyes. "I can talk and not look, all at the same time," he said.

"Jesus, Dad," Marlene said. She knew what was going on, even without glancing in the mirror.

Normally, what would you have done? What would *any* woman have done? Clutch herself even tighter, right? Perhaps shake her head disbelievingly? Cheryl didn't. Cheryl let her arms fall to her sides, and she took a deep breath. I wasn't sure if Claude saw it through his fingers, but I sure as hell did. Cheryl gave herself to him. Right there. In the back seat. Storm cell number one, on its way to The Oorah.

On the other side of town, a different story, but a storm cell, nevertheless. Samuel opened his windows and turned up the volume on the car stereo. Eddie Kendricks oozed through the speakers, thin and high and sad. "I don't think you need to go spend money on a doctor," he said, and beside him in the front seat, examining his reflection in the small mirror on the back on the sun visor, Wallace said, "You're probably correct. I'm not sure there's anything a doctor can do except tell me not to blow my nose. I like this new plan, I must say. It's exciting. Very different, but exciting."

I'd never seen Wallace without Wade right beside him. That the two of them were separated tipped the balance of our little world. Like Wallace's nose, things were slightly out of whack.

Samuel and Wallace were a few minutes behind Claude and Marlene and Cheryl, but of course, none of them knew they were part of this little, perfect storm. (I know, I know. I said I didn't like that phrase, but I swear, the more this day paid forward, the more it seemed as though there was something wonderfully perfect about it.) Everybody I cared about, everybody I was connected to in one way or the other, tacking on different compass headings toward a watering hole that had long since stopped passing health inspections.

"I have never darkened the door of The Oorah," Wallace said, a fraction of his voice trapped behind his swollen nose, making him sound younger and whinier.

"Is that a racist statement, man?" Samuel said. His deep radio voice lowered to a growl, but his intention was only to mess with Wallace. The growl was his fuck-with-you voice.

Wallace panicked. "Oh, my god, no, no!" he stammered. "It's a thing, I mean, something people say. I didn't mean to say that me being with you would literally darken the door, I mean to say, that isn't what I meant to say at all, oh my god, no."

Before he yammered any further, Samuel's shoulders bent forward from laughter, hunching over the steering wheel of the Lincoln. "Oh," Wallace said, a blush rising under his collar, "you're teasing me. I can't remember the last time I was teased. Probably when we were kids. Wade and I, I mean."

That was perhaps the saddest thing I'd heard in weeks, someone remembering a slice of his life that had disappeared or evaporated or atrophied. I'll bet he thought it would never happen again, being teased. I'll bet he never thought he would get head-butted by the leader of the White Liberation Front either. This was a banner day for Wallace.

"Man, The Oorah's all right. Nobody cares who anybody is. I mean, check me out. I come strolling through the door all the time, and nobody says a word. They'll let you in, broken nose and all." Samuel laughed again, and this time Wallace joined right in, although I must say, chuckling appeared to hurt his nose.

I said that Claude and his entourage were ahead of Samuel, but the timing tightened up when Marlene made the wrong turn down Stone Avenue because Claude wasn't watching where she was driving. He was never good about keeping an eye on her, even when she was a little kid. He was easily distracted. His attention was compromised by my sister and her renegade nipples that could cut glass at that moment, nipples she displayed proudly, and Claude was more than happy to ogle. I knew what he was up to. If Cheryl protested, he would blame his new-found inhibitions on his little bike accident. But Cheryl didn't mind. I wondered if, when I wasn't looking, she'd had some augmentation done. Maybe I never noticed before. It isn't the kind of thing that sisters make a note of, especially when one of them is dying.

"Uh oh," Marlene said, "I think I got turned around." Out of the mouths of babes. They were *all* turned around, literally and figuratively. Claude wrenched backward in his passenger seat. Cheryl feeling the sudden freedom of an empty nester because of her recently-fled husband—a complete turnaround for her. People were *turning around* so much, they resembled whirling dervishes.

Claude didn't scold Marlene for heading in the wrong direction. He simply turned forward in his seat and pointed out directions. This left. The next right. Soon they were back on track, pulling off Old Bleachery Road and into the gravel-and-mostly-dirt parking lot of The Oorah, which was all but empty. Only LeJeune's Mustang sat in the far corner of the lot.

As they piled out of Claude's pickup, Samuel's big cranberry Lincoln eased into the lot. I could tell Claude lit up a little when he spotted his pal and colleague about to join him for a Sunday Funday. But the Lincoln sat there, idling. Inside, no one appeared to be ready to leave the car.

Back at Claude's truck, Cheryl, said, "Did you plan this?" but it wasn't an accusation.

"This is great timing!" Claude yelled. "Samuel! Kismet!"

Samuel couldn't hear him from inside the Lincoln. He was busy with the twin. "You sure about this, man?" he said to Wallace as he opened the door.

"Well, like you said, if I'm not going to a doctor, this is the next best medicine. I do hope they can mix up a Dark 'n Stormy," he said, opening the door and unfolding into the parking lot.

"Man, you got to stop with all that racist stuff," Samuel said, grinning again. "Dark and stormy. Shit."

The sight of Wallace emerging like a strange birth from Samuel's cranberry-colored Lincoln confused Claude.

"Which one are you?" Claude said, exercising his lack of inhibitions again.

"Dad! Jesus," Marlene said.

"I'm Wallace, the one with a broken nose. Is it simply horrendous?" Wallace said, trying to gather as many opinions as quickly as possible.

Cheryl said, "What the hell happened?"

"Some pissed off punk with gauges and a bad attitude attacked him. I handled it," Samuel said, perhaps puffing his chest out slightly. Claude and Cheryl glanced at Marlene, waiting to see how quickly she would connect the dots. She felt their stares.

"Hey," she said, "not my problem anymore, not this Sunday, nossir." The crowd of them, a little tribe of sorts, performed a communal shrug and made their way to the front door of The Oorah. They crossed the threshold, and the first drops of Sunday rain pelted the dust and the gravel behind them.

A perfect little storm, with a little storm of its very own.

LeJeune

Don't know why I still open on Sundays. Tradition, maybe. Not a ton of money in it. Most regulars too drunk from Saturday night or too religious to drink beer on a godly day. Don't mind having to work on Sunday. Don't care. Gave me time to think. Get things done. No bar back, no one stocking liquor. Hell, couldn't ask Ortiz to come in, especially after what he usually goes through on a Saturday night.

Unlocked the front door, turned on the pair of big-ass ceiling fans to shuffle skanky air around, and in they came. Got to say, was a little surprised. Couldn't tell right off the bat who they were because of them filing in from semi-dark rain to full-on bar-dark like a little squad of soldiers. But then . . . saw Claude and Samuel leading the bunch of them, leading them right to the only big table in the room. Claude yelling out, "It's a family reunion!" He laughed.

Claude's sister-in-law pulled up the rear. Tagging along like she was lost or something. Didn't know her well. Seen her here once or twice, years ago. And that one time at the hospital. Knew enough not to trust her. Heard things though. Word-a-mouth stuff. Claude said *family reunion* and Samuel laughed too loud. Weird.

Wasn't about to do damn table service and Claude knew it. Came over to the bar then turned around, counting heads. "I guess we need a half dozen or so cold beers and a few shots, but I haven't counted because numbers have taken on a whole new meaning since my accident, you know. Lots of things have. It's wonderful." Casted a glance toward that

Cheryl the way a guy catfishing throws out a trot line. Saw that look. Seen men sling it plenty of times before. Knew what was what.

Me? Not the smartest person in the state, but have good eyes and good sense. Valuable combination. See something and know what it means exactly. Makes me a helluva bartender. Probably the reason my heart was about to be broke. Saw it coming. Cheryl sitting there all perky and what not. A shirt she chose not because of the weather but because of the eyes that might look at it. Couldn't say I blame her. Had a pair of twins like that, would let them out for air every now and then too.

Fellow from the bookstore with lime green pants and purple nose kept his head on a swivel. Looking and looking, around and around, like he couldn't believe he ended up in a place like this. Everybody else smiling like they just got paid. Pissed me off, they were so damn happy.

"Your kid is too young to drink," I told Claude.

"Stifling rules imposed by anonymities of the outside world. Inside here, the world is new and our very own," he said without turning around. "I'll make a report to the commissar, but I'll keep your name out of it."

The hell? Sounded like a crazy man. Or a man I didn't know. Maybe that bump on the head did do something to him. Wasn't sure his changes were for the better. Grabbed beers, all dripping and slick, with two hands and headed for his table. Set one in front of Marlene. Cheryl moved it out of the way. Claude looked at her and cocked his head. Cheryl shook hers—her head, I mean, not that pair a puppies under her chin—and Claude never quit smiling. That was all she wrote for me. All I needed to know. Like I said—good eyes and good sense. Saw that one little important thing: Daddy putting a beer in front of daughter. Newest momma protecting a sort-of daughter. A damn little family. Had the good sense to let it all go. Like a breath I been holding too long. *Suck it up, Buttercup.*

Of all things—door opened and the sound of hard rain followed Wilton all the way to the bar. Head dripping wet. Said, "I told you I'd give you one more night to think about it. What do you say, huh?"

What I said was "You want a club soda? And a towel?" Because I hadn't figured out the other words that needed to come out my mouth.

Knew what they were, knew they needed to be said. Didn't know how to string them together yet.

But I was getting there.

WADE

For the life of me, I cannot recall the last time Wallace and I separated, cannot remember the last time we were not melded at the hip—not unlike the way we came into this world. Now, I was left with a groggy-headed white nationalist and a hole in the wall and a frantic customer whose pacemaker all but ceased pacing when a furry torrent of wild-eyed rodents ran down the *New Nonfiction* aisle and through her legs, which fortunately happened to be agape at the time.

Did I feel abandoned? Honestly, yes. I understood the logic of our parting. At that time, there were so many needs. Wallace needing a fresh shirt. Someone needing to mind the store, such that it was. Someone needing to be present when Colt finally woke from his dreams of being attacked by ravenous rats. Someone needing to drive Wallace to the hospital. In that case, that someone was Tisdale and his gaudy Lincoln Continental. I feared for my brother, out there by himself with that man.

Was I afraid? Yes, I confess. Afraid to be left alone in a world suddenly out of control, what with Black men and rats and paper-thin sheetrock and screaming female customers. I wasn't sure I was equipped to deal with such an environment on my own. The young man with the ravaged ear. The destroyed wall. The manic woman.

I did manage to calm her, and what I told her was quite ingenious, if I say so myself. I said, "Madame, how did that make you feel?" And she yelled, "I'm calling the police . . . and the city! You have a problem. Yes, I am terrified." So I said, "Madame, there is no need to call the authorities, for I am the authority here, and you had your fear test-marketed in anticipation of a new blockbuster novel to be released in the near future . . ." I was shooting from the hip, that same lonely hip where Wallace was formerly planted. Flying by the seat of my bright trousers. "It is entitled *Rodent Wall* by the bestselling British horror author Velda Kant. If you were frightened, you will love her new book. Shall I put you down for a preorder?" And she said, "Oh my, were all of those rats fake?" To which I said, "Not so much fake as animatronic rodents. You've been to Disney World, I assume? If you have seen how they magically make animals move, you know exactly what I mean. No need to worry. You were never in danger. I shall report to the publisher of your reaction. They will be pleased. And please, keep all of this to yourself. Very hush-hush, you see." Fooling her into calmness was not difficult. She was no rocket scientist.

When I took the information for her preorder of Velda Kant's newest foray into paralyzing literary horror, I made a note to write this customer in three months and tell her of the unfortunate legal issues involving Mrs. Kant and her publisher, issues that would delay the coming of the rodents for months on end. Perhaps indefinitely. Haha!

I must say, it frightened me how easily I lied. I should probably write my own stories. I should think that people would enjoy my altered versions of the truth.

WALLACE

Samuel—he insisted I call him Samuel instead of the more formal Dr. Tisdale—struck me as an immensely thoughtful man, which made perfect sense, him being a professor and whatnot. I don't mean to say he continually jettisoned deep and meaningful concepts into his conversation. Rather, he wore the expression of a man constantly on the verge of a wonderful epiphany, a man who foresaw the imminent connection of dots of some kind. When he told me he taught math, it made perfect sense. He struck me as a good, logical thinker.

One of his thoughts was that we did not need to go to the hospital. He said, "A broken nose is a lot like a broken toe. It's a pain in the ass, but there's not much you can do about it. And if it's all the same to you, I'd like to avoid the whole hospital thing." He shivered, and I detected something underlying his avoidance of a hospital, but I tended to agree with him.

Which is how I ended up making my inaugural trip to The Oorah. Samuel said, after thinking for several minutes, "The treatment at The Oorah will be cheaper than the emergency room and way the hell less painful."

The nose was beginning to feel better already, and I knew with the application of a Dark 'n Stormy or two, the pain would subside. There were a few moments of silence as Samuel made some navigational adjustments with his Lincoln Continental, but they were not awkward. In fact, the silences were somewhat comfortable. Music filled the gaps. Diana Ross, I believe, and her Supremes. You rarely met men his age who listened to classic Motown. I complimented his musical taste. "Thanks," he answered, "I get it from my mother," and he was silent until he drew a long breath and said, "Look, there is something else I need to tell you, something about that Bible," he said, patting the volume that lay on the seat in the wide space between us.

I had all but forgotten about the Bible, what with all the excitement of fisticuffs and rodents and broken noses and damaged sheetrock.

"Open it up to the front page, where all the handwriting is," he said, never taking his eyes from the road. I am not a fan of reading while a car is in motion. I tend to get woozy and nauseated, which is why I always drove when Wade and I traveled. The sudden memory of Wade brought on a breathy sigh that I loudly released into the car. Samuel misinterpreted my reaction.

"Okay, sorry, you don't have to look at it, I guess," Samuel said, and I assured him that my sudden exhale had nothing to do with the Bible.

"I was thinking about Wade. I feel suddenly disconnected from him," I said.

"Well, you kind of are, right at this particular moment," Samuel said.

"It's a new feeling," I said. "I suppose I'll grow accustomed to it. I shouldn't overreact. He didn't die or anything."

"Yeah, but did he like you driving off with a Black man?"

"He had his chances to say something. Silence often speaks volumes." I thought that was a rather profound statement, but Samuel didn't answer. He pushed the Bible closer to me with his free hand. At that moment, a new song came over the speakers, a Marvin Gaye song that I recognized, "What's Going On."

I found the page he'd mentioned, before the scripture began, per se. Why, it was a crude yet complicated family tree, I thought. I saw all manners of scribbling and comments, some of which were rather humorous. I looked but wasn't sure what I was supposed to see. Or say. It was only lines and names.

Samuel said, "There, toward the end. Those lines shooting off to the side like they were added in. The ones that look newer." When he finished talking, he sang the chorus along to the tape player.

When one is not looking for a specific thing, one can be blinded to any clues right in front of one's eyes. What I mean to say is, it lay right in front of me, and I could make neither heads nor tails of it. I must have been staring directly at it, yet I couldn't see it. Perhaps I was trying *not* to see it. Perhaps something in my subconscious raised blinders. I simply could not do the calculus required to make sense of the writing, of the lines, of the lineage.

"I came to the store to tell you both about what's written on that page. Then, you know, things got out of hand," Samuel said.

Whatever lay on this page was important enough to Samuel to make a trip behind enemy lines, so to speak. Whatever it revealed possessed that sort of gravity. "Is this valuable for some reason?" I asked.

Samuel thought for few seconds. "Yeah, I guess you could say that. There's value there."

So maybe he was, indeed, after money when he came to Dunean's with an antique Bible. It was a business trip for him.

"Keep looking," Samuel said.

Suddenly, there came a parting of the clouds. The blinders tumbled down. I saw it plain as day. My father's name—the name Wallace and I had not uttered in years—written right there, marginalia of the lowest, most surprising kind. Hixson Hance. Aloud, the name sounded like a throat-clearing exercise. It reeked of phlegm from deep inside the body. I shuddered slightly. One line from Hixon's name—from my father's name—extended lightly down the page, ending with two simple words: *twin boys*. A genetic grouping. Still, I wasn't sure what to make of it all. There we were. Our father and us. But why? What was the meaning of us appearing on the page of a Bible possessed by one Dr. Samuel Tisdale? If this was a joke, I was unaware of the punch line.

Samuel offered no help. Before I could ask questions or come up with answers on my own, I saw the other line, leading in an opposite direction, to a woman's name: Carlotta, and from her sprang one son. *Samuel.* Then, a thin, inky line that stretched from the word *Samuel* across the gulf of faded white space and ultimately connected with the *twin boys*.

"You see what's going on, right?" Samuel said, or maybe it was Marvin Gaye singing. No matter. I could see.

SAMUEL

The big, dramatic, domino-tumbling revelation was not as satisfying as I thought it'd be. You'd think telling a gay white Confederate that he had a Black half-brother would bring about wailing and pulling of hair and a flood of denials, but none of that transpired. Sometimes people don't do what you expect or what you imagined. Truth be told, I suddenly felt a little sorry for all of us, from the moment it hit him until we pulled up to The Oorah. I didn't say a word, and I think he appreciated that. We sat in the parking lot for a minute, not long, but long enough to be an important pause. I saw Claude's car and what looked to be Marlene and Cheryl getting out. I couldn't bring myself to look at Wallace, but in my peripheral vision, I detected that big, swollen nose poking forward. Finally, Wallace turned toward me, and I waited for the rush of denials or the nervous laughter or white anger . . . but I wasn't expecting what I heard.

Wallace closed the Bible and laid it in back on the car seat carefully, like it might break, then he blew out another one of those big sighs he'd being firing off since he got in the car. "Well, Samuel," he said, "I suddenly have so many questions. I'm not sure how many answers I truly want."

I knew that feeling: a thousand questions fluttering inside your head like a cloud of anxious bugs, all buzzing to escape into the air. Wallace reached for the door handle, his shirt blooming with the blood from his broken nose, then glanced toward The Oorah. Another sigh.

"There's always more to our stories, isn't there, Samuel?" Wallace said, and I couldn't argue with him about that. There's always more.

PEG

Not like I could do anything about it. I'm not God. I can't control events. As I've mentioned, that's the worst part of this—being able to see and not act. Not like there's a door I could shut and block my view of Cheryl and the way she looked at Claude across from table in The Oorah. Seriously, Cheryl—the Cheryl I knew—wouldn't have been caught dead sitting for too long in a place like that. She would have been afraid someone she knew, someone important, might see her and spread the word. Oh, don't let Cheryl fool you. She cared what people thought about her.

There she sat, in the flesh, watching the activity around her like a kid at a Christmas parade, her head pivoting back and forth and back again to make sure nothing escaped attention. I know now what that expression is called, the one on her face. It's called living for the moment. Yes, yes, a cliché of the highest order, often tossed out in therapy sessions and yoga classes, but sometimes you have to call a thing what it is. *Cheryl was enjoying that precise moment.* She wasn't bemoaning her fate or grieving for a deceased sister or cursing the air. She wasn't stalking the local sidewalks and ice cream stores and thunderstorms to confirm the identity of her husband's lady friend. She was being Cheryl, and I hadn't witnessed that in a long time.

However, the more I watched and studied—and yes, I think this was a good thing—the less uncomfortable I felt about the situation, the way Cheryl kept trying to catch Claude's eye every thirty seconds or so. I began to think I no longer possessed the capacity for jealousy. Maybe jealousy evaporates at the time of one's passing. If there was ever an opportunity for jealousy to rise like a green funk and cover me up, it was now. Here I was, not that long dead, and there they were, gazing at each other across a sticky, pock-marked table like a couple of moony-eyed teenagers. Had they even considered me?

But no matter. I felt the beginnings of their happiness bubbling up from somewhere. I knew, like some sort of soothsayer, that Cheryl would have no trouble getting beyond that marital speed bump named Patrick. But Claude? That was another story. I wondered what would become of the mystery girl with the chiseled calves and the chiseled attitude. From where I stood (rather, floated), I wasn't sure what Claude saw in her. Let me rephrase. I know what he *saw* from the perch on his bike. But I wasn't sure that he saw anything below the surface of her spandex. Jesus. Let me rephrase. He liked her ass. That was his sole motivation thus far. That says volumes about Claude in particular and men in general. *Asses make you pedal faster*. Make a bumper sticker out of that one.

Maybe Miss Ass and Calves was only a memory now. Or perhaps the bump on Claude's head knocked any knowledge of her into oblivion. He didn't remember the car launching him into his new life, and he didn't remember the girl he chased up the mountain.

Bottom line? Claude and Cheryl were currently inching toward happy. I could live with that.

LeJeune

L ife. Lays it out there. Always does. Sometimes got to suck it up, Buttercup, but for the most part, life tells you what to do. Gives you road signs. Always got signs when I needed them most. That's how I ended up at The Oorah. Was driving through on the way to someplace I've forgotten. Stopped in to see the old man's Marine buddy. Next thing I knew? Had a job. Why? Because I followed the signs.

Needed a sign that morning. Damned if I didn't get it. Needed more than one actually, because Wilton came on like a ton a bricks, and truth be told, was not sure what the hell to do. Not a suck-it-up moment, this one. Fork in the road moment though. Hell, more than one fork.

Didn't take a magnifying glass to see Claude was all googly-eyed with ol' Cheryl. Not like two of them done anything yet. Could tell without doubt he had not banged that. Still a thin demilitarized zone between them, but let me tell you, Buttercup, walls were coming down fast. Bartend long enough, you start putting couples into camps: them that's done it, them that haven't, them that definitely will, and them that won't ever, no how no way. Claude and the Sister Substitute sat in the *definitely will* camp. Only a matter of time. Timing, I should say. Timing and alcohol, not necessarily in that order. Actually, timing, alcohol and desire—get two out of the three and off come the clothes.

Never was right for me and Claude. Timing, that is. Sure, carted him off to my place when he was too hammered to figure out how to call a cab. Could have called it for him? Of course. But can't blame a girl for trying. Like I said before, him always too drowned in PBR and Beam in the dark. Too embarrassed and shy when the sun came up. Gunny Sergeant would say I was trolling the wrong bait in the wrong pond. I liked Claude. Sue me for letting him sleep it off on my couch. Always face down. Didn't want somebody choking on their bad habits in my place.

Ask me if I was sad. Or jealous. Go ahead. Won't tell you the truth, probably because I don't know the answer. Never been the jealous type. Didn't have any kind of flittering and fluttering going on in my stomach. Heard that's what happens when jealousy comes. Sad? Maybe so. Sometimes people like me—people with tattoos, so skinny they look like they need a cheeseburger. People who got a brain but the words coming out their mouth don't sound college enough. People who don't give two shits about the right kinds of things in the world. These kind of people aren't allowed to be sad. *Suck it up, Buttercup.* Had your shots after he pounded all his. But you were calling to the wrong area code, playing out your league. Man who teaches at a college plus a girl who knows how to set the timing on a '67 Mustang? Bad math right there.

Go ahead. Tell me. Say, *LeJeune, you trying to make yourself feel better.* What's that old saying? Those grapes were sour anyway. Glad I didn't spend any more time trying to reach them. Anyway, pulling back the troops. Those folks had something going on at that table, and I wasn't included. Turn the page, girl. Suck it up.

Which brought me to Wilton. Brother of mine trying to spackle over the cracks of his life.

Throwing out plans like a bad insurance agent. Wanting me to come to Florida with him and open up a bar. Told him—only thing worse than tending a bar is owning one. Not in the market for new aggravation.

He kept pushing. Give him that much. Stubbornness came naturally. Reminded me of me. We might for real be related. Both got stubborn streaks that glow like birthmarks.

Him saying things like, *You're already used to the humidity. You don't have beaches here—I got a beach right outside my back door. I know a bar for sale. You can decorate it any way you like.* Me saying, *Decorate? Ain't real bright, are you? Have you looked at me?* He said, *You don't have to put up any of the upfront money. I got that covered.*

Started wearing me down. Water torture, him dripping all those good intentions on my forehead. Still, needed a sign. Couldn't make that kind of decision all on my own. Needed something. Natural disaster. Burning bush. Voices in my head.

And that Sunday, there it was, sitting right in front of me. Claude with his chin in his hand, smiling over at his sister-in-law. Smiling at his daughter. Looking like a stranded man who got plucked off his desert island. Never smiled at me that way, even after I rescued him from The Oorah all those nights. Never going get a smile like that out of him. Knew that sure as I knew the beer taps would run dry before midnight.

Wilton busted through the door out of the rain, talking before he hit the bar, not even noticing the little crowd inside. Could hear every word he said if they were interested. "Well, I told you I'd give you one more night to think about it. What do you say, huh? Personally, I didn't sleep a wink. I was too excited thinking about what the future might bring. But what about you, LeJeune? What are you thinking?" Him all but jumping onto a barstool. Thought he might miss and fall on his ass. Probably wouldn't faze him a bit. Was a man running on fumes and possibilities.

"You want a club soda? And a towel?" I asked him.

"You're stalling," he said back. I didn't answer him, so he kept talking. "You know, LeJeune, last night you couldn't answer me when I asked you that one question. Silencio. Nada a word." Another thing he told me about Florida. You pick up a little Spanish. "Being bilingual helps in the bartending business down there," he told me once.

Kept on rolling. "So I'm asking one more time: what the hell is keeping you here? Sure ain't this place," he said and waved his arm toward the front windows, those greasy front windows. Followed the direction he was waving, landed my glance on Claude.

That was it. My sign. Not a natural disaster, but something most definitely natural. Wilton was right. If I stayed around here, I'd sooner or later have to clean the damn windows. Or watch them get dirtier and dirtier. Claude, a changed man with a bump on his brain. Me? A bartender with an attitude too big for my bony body. Florida probably do us all some good.

"Well, bubba, where we going to live?" I said. Wilton smiled. Spitting image of my daddy jumped right out at me.

MARLENE

When I thought about the last few years, my head filled up with pictures of glaciers. The creep of time. Time hit the brakes when my mother got sick. Those were the slowest months I've ever lived through, watching her disappear one minute at a time. It didn't matter which house we were in, mine or Cheryl's, because time doesn't care about addresses. Neither does dying.

Maybe that's why I started hanging around with Colt. I wanted something or somebody to make the clocks run faster. And where the hell was I going anyway? Why did I want to move faster? I'm an idiot. Colt didn't help a bit. In fact, things moved slower when he was around because he was so freaking scattered and lazy. The only thing that got him moving was finding something to hate.

But now. Now was different. And it all happened so quickly. My roller coaster was screaming downhill. Yes, that's exactly what it was—a roller coaster. For so damn long, I click-clacked uphill, barely out-pulling gravity. Then, Claude had his accident, things started going downhill, and I don't mean that in a bad way. Downhill meant speed. Downhill meant stuff happened. Here I was, sitting at a bar with my father and my aunt, and they couldn't take their eyes off each other. I don't know what my mother would think, but I can't imagine she would be sad about it. She was the kind of person who wanted everybody to be happy. Sometimes, she'd been a real pain in the ass, fluttering around, checking on everybody's happy meter. But if she knew what was going on now, she wouldn't have anything bad to say. Saying bad things was never her style.

I had a thought that made my breath catch in my throat. All these events—all these big and little things that were combining and happening so fast and bringing all of us together—how could I *slow* them all down now? I didn't want it to change. I didn't want any more speed. I wanted to be happy like this for a long, long time. It's not like I'm owed anything because my mother died and my father scrambled his brains, except maybe a little chunk of time when everybody takes a breath and slows down and smiles at each other, like we were doing right now.

I don't think that's too much for a girl to ask.

CLAUDE

A little knock on the head—actually a little flight through the air *and* a little knock on the head, but honestly, you don't know how little of a knock or flight because that depends entirely on your point of view, and since you don't remember the actual rendezvous of skull and pavement—with, of course, the protective layer of the expensive helmet that TJ sold you sandwiched between your brain and the road—you are entitled to call it *little* without much reservation. The funniest thing to you is, considering all that rattling around your brain did, the things affected most were your eyes. Now you see the world differently, and the view is, you have to say, satisfying.

Maybe the wiring inside the skull is so intricate and webbed that you poke one side hard enough, you bruise the other. You never knew you had the capacity to—and here you pause to search for the right word, probably because *you had a knock on the head!*—the capacity to, well, envelope the world, the capacity to sit back, reach out, and bring all the important things in the world closer in some kind of giant, sloppy hug.

You are having those kinds of thoughts these days. New contemplations. Like how Cheryl, when you stare over at her, resembles the future. Of course, you can't tell her that, can you? She is currently a married woman, but she glows like the unbroken, un-walked-upon future. A wide, long beach free of footprints. And Marlene, who strolls around these days with a smile on her face, smelling faintly of chicken broth. She glows too.

Not all your new thoughts are crystalline. The one thought that nags at you, buzzes around your head—or, you mean, inside your head—like a persistent housefly is about the mountain. *That* mountain. Where you had the accident. You are mad at that mountain.

You are *supposed* to be mad at the mountain. One, because you couldn't climb it on your bicycle. That is obvious. It (the mountain, you mean, not the bicycle) beat you into painful submission. You remember the mountain. You remember being there, needing to get off of it the easiest way you could, which was down. Let gravity be your pal. You hate that mountain. You hated it the second you woke up in the hospital because you could hear it laughing at you, even while you lay there in your clean, crisp bed.

Yet there is something you cannot figure out: why the hell were you on that mountain to begin with? For the life of you, you can't recall why you pedaled on that curve that wraps around the shoulder of the mountain with what you guess is a six- or eight-degree incline. You *knew* you couldn't climb something like that. You're no hammerhead. You don't show off on the bike. Something lured you up there, you are positive, but as hard as you rack your addled brain, you can't come up with any sane reason you were on your bike, on that curve, on that incline at that precise moment.

For now, you blame the mountain. There is nothing else to blame. You certainly don't blame yourself. That makes no sense, and you're all about making sense these days. You laugh at that: trying to make sense while a bruise the size of a tennis ball sits on the bumpy surface of your brain. Stop making sense. The Talking Heads. (You should also mention, since the accident, you sometimes have these tiny streams of consciousness. More rivulets of consciousness than full-fledged streams. Hence, the Talking Heads.)

Anyway, don't blame anybody. Blame the mountain.

W<small>ADE</small>

I couldn't be sure of the nature of their nascent relationship, "their" in reference to Wallace and that Tisdale man. Surprisingly and sadly, Wallace looked invigorated by his exit in that freighter of an automobile. I imagine that model of car measures mileage in feet per gallon. Wallace, I noticed, did not hesitate, did not pause when Tisdale offered a ride to the hospital and swung the door open wide on his Lincoln. Wallace did not look back, and that, I must say, had given *me* pause. My brother, my twin, was happy to take his leave of me.

One would think, at our age, making new friends was no longer a reasonable possibility. How many people truly connect with someone new after, say, the age of fifty? Very few, I'd venture. It must be something chemical in the brain. Or electrical. Pathways no longer function, pathways that, in our younger years, allowed us to embrace new people and new experiences.

This was different. Tisdale was a Black man. And he drove my brother away. There was no way on god's green earth I would follow that man into a car, and yet, there was Wallace all but skipping, his nose a new, purple eruption on his face, a blossom blooming bigger all the time. He appeared suddenly—what is the word?—relieved. I cannot recall the last time I saw him happy, the last time either of us was truly happy. We have been, for the most part, *content* in our lives, a contentment fed by the work we accomplished at the bookstore, and contentment is only a distant relative of true happiness. Yes, we felt as though we were called upon, perhaps not by god but by something just as invisible and just as spiritual. We felt a duty constantly stirring inside of us to keep our shelves pure and our secret room stocked with the finest retail offerings the Confederacy had to offer.

I was sure Wallace felt the same way. We had discussed this over Dark 'n Stormies while evenings descended around our porch. But now that I recall, I did most of the talking, most of the planning . . . but Wallace nodded at everything! He let me lead, but he was always right behind me, I'm positive.

So how, I ask you, could Wallace so quickly shirk us? How could he jump into a car with a new-found Black acquaintance without so much as a look back at his brother? Unless . . .

This I had not considered. *Unless* he was doing research! Unless he was keeping his enemies close again. That must have been it! Lord, I suddenly felt better, as if the planets had magically slithered back into alignment and all was well with the orbit of the world once more. That must have been it. Wallace was reconnoitering. He was scouting. He was broadening his knowledge base. He would, no doubt, be calling or texting at any moment, begging for me to rescue him from the emergency room at the hospital, where his nose was set and bandaged. I thought I should hop into our car and head that way, in anticipation of his alarm. Our twin-ness made us like that, always a step ahead of each other's thoughts and actions, other-worldly in our communications.

I walked to the porch and closed my eyes and sniffed the air. Despite the mugginess after the rain, I could sense it. Wallace needed me. He was out there, and he needed his twin, needed his other half. These past few hours were the longest we had been without each other in, lord, probably years. I was sure Wallace felt the same hollow emptiness inside of his stomach, heard the same silence that came from one familiar voice being suddenly absent.

I could not locate the keys to our automobile. Wallace must have laid them somewhere special when we drove to the store that morning to meet Tisdale. I hunted for minutes, in all the usual spots, but to no avail. I checked shelves and sills. I scoured the bathroom. I tried to recall if Wallace had left my side the entire morning. I didn't think he had. The only spare key to our Buick currently hung on a finishing nail on the wall of our laundry room at home. The keys were nowhere to be found in the store. I wondered if Colt had done something nefarious when he finally regained consciousness and made his wobbly exit, refusing any of my assistance.

I walked into the secret Confederate Room and reacquainted myself with the destruction that would have to be repaired come Monday. By whom? Who could patch a hole in the wall without seeing what lined the shelves? I combed my memory for any of our special customers who also performed minor carpentry work.

I gave up on the keys. I assumed Tisdale would ferry Wallace to the closest ER, which was only a twenty- or thirty-minute walk. I found my white, floppy hat to protect me from the sun, which had reappeared following the unexpected Sunday shower. I would go it on foot, intrepidly.

Wallace needed me. And I him.

CHERYL

For the record, I was trying not to worry, not get ahead of myself.

"You're not saying much," Claude said, smiling across at me.

The others around our little table nodded and agreed with him. I started to blame it on the beer. Or blame it on any sort of excuse I could come up with on the spur of that moment, like, *I don't normally drink this much in the course of a couple hours, and* never *on a Sunday.* Or *I'm tired.* Or *I don't have much to say.* Blah, blah.

The truth? I was working hard not to over-think the whole situation. I didn't want to confront the nagging little fact that I was married. I mean, that hadn't changed in the last few hours. But for god's sake, I had not *felt* married in quite some time, and since the thunderstorm in the ice cream store, I reminded myself of a lonely, single woman. However, the marital reality remained and wouldn't stop banging in my head. And speaking of heads and banging, there was Claude, good old sweet scramble-brained Claude, who didn't take his eyes off me or my chest the entire ride to The Oorah or the entire time inside that scummy bar. Finally. Time somebody noticed my new boobs. They weren't exactly new anymore. I'd had them for a while. Everybody was so distracted back when Peg was sick, I decided that was as good a time as any. I didn't go crazy, I didn't go all stripper tits. But I thought it was a definite upgrade in noticeability, and when I wore the right bra and unbuttoned an extra button, there was no doubt I'd had work done. Don't ask me why I did it. Probably for all the wrong reasons. A sister dying. A husband looking elsewhere for ice cream. The stench of things dying or rotting all through the house. I guess I wanted something new to think about. I *borrowed* Patrick's American Express. If he noticed, he didn't say a thing. Like I said, people had their eyes elsewhere for a long, long time, and Patrick's weren't on the location of his credit card or the evolution of his wife's breasts.

Which was fine and dandy with me. In all seriousness, I thought it was pretty damn funny. I'd heard about this place, the point where you weren't mad as much as you were good and ready to *not be mad.* I read it somewhere or heard a friend talk about that moment you realize anger is the worst type of machine, one that eats up way the hell more energy than it ever puts out. But this realization, this anger epiphany, normally occurred months and months down the road, sometimes *years* after the trauma, and here I was, not even sure all the trauma had occurred yet.

I knew one thing for sure: I wasn't mad at Patrick. I didn't care about him one way or another. I had washed up on the soft shore of indifference. He was not a bad man. He was settling into another brand of life with a woman and her Stratford son. Hey, not my monkeys, not my circus. Not worth feeding the Anger Machine.

So when Claude said, "you aren't saying much," I said right back to him, "For the record, when I'm happy, I don't say a whole lot. Being quiet isn't something you should worry about. Quiet is a good thing."

Claude smiled and said, "If I was able to make mental notes, I'd do that right now. But you know, with the brain bruises and all." Then he winked, so I didn't know if he was being serious or not.

Everybody around the table groaned like a small, buzzed Greek chorus because we had all recognized Claude was milking his traumatic brain injury for everything he could get out of it. However, we couldn't be a hundred percent sure. All that smiling and rosy outlook could be the real thing.

I mean, for the record, how do you know what somebody with a bruised brain is truly thinking?

CLAUDE

What you are thinking:
That the BMW coming around the bend is the luckiest few seconds of your life. That the rain is over, and the sun is coming out on a Sunday afternoon. That you don't have a brain injury; it is more of a brain enhancement. That this is all because of the bike, and the bike is all because Peg passed away. And maybe these people being here, these people smiling at each other and sipping beer and dodging the random slants of late Sunday afternoon light that somehow escape through the gritty windows of The Oorah are here because Peg *isn't*, and while that may sound like a reason to be sad, how can it be sad the way everyone smiles?

Samuel says, "You're racking up a lot of sympathy mileage with that brain thing," and Wallace says, "I've heard that it can take years for brains to recover and sometimes they don't. I think we have a book on the shelves about the brain," and Samuel says, "I bet it wasn't written by a Black man," and everyone laughs. *Laughs.* The things you used to scowl about make you chuckle. You don't know how this happened. You don't care.

Your head feels fine. Everything feels fine.

LeJeune

Closed early, nobody minded. Filed out like a little platoon of happy soldiers walking away from a war they won. Claude, the last one to go through the door of The Oorah, like he was the daddy or something. Me, standing there with my key.

"Gotta tell you something," said to him before he headed out into the last of the afternoon.

"I know you do," he said back.

Me thinking, *What? He can see into the future now? Must a been one helluva bump on the head.*

"I've decided to leave. It's a long story," I said.

Claude smiled back, didn't say a word, so I kept on.

"Wilton over there. Well, we're related. Never knew. And all this stuff coming together and whatever. Thinking the time is good as any, in other words." Heard myself rambling. So did Claude. Summed it up for the both of us.

"Things are changing," he said. "Faster than we ever thought. And it's alright, you know. It's alright."

Studied on Claude. Of all things changing, he was changing most. Like a flywheel on a crankshaft, him spinning in a new direction and us all spinning off him. Energy transferring one place and another. Nothing changed on his face, though. Still those eyes set back far enough in his head to be camouflaged. That nose I always used to make sure was pointed down when he passed out on my couch.

SCOTT GOULD

"Gotta say, always thought me and you," I said, then pumped the brakes. Couldn't bring myself to come right out with the words. Didn't want to see them there, floating in the air.

"Ah, LeJeune," he said, "when you pass up as many chances as you and I had to get into trouble, you have to know that means something. It means that we had a different job to do for each other. You always gave me a nice reason to come and go. Now you have to do the same thing. More particularly, the go part." Look on his face like a man listening to himself talk, proud of what he heard.

"Wasn't supposed to stay here forever," I said.

"Nobody is supposed to stay in one place forever," he said.

"Think you might miss me a little bit?" I asked. "Wouldn't mind that, if you pressed me on it."

Thought I saw him start to blush. "I won't come back here ever again," he said, "in homage to you." And he took a little bow. Right in front of me.

Now, you tell *me*—you ever had somebody give up something important for one reason? Because you wouldn't be there? Yup, was going to miss me bad.

"Appreciate that," I said.

He had to get in one more, one last word. "You ought to know," he said, "you talk a little bit when you're sleeping. Nothing embarrassing or important, at least to anybody else but you. But I thought you ought to know. It's sweet." And Claude walked out the door where folks coveyed together, waiting for him.

Only one way that man knew anything about me and my sleeping habits. He listened. He lay close in the dark. Awake and eavesdropping and looking in my direction.

A thought like that might carry me all the way to Florida.

Samuel

Because I didn't know where else to go, I drove in the general direction of Dunean's, but I suppose you could say that destination made sense. I had to get Wallace back to the place we started this Sunday adventure. He hit the button to ease the window down. The early evening had cooled enough to make the air less thick, especially after the rain. He cocked his head into the open space, like a dog dangling his tongue in the rushing air. I think Wallace was doing brand-new things, and he was enjoying the hell out of them.

It was obvious that Wallace never worried about consequences until they were in clear sight and barreling down on him, like when he said, "This could be awkward. You—I mean, we—well, we have to tell Wade about this. You know what I mean. I don't think the news will sit well with him. I usually know what he's thinking, but I must confess, I'm a bit in the dark about this one. I guess what I'm saying is normally when I need to make a decision about a situation like this, I consult with my brother. But now, the decision is *about* him."

He was also one of those people who could complicate adding one plus one. "Man, you are going to make yourself crazy if you don't simplify shit some," I said, and he didn't have a clue as to my meaning. I have always been the kind of person who looked for the most direct route to a logical conclusion. It's the math person in me. I'm pragmatic. From my point of view, this was relatively clear-cut. Tell Wade the story. Let the chips fall where they may. Trust gravity.

I pushed the cassette tape in and said, "You never know. You're worried, but you don't have anything to worry about yet. Nothing has happened. Hell, man, you're starting to react before you got a good reason." When I said *react*, I thought of the rats, all the furry, yellow-toothed Wallaces and Wades I had emancipated behind the bookstore. In my confessional to Wallace, I failed to mention that I was the catalyst for Dunean's rodent infestation. Call it a sin of omission. I prefer to call it pragmatic.

"Oh, I know Wade better than any other human on the face of the earth. He was always a bit more—how shall I say?—enthusiastic about our ethnic endeavors than I. Did you know he was the one who wanted the Confederate Room?"

I listened for the thuds of wheels over a body. It sounded as though Wallace was tossing his brother directly beneath the bus. I didn't buy it, but I let him go on. He was enjoying talking about his brother, when Wade wasn't around to defend himself. I don't think he'd ever had much of an opportunity to do that.

"Of course, I never protested, so you might say there is culpability in my silence, but I always thought there was something a bit too . . . overt about the entire enterprise. We're twins, but we do have our differences. You can't always see them when we're standing side by side, I suppose," Wallace said, looking out the window as we passed strip malls and gas stations. The smell pouring through the open window was the hint of egg rolls, and I was suddenly hungry.

"Do you two make any money on that stuff?" I said.

"You would *not* believe," Wallace said. "The things people buy in the name of states' rights. We can't keep the Dixieland Musical Vibrators in stock. I will never understand heterosexuals, especially ones with discretionary income."

I sniffed the fast-moving air again. "You hungry? I could use something to eat. There's this Chinese place over by the hospital with great eggrolls. I'll buy." I saw Wallace thinking about it. It was one thing to hunker down in a dusky dive bar with your new Black half-brother and quite another to make a public appearance in the Happy China II. You could bet between the two of us, we'd eventually know somebody who walked through the door. I made the turn toward the restaurant, onto one of those narrow streets that wasn't designed for a car the size of a Lincoln. He didn't mull it over too long.

"If you think it's okay. That sounds delicious. I hope they don't refuse us service because of my shirt," he said and stuck his head farther out of the window, so far in fact, I thought he was approaching a dangerous situation. When he screamed, I thought he might've hit his head on a telephone poll, what with the shoulder of the street right on top of the pavement. Exactly what we needed—another brain injury.

Wallace jerked his head back inside the car, and I glanced over, checking for blood. I hit the brakes, maybe a little aggressively, because Wallace, who wasn't wearing his seat belt, slammed forward into the soft dash of the Lincoln. I hoped he didn't bang his nose again.

"Oh, my lord, did you see that?!" Wallace was having trouble catching his breath while he collected himself.

"What the hell, man? Did I hit something?" I glanced in the rearview mirror, but the only thing in sight was a guy wearing a stupid looking hat, walking down the sidewalk with his head bent low. He was closing the distance between us.

"Well, *this* could be awkward," Wallace said for the second time in the last five minutes. I looked in the mirror again. The guy was almost even with the Lincoln, his head still focused on the sidewalk, examining every step he took. When he walked next to the open window, Wallace said, "Oh, hello, brother!" and Wade the walker lifted his head as if he'd been awakened from a nap in a room he didn't recognize. He peered from under the brim of his hat, and his gaze bounced all over the car, finally settling on his twin.

"I thought you might need me. I think you have our car keys," he said, as though that explained everything. Wallace understood, like a brother would.

"Oh, my lord, I'm sorry. I didn't think," he said, reaching into his pocket. "Sure enough, here they are."

Wade perspired, even though the sun was about to dip behind the trees. Half-moons of sweat hung under his armpits. He'd been working hard. I could tell he'd been worrying a lot too. *Both of these fellows are worriers*, I thought.

Wade bent down to peer through the open window at me. "I was walking to the hospital. I thought I could be of some use," he said.

"You are always of use," Wallace said, reaching for the door handle. Wade backed off, not so much to get out of the way of the opening door, but to give his brother some space to escape. Wallace stepped out, and the two of them stood in front of each other on the sidewalk like boxers getting ring instructions. Finally, Wallace said, "Well, this is awkward. However, you could ride with us. In fact, you should. We have some interesting things to tell you. Best you are sitting down."

"How is your nose?" Wade said.

"Annoying," Wallace answered, prodding the tip with a finger. The swelling had decreased a bit. "I've been self-medicating. We did not go to the hospital. Like I said, we have stories to tell. One big one. I know how much you enjoy a good story well-told. Let's climb in."

Wade was at a loss. "Should we sit? Where should we sit?" he said. "In the back? Plenty of room in the back."

A couple of white guys in the back of the Lincoln . . . the optics were not appealing. From a distance—hell, from up close—it would look like a Black guy chauffeuring a pair of identical white boys around town. I didn't want any sort of *Driving Miss Daisy* scene, especially not today.

"Listen," I said, "this is one large Detroit automobile. Plenty of room in the front for everybody." I moved a couple of cassette cases out of the way and swept off the middle seat with my hand. I laid the Bible carefully in the back.

"Of course there is," Wallace said, almost squealing. I knew this was something we'd have to work on, him being all bent out of shape about the awkwardness in the world.

Wallace gave Wade a nudge toward the door, and he slid in next to me. His brother climbed in beside him. Wade leaned toward Wallace's ear and tried to keep me from hearing him whisper, "Is this part of your plan?"

"Most definitely, brother," Wallace said. I turned and saw Wallace smiling a new, comfortable, broad smile on his face. Wade stared blankly through the windshield, like he was about to go on a long trip without a map. He sucked in a chest full of air, but I never heard the sigh come out. I hoped he wasn't going to hold his breath for the rest of the ride. I could suddenly tell the two of them apart without any trouble.

"Hey, Wade," I said, putting the car in gear and turning up the volume on The Temptations' greatest hits, "you like Chinese? I know a place."

Marlene

I knew exactly what I was doing. Hang out with a boy that everybody hates, and you can look all those people in the eye and say, *See? I can shake up your world and you can't stop me. I can be responsible for my own destruction. I don't need your help fucking up my own life.*

I didn't think for a second I was the first girl to start sleeping with a boy because her father moved out and her mother died. Or something along those lines. It was a silly cliché, but maybe clichés were not a bad thing some of the time. At least you knew you were not the only one going through it all. I felt a little less stupid when I realized I was not the Lone Ranger.

When I was with Colt, I spent most of my time looking over my shoulder and spitting in the general direction of my past. Now, since my father's bike accident, I'd been thinking more about the days ahead. I had a pretty good feeling there was something to look forward to. You know, like when you knew it was going to be a nice day and you hadn't even looked at the weather on your phone yet. When you felt a warm front blowing in on you, nice and easy. Yes, good weather was coming.

I'm going to learn to cook something other than chicken soup. Expand that horizon first. From there, I'll have to see what comes up. But I can tell you, I'm not all that worried about it.

CHERYL

The things I was carrying around in my head. And on my shoulders. The sheer weight of it all. Like Patrick and his new destination—a pear-shaped woman with what appeared to be, at least from the bathroom of an ice cream parlor, a heart the size of a Volkswagen. I had conversations with myself about whether he ran in that direction or whether I pushed him. Either way, it felt heavy and unsettled, like a poorly balanced backpack.

There was Peg, who had the fucking audacity to die when I was outside sipping bourbon and arguing with the aforementioned Patrick. I missed her moment of departure, and I was still mad about it—mad at her, but mostly mad at myself . . . for being mad at myself.

I wondered if being pissed at Peg was the whole reason I kind of threw myself—me and my new boobs—at Claude. God, people in town were going to talk. Hell, they were already talking, all those women that Peg hung out with. I can hear them now: First, the husband leaves her after she gets sick. Then the sister moves in after she passes away. Peg can't catch a break even when she's dead.

And Marlene. I can't say I was jealous of her—her and her chicken soup and her playing nurse for her father—but I felt like the closer she got to Claude, the harder it was going to be for me. And that's not fair, right? To anybody?

So yeah, I was a little screwed up. One evening, I found the nerve to say something to Claude. Confession? I was whining and venting and hoping he would steer my head to his shoulder and tell me everything was going to be okay. But these days, post-accident, you never knew what to expect from Claude. It was a roll of some dice.

I let go with the whole story. Told him about the weight on my shoulders and in my head, and I waited.

All he said was, "You know, Cher, you don't get this far in life without picking up some baggage. You and me, we can't pack in a carry-on anymore. We'll be checking luggage from here on out."

You might think that would confuse me, but I understood perfectly. I suddenly felt lighter. My shoulders didn't hurt as much. He called me Cher. I could breathe again. It was like the gusts over the water quit blowing up whitecaps, and the surface was suddenly smooth as glass.

Let me get this on the record: It's not hard to fall for a man who calms you down.

PEG

Claude used to say something that stuck with me, even through all the sickness and dying and so forth: "Only trouble is interesting."

The context was always some book or story he was teaching in one of his classes. "First, find the trouble," he'd say, "then things get interesting." Most of the time, I ignored him, but I *heard* him. Now I see how smart that statement was. *Only trouble is interesting.*

However, these days, trouble was fading like a sunset. You know how that works, right? You're sitting there, staring at the colors, oohing and ahhing at the beauty of it, when all a sudden, in seconds, it vanishes? From where I sat, trouble was sinking away like the sun on a horizon. Soon, there wouldn't be anything interesting for me to watch, no trouble. Which is all to say, that storm I predicted? It fizzled. The clouds rolled right on by.

Those people, they were being such adults. I mean, god, the things they said to each other. Once, when she finally realized that his eyes were going to fix on her face and her chest for a long time to come, Cheryl said to Claude, "I feel bad. What would Peg think about all of this?" and while it was nice of her to conjure up my name, I could already tell that no matter what I might have thought, it wasn't going to stop her. Claude said, "Peg always wanted folks to be who they are. We're being who we're supposed to be." I'll tell you what, rattle a guy's brain around, there's a chance he starts making sense. Good lord, don't tell women that. They'll start carrying around ball-peen hammers in their purses.

And Marlene. The fog cleared for her. Not that I was ever worried. She always had decent energy and decent eyesight. I knew she'd catch a glimpse of what was good in the world and take off, chasing it down. You know what I mean. The young. They always have time for second chances.

I'm so happy for Claude. You never want the people you cared about to remain unloved. That head injury forced me to recalculate Claude. He talked differently now, held himself differently. He'd flown through the air, and when he landed, his world was rewired, all for the better, as far as I can tell. It will be hard to watch what happens from here on out. It's not like I can turn away or anything. Maybe one day I will, but for now, my vision consisted of fixed points, and all those points were the people I left behind.

However—and I say this not having all the facts yet—something was happening to me as well. The edges of what I gazed at were growing smooth and dull. Everything I put my eyes on, like the people I watched from here, was made of sea glass, as though a slight fog drifted in from the periphery, from the darkness. The changes were coming slowly, thankfully. It was not as though somebody jerked the big cosmic shade down, but I'm pretty sure that my vision was fading.

Perhaps that is the way it goes here. Perhaps when you die, you are allowed one specific movie to watch, one human drama you left behind. Because we all deposit *at least* one of those in our pasts, right? Once that movie runs its course, once that conclusion arrives, the fade-out begins until the lights finally flicker off.

Nobody gives you any clues here. Nobody warns you. It would have been nice to know that when Claude discovered his smile and Marlene began making soup and Cheryl started unbuttoning that extra button and Samuel whisked his new kinfolk away to Happy China II, my days (or nights, who knew the difference?) would be over. The only thing left to do was wonder why. Why was I given the opportunity to watch what I left behind? Not only watch, but watch *and* not be able to do anything about it, not be able to warn or encourage or berate or scorn?

I have no earthly idea what is next. If I was a betting woman, I'd lay money—a lot of money—on the fact that what's next is absolutely *nothing*, that when the fade out is complete, I'll be completely faded out, so to speak.

I have come to realize something through my life as a dead voyeur. It nags at me and won't let me go. I can't shake it from my brain. Maybe, *maybe*, I now know one true thing that will lead me into the forever dark:

Life goes on. Death doesn't.

CLAUDE

You almost die and you buy another expensive foreign bike, and it feels like you've been here before, bird-dogging TJ through the steel and titanium frames dangling like mobiles from the ceiling. TJ wants you to upgrade, and you don't argue with him. With the insurance settlement from the driver of the sporty BMW, you buy a bike so expensive it should pedal itself or brush your teeth or do something to make it worth all that cash. You have enough money left over to pay down a sizeable chunk of your mortgage, which may be a moot point, since plans are in the works for you to move across town to Cheryl's, a change everyone agrees is imminent and healthy.

In the six months since the accident, you often wonder if you want to get on the saddle again. You think about it, not obsessively, but enough that it becomes somewhat of an annoying pebble in your shoe.

Then, something clicks in your brain. (And speaking of brains, yours is fine. You have no defects in your speech or your balance or your ability to distinguish right from wrong or right from left.) The only noticeable—and what appears to be lasting—effect of the accident is that you are a great deal more content with your life. You aren't sure that the bump on the head made you happier. You tend to think that you were simply realigned, that whatever factory-installed machinery happens to be in the brain dictating your emotional direction—gyroscopes or a series of compasses or whatever—they clanged into a fresh, wonderful arrangement when you struck the pavement.

Anyway, about the clicking in your brain: it is actually two things. The first is you no longer have interest in the mysterious woman with the sculpted calves and high-riding ass. Yes, you *finally* remember her, remembered chasing her up that damn mountain. In your mind, she was simply inspiration incarnate. Maybe a mirage. Or a ghost. She led you to the mountain. Not the mountain *top*, only to the mountain, to the incline. She served her purpose. She makes you think of Dante and how he saw—what was her name?—Beatrice, you think it was. Dante saw her in church one morning and was lightning-struck, and from that moment on, he was inspired by her and wrote for her and quite literally went to hell and back for her. But—and this is important—he *never* had a relationship with her. The mystery girl on the bike is your Beatrice, your cycling muse. If you ever see her again, that's what you will call her, no matter what her name is. So, thing number one: you are no longer interested in tailing Beatrice anywhere.

Thing number two is connected to thing number one, and thing number two is the reason that you give TJ an amount of money more fit for purchasing a car, not a bike as light as a breath, a bicycle that oozes speed, even standing still. Thing number two is a true confession: *you want to get to the top of the mountain that tried to kill you.* And for the life of you, you don't know why.

Why would you return to the scene of that disaster? People will say, of course, that it's something you've left undone or that it's one of your bucket list items or that it's a past failure that you need to untangle. Closure, perhaps. But those people would be wrong. You know the real reason. You want to see if you can get to the top *without* becoming a hammerhead. Because you've also been thinking a lot about hammerheads.

You don't like those people, with their aerodynamic egos and their expensive sunglasses and the way they don't even appear to touch the pavement when they ride, cushioned by the soft cloud of their piss-poor attitudes. You've wondered what it's like to be one of them, to not give a flying fuck about anything but the road and the speed and who you leave in the thick dust of your ridicule. Being a hammerhead would be an awful existence. But those are the kind of people who are built to ride to the top of mountains. Not you, with your softening middle and the soft spot in your skull, your own little fontanel, the spot where you and the mountain encountered each other months ago.

You are aware that nobody who loves you gives a crap about your desire to meet the mountain again. They say as much. Actually, Cheryl becomes so annoyed when you mention the mountain, she can't form sentences. But Marlene rolls her eyes and says you "aren't right in the head," which strikes you as a darkly humorous thing to say to someone with a brain injury. (Marlene is turning into the source of comic relief in the house, which you would have never predicted.) Samuel says, "Okay, you get to the top . . . what difference will that make?" Samuel, always the rational mathematician. You can only imagine what LeJeune thinks. She might be all for it. *Suck it up, Buttercup, and go up that mountain.* You can almost hear her, all the way from somewhere north of Vero Beach.

You quit talking about it, and after a couple of months, they believe the idea of riding up that mountain has evaporated and blown away. You don't tell them about the bike you bought with a stack of insurance settlement cash. You don't tell a soul. You lean your new bike against the bookcase in your office at school, and since you don't keep regular office hours yet, nobody is the wiser. The college is very kind in the wake of your accident, allowing you to teach a light load until you feel up to the challenge of a normal, hefty schedule. Samuel doesn't have a clue. He is too busy working hand in hand with the twins at their bookstore, helping rid them of the rats in their walls. Rumor has it, he has devised a humane system involving a couple of traps and peanut butter crackers. Samuel never says where he takes the rats he catches. It is all a mystery.

Several afternoons a week, you wander to the Addison campus a couple hours before dark, when you know most of the faculty offices are empty for the day. You pull on your kit, roll the bike into the elevator, and make your way down to the road. Once you have your glasses and helmet on, nobody can recognize you anyway. You ride easy circuits around the outskirts of town, avoiding groups of riders you see in the distance, preferring to pedal by yourself.

You give yourself three weeks for your legs and your brain and your lungs to adjust to the idea of riding again, then you decide the time has come to face the mountain. You don't make a big deal of it, simply turn left one afternoon instead of right, and the next thing you know, you're pushing harder than normal against the pedals, and the road rises in front of you, like a character in a comic book. The villain.

For a half mile, you wonder what all the worry was about. You have a feather-light bike that devours pavement beneath your wheels. You can almost smell the top of the mountain, like you believe the air will be different there. Those thoughts keep you stamping on the pedals until gravity decides to make fun of you. Again.

Halfway up the grade, your legs turn to sludge, and a couple of hammerheads pass you and you cock your good ear at them to hear if they say anything disparaging. You feel their scorn like a hot wave pulsing in front of their bikes. They don't say a word as they ease past, because they don't care that your thighs are on fire or that sweat drips in wet sheets behind your glasses. You ask yourself why you've done this. Perhaps you do need Beatrice, and you try to conjure her up. When the next pair of hammerheads dust you off, you check, but neither of them has the calves or the ass of your Beatrice.

In five more huffing, angry minutes, you round a switchback, and the world looks suddenly familiar. This is the place, you think. This is where I flew through the air.

All you need to do is work through the sweat and the burning and pedal a few more switchbacks, and you'll have your mountain, and you'll be an honorary hammerhead without being a true hammerhead. A hammerhead for a day, for an afternoon.

You look at the trees, and a sliver of a memory emerges of how they looked when you winged toward them. You think you hear a car gearing down on the curve above you, but nothing rounds the switchback. That's when you make a decision, and you are surprised how easy it is.

You give up. That's all. You just stop. You stroke a half pedal to keep upright and lean to the left, and you turn your new bike around. You quit. You check the road carefully (because your brain cannot stand another banging melodrama), and you swing it in a tight U-turn, and you stop pedaling because you don't have to anymore. You zip the front of your jersey tight to your neck to fend off the rush of air. Gravity takes over and pulls you down the mountain, pushing you toward home. You barely tap the brakes on the curves, letting the bike angle against the wind whipping past you. You smile not because you are happy, rather because you are *not* unhappy. Not unhappy with yourself, that is. Because, you see, you are a failure. You couldn't make it to the top of the mountain. You couldn't even struggle past the place where you failed the first time.

But you don't care. You are okay with it all. In minutes, you'll coast to the bottom, and you'll make a turn toward home. You'll let them—all of them—see your brand-new bike. You'll let them hug you or roll their eyes at you. You'll explain to them how you were a failure on the road, how you fell short of doing what you needed to do. How you weren't a hammerhead. And you know what? Your story, your shortcomings, won't matter a bit.

All that matters to them is you made it back, still smiling, in one piece.

-The End-

ACKNOWLEDGMENTS

The Hammerhead Chronicles traveled a weird, twisted, and wonderful path into the world, and I owe a debt of thanks to a good many good people. Here are some: to my father, Jack, for putting up with the stories and putting up with me (here's another one for the coffee table, Pops); to my daughters, Emily and Maggie, and their husbands, Herb and Connor, for the constant waves of support; to Bennett, June, and Sofia for showing up; to the guys at Sunshine Cycle Shop for taking care of me, before the wreck and after—may the Quonset hut rest in peace; to all of my riding pals through the years, even the hammerheads who left me sucking wind on the inclines; to early, careful readers, Mark Sibley-Jones and SLC; to Jim Caldwell for taking a look at the manuscript and giving a stamp of approval to the cycling sections; to the feisty team at UNG Press, especially Corey Parson and Elizabeth Odom; to Frazier, the anxious wonder-mutt, who finally learned to sleep through the sounds of typing; and, as always, thanks to Shannon for never doubting.

CPSIA information can be obtained
at www.ICGtesting.com
Printed in the USA
LVHW042320281022
731834LV00004B/93